THE QUEEN'S TREASURE

SHERRY TORGENT

BLUE INK
PRESS

In memory of my sister, Suzette

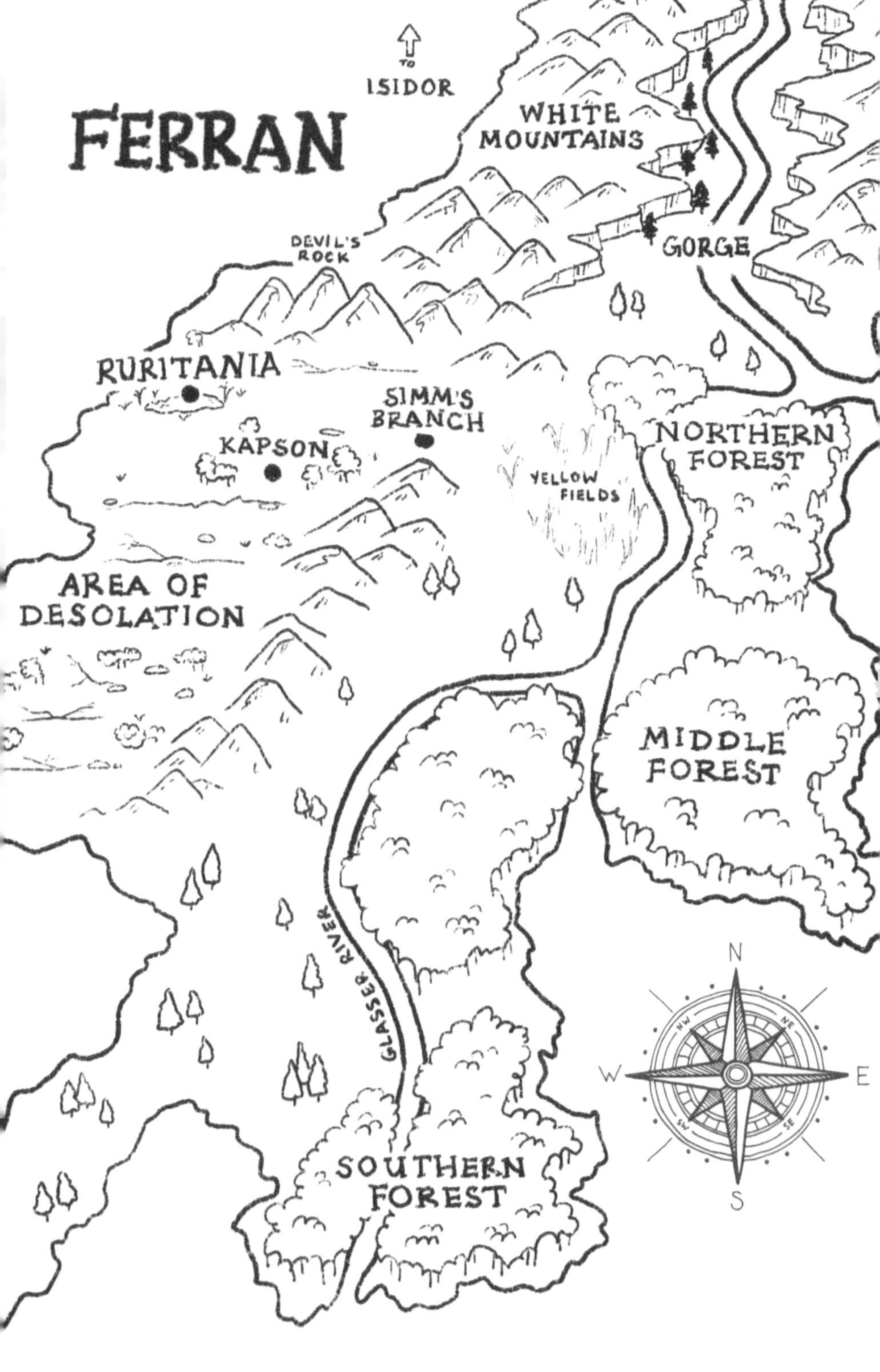

FERRAN
TO
ISIDOR
WHITE
MOUNTAINS
DEVIL'S
ROCK
GORGE
RURITANIA
SIMM'S
BRANCH
KAPSON
NORTHERN
FOREST
YELLOW
FIELDS
AREA OF
DESOLATION
MIDDLE
FOREST
GLASSER RIVER
SOUTHERN
FOREST
N
W
E
S
NW
NE
SW
SE

"Do not lay up for yourselves treasures on earth, where moth and rust destroy and where thieves break in and steal, but lay up for yourselves treasures in heaven, where neither moth nor rust destroys and where thieves do not break in and steal. For where your treasure is, there your heart will be also."

Matthew 6:19–21

The Queen's Treasure

Twenty-one years after The King's Oracle

CHAPTER 1

LARK

Lark brushed off the snowflakes from his coat collar and stamped his boots loudly as he stepped through the entrance of the Prickly Pig. The dimly lit tavern was nearly empty. Two men sat at the far end of the bar slumped over their mead, while an old man in a soiled coat nursed his drink at a table by the fireplace.

"How was the birthday party?" Tomas asked, wiping a rag across the bar. Tomas still had traces of red hair in his white beard. It was hard to believe he had once been the reeve for Lark's grandfather—King Niko. Now Tomas and his younger wife, Hilran, spent their days providing spirits and grub to the fair citizens of Isidor's largest city.

Lark lifted his coattail, moved his scabbard aside, and took a seat on a bar stool. "Have any food left?"

Tomas gave him a scrutinizing look. The tavern would be closing soon and Lark's last-minute request for food clearly did not sit well with a man who had spent his life adhering to meticulous rules. "I can ask Hilran to see if there's anything left, but don't expect much at this late hour." Tomas muttered under his breath as he headed to the kitchen.

Lark tapped his fingers on the bar, pondering his decision to sneak out of the castle. *Perhaps I shouldn't have left my own birthday party early.* The whole thing was for appearances anyway—an opportunity to show the good people of Isidor what a fine king he'd make one day.

King.

He couldn't bring himself to whisper the word, much less entertain the idea. He glanced back at the grizzly man by the fire. He had the humped back of someone who had carried a nobleman's breakfast tray for too many years.

"Never seen him before," Hilran said, sliding a plate of braised rabbit with diced carrots and parsnips under his nose. She flashed him a warm smile and flicked a kitchen towel over her shoulder. "Happy birthday, Lark. On the house."

"Thanks," he grumbled, pulling the plate closer. He *hated* rabbit, but he didn't dare say so, for Hilran was a kind soul.

She handed him a two-pronged fork. "Twenty is nothing to scoff at. You're practically a man."

"Then I'll take a mead."

"No," she admonished, as if reminding him of his duty as prince.

He scowled. "Let me guess. Gideon's orders?"

Hilran placed a hand over his. "Your king only wants what's best for you."

"He wants what's best for him and my mother," he said, pulling his hand away.

"You'll be king one day and then you can do as you like."

"Or Bren will be queen. We are twins after all." He tore off a rabbit leg and sucked the vinegary juice from it.

"You *are* the older," she continued.

"By a few minutes," he said, dropping the leg. "Besides, I'm not king material."

Hilran shook her head. "You're so much like your late uncle, it's frightening," she said happily.

Tomas shimmied up behind Hilran and wrapped his arms

around her waist. "Yeah, but Lark is as stubborn and crusty as his old man," he growled next to her ear.

Hilran laughed, twisting out of Tomas' arms. She swatted away his flirtation with her towel.

Lark stabbed his fork into the vegetables. How many times had he heard he was like his uncle *and* his father? Living in the shadow of his parents and the infamous, dead uncle he was named after was burdensome. Gideon and Wynter had reached legendary status by finding the Iron Gate to Isidor and fulfilling the late King Rodolf's oracle. They'd found the promised land and united the Uluns and Alrenians as Ferrians once again. Lark was just another cog in their wheel of good fortune. Until he found his own way, he'd always just be the son of the king and queen—nothing more than a prince named after the king's beloved brother.

He shoved a forkful of parsnips and carrots into his mouth then pushed the plate away. Hilran plucked it off the bar and retreated into the kitchen with Tomas.

Lark turned in his seat and studied the leathery face of the old man in the corner.

He definitely isn't local.

If Lark had to guess by his dust-covered clothes, the man had traveled from Ferran. Though it had been 22 years since Isidor was discovered and settled, there were still thousands who lived in Ferran, but they didn't often venture into the new land of Isidor unless there was some business to be done.

Might as well play the seer card and see if he bites.

Lark was always up for making a few coins from an unsuspecting traveler. People rarely turned down a vision from a seer. For the right price Lark would tell a pliable customer anything he thought they wanted to hear. The king's seer, Gotz, frowned upon such games. He had warned Lark repeatedly about using his gift for personal gain instead of God's purposes. But since when had he ever listened to Gotz?

He strode over to the man's table and sat down without asking for permission.

"That seat is taken!" The man's voice was as coarse as his appearance.

Lark put on a show of looking around. "Funny, I don't see anyone else."

The man took a deep, wheezy breath. "She'll be here soon enough." He took a long swig from his mug.

Lark leaned one hand on the table, ready to make the man an offer. "Listen. I can help you."

The man's forehead creased. "Did Gilla send you?"

He opened his mouth to say *No,* but suddenly intrigued by this mystery woman named Gilla, he decided to play along to see where the conversation would go. "Yes," Lark said, straightening with a subtle cock of his eyebrow. He gave his waistcoat an official-looking tug, presenting a modicum of virtue. "Gilla sent me in her stead."

"The swine," he grumbled. "I knew she wouldn't show her randy face. Too good for the common folk, that one. Thinks she's better than everyone else cause her father was some famous Ulun warrior."

This is getting more interesting by the minute. Lark cleared his throat. "Shall we proceed?"

The man eyed him suspiciously. "Do you have the money?"

Now here's where he should have fessed up that *Gilla* had not sent him, but his curiosity had been piqued. Besides, what if something nefarious was going on that Gideon and Wynter needed to know about? He may not have always seen eye-to-eye with his parents, but he wasn't going to sit back and let someone waltz into Isidor to conduct their shady business deal.

Lark dug inside his coat pocket and pulled out the pouch of coins he'd just received for his birthday. He tossed the black sack on the table. "It's all there." Lark had no idea what the agreed-upon price was, but the jangling coins produced the desired effect. The man's eyes widened. He licked his wrinkled lips like a dog waiting for scraps from his owner's table. The man's bony fingers inched toward the prize.

Lark snatched the pouch away. "Not so fast."

The man frowned then gruffly pulled a worn knapsack off the back of his chair and set it on his lap. He dug inside and pulled out a grimy, square piece of oilcloth that had been stitched up on the sides. He laid it on the table and slid it over. The stained package hardly looked worth the twenty gold coins in Lark's pouch. The man noticed his hesitation and eyed him warily.

"It's what Gilla and me agreed on. The map for the money."

A map? Interesting.

The deal was probably a con, but what did Lark care about money? He put the pouch back on the table, and the man reached for it again. For the briefest moment their fingers touched, and Lark's world went dark as a vision enveloped him.

Dark alley.

The old man counting his coins.

Steps . . . a shadow . . . gold coins tinkling one by one to the ground.

Blood.

And just like that, the vision was over.

Lark blinked. The old man and the pouch of coins were gone. He turned in his chair just in time to see the tavern door swing shut. He grabbed the stained oilcloth and went out into the night.

CHAPTER 2

BREN

Besides a few candles burning within the homes of the restless, the streets of Glasser, Isidor's capital, were abandoned and dark. The city had been dusted with a light snow—a final farewell before spring ushered in its first buds. The night had been serene until Bren had happed upon the sinister prowler. She held him from behind, her knife blade gently teasing his throat. "Thinkest thou shalt cause harm to this fair city?" she whispered next to his ear.

He held up his hands in surrender. She slipped the knife into the sheath at her waist and pulled back the hood of her woolen cape.

"This game of yours is getting old," her brother said, turning to her.

"It's not a game, Lark. I could have been anyone, and you'd be dead." She hadn't meant to scold him, but she hadn't altogether forgiven him for leaving their birthday party early.

Lark continued down the desolate main street. She scrambled after him.

"Why are you here?" he asked, sounding annoyed.

"Why do you think? You left the party early."

"No one probably noticed," he said, glancing over at her.

"It was rude."

He chuckled. "You mean like father, like son?" She grabbed his arm and pulled him to a stop. He sighed.

"You have to stop comparing yourself to him," she said.

"Why? Everyone else does."

"Not me. Never."

He smiled at her, and she knew she had the old Lark back— the one who believed that, as twins, they were stronger together than apart.

"What would I do without my champion?" he asked, rumpling her hair.

"Clearly, die on the streets."

He wrapped an arm around her shoulders. "Come on. Let's go home."

Bren's brother was her world. They were uniquely gifted, and those gifts had bonded them as much as being twins had— perhaps even more. She could often sense his thoughts and feelings with her gift of healing, and he always seemed to show up just when she needed him the most. It was as if their two bodies shared one soul. She didn't feel quite herself when he was out of sight. It didn't help that he was prone to recklessness that made her stomach knot with worry—like leaving their birthday party to roam Glasser.

They walked in silence, his arm across her shoulders, her arm around his waist. They were like an old, comfortable pair of shoes.

Lark stopped and looked around expectantly. "Did you hear that?"

"Hear what?" Bren asked, scanning the darkened buildings and streets.

Lark put a finger to his lips.

A cat screeched. What sounded like a stack of crates crashed to the ground.

"That, I heard," she said quietly.

The dim light of a lantern flickered from within an alley just ahead.

They parted without words. Lark drew his sword and Bren pulled her knife. Hushed, angry voices spilled out into the night.

Lark glanced at her, and she nodded. She approached to the right of the alley as Lark made a wide arch to the left, staying in the shadows until he was on the opposite side.

Someone grunted, then groaned mournfully. What sounded like coins tinkled to the ground.

Lark gave her a nod from across the alley, and they stepped into the lantern light.

A beastly man with a wolf mantle draped over his shoulders and leather cuffs on his forearms, stood over a body. Blood dripped from his large knife. The lantern by his feet illuminated the butchery of his victim. A rat scuttled across the dead man and sniffed at his pockets. The murderer snarled at Bren and Lark. "He got what was coming to him."

"We don't care," Lark said, carefully inching forward. Bren matched his steps. The man would be no match for the two of them. But her confidence was short-lived. Two more men came out of the dark recesses of the alley—one bald, brawny, and carrying an ax, and the other a slim, bearded man wielding a fat, serrated blade that could easily gut someone from stem to stern with one cut. Bren and Lark had both been trained for combat by their parents, but even a skilled warrior could lose in the numbers game.

She swallowed hard. "Brother?" Her whole body tensed.

The killer knelt on one knee, keeping one eye on them, and grabbed the gold coins that had spilled into the alley. His friends brandished their weapons as a warning.

Bren kept looking to Lark for the signal to attack, but he seemed spellbound by the money.

The brute took a quick glance at Bren's fine clothes and long, dark hair, and chuckled. "Run along, *princess*, before you get yourself hurt."

She clenched her jaw and tightened her knife grip. The man likely had no idea she was a real princess: he'd meant to ridicule the fact that she was an armed woman in fine clothes.

Nobody calls me princess.

Bren dashed toward the man without thought, knife raised. His eyes widened as he grabbed the last few coins off the ground. The man with the ax rushed forward. She ducked under his clumsy swing, and the ax landed in her mocker's neck as he was trying to stand. She gasped in horror as he fell to the ground, and the pouch of coins rolled out of his hand.

"Bren!" Lark screamed as his sword rang loudly against the other man's blade.

"I'm fine," she called breathlessly, resetting her stance.

Her attacker grunted and wrenched his ax from his cohort's neck as if he'd split open nothing more than a dry log. He switched the ax to his other hand, sneered at her, then stepped toward her and swung. She sidestepped the attack and ducked behind him. He swayed a bit, turning awkwardly. He raised the ax as she shot forward and grabbed its handle. He bared his teeth, pushing the sharp blade closer and closer to her face. She screamed and plunged her knife into the top of his thigh. His leg buckled, but he managed a clumsy swing that scraped across her cheek as she stumbled backward. Warm blood trickled down Bren's right cheek.

The man swore as he quickly glanced at his thigh wound. He let loose a barrage of horrible things he was going to do to her and laughed. She set her feet, preparing to meet him straight on, only to be pushed roughly aside from behind. A tall, cloaked figure stepped forward and grabbed the bald man's wrist with one hand and plunged a long sword into his gut with the other. The man fell to the ground.

The hooded stranger turned toward the wiry man who had Lark backed up against the alley wall in a death struggle, the thief's serrated blade pushing against Lark's blade – steel on steel. Bren had only been vaguely aware of their battle and watched in awe as the skilled stranger grabbed the man and pulled him off Lark with one hand. The bearded ruffian flared his nostrils and swung his thick blade at the new arrival, but their knightly rescuer batted it away as if it were nothing, pushed the man against the wall, wrenched the man's own blade from his hand, and sliced his throat with it. The man collapsed to the ground while grasping at his gaping neck.

The stranger stood over the dying man until his eyes rolled into the back of his head and his chest grew still, then he dropped the man's serrated blade, turned around, and removed his hood.

"Father," Bren breathed.

"You think you two have what it takes to kill a man?" Gideon asked, looking pointedly at Lark. Gideon waited two breaths then glanced over at Bren. She remained silent.

"We had it handled," Lark said, sheathing his sword.

"You two. Home. Now!" Gideon bellowed.

Lark chuckled that their father thought he could order them home like children. He shook his head, then took off in the opposite direction of home.

CHAPTER 3

LARK

Lark drummed his fingers on the long dining table in the great hall of the castle while his mother paced in front of the broad, stone fireplace—the only warm spot in the massive room. Wynter was still wearing a robe and her long hair was unbound. Normally, she'd be dressed by now with her hair braided, riding freely through the castle's immense property with the steward to help manage the gardens, fishponds, deer parks, and a myriad of other industries on the grounds. But not this morning. Her measured steps were as tight as her lips.

Bren was sitting next to Lark with her eyes closed and her arms crossed. Evidence of last night's skirmish in the alley brazened across her cheek.

I wonder why she hasn't healed the gash? Probably afraid Wynter would scold her for using her gift to heal herself.

Though Lark had showed signs of having the gift of prophecy and Bren the gift of healing, neither of them was supposed to be using their gift until they fully understood the responsibility that came with it. He smirked. *If Gideon and Wynter only knew the games they had played.*

Bren opened one eye and peered at Lark. Gideon finally made an appearance in his standard white shirt, tan pants, and tall black boots. He seated himself at the end of the table and propped his large feet on the edge with a thunk.

Lark rolled his aching shoulders.

"I don't know where to begin," Wynter said, looking between Lark and Bren.

Bren opened her eyes and yawned into her fist.

Wynter's eyes narrowed. "We throw you a 20th birthday party, and you celebrate by sneaking out and roaming the streets, looking for trouble?"

Lark scratched the back of his neck. "It wasn't really like that."

"Then enlighten me!" she snapped. "What was it *really* like?"

He had to be careful here. He didn't want anyone to know that he'd encountered the murdered man at the tavern right before the altercation in the alley. "I went to the Prickly Pig for a late bite to eat. That's all."

Wynter watched him intently. She wasn't easy to fool. Like Bren, she had a way of seeing right through his lies.

"I *ate*," Lark added.

Bren suppressed a smile.

Darn you, Bren. Stop distracting me.

He had to concentrate and maintain eye contact with Wynter if he was going to sell his story.

Wynter folded her arms. Gideon was staring at something on the beamed ceiling.

Lark continued, keeping his voice calm and even. "Afterwards, I was walking home, and Bren showed up."

"Looking for him, by the way," Bren said adamantly, "because I knew it was wrong to be out."

He presssed his lips tightly together. He'd forgotten how skilled Bren was at getting out of trouble.

"Anyway," he said shooting his sister a look of disdain, "it sounded like someone was in trouble in the alley. We couldn't ignore that, could we?" He grinned a little.

Wynter's face colored. "Did you not think of the danger

you'd put yourself or your sister in? You had no idea what was going on in that alley."

Time to wrap this up.

"Sorry," he said simply.

"Sorry?" Wynter turned to Gideon. "Are you listening to this?"

The look of boredom on Gideon's face was typical for these kinds of tongue-lashings.

"What's done is done. They're both fine," he said.

"Fine?" she said, raising her voice another octave. She immediately stormed up to Bren and grabbed her chin and turned it toward Gideon. "Does this cut look fine to you?"

Gideon dropped his feet to the floor and stood.

Lark sank a little further into his seat. He may have defied Gideon last night by walking away from his demand to return home, but his father was not a man to toy with in the light of day. So, whatever was coming would likely be the final word.

Gideon stood in front of Lark and Bren and placed his hands on his hips. Bren twirled her hair with her index finger.

How does she do that? Act nonchalant?

"You ran into that alley without knowing what you were dealing with. The man on the ground had a wound he couldn't survive. The smart thing to do would have been to wait and follow the thieves back to wherever they were holed up, then go for help."

Wynter's mouth dropped open. Perhaps this wasn't the tongue-lashing she'd hoped for from Gideon. Lark straightened up in his chair, feeling a little more optimistic. *Are we really going to get away with just a hand slap? Maybe he's finally going to treat me like a man.*

"You've both been taught combat strategies to defend yourselves, not to engage in vigilante justice. If either of you expect to inherit the throne of Ferran, you'd better start acting with your head instead of your heart."

Bren's eyes were twinkling with expectation.

She thinks we're going to get away with it, too, Lark thought.

"Gideon," Wynter pleaded.

He furrowed his brow. "I'm not done." Something unspoken passed between them, and Wynter's faced calmed.

"You're both confined to the castle grounds until further notice," Gideon said.

Bren sprang to her feet, her face red with fury. "That's unfair! I didn't do anything." She pointed at Lark. "He's the one who rushed into the alley."

"Actually," Lark said, "you were the one who rushed in. I was still observing the situation."

"Oh really? It looked to me like you froze with fear!"

Lark stood and pushed his chair over. "I didn't freeze!"

"Stop!" Wynter cried. "You heard your father."

He and Bren glared at each other. A sick lump formed in his stomach. This was not how he saw this going.

CHAPTER 4

BREN

The hour was late, and technically what Bren was about to do was snooping, but she was sure Lark was hiding something. The pouch of coins in the alley was identical to the pouch they had each received from their parents for their birthday. That and the fact that Lark had hesitated to attack the men in the alley was enough to make her suspect that there was more to the story.

She knocked lightly and opened the door to his room. "Lark?"

The room was empty—his bed still made. The fire set by palace attendants every night beamed warm light across the wooden floor. She hurried to the oversized trunk on the other side of his bed where he liked to stash things and dropped to her knees.

For Lark to have given up his coins, he would have had to receive something in return. But what?

She rummaged through the musty-smelling contents, finding nothing of particular interest—old pack, waterskin, slingshot, a pouch containing flint and steel. She opened a box to find a dozen small animals that Lark had carved from wood when he was a boy. She dug out the fox and held it in her hand. It had been her favorite, and Lark's had been the bear—which he often bragged could kill her fox if it had a mind to. She would argue that the fox would outfox the bear, and therefore it was the superior of the two. She quickly returned the fox to its dark abode.

Nothing in the trunk looked like something Lark would exchange a whole bag of coins for. She let the lid close with a thud, then stood and surveyed the room. A few clothes were strewn about on chairs. A plate of half-eaten food sat on a table in front of the fireplace. She crossed the room to his wardrobe and shuffled through his coats and cloaks, checking the pockets.

"Looking for something?"

She froze, then slowly peeked around the door of the wardrobe.

Lark was standing there with an arm of rumpled clothes. He slammed the bedroom door. "What do you want, Bren? And don't say you wanted to borrow a coat."

"I'm sorry," Bren said.

He strode over and tossed the clothes he was carrying on his bed, then opened his trunk. He gave her a disapproving look. "You went through my things?"

When she didn't say anything, he sighed and quickly fished out a pack, waterskin, and the flint and steel. He dumped the items on this bed.

"What are you doing?" she asked, anxiously.

"What does it look like I'm doing?" He removed his shirt and replaced it with the one on his bed. She could smell the vile odor of its previous occupant from where she stood.

She stormed over and picked up the dirty pants he was about to put on. "Whose clothes are these?" she asked, shaking them in her fist.

"The stable boy. I'm leaving."

She frowned. "Leaving?"

He ripped the pants out of her hand. "I would appreciate if you didn't run to Mommy and Daddy and try to throw me under the horse and cart like you did this morning."

"I *said* I was sorry."

Lark unbuckled his pants and let them drop to the floor. "I get it, okay?" he said, tugging on the stable boy's pants over his underclothes. "You still want to please them. You're fine with being the compliant princess, perhaps even being queen one day, but I'm not."

Her heart raced. They'd never been apart. Not once.

"You can't do this," she said, panic rising in her chest.

"Don't try and stop me," he said, tucking the soiled shirt into his pants.

"Where will you go?"

"Nowhere. Anywhere! Does it matter? I won't be here!"

She balled her hands into fists, heat rising to her face. "You will devastate her!"

He paused for a moment, a puzzled look on his face. He snatched up his pack. "Mother will be fine."

Bren grabbed his arm. "You don't understand. *You're* her favorite."

He wrenched his arm away. "What? Don't be ridiculous."

"It's true, and you know it."

Lark's expression softened. He took her gently by the arms. "She'll be fine. She has you. She has Six and Kidron."

Bren tried to stop the tears, but they came anyway, burning the gash on her cheek. "I won't be, though. I won't be fine."

"I don't want to leave," he said. "I *have* to leave. Please understand. I need to figure out who I am—away from here—from them."

She nodded. "I do understand. It just feels like this is the end. Like our childhood is over."

"We're adults now, Bren. We can't chase each other around the gardens anymore and fight drifters in dark alleys."

"I want to go with you," she said, wiping away her tears.

"No!" he said, skirting by her. He ripped clothes out of his wardrobe and shoved them into his pack.

Her anger returned. She slipped her hand in her pocket and

took out the pouch of gold coins she'd snatched out of the alley. "Then I guess you'll be needing this," she said, tossing the black pouch onto the floor.

He glanced over and paused, one hand still stuffed in his pack.

"It's yours, isn't it? I swiped it off the ground when father turned to help you."

Lark turned back to his packing.

"What did the dead man give you for the coins?" she asked.

He passed by her, ignoring the carelessly tossed pouch, and filled his bag with the rest of his supplies on the bed. "Is that why you were going through my things?"

"I knew you were hiding something."

"The guy gave me some stupid packet sewn up in oilcloth. I have no idea what's in it. I was bored. He thought someone had sent me, so I made an exchange."

"And he ended up dead in an alley!" she cried.

Lark's face flushed with anger. He put on the stable boy's cap, shouldered his bag, then snatched the coin pouch off the floor. He paused at the door. "Give me a day before you tell them. You owe me that much." The door slammed shut.

Bren gritted her teeth. She would not be dismissed like some servant, nor would she be left behind to plead Lark's case. There was only one choice here, and it would be, by far, the most reckless thing she'd ever done.

CHAPTER 5

LARK

Lark's breath clouded in front of him and drifted into the darkness. Leaving the castle grounds with his black stallion, Dash, had been a risk. Thankfully, the guards had barely taken note of Lark with his filched stable boy clothes and his cap pulled low. They accepted Lark's mumbled lie that the horse was restless and needed to be walked despite the late hour. Dash had a well-known, objectionable disposition, so truth had served the lie.

The horse was an expensive breed, trained for war and charging toward an enemy. He was at least two hands taller than the average horse and had a thick neck, long mane, and strong legs built for quick maneuvering. The downside was that Dash was highly spirited and intelligent, and he gave the stable hands more trouble than all the other horses combined. Lark and Bren were the only ones Dash responded to with any kind of deference, although currently the horse was not taking kindly to being dragged out of the stable at such a late hour. He ambled behind Lark, keeping his distance as a form of silent protest. But there was no need to worry. Dash would follow him to the ends of the earth without a bridle or lead, even in the dead of night. There was never a more reliable companion.

Running away was possibly foolish, but Lark refused to be confined to the castle like a child. The truth was, his parents' admonishment had fueled something that had already been lit inside him months ago—a desire, a drive—sometimes so intense that it made his head swirl. He felt like he needed to run even while he was sleeping. But now that he was free, where would he go? Even as the question entered his mind, he knew where.

Once he reached the edge of Glasser, he stopped at the familiar thatched-roofed, stone cottage tucked behind its picket fence. One of the two small windows was aglow with candlelight. He considered whether he should stop. It wasn't like he owed his father's seer anything, but Gotz and Lark were the only two in Isidor with the gift of prophesy. Gotz had done his best to teach Lark how to use his gift, but Lark didn't want to be a seer, so he gave people false visions in exchange for money and only used his gift (as limited as it was) when it benefited him to do so.

He was lingering outside the fence when the arched door of the cottage creaked open. Lark instinctively put a hand on the hilt of the sword at his hip.

"Are you going to come in or not?" Gotz called out. "It's freezing out here."

He'd never get used to the seer's uncanny abilities.

"Stay here," Lark said to Dash. The horse shook his mane and snorted.

Lark followed Gotz into the only living space other than the bedchamber—the kitchen. Dried bundles of herbs hung from every rafter, filling the room with the scent of dead flowers and verdant spice. The large hutch was overflowing with stacks of wooden bowls and clay vessels that Gotz used for creating his medicines, though the table currently stood empty of any such experiments. A fire burned in the hearth on the far wall, its pot hook hanging empty. Even though the room was full, it lacked the spirit that it normally held, making Lark feel like he had just entered the home of a stranger.

Gotz gathered his long robe and sat down on a stool by the fire and warmed his hands. His tabby cat purred and rubbed against his leg. His white hawk, Kia, was sitting on a T-shaped perch on Lark's left, stretching her black-speckled, white wings. The way she seemed to be assessing Lark with her predator eyes was unnerving.

"Where are you going?" Gotz asked, staring into the fire.

"I haven't decided yet," Lark said, stepping further into the room to put distance between him and the bird.

"Yes, you have."

"Then why did you ask?" Lark grumbled.

Gotz peered over at him. He barely had a hair left on his head, and his eyes were rheumy and wet. His hands were gnarled and shriveled.

"I'm going to Ferran," Lark said tiredly.

Gotz returned his gaze to the fire.

"I just thought you should know," Lark said. "You know, in case—"

"In case I die?" Gotz asked. "You can say you gave me a proper goodbye?"

Lark swallowed.

Gotz waved a dismissive hand. "It's okay, young Lark. This wretched winter might still have me before it's done."

"I haven't seen your death." And he hadn't. Not that he would. His visions were unpredictable and haphazard.

"I'm glad to hear it," Gotz said wistfully.

"Well, I better be going." Lark was regretting making the stop and turned to leave.

"What you seek may not be what you find," Gotz said, still gazing into the glowing embers.

"What am I seeking?" Because he didn't know himself, so if Gotz knew something . . .

"Come," Gotz said, beckoning him with a finger.

Lark hesitated.

"Kneel down, I'm too old to stand much anymore," Gotz said.

Lark kneeled in front of him. He sensed a sadness in the old seer's eyes, and it scared him.

"Maybe this wasn't such a good idea." Lark began rising.

Gotz reached out and pressed down on his shoulder. "Close your eyes."

Lark's knees began to ache. His heart raced. He closed his eyes.

Why am I afraid?

Gotz had barely touched him when his mind was seized with a vision and his body clenched.

A map.

Barren land. Burned.

A cave.

A young woman. "Lira," a voice whispers.

Blood.

Death.

Lark fell backwards on his rump and scrambled to his feet. "Blazes! What does it mean?"

Gotz's hand was still stretched out to where Lark's shoulder had been. He lowered his hand to his lap.

"What does it mean?" Lark repeated. This wasn't the first vision he'd gotten in snippets. This one was just like the one from last night when he'd touched the old man in the tavern. He had seen the coins, a shadow, and blood. But the pieces of the visions never made any sense until after the actual events had occurred.

"It's not for me to say," Gotz said dryly.

Lark's face burned with frustration. "Then what's the point?!"

Gotz laughed a little. "Maybe if you lived by the spirit, you'd be able to see."

Lark brushed the dirt off his knees. "You mean be more like you, more like Gideon, or my Uncle Lark."

"If you open your eyes you will see. If you open your ears you will hear."

"I shouldn't have come. You only speak in riddles."

"Even if I spoke the truth, you would not be able to receive it because your heart is hard." With much effort, Gotz pushed himself to his feet. "I fear you are more like your father than I thought."

Lark's breathing labored. He hated Isidor. He hated being a prince. And he hated the seer and his meaningless visions. He was halfway to the door when Gotz spoke. "Wait. I have something for you."

He considered leaving anyway, but Lark had an unquenchable curiosity. He took a deep breath and turned around.

Gotz lumbered over to a bureau and opened the top drawer. He removed something long, wrapped and tied in leather. "Here," he said, holding it out.

Lark eyed it warily.

"It's your late uncle's knife. It has a one-of-a-kind jeweled hilt I think you'll like."

A large knot formed in Lark's throat. He took a few steps and reached out, his hand hovering above the bundle. "Why do you have this?"

"I told your mother you would need it one day, so she gave it to me for safe keeping. Gideon had given it to her as a gift when Lark died."

He took the knife. His heart ached thinking of his mother. Bren was right about him being their mother's favorite. He'd always known. It wasn't like she loved Bren any less, but there had always been an unspoken bond between him and his mother that he couldn't explain.

"Thank you." He didn't know what else to say. He turned and raced out the door, practically running to Dash, who was whinnying with displeasure at being left idling in the cold. Lark stuffed the knife in his saddle pack.

"Young, Lark!" Gotz called from the cottage door. "One more thing."

A white shadow swooped out of the doorway. Within seconds, Gotz's hawk landed on Lark's saddle and inspected its surroundings.

"Kia is yours now."

Lark stared at the large bird. He was about to open his mouth to protest when Gotz added, "Remember, young Lark. With humility comes revelation." With that, the door shut.

A moment later, the candle in the window guttered and went out.

CHAPTER 6

BREN

It was almost dawn. The sky was still a dull gray. Soaking wet, cold, and shivering, Bren propped her spear next to the door and knocked at the back entrance of her best friend's house. The horse barn, just a stone's throw away, was locked up tight. She blew warm air into her hands and prayed that her friend was awake. She wouldn't let Lark leave her behind, but she needed to move quickly if she was going to catch up with him. Before she left the castle, she had sealed a note to her parents with a drop of wax.

Lark and I need some time alone. We're going north to the mountains of Isidor to hunt.

The note would hopefully put their parents off their trail should they decide to come looking for them. Bren was certain there was only one place Lark would go.

The kitchen door flew open. Seven stood there like a dark, Greek god with an apron tied around his waist. "What is this?" he asked, eyeing her wet attire.

Bren scooted past his six-foot-four frame.

"You're going to get sick," he said, shutting the door.

"I'm fine," she said, sideling up next to the kitchen fire. Something nutty and sweet-smelling was simmering in a large pot. Her stomach rumbled.

"Why are you wet? What happened to your face?"

She sat down on a stool and sighed. "It's nothing."

Seven stood across from her by the fire and frowned. The reflection of the fire flared in his brown eyes. He may have been born in Glasser, but he was typical Jutta, like his mother, Six. Fact-driven and practical.

"Is Six here?" she asked, looking around the tidy kitchen.

"No."

Good. No Six. No problems.

Six may have been Wynter's best friend, but she was also meddlesome and never let Seven get too far out of her reach. Perhaps it was because she'd raised Seven on her own, and he was all she had. No one spoke of the father, especially Seven. If one believed the rumors, he was a man of some importance from far away.

"I just need to dry off," Bren said.

"Why are you wet?" he repeated.

"I may have swum across the castle moat."

He smiled. "You're mad."

"So I've been told."

He grabbed a couple of bowls off a shelf, ladled out porridge from the pot over the fire, pilfered a couple of wooden spoons off the kitchen worktable, and sat down across from her.

She accepted a bowl, holding it tightly in her lap to warm her cold hands. Seven dug into his with the verbosity of a wild boar.

"Why are you here?" he asked with a full mouth.

"Can't I just visit a friend?"

"You never come just for a visit. The face?" he asked, motioning toward the gash on her cheek.

Having a conversation with Seven was like talking to a judge and jury at the same time.

"I met an angry ax," she said, hoping to avoid the details. She lifted her bowl and shoveled some of the honey-sweetened porridge into her mouth. "Are you up for an adventure?"

His eyes lit up. He stopped eating mid-spoon. "That is a question that never needs to be asked."

She smiled. Seven was a brawny, 19-year-old with a fever for action. He was also clever and had a battle instinct that made even a skilled fighter like his mother, Six, raise an eyebrow or two.

"Then what are we waiting for?" she asked. "Get your things."

He hurriedly finished eating, then rinsed out his bowl and spoon in a tub of water and laid it neatly on a linen towel to dry.

"Where are we going?" he asked, eyeing her bowl.

Her leg bounced with nervous energy. She needed to keep their destination secret. *For now.* If he knew where they were going, that would have been the end of the conversation.

"No," he said, shaking his head, "I've seen that leg-bouncing thing of yours before. You're up to no good."

She placed a hand on her leg to stop it, then stood up and smiled.

He was still eyeing the bowl in her hand. He would make sure she cleaned it before they left. Neatness was one of Seven's peculiar habits. Suppressing an eye roll, she went and dipped her bowl and spoon into the dishwater and rinsed until there was a look of satisfaction in his eyes. "Are you going to go with me or not?" she asked, wiping her hands on a towel. She wanted to get out of Glasser before the shops opened *and* before Six showed up.

He took a deep breath. "How mad will this adventure make my mother?"

"On a scale of Six hugging you to Six carving your heart out of your chest?" She paused for dramatic effect. "I hope you're not attached to your heart," she said with a tilt of her head and a mischievous smirk.

"I'll get my things," he said with an air of eagerness.

She chuckled quietly as he left the room. The one thing that fueled Seven more than anything else was a chance to clash swords with his mother. He would do anything if he thought there was even a small chance that Six would pick up a sword against him.

This was the way of the Jutta.

CHAPTER 7

LARK

Lark traveled all night by lantern light through the White Mountain gorge. Had he known how harrowing it was going to be navigating in the dark between sheer, rocky cliffs, he may have reconsidered his timing. But it mattered not now. The sun had risen, and he was out of Glasser and safely in open pasture at the base of the gorge. He needed to get some sleep before he made the strenuous climb and stepped into the heart of Ferran for the first time.

He crossed the gorge river and found the ivy-ridden remains of an old building in the woods—a place his mother had spoken of. Her descriptions of the forest of giant cypress didn't do them justice. Had she and his father really killed three wolves here among these towering ancients? The trees were witnesses, but trees didn't speak of such things, though his mother would say otherwise. She claimed she could hear the crackle and pop of the language of trees just by placing an ear to their trunks.

A small ache formed in his stomach thinking of how disappointed and worried Wynter would be when she discovered he'd left. But he couldn't think about such things now. He was tired and chilled to the bone. He needed a warm fire and some sleep. He tied Dash's bridle to a shrub as a precaution. Kia sat above them on one of the remnants of stone wall and scanned the woods for her breakfast.

He cleared out some underbrush, gathered wood, and started a fire as warm as the rising sun. It felt good to be free from Isidor—from his parents. And he hated to say it, but it was also a relief to be free from Bren. He loved her, but being a twin was a lot like taking care of two of himself.

After eating some stale bread and a wedge of cheese he'd swiped from the castle kitchens, he opened his pack and removed the sewn-up oilcloth the old man in the tavern had given him in exchange for his coin pouch. He had stealthily slipped it from underneath his pillow and put it in his pack during Bren's rant.

Lark had seen a vision when the man's fingers had touched him. *Blood.* Yet he'd let the man walk out with the money all the same. Now that man was dead. Lark should have harbored some sense of guilt, but he did not.

He slipped his uncle's jewel-hilted knife under one of the stitches in the oilcloth and sliced down one side, then the other. Inside was an old, folded piece of parchment. He threw the oilcloth into the fire and waited until it bubbled and melted into ash, then he unfolded the mysterious paper. A smaller piece of paper, the size of his hand, fell out and fluttered to the ground. He smoothed out the bigger parchment on his leg. It looked like an old map of Ferran. His eyes went immediately to the scarlet X, near the only city remaining in the west—Ruritania. The letters D.R. were written in small, faded script next to the X.

D.R.? What could it mean?

Dash snorted. Kia let out two long calls.

"Hush," he said.

He snatched the smaller piece of parchment off the ground and read.

For this is left of that fair Oracle

Bottomless seas, caverns deep
The soul shall find itself alone amid the Morbids creep
O Great Destruction, eternal flame
Yet there is still one whom the treasure will claim
Look, great wanderer, for only you will see, the crown of jewels at
the bottom of the sea
Alas, the hour has finally come. Extinguish the flame of the evil one.

He shoved the strange words into his pants pocket and studied the map more closely. Ulun and Alrenian territories were explicitly marked, so the map had to be created from the time when Ferran was divided. He traced a finger from the gorge where he now sat, to the X. The way to Ruritania went directly through the area of desolation—arid land hit the worst by the Great Destruction.

What of any importance could lie there? Yet someone named Gilla had been willing to pay handsomely for this map.

Dash stamped his front hoof stubbornly into the ground and snorted, alerting Lark to danger. Kia flew off.

Lark quickly folded the map, stuffed it inside his pack, and kicked dirt into the fire to snuff it out. He quietly drew his sword from its scabbard.

Dash whinnied.

"Shhh," he whispered, stepping over and rubbing the horse's nose.

The voices were distant, coming from the direction of the river. He stepped lightly through the brush, touching the giant cypresses to help guide him back to the river. He stopped at the edge of the woods where small sycamore trees grew.

Two bearded men, wearing dark fur mantles and leather arm bracers, were sitting by a fire on the other side of the river. One was sharpening a knife across a stone, and the other was tending to the spit-roasting of a small creature over the fire. A woman with a black patch over her left eye stood above them with a log in her hand. Her dark blonde hair was braided in dozens of long strands and bound behind her neck. Her leather shoulder armor, silver arm bracers, and leather pants gave her a venomous look—the long sword strapped across her back, a deadly tongue.

"He can't be far," the woman said. She tossed the log on the fire, sending up fiery sparks into the air.

The man sharpening the knife said, "You said that last night."

She slapped him on the back of the head. "Keep your trap shut!"

"What about the king?" the other man said, wiping his mouth across the sleeve of his tunic. "I don't want his son's blood on my hands."

"Don't worry," the woman said. "Once we get the map, I'll take care of the prince."

Lark gasped.

She spat into the fire and looked straight into the woods where Lark was standing.

Kia cried out a warning.

CHAPTER 8

BREN

Seven secured two horses for them from the barn. That meant that his mother, Six, would be without her horse.

Good. It will make it harder for her to try and follow once she realizes Seven has left Glasser.

Bren's thought was a stretch, though. With a snap of her fingers, Six could have any of the crown's fine horses at her disposal. Bren's mother and Six were friends to a fault. Everything they had been through together had bonded them for life —Wynter's mistaken identity as the Alrenian queen, the quest for Isidor, the battle with the rogue Uluns. Bren just hoped that the note she'd left for her parents would put them off their trail, but chances were they wouldn't be fooled for long.

As soon as Seven recognized the direction Bren was taking him in, he stopped his horse.

"You lied to me," he grumbled.

"I didn't lie. I just didn't say where we were going."

"Enjoy your trip," he said, giving his horse a small tap with his left leg.

She closed her eyes and bit down on her bottom lip. Seven was more of a day trip kind of guy, and anything beyond that, he required days to prepare—days she didn't have if she wanted to catch up to Lark.

"Wait!" she called to his back.

To her relief, he circled back around and stared at her.

She had exactly thirty seconds to talk him out of turning back. It would have to be something big to get him to change his mind.

"What do you want?"

"To return to Glasser."

"No," she said with a sigh. "What *thing* do you want that would sway you to continue? Name it, and I'll give it to you."

His mouth twisted, and he got a faraway look in his eyes while he thought about it. "The spear."

She slid her hand unconsciously to the spear attached to the side of her saddle. "No," she said.

"It was given to Six by Gideon's lieutenant, Brendle," he said, repeating a claim of ownership that he'd made before. "You know this is true. Brendle trained Six in the art of the spear."

"Yesss," she said, drawing the word out, "but I'm *named* after Brendle because he was my mother's spirit wolf, and he died trying to save her. It has sentimental value."

"Then I will see you when you get back." With that remark, he made to turn his horse.

She bit her lip and squeezed her horse's reins in her hand. "Fine!"

He rode up next to her and held out his hand.

"This isn't right, and you know it," she said, sliding off her horse. She removed the spear and held it out to him like a torch.

"I'll need you to attach it to my saddle," he said with an air of superiority.

She reluctantly secured the spear below his saddle. "There!" Her face flushed with heat. Losing the spear was akin to losing a beloved pet. She'd learned to battle with that spear—sparring with Lark, Six, and her parents. It was a relic of a lost time, and it left a sick pit in her stomach to have to part with it.

Seven undid his sword belt and handed it to her. "Now we can go to Ferran." He tapped his heels, and his horse cantered toward the White Mountain gorge.

That afternoon, they emerged from the gorge into the open plain that sat at the base of the White Mountains. That's where they ran into the first signs of trouble.

Seven knelt down and rubbed ash from an extinguished fire between his fingers.

"How far ahead do you think Lark is?" Bren asked.

"Not far."

Bren had first assumed that the fire had been Lark's, but something didn't feel right. She walked around the remnants of the fire, taking in the flattened grass. She knelt and picked up a discarded bone with flakes of meat still left on it and sniffed it.

Rabbit.

A hawk circled them overhead and cried out.

"This isn't Lark's camp," she said.

"How do you know?" Seven asked.

She held up the rabbit bone. "He hates rabbit."

They both searched the underbrush for more clues. Anything that would indicate Lark had been there.

Bren found a neck scarf in some tall grass by the river. She gave it a quick sniff and pulled her head back in disgust. It was foul, but not *Lark* foul.

"Hey!" Seven shouted. "I think you should see this."

He was standing twenty feet away in the grassy area leading away from the river. She jogged over.

Seven pointed at the ground. "It ends a few feet away."

Blood.

Bren's heart pounded.

"We don't know it's Lark's," Seven said.

The hawk that had been circling overhead landed on the ground close to them and called out again.

"Is that—?" Seven asked.

"Gotz's hawk, Kia," she said, growing pale.

"The seer is too old to travel this far," Seven said, scanning the area.

Bren knelt down, but before her fingers even touched the dried stain, she knew that the blood was Lark's.

CHAPTER 9

WYNTER

Wynter stormed out of the castle, slightly lifting the hem of her simple day dress as she crossed the castle's drawbridge. Gideon was on his knees at the far end, replacing a rotten board.

"Have you seen this?" she said, waving the note Bren and Lark had left for them.

He wiped his forehead on his sleeve. "Can you hand me that hammer by your feet?"

She sighed as she bent down and retrieved the tool. "Why aren't you at court? I thought they needed you for a special hearing?"

He took the hammer and pounded a nail into a piece of new board he had laid. "Griffon Conn's complaint that it was a two-legged thief who took his ram and spoiled his lambing season is hardly worth my attention."

"They look to you as the final authority, you know."

Gideon sat back on his heels and surveyed his handiwork. "What's this piece of paper of yours about?"

"It's from Lark and Bren," she said indignantly. "They've left the castle grounds."

His expression remained unchanged.

"Well?" she asked. "Aren't you going to say anything?"

Gideon pushed himself to his feet. "They're twenty years old. What do you want me to say?"

Heat rose to her face. She crushed the letter in her hand and held it in front of him. "They've defied us!"

"They're growing up, Wynter."

She dropped her hand to her side. "How can you be so . . ."

He cocked his head and smiled. His dark hair was long again, reminding her of when they'd first meet, and she'd thought him a brute beast. Righteous anger coursed through her right down to her fingertips. "How can you be so . . . indifferent!?"

"You're beautiful when you're angry, you know that." He reached out to her.

She twisted away from him and marched back toward the castle. The bridge vibrated beneath her feet. She glanced back. Gideon was marching toward her with a scowl on his face. Her heart skipped a beat, and she immediately took off running. Before she could reach the castle, he scooped her up into his arms.

She kicked and squirmed. "Put me down!"

He carried her straight into the castle courtyard, set her down, and boldly drew her in for a long kiss. She pushed against him, but part of her relented because he hadn't let her walk away. *Daughters of Ferran. I never could resist his strange charms.*

Suddenly, the staff in the inner courtyard who had been passing through broke into applause.

With her lips still pressed against Gideon's, she broke into a smile. "I hate you."

"I know." He kissed her forehead, then turned to the staff. "Everyone back to work!"

There were a few chuckles and whispers as the workers returned to their daily tasks.

"That will be the talk of the town for the next week," she said with a small smile, retying a loose tie on the side of her dress.

Gideon's face grew apprehensive—something he only did when he was troubled.

"What is it?" she asked.

"My brother's horse died this morning."

Her stomach soured. *That is why he avoided court and sought solitude.* The news had more sting to it than she'd cared to admit. The horse had been the last remaining link to his brother for both of them. She'd once had feelings for Gideon's brother, Lark, but that had been a long time ago, and some of Lark's last words had proven truer than she could have ever imagined. *You're meant for him.*

She gently touched Gideon's cheek. "I'm so sorry."

He took a step back and held open his palm for the children's note. They wouldn't speak of Lark's horse again. He would grieve in his own way.

He straightened out the crumpled note and quickly skimmed it. *"Hunting?"* he said, rubbing a hand across his mouth.

"What?" she asked, reading it again over his shoulder. "Do you think it's a ploy to divert us?"

"I know it is."

"Where do you think they went?"

"I don't know, but we both know someone who might."

They locked eyes.

"Gotz," she said. "Let me grab a cloak."

Chapter 10

Lark

Lark lifted a hand to his throbbing head. He winced when his fingers found a large knot crusted over with blood.

I wonder how long I've been out.

He opened his eyes and tried moving, but his legs were bound, and his hands were tied behind his back. He tugged at his restraints, then twisted his head around. He was in an open pasture littered with weeds and remnants of a long-forgotten camp.

Well, this wasn't how I wanted to see Ferran for the first time.

How could he have been so foolish? He thought he could handle the paltry little group of mischief-makers, but he'd underestimated the skills of the girl. She'd been a worthy opponent, but he had been confident that she was no match for him right up until someone hit him from behind.

Footsteps approached. He closed his eyes. It was best to feign unconsciousness until he knew who he was dealing with.

"What are you going to do with him?" a man asked.

"You shouldn't have knocked him over the head," the woman said.

"I was helping you."

"No, you were interfering. Don't do it again."

"We got the map, didn't we?"

"No thanks to you." She prodded Lark with her boot.

"I'm not sure I'm comfortable with killing the king's son, Gilla," another man said.

"*Lord* Gideon didn't think twice before he killed my father," Gilla said. "Now it's my turn to return the favor."

She spat, and it landed on Lark's chin.

"I'm going hunting," she said. "Keep an eye on him."

CHAPTER 11

—————

BREN

Bren and Seven peered over a cairn of stones at the top of the gorge. They had left their horses a hundred feet behind them so they could get their first look at Ferran without being taken unawares.

"Looks like there're only two of them," Seven whispered.

Two men were sitting against an old, decaying wagon in a weedy field of weathered and abandoned belongings from long ago. One was blond, with his long hair pulled back with a leather tie, and the other had dark hair cut at the shoulder. They both had bushy beards and black fur mantles over their shoulders. Bren spied Lark lying motionless by some old barrels just a few feet away from his captors. He was bound, which meant he was still alive. Lark's black horse, Dash, was tied up at the edge of the woods along with three other horses. Dash was whinnying and furiously pulling on his lead. The third horse gave her pause. It could mean there was a third person close by. Simply charging in with weapons drawn would be too risky. They needed a plan.

"What's the plan?" Seven asked.

"We approach and ask for food," she said.

"I'm not hungry."

She elbowed him. "We *pretend* we're hungry, then we draw our weapons."

He grunted.

"You have a better idea?" she asked.

He told her his idea.

"You're right, that's better," she said, hating to admit it. She quietly drew her sword from its scabbard. "Ready?"

"This question is unnecessary," he said, scowling at her. "Of course I'm ready."

Seven somehow never understood the subtleties of conversation, but now was not the time to point it out. It would only serve to get on his bad side.

She took a deep breath, gripped her sword tight, and climbed the last few feet out into the open. As soon as her feet hit solid ground, she took off running toward the men—toward Lark.

"Help!" she cried, running and glancing behind her.

The men stood up and drew their swords.

Seven came out after her almost straight away and made chase with his newly acquired spear in hand.

"Please!" Bren cried out, stumbling for effect.

The men gave each other confused looks but seemed to be buying that she was a damsel in distress. They were looking past her at Seven.

That's it, you filthy pigs. Focus on Seven.

When she reached them, she turned and faced Seven's advance, breathing heavily. She held her sword at the ready like she was bracing for Seven's attack.

"Don't worry, Lass, we can handle this," the blond man said.

Seven screamed, widened his eyes, and bared his teeth as he raced toward them. He was like a charging tree trunk—all power and muscle.

Daughters of Ferran! What happened to the skinny little boy I once knew?

The men planted their feet, held their swords with both hands, tips toward the sky, and exchanged nervous glances.

Bren dared a peek at Lark. He was awake, looking wide-eyed between her and Seven's raging approach.

Seven attacked with the force of a seasoned warrior—both hands on his spear.

The blond man came forward fast and hacked at Seven, relying on his strength more than skill. Seven let the shaft of his spear take the fury.

Bren suddenly feared for Seven and took a step forward. But the dark-haired man had one eye on her, so she quickly shouted to the blond man to maintain her ruse. "That's it. Give the villainous maggot-pie what he deserves!"

Seven gave her a sharp look as he danced around his opponent. Then he lunged with his spear with a new ferocity and quickness as if her insult had woken him up. His stabs became lightning fast—like a snake striking and recoiling, driving the man back again and again. Bren's heart pounded with excitement as the man desperately tried to defend himself.

"You're pathetic, you vomit-eating rogue!" she shouted at Seven.

Seven gritted his teeth.

Her words were turning Seven into a mad man. It gave her a strange thrill to see her words have such an affect.

The man managed a desperate wide sweep with his sword. Seven blocked with his spear, then drove its sharp tip into the man's leg. The man cried out, and his leg buckled, bringing him to one knee. Seven twirled the spear and rammed the blunt end straight into the man's Adam's apple. The injured man dropped his sword and fell backward to the ground.

Breathing heavily, Seven turned to the remaining dark-haired man.

Bren should have engaged the second man as soon as Seven had traded first blows with the man on the ground. That *had* been the plan. But seeing Seven in the heat of the battle had somehow stunned her. She'd gotten caught up in the show and had forgotten her part.

With sweat beading on his forehead and his spear dangling in one hand, Seven marched straight toward the man standing next to her. Bren backed away, inching toward Lark. This was Seven's fight now. He would finish it.

There was fear in the man's face as Seven came at him. His wounded friend had managed to stand and was now limping toward the horses.

Seven thrust his spear low.

The man blocked with his blade.

Then there was a blur of lunging, ducking, and hacking until the man's friend rode up in a rush with the other horses in tow, including Dash. The last man standing turned and ran away from Seven, catching up alongside one of the horses until he managed to jump and grab its pommel and swing himself up into the saddle. The two men bolted across the meadow and rode into the forest.

Seven, breathing heavily, glanced over at Bren and they held each other's eyes. She tried to make sense of how this warrior before her now could possibly be the same boy she'd just schemed with at the top of that hill.

"Bren!" Lark called out, breaking her trance.

She turned away from Seven and hurried to Lark's side.

"Boy, am I glad to see you," he said.

She cut the rope from his wrists and ankles with the knife at her waist, and they embraced. "Never leave without me again," she said. "Promise me." He nodded and hugged her tighter.

Dash showed up unexpectantly, dragging his lead with Lark's pack slung across the pommel. He nudged Lark playfully in the back and snorted.

"That's my boy," Lark said, giving him a good scratch behind the ears.

CHAPTER 12

GIDEON

Gideon rode by Wynter's side through the capital city they had named Glasser. He couldn't believe it had been twenty-one years since they'd traveled through the White Mountains and discovered Isidor. The land was plentiful, and food was abundant here. But the Ferran they'd left behind always simmered in his thoughts. Reports were that the ground sickness came less frequently now. Very few people lived in the trees anymore, and the abandoned treetop homes were maintained by hired stewards who rented them out to travelers for their novelty. Ferran was ripe for rebuilding, but first they needed to build the treasury and that had proved to be slow business. For now, Ferran was stuck in the past.

"What are you so deep in thought about?" Wynter asked, guiding her horse closer. She was wearing pants today. Something he'd not seen her do in a long time. She'd taken to dresses on the advice of her chamberlain who wouldn't hear of having his queen in pants. Staying in his good graces was tantamount to her sanity, so she complied—most of the time.

"Just thinking of you," he said with a wink.

She smiled at him. "Uh huh."

Wynter could always see straight through him. She didn't

need to use her gift of healing to see his heart anymore. He had surrendered it to her a long time ago.

They arrived at Gotz's cottage at the edge of town and slid off their saddles. There was barely a trickle of smoke coming from the chimney.

"How long has it been?" Wynter asked, as they tethered their horses to Gotz's hitching post.

"Too long. He refuses to leave his cottage and come for a visit. I've tried."

Gideon led the way to the door and knocked. He prayed Gotz knew something as to Lark and Bren's whereabouts, because Wynter would not rest until she found them.

"Maybe he's out," Wynter offered.

"Gotz!" He pounded on the door with his fist. Wynter gently brushed him aside and listened quietly at the door. "Something's wrong," she said. Gideon opened the door, and they stepped into the small foyer. Gotz's tabby cat shot around them and out the door.

"Gotz!" Wynter cried out, pointing to the left. "Check his bedchamber."

Gideon's heart raced. The place was freezing. He should have checked on Gotz more often—made sure he was taking care of himself. Gotz's bed was neatly made and the pillow plump. Only the stub of a candle remained at his bedside table.

"Gideon!"

He ran from the bedroom and rushed into the kitchen. Wynter was on the wooden floor beside Gotz, feeling his head. The fire in the hearth was mostly ashes and embers.

Gideon dropped to his knees and lifted Gotz's head off the ground. Gotz slowly opened his wrinkly eyes. A lump rose in Gideon's throat. The seer had been like a father to him, standing by his side all those years when he was young and stubborn and had refused advice.

"Let me help you up," Gideon said, trying to lift him by the shoulders.

Gotz shook his head and stretched out a hand to protest. A deep cough wracked his body. Gideon couldn't believe how feeble Gotz had become. He barely had a hair left on his head—it was all brown spots and white fuzz now. His skin was wrinkled and pale, and his fingers were gnarled with the disease that ate bones.

"It's time," Gotz wheezed.

Gideon's breath came faster. *No.* He couldn't lose Gotz. *First his brother's horse, now this?*

He remembered that day long ago in Ferran when Wynter was unconscious from healing an Alrenian child, and he hadn't known if Wynter would recover. He'd sent Gotz away in his grief and anger. A few days later he had encountered Gotz in the woods, and the old seer accused him of running away. *I've lost so much,* he'd told him. Then Gotz said something Gideon would never forget. *We've all lost more than a man should. It's what you do in the face of it that matters.*

Wynter reached out a hand and placed it on Gotz's chest and closed her eyes. She didn't heal anymore, it was too dangerous for her now, but she could still feel the severity of the sickness.

She opened her eyes, looked at Gideon, and shook her head.

"I told you," Gotz said, breaking into another coughing fit.

"You old fool," Gideon said, "why didn't you send for me?"

Gotz managed a little wave of his hand. "You've got your hands full with those two whippersnappers."

Gideon rubbed a loving hand over Gotz's bald head. "I need you, Gotz." His voiced cracked.

Gotz gazed up at him. There was a spark of love in his eyes. "No," he said. "You never did. You always had what you needed right here." He tapped Gideon's heart with a crooked finger. Gideon's throat tightened with grief. "Of course, you're nothing without this one," Gotz breathed, looking over at Wynter.

"Sons of Ferran, Gotz. I'll never forgive you for leaving me like this," he cried out.

"I'm sorry." The words triggered another bout of coughing. Gideon took his hand and squeezed it.

"Lark," Gotz whispered. His rheumy blue eyes glazed over and he released a final breath that sounded like a sigh of relief.

Gideon's stomach lurched. He ran from the room and out the front door, losing his breakfast on the ground. He placed his hands on his knees. His head swam. Wynter placed a hand on his back, and a flood of peace coursed through him. He turned around and drew her into his arms.

"I'm so sorry," she said.

He inhaled the wildflower and honey in her hair and held onto the only thing he had left from his past. Losing Lark's horse and Gotz on the same day was the end to an era—an end he was not prepared for. When he had finally composed himself, he took a step back. Wynter stroked his face, tears pooling in her eyes.

"Why did he say Lark's name?" Gideon asked. "You think he knew my brother's horse died this morning?"

"Maybe."

They reluctantly returned to Gotz's frail body. Wynter helped wrap and bind him in blankets from his bedchamber. They would take him back to the castle grounds and build a pyre for his funeral. Gideon quickly surveyed Gotz's humble kitchen belongings. Jars and bowls lined the shelves. Herbs tied in bundles were hung from the rafters. The large bird stand stood empty.

"Kia is missing," he said.

Wynter was busy rummaging through all the drawers and cupboards.

"What are you looking for?" he asked.

"A knife."

Gideon stared down at the mummy-looking bundle—Gotz's remains. Gideon had lost his mother, father, and both brothers. Now Gotz. If Wynter's friend, Six, had been there, she'd say tears for the dead were wasted. *It's the living we should cry for,* she'd say. That was the way of the Jutta.

"It's not here," Wynter said, blowing a strand of hair out of her face.

"What's not here?"

"Your brother's knife," she said. "Gotz said one day our son would come for it, so I gave it to him for safe keeping."

Gideon chewed on the inside of his cheek. "Do you think—?"

Wynter nodded. "Lark and Bren have been here. Gotz probably sent Kia with them."

"Gotz knew he was dying," Gideon said reflectively.

They looked at each other with a mix of grief for Gotz and concern for their missing children.

"Where could Lark and Bren have gone?" Wynter asked.

Gideon's jaw tightened. "I don't know."

But now that Gotz was gone, Gideon suddenly realized how important it was to find them. Besides his sister, Kidron, the children and Wynter were all the family he had left now.

CHAPTER 13

LARK

"Is that our mother's spear hanging on the side of Seven's saddle?" Lark asked, glancing back as they walked their horses through the northern forest of Ferran.

"Yes," Bren said with a sigh. "It was the only way I could get him to come to Ferran with me."

"He's been keeping his distance ever since you two came to the rescue."

"I think he's mad at me," Bren said, picking the petals off a wildflower and letting them float to the ground.

"Because?"

"You heard. I called him a villainous maggot-pie and a vomit-eating rogue."

Lark burst out laughing.

Bren tightened her lips and punched him in the arm. "Daughters of Ferran, I was nervous! I didn't want your captors catching on to our ruse, so I improvised. I was playing a damsel in distress, so I called him a few names. He probably thinks I meant it. You know how he is."

Lark smiled and shook his head. It felt good to laugh; it distracted him from thinking about his captor. *Gilla.* She'd said Gideon had killed her father, and it was no coincidence that twenty-one years ago, Gideon had killed the rogue Ulun leader, Valen, in the court of swords. The fight to the death between Gideon and Valen had become so legendary that children in Isidor re-enacted the battle with their wooden swords, using pumpkins and cabbages to mimic the beheading of Valen.

Gilla wants more than the map. She wants revenge. When I purchased the map, I opened a long-forgotten door.

He had to decide what his next move was going to be. Even though Gilla had the map, revenge was likely still on her mind. Perhaps she wouldn't give up on losing the king's son so easily. There were more dangers lurking in Ferran than he'd realized. If Bren and Seven hadn't shown up, he'd likely be dead by now.

They approached a large clearing with a horse stable and a small cottage with a porch. Signage nailed to a porch post read, *Queen's Treetop Inn.* The proprietress left her mending on her rocking chair and hobbled toward them. She was short and plump, with a crease-lined face and twinkling eyes. Little tufts of gray hair sprouted out the sides of her linen cap. "Welcome to the childhood home of our queen, Lady Wynter. Tree shelter for the night and boarding for the horses?" she asked with a polite smile and an extended palm.

Wynter had lived in the middle forest, not the northern forest where they currently stood, but Lark supposed the women cared not. A tree house was a tree house, and he was curious to see how his mother had once lived, so he dropped a gold coin in the woman's hand.

She spat on it, bit on it, and nodded. She called a young girl off the porch of her home to come take their horses. He had a brief moment of concern at handing over Dash to a child, but to Lark's surprise the horse went obediently, smelling the girl's hair, as if he were enamored with her.

The woman led their small group of three down a long path into the woods and stopped at a tree with a rope ladder. "If you want food, follow the signs on the slat bridge that heads south. Hot sheeps' feet and beef ribs are the speciality."

Lark adjusted his pack to lay against his back and took the lead climbing, followed by Bren.

"Wow," Bren said from below him. "It's hard to believe our mother lived like this."

Seven made small grunts from the rear—a clear expression of his thoughts on the antiquated accommodations.

"As I recall, Seven," Lark said, "Six used to be a bridge builder. She probably built some of the bridges up here."

No response.

After a rather strenuous climb, Lark poked his head through a square in the floor of the tree hut. Two rays of fading sunlight filled with dust motes filtered through the windows that were propped open with wooden rods. He put his hands on the floor and pushed himself up; Bren and Seven followed right behind him.

"Not what I was expecting," Bren said, looking around.

Lark had to agree. The place was bare except for a table, two chairs, and a straw-stuffed pallet against the far wall. He shimmied out of his pack and dropped it to the floor. "It will do for a night."

Kia landed on the windowsill and craned her neck left and right as if contemplating where she might sleep.

"It will only *do* when I'm done with it," Seven said, shooing Kia away and removing the window rod. The window fell shut with a thud.

Lark stood baffled as Seven arranged his spear and pack neatly in a corner.

"Maybe we should go get some food while he . . . you know . . . straightens up," Bren said, motioning to the exit in the floor with her head.

Lark stifled a sigh: Bren was probably right. Seven wouldn't be satisfied until the place was to his liking.

"Good idea," Lark said, rubbing his hands together. He was famished. "Any requests, Seven?"

"A broom," Seven said grumpily.

"Come on," Bren said, pulling at Lark's arm.

Lark shook his head, and they readily left Seven to stew about the hut while they made their way down onto a slat bridge just below them. They wobbled south, passing a handful of other patrons, until they found signs pointing the way to *Treetop Tavern*.

"The place was fine," Lark grumbled.

"You know how Seven is," Bren said.

"And *you* know he and I have never gotten along."

"He saved your life," she retorted.

The words stung a little. Owing Seven wasn't exactly a position he would have put himself in voluntarily. The two of them had always tolerated each other at best. "Listen," Lark said, swatting a tree branch out of the way. "Mother and father will come looking for us now. They may have been willing to let me go, but not both of us."

"Lucky for you, I thought of that already."

"What do you mean?"

"I left them a note saying that we were going to the mountains of Isidor to hunt."

"And you think they'll fall for that?"

Bren shrugged.

"Look, I appreciate you and Seven coming to the rescue and everything, but you two should go home."

Bren dug her fingers into his arm and stopped him. "I won't go back without you, so save your breath."

"You're going to be queen one day, and we both know it. Please go back. Be the good one."

She dropped her hand and shook her head. "You don't get it. We're twins. We're connected."

The truth was, he didn't want to be the reason that Bren had left Isidor.

She tapped her hand twice over her heart. "This is my choice. I'm choosing this."

He nodded. It was hard to argue with Bren, much less say no to her.

She pulled him into her arms, and they held onto each other for a moment.

"Thanks for rescuing me," he said.

"Speaking of," she said. "Why did those drifters take you prisoner?"

"One of the drunks at the Prickly Pig must have told them they saw me trade something with the old man. Turns out it was a map." He'd keep Gilla to himself for the moment. As far as Bren knew, there were just the two men.

"A map, as in there was a map inside the oilcloth you mentioned?"

He rubbed the back of his neck and nodded.

"What kind of map?" she asked, curiously.

"I can't be sure, but I think it's a treasure map," he said. "The drifters were after it, and I want to know why."

CHAPTER 14

BREN

Bren couldn't believe the transformation that Seven had made to the tree hut. It was nothing short of a miracle. Three hammocks had been hung one above the other at the end of the room. There was no trace of the straw pallet. A lantern hung from a hook in the ceiling, illuminating the spotless floor. Seven was sitting at the small table, and a third chair that had not been there before had been added. He was cleaning his spear tip by dipping a rag into a wooden bowl filled with some foul-smelling liquid. A straw hand broom bound with hemp cord was propped in the corner next to his pack.

Lark looked at Bren and raised an eyebrow. "We brought food," Lark said, placing the parcel on the table.

"Don't get it on the floor," Seven said, scooting his cleaning bowl closer to himself. He tapped an empty, wooden plate sitting at the center of the table with one finger—an unspoken request to keep food neat and ordered as he was accustomed to.

Bren unwrapped the paper and placed a round loaf of bread, a large wedge of cheese, and three apples on the plate. She plucked up an apple and bit into its leathery skin.

Lark took a seat and smoothed out the paper the food had been wrapped in. "Pen and ink?" he asked Seven.

Seven stopped his spear cleaning and retrieved a narrow box engraved with an eagle from his pack and handed it to Lark. Lark undid the brass latch and prepared the quill and ink. Tapping the quill on the edge of the ink bottle, he began drawing.

Seven watched intently, while Bren crunched on her apple.

"A map of Ferran," Seven finally said. "How do you know so many details?"

"Let's just say this map recently fell into my lap," Lark answered, continuing his detailed drawing.

"How is that possible?" Seven asked.

Bren wiped her mouth with the back of her hand and swallowed. "It's just a saying, Seven. It didn't actually fall into his lap. Kind of like yelling out vulgarities during the heat of battle that shouldn't have been taken seriously."

Seven grunted and studied Lark's finished map more closely. "The X you drew, near Ruritania," he said, sliding a finger across Ferran past the area of desolation. "What are the initials you wrote next to it? D.R.?"

"I'm not sure, but an X most certainly suggests that there's hidden treasure to be found," Lark said.

"Hmph," Seven said. His expression remained stoic.

Bren and Lark eyed each other. Trying to read Seven was like trying to figure out how deep the ocean was.

"There has to be something to it," Bren said. "Lark said his captors were tracking him for the map."

"There's something else you should know," Lark said warily. "There was a third person with those men. A woman named Gilla. She was planning to kill me."

"What?" Bren asked, sitting down. Seven eyed the half-eaten apple in her hand like it was human waste. She placed it stem up on the table just for spite.

"She has a vendetta against you," Seven said, turning his attention back to Lark. "Not surprising considering how many people you've fooled with your false visions."

Lark ignored the jab and tore off a piece of bread. "Gilla said my father killed her father. And if I were to take a wild guess, I'm betting her father was Valen—the man father killed in the court of swords all those years ago. The map was the goal, and I was just a bonus."

"Whoever digs a hole and scoops it out falls into the pit they have made," Seven said with a hint of disdain.

Lark's jaw tightened. "What is that supposed to mean?"

"You will either understand it or you won't," Seven said gruffly, balling his right hand into a fist.

"Enough!" Bren said sharply, looking back and forth between their vain posturing. She touched Seven's fist and it unfurled and relaxed. She tempered her voice in an attempt to bring calm back to the room. "What are you proposing to do about this so-called treasure map?" she asked Lark. "This *Gilla*, whoever she is, will be searching for the treasure. If she comes across us— across you—"

Lark pulled a knife out of his pack with a jewel-encrusted hilt that she'd never seen before. He pushed up his sleeves and sliced off a chunk of cheese. "Let's not worry about details," he said. "If there's treasure to be had, I'm going to find it."

Bren's pulse quickened. Lark had no plan, just some vague idea of a treasure that may or may not exist and a woman who had an ax to grind. She turned to her only ally. "Seven, tell him," she said, standing up. "Going after a treasure that we don't even know exists is a foolish idea."

Lark pressed his cheese and bread together and ate silently as if he hadn't a care in the world.

Seven tucked his hands in his armpits. "You'd have to travel through the area of desolation."

Bren slapped a hand on the table. "Exactly!"

"There's more," Lark said, sticking his free hand in his pocket. "Look at this." He slid the paper over to Seven. "It was with the map."

Seven leaned forward and wrinkled his brow. Bren read over his shoulder:

For this is left of that fair Oracle
Bottomless seas, caverns deep
The soul shall find itself alone amid the Morbids creep
O Great Destruction, eternal flame
Yet there is still one whom the treasure will claim
Look, great wanderer, for only you will see, the crown of jewels at the bottom of the sea
Alas, the hour has finally come. Extinguish the flame of the evil one.

Seven's eyes widened. "Sons of Ferran," he said, placing both hands on the table. "It's possible that you've got the map to the queen's treasure and the key to find it."

Lark leaned in and rested his arms on the table. "What's the queen's treasure?"

Seven glared at him like he had two heads. "It's believed that King Rodolf's wife, Zara, fled after she read Rodolf's last oracle. She knew her children would go to war against each other. It is said that she fled to Ruritania and took half of the kingdom's treasure with her."

"You mean oracle, as in *the* king's oracle?" Lark asked with great interest. "The same oracle that our parents used to find Isidor?"

Bren had seen that spark in Lark's eyes before, and she feared it.

"Yes," Seven said.

"No, no, no," Bren said, shaking her head. "We're not going to go on some crazy wild goose chase for something like this."

Seven's eyes glimmered with excitement. "The story goes that the queen wanted to make sure that the kingdom had money to rebuild if her children were ever united under one crown." He tapped a finger on the map. "But the treasure has never been found."

"We've already rebuilt," Bren argued. "In *Isidor*."

Seven made direct eye contact with her, something he rarely did. "Ferran has yet to recover. And if that treasure *does* exist and falls into the wrong hands—"

Bren spread her arms wide. "I don't think you two heard me. We're not chasing after treasure! If it hasn't been found by now, it probably never will."

"If we travel straight west from here," Seven said to Lark, "we should reach Ruritania in three days."

"We leave at first light," Lark said with a grin. The two of them grasped forearms—a Jutta gesture of brotherhood.

A moment ago, they had been at each other's throats. Now they were co-conspirators? Bren stood in disbelief as Seven and Lark hurriedly made work of packing up everything on the table. Without a word, Seven climbed into the bottom hammock, and Lark leaped into the next one up, leaving Bren the hammock practically touching the roof.

"Extinguish the lantern," Seven mumbled as he rolled over and faced the wall.

Bren lowered the wick and stood in the dark, her heart pounding. *Why am I scared?* Deep down she knew why. Her father had been right about one thing. She didn't know if she could kill anyone. And on a dangerous journey like they were about to embark on, there was a good chance she'd have to. Especially if Gilla *was* Valen's daughter and she was out there looking for revenge. Their parents had always fought her and Lark's battles. Now she was going to have to fight her own, and she wasn't all that sure that she was ready to. She touched the scar the man's ax had left on her cheek and poured her healing power into it until she felt it disappear.

Chapter 15

Lark

The sun had just peeked over the horizon. The morning was cool, and a light fog was drifting among the trees like ghostly apparitions. Lark rubbed Dash's nose and offered him the last apple which the horse readily accepted. Seven was attaching his spear to his saddle. Kia called out five times from somewhere above the treetops.

Why had Gotz given him his beloved hawk? And what had Gotz's parting cryptic words meant? *What you seek may not be what you find.*

Finding the queen's treasure was going to give Lark the one thing he desperately needed—a purpose. If Lark could find the treasure, he'd create his own legacy. He would be the one to save Ferran. His parents currently paid tenants to maintain Ferran. Small villages dotted the land, and supplies were sent from Isidor to supplement what Ferran still lacked. The ground sickness had been eradicated, and Morbids were supposedly extinct now, but the country had still not been rebuilt to what it once was. Ferran had yet to recover from the Great Destruction from fifty years ago. Money would be the key to its recovery.

He had a slight pang of guilt over ignoring Bren's trepidation about seeking the treasure, but he wasn't going to return home just because she was worried about Gilla. Yes, Gilla *was* a potential problem, but not one he couldn't handle if the need arose. She was skilled with a sword, but not as skilled as he was. He'd fought her long enough to see her weaknesses.

She has a clumsy stance. Her strikes are undisciplined and born out of anger.

Gilla only bested him because one of her thugs had clubbed him from behind. He hoped he *would* come across her again so he could finish what she'd started.

Bren walked toward him, leading her horse from the stable. She hadn't spoken to him since they had awakened. A small part of him feared she'd return home to Isidor and leave him alone with Seven. He was watching Bren intently when the old woman who ran the treetop accommodations approached.

"I hope you found your quarters acceptable," she said to Seven with a glint in her eye and a lick of her lips.

Lark wondered what Seven had done to get the tree house *extras* they'd enjoyed.

Seven reached in his saddle bag and handed the woman two large, wooden spoons.

Her eyes lit up as she examined the handiwork. "Ahh. Yes. These will do quite nicely." She looked at Seven with one narrowed eye. "Though I caught that hawk of yours stealing one of my head scarves off the line this morn."

Seven humphed then dug in his pack and presented the woman with a small pair of scissors. "Perhaps you'll sew a new one."

She greedily slid the little scissors into her dress pocket and transformed herself into beacon of cordiality. "Where ye headed? Maybe I can be of assistance."

"Ruritania."

She shook her head in dismay. "You'll be needing a guide if ye go there."

"We'll be fine," Lark interjected.

"Tsk tsk. So many of those never to be seen again have said the exact same thing," she said glumly. "Suit yeself."

"Where can we find a guide?" Seven asked.

Lark shot him a look, but Seven ignored him.

"There might be someone," she said, shuffling one foot across the dirt.

Seven produced a money pouch from his saddle bag and proffered her a coin.

"Names, Rune," she said, snatching the coin. "You'll find his shack on the edge of the Yellow Fields." With that, she turned and hobbled back to her humble abode, biting the coin with a chortle of glee.

"We don't need a guide," Lark said.

"We do," Seven said, setting his jaw.

Bren led her horse silently into the midst of their bickering.

"I'm sorry about last night," Lark said to Bren.

She mounted her horse. "I know," she said, looking down at him.

She's leaving. Perhaps it's for the best.

He put his hands on his hips and took a deep breath. "What will you tell Wynter and Gideon?"

"Nothing," she said, looking confused.

"I don't think you should travel back to Isidor alone. Not after what happened with Gilla at the gorge."

Her brow furrowed. "What are you talking about?"

"Aren't you going home?" he asked.

"Don't be ridiculous. You'll get yourself killed without me."

Despite her sour look, he smiled.

She narrowed her eyes. "That doesn't mean I don't think this is ridiculous."

He dropped the smile and offered her a serious face and a deeper voice. "Of course."

She rolled her eyes and shook her head and that was the end of their disagreement.

They rode the horses south to the Yellow Fields. Seven

insisted they find the guide the woman had called Rune. After that, they'd head west through the area of desolation and on to Ruritania. For the first time in a long time, Lark was happy.

CHAPTER 16

WYNTER

Wynter and Gideon had joined a large group of well-wishers at the Prickly Pig Tavern. Tomas and Hilran had insisted on having a small gathering at their establishment to honor Gotz's life. Tomas had once been Gideon's father's reeve, and Hilran, a childhood friend. Gotz had been a big part of all their lives.

Gideon was withdrawn and reflective, so Wynter left him to his small corner at the end of the bar while she stood at the back of the tavern and accepted villagers' humble condolences. The gathering had grown in large measure, and she wondered how many had mustered tears of grief just so they could come feast on Hilran's veal stew and nut tarts.

Wynter smiled and nodded as she listened to person after person share words of sympathy, but silently she was thinking of how sad it was that Gotz hadn't lived to see Ferran rebuilt to what it was before the Great Destruction. She knew Gideon felt the weight of responsibility to quicken the recovery of Ferran as much as she did. They waited anxiously for Gideon's sister, Kidron, to return from Ruritania with what they'd hoped would be good news and a way forward.

It was amidst this scene of gloom and comfort feasting that

Six came barreling in with a scowl on her face and the gait of someone looking for a fight. A crossbody scabbard swayed against her hip as she navigated the rebuking glances that followed her. Wynter continued to smile and nod to the elderly couple who were currently expressing to her what a great neighbor Gotz had been. She tried to stay focused on the conversation, but Six hadn't been at the funeral and Wynter was angry at her friend for not showing up to pay her respects to someone who had been important to both of them.

"If you'll excuse me," Wynter finally said, anxious to waylay Six.

She gave her skirt a slight lift and pushed politely through the crowd until she had Six's arm in her grasp. She ushered her, none too kindly, back into the kitchen without a word. The few wait staff and food preparers who bustled between fireplace and prep table were too busy to notice the small intrusion.

Six jerked her arm away.

"How could you miss Gotz's funeral?" Wynter asked. "Gotz was—"

"Seven is missing," Six snapped.

"What?" Wynter asked. Seven was good friends with Bren, so if he was missing, there was a good chance he was with Bren. The kitchen suddenly became uncomfortably hot.

Six crossed her arms. "Any idea where he might be?"

"Not exactly. No." She knew Six's question was more of an accusation aimed at Wynter's children.

Six threw up her hands in exasperation.

"Follow me," Wynter said.

They skirted past the cook's prep table and exited out the back. The smell of roasted meat and potatoes followed them out the door. The back of the tavern jutted up next to the woods, offering a veil of privacy. No one was around except for a man slumped on the ground against the building with an empty mug of mead lying next to him. His chin had fallen to his chest, and he was snoring.

"Well?" Six said.

"Lark and Bren left us a note that they were going hunting."

"Sons of Ulu! Daughters of Alrenia!" She bit her lip and mumbled a few more choice words.

Wynter let the reference to their old factions go. There were no longer Alrenians and Uluns, they were Ferrians now.

"Where did they go?" Six said, pacing. "Because when I find Seven, I will break him. He will beg me for mercy."

Wynter had been equally angry on finding out her children had left Glasser. She let Six vent.

Gideon came out the back, and Wynter immediately relaxed, but as soon as she saw the concern in his eyes and the note in his hands, her stomach dropped.

"What is it?" she asked, fearing bad news.

Six drew to Wynter's side.

"It's not the kids," he said, allaying her fears. "Kidron has sent word from Ruritania."

"What did she say?" Wynter asked.

"There's no sign of the map. Not yet."

Something more lingered in his eyes. "What else?" she asked.

"She believes Alith is close to finding the map. If Alith finds the treasure, she plans on declaring Ruritania's independence from Ferran."

Six grabbed the note out of Gideon's hand and read it silently.

"Always a pleasure, Six," he mumbled.

"What's this about a map?" The drunk man was standing now, swaying slightly.

"Nothing to concern yourself with," Gideon said, barely giving him a glance.

"I seen an old man give your boy a map," he said, slurring his words.

Gideon strode over to the man and glared at him. "Did you now?"

The man, who had barely two teeth in his mouth, cowered

and rubbed a hand through his greasy hair. His eyes shifted nervously to Wynter. She hurried to Gideon's side and touched his elbow to let him know she would handle the man.

"What's your name?" she asked kindly.

"Thomas Atticus, Your Majesty." He tried a slight bow, but the gesture threw him off-balance, and he wobbled sideways.

Gideon steadied him with a hand. "He's drunk."

Thomas set his lips and narrowed his eyes. "I seen it just like I said. I was at the bar inside minding my own business."

"Anything you could tell us, Mr. Atticus, would be of great service to the kingdom," Wynter said.

The man's lip quivered.

Wynter dared a small glance at Gideon and Six. Gideon's face was red, and his fists were clenched tight. Six had planted her feet, and her hand rested on the hilt of the knife she wore at her waist.

"*Nobody* is going to hurt you," Wynter said, giving Gideon and Six a chastising look.

The man nodded uncertainly. "Your boy exchanged a black pouch for a package from some old man I've never seen before," he mumbled.

Wynter's stomach dropped. Lark's birthday gift had been a pouch of coins, and he *had* been at the tavern by his own omission.

For Ferran's sake. What mess has he gotten himself into?

Gideon took a step toward Thomas. Wynter pushed a hand into Gideon's chest to stay him.

She smiled at Thomas and kept her voice soft. "When was this that you saw the exchange?"

"Um . . . I think it was two or three days ago."

"Which was it?" Gideon barked. "Two or three?"

Wynter cast Gideon a threatening glare.

Thomas kept a wary eye on Gideon as he talked to Wynter. "The old man bragged about some map that he was going to get a heap of gold for. He'd had a bit too much to drink if you know what I mean. Sometimes that makes a man talk when he shouldn't."

"You mean like now?" Gideon said in a threatening tone.

Wynter pushed away her anxiety. The course of her children and Seven was beginning to take shape, and she feared what it might mean.

"I wasn't part of it. I swear!" Thomas insisted.

"And our son, Lark," she said, swallowing hard, "purchased this map from the man?"

The man quickly nodded. "I didn't have nothing to do with it." His eyes searched for a way out.

Wynter reached out and placed a hand on his arm. "Your help has been so valuable that the king and I would like to send you two pheasants from our estate as a thank-you."

The man's uneasiness faded in small measure. He straightened himself. "I like to do what I can. For the kingdom."

"Now," Wynter said, "can you tell us what was on this map?"

Before Wynter could draw another breath, Six was at the man's side with a knife to his groin.

"You have ten seconds to tell us what was on that map."

"Six!"

Fear set the man trembling, and all progress Wynter had made in creating calm evaporated. The man broke away and ran for his life, disappearing around the inn.

"I'll send the pheasants!" Wynter called after him. She turned and glowered at Six which had little to no effect. Six wiped her knife on her sleeve, even though no blood had been drawn and shoved it back into the sheath at her waist.

"I wonder if the altercation in that alley had something to do with the map Lark purchased," Gideon said. "We both know there's only one map that people would be willing to kill for."

"You think it's possible Lark has the map we've been looking for?" Wynter asked.

He scratched his cheek. "It's possible. But whether he still has it remains to be seen."

"Wait," Six said, as if all the pieces had just fallen into place. "Are you looking for the queen's treasure map? The one nobody has ever found and probably doesn't even exist?"

"Six," Wynter said, trying to stay the voice of reason, "we had no choice but to look for it. The future of Ferran depends on it."

"And we don't know if what Lark purchased was the queen's treasure map," Gideon said.

Six scoffed and postured herself in front of Gideon. "If our kids even *think* they have the queen's treasure map, then that means they're headed to Ruritania. And if that Ulun traitor, Alith, gets a hold of our kids, she'll have you by the balls."

"Six! This isn't helping!" Wynter cried.

"Six is right," Gideon said, rubbing his forehead. "We have to assume Lark purchased the queen's treasure map whether it's real or fake. And if Kidron is right, and Alith is after it, she could do much more than declare Ruritania's independence from Ferran. She could come after Ferran itself."

"Then our children may have landed right in the middle of this. God help us," Wynter said, placing a hand to her beating heart.

"When do we leave?" Six asked.

"As soon as I call the men to arms," Gideon said.

CHAPTER 17

LARK

They'd almost missed the tiny stone shack of the guide, and Lark wished they had. They led their horses down a narrow dirt path that led to the humble abode where a small spiral of smoke rose from its crooked chimney. Calling it a shack was being gracious. The stone walls were crumbling, and the whole place was overgrown with wild shrubs and weeds. There was an old wash tub sitting under the only front window, and errant shoots had sprouted in that, too. Even Kia circled *around* the homestead instead of over it, as if it held some omen of bad luck.

"I don't know about this," Lark said, rubbing Dash's nose.

Seven scooted past him, pulling his horse along with him, as he approached the door.

Lark gave Bren a sour look, but she only shrugged.

Why do we need a guide when all we have to do is head west?

Lark dropped Dash's lead to let him scavenge for something edible in the forsaken landscape. Seven knocked on the weathered gray door with one fist. Lark cocked a hip and stuck his thumbs in his knife belt which now held Gotz's gift—his late Uncle Lark's knife.

The door creaked opened about a hand's width, and a

yellow-haired man peered around it. "What do you want?" he grumbled.

"Rune?" Seven asked.

The man pulled the door completely open. "Who wants to know?" he asked, eyeing Seven up and down.

The man looked to be in his fifties and had short, sun-bleached hair and piercing blue eyes. His shirt was soiled, and his boots had seen better days. By the look of his hands, he'd known hard work.

"We were told you were for hire as a guide," Seven said.

"Where?" Rune asked, looking around Seven at Bren and Lark.

"Ruritania," Bren said.

The man took a step back and attempted to slam the door. Seven stepped forward and stopped it with his hand. "We can pay well."

Rune considered for a solid half second. "Not interested."

The door banged shut in Seven's face.

"You tried," Lark said, relieved they wouldn't be adding a fourth to their journey.

Seven ignored Lark and knocked again, only harder this time.

"You have to let him try or we'll be hearing about this all the way to Ruritania," Bren said.

Lark sighed.

"These two are royalty!" Seven shouted at the door.

"Seven!" Lark growled.

The door opened slowly. Rune stepped out, studying Bren and Lark. "Who are you?"

"Nobody," Lark said bitterly.

"Children of the king and queen," Bren said resignedly.

Lark shook his head in dismay. That wasn't information they needed to share. Not when enemies of Gideon and Wynter might still roam Ferran.

Rune wiped a rough hand across his gristly blond cheeks then returned to his shack and shut the door.

"Sorry we bothered you!" Lark called out. "Let's go, Seven."

Seven reluctantly turned his horse, his jaw tightening as he glared at Lark with his big Jutta eyes.

This is going to be long journey, Lark thought.

They headed away from the crumbling abode. Lark whistled for Dash.

The door creaked behind them. Next thing Lark knew, Rune was tromping through the weeds, passing them by with a knapsack slung over one shoulder and a scabbarded sword slung over the other. "Let's go!" Rune called back without stopping.

Seven's face lit up like a morning sunrise.

"Great," Lark said quietly. *Stupendous.*

CHAPTER 18

BREN

The stars shone in their appointed places and the moon hovered above the trees. Just before dusk, they had made camp with their new guide, Rune, in a meadow bordered by woods. Bren distracted herself from the trepidation she was feeling about traveling to Ruritania by replacing the cord in one of her boots. Seven had built a fire that most pyre builders would have admired and was now out in the meadow with his newly acquired spear, sparring with shadows. Rune had unceremoniously ventured away from camp without any explanation. Lark was lying on his side, propped up with one arm, plucking blades of wild grass and throwing them into the fire. And Kia, strangely enough, had perched herself on Bren's pack and was intently watching her every move. They were a regular band of misfits.

Bren bit off the excess lacing and tied it. Kia hopped to the ground, picked up the extra lacing, and flew away like some kind of bird bandit.

"Why did you bring your beau?" Lark asked.

Bren gave him an incredulous look. "You know Seven and I are just friends."

"Does *he* know that?" he asked, motioning with his chin toward the sparring dark shadow.

"Of course he does," she snapped.

Right on cue, Seven stopped mid-swing and turned toward her voice. His stature was striking even in the moonlight—tall, arms as big as his thighs. He was no longer the young boy she'd played tag with in the fair fields of Isidor. Her face flushed with heat.

"Oh," he said with a smile. "It's worse than I thought. You have feelings for him, too."

Bren's nostrils flared. "Don't," she warned.

"Fine. Deny it all you want, but I can read both of you. I'm a seer, after all."

"Not a very good one," she reminded him. The fire popped and an ember landed at Bren's feet. She stomped it out with her boot.

"I don't want Seven or this Rune fellow dictating our every move," Lark said, returning to his foul mood.

Bren sighed.

"You and Seven should go home," he continued. "I left to get away from everyone."

"Even me?" she asked.

"We don't need a guide," he said, ignoring her question.

She stood and brushed herself off. "Fine. I'll talk to Seven about releasing Rune."

If that one small concession would appease Lark, then it was worth getting rid of Rune to stop Lark's absurd idea of sending her and Seven home.

She cautiously approached Seven in the field beyond the fire. She didn't want to catch him unawares with a spear in his hands. She waited silently for a few minutes. He was as good as men twice his age. He finally noticed her and lowered his spear.

"You're better with the spear than I am," she said. A compliment here and there never hurt one's cause.

"You never compliment anyone," he said, breathing heavily.

She inwardly cringed. There was no use trying to charm him first. With Jutta it was best to stick with the facts. "Lark doesn't want Rune's help."

"He's wrong," he said, jabbing the end of the spear into the ground.

"Seven, it's give and take with friends. Sometimes you have to give."

He studied her with his big, brown eyes and wiped a hand through the sweat on his face.

"Lark has the gift of prophecy," she said. "He'll know if we're headed into trouble."

Seven laughed—something he rarely did. "He's been about as reliable as the weather when it comes to his seer abilities."

"*Give,*" she said with a little more force.

The two of them were all but arm-wrestling. If she'd been Jutta, that probably would have been Seven's preferred method of settling it.

Seven turned his attention to the camp behind her. "Rune's back," he said, pointing with the spear tip.

That was her cue that the conversation was over. Seven was relenting in his strange way. They strode back to camp. Rune sat down on his pack and rubbed his hands together near the flames. Seven picked up some logs and began strategically placing them on the fire. Lark had rolled over to his back and was staring up at the stars.

"Rune," Bren said meekly.

Rune looked up at her with what apparently was his trademark squint.

"We um . . ."

Lark sat up. There was hopeful anticipation in his eyes.

"We've decided we don't need a guide," she said quickly. "We'll pay you for your time of course." She swallowed and waited.

Rune stared into the fire for a long, heart-pumping moment. Then he rose slowly and gathered his pack.

Lark pushed himself to his feet and offered Rune two coins that he'd dug out of his pants pocket. Rune glanced at the coins, then at Bren. His icy-blue eyes pierced something inside her. Never had she seen eyes that hid such dark secrets. Without a word, and without taking the money, Rune walked away from the camp and into the woods.

Lark flipped one of the coins into the air and caught it with the other hand with a touch of glee. She hoped letting Rune go was the right decision because even the best-laid plans had a way of going awry.

CHAPTER 19

LARK

Lark rested contently by the fire. With Rune gone, Lark would be able to take the lead on their journey to Ruritania. Bren had come through for him by talking Seven out of their need for a guide. He blinked his weary eyes and looked across the fire at his sister. She was sleeping back-to-back with Seven on the other side of the fire, breathing softly. *Two peas in a pod.* He swallowed a yawn, fighting to stay awake for the first watch. Nothing seemed amiss, and the night was peaceful, so he closed his eyes just for a moment and listened to the soulful hoots of the forest owls. But what he had planned on being only a few minutes of rest ended up being a couple of hours, and he was awakened suddenly by a cold blade pressed against his neck.

"Make one sound, and I'll cut you where you lie."

It was a woman's voice, one he recognized.

Gilla.

He clenched his jaw, angry that he had allowed himself to fall asleep. The fire had burned down, casting only a soft glow.

"Get up. Put your hands where I can see them."

Lark slowly pushed himself up and raised his hands. The tip

of Gilla's short sword had stayed cold and steady at the soft spot of his throat. Her dark eye patch stood out like a stain against her pale skin.

"Did you think I'd just take the map and go on my merry way?" she whispered, loosening his knife belt and tossing it aside. "You and I have a score to settle." Her breath reeked of charred meat.

"Let him go!" Bren shouted. Seven and Bren were standing across the fading fire with weapons drawn.

Gilla kept her eye on Lark. "Try anything and he dies where he stands."

Lark ground his teeth, fighting the urge to take action. But Gilla's men were likely lurking in the shadows, and he wouldn't put Bren's life at risk like he'd done in the alley back in Glasser. Wynter had been right about one thing. The slash across the cheek Bren had received in the alley could just have easily been a slash across her throat.

"The court of swords was agreed upon by Valen. He lost!" Bren snapped.

Lark grimaced. They weren't even sure Valen *was* Gilla's father.

Gilla ignored her and smiled at Lark. Her front two teeth slightly overlapped. "I'm guessing this is little sis. The princess comes to the rescue!"

Lark's temper flared. "Stand down, Bren."

Gilla grinned at him. "Turn nice and slow and walk toward the woods."

"You're not taking him!" Bren screamed.

Gilla pulled Lark tightly to her, then pressed the long edge of her sword precariously against his neck. "If you follow us, he dies. Your choice," she sneered.

Bren's face was hot with anger. She looked over at Seven. He shook his head.

For once, Lark was glad Seven was there. He'd keep Bren

from doing something stupid. Gilla turned with Lark still in her grasp and headed toward the woods.

"You won't get away with this," Bren called from behind.

Gilla tightened her grip and spoke in Lark's ear. "Oh, but I will. And how sweet revenge will taste, dear Lark. Because Valen's death will finally be avenged."

CHAPTER 20

BREN

Lark was gone. Gilla had taken Lark, and Bren had no idea what to do. It was still a few hours until sunrise. Seven had rekindled the fire and Bren was sitting next to him staring into the flames. Why hadn't she done more to save him? He would have fought to the death to save her. Kia returned quite suddenly and landed on a stack of firewood like a white phantom. She folded in her wings and called out. Bren tensed with expectation. "What is it, girl? Did you see where she took Lark?"

Someone stepped out of the shadows.

Bren and Seven both jumped to their feet. For a split second her heart raced with hope. *Lark has escaped.*

Rune held up his hands up as he stepped into the firelight.

She should have been relieved to see him, but instead she was angry—angry that she had listened to Lark and let Rune go, and angry that Rune had shown back up too late to help save Lark. "What do you want, Rune?" she asked testily.

"Lark has been captured," Seven said before Rune could answer.

"I know," he said. "I saw."

Without thinking, Bren drew her knife and rushed at Rune,

sending Kia into flight. Seven grabbed her from behind, lifting her off the ground just shy of the blades' reach.

"Why didn't you help him!?" she screamed as Seven pulled her backward. He put her down a safe distance from Rune and planted himself firmly between the two of them, but Bren did not yet sheathe her knife.

Rune glowered at her with his cool eyes. "You know nothing of Ferran except the fairy tales your parents told you before they tucked you in at night."

His words were meant to sting, and they did, because deep down she knew there was truth in what he said. She was a stranger in a land that she knew nothing about. But his words were callous and his arrogance contemptuous, and she had no appetite for either. "Lark was right when he said we didn't need you," she said stubbornly.

"Bren," Seven said quietly.

Rune adjusted his pack and frowned more deeply. "You're not in Isidor anymore," he said matter-of-factly. "If you try to save Lark, Gilla will have you both killed. Go home. You don't belong here." He turned and walked away.

Her heart sank like an anchor. "Wait!" Bren called out, swallowing her pride.

Rune stopped, but he didn't turn around.

She sheathed her knife and held up her hands, showing Seven she had no intention of harming Rune. Seven nodded and Bren went and stood in front of Rune wondering what kinds of words resonated with a heartless man. She looked into his cold eyes, then reached out, almost imperceptibly, and touched his hand. Using her gift, she searched inside him. Immediately she was hit with a jolt of loss . . . bitterness . . . rage . . . and . . .

Regret?

She was about to dig deeper, when Rune must have realized what she was doing and grabbed her forcefully by both arms and pulled her close. "Don't," he said, his breath hot on her face.

"Let her go, Rune!" Seven growled as he stormed toward them.

"If I beg," she whispered desperately, "will you help us get Lark back?"

He searched her eyes.

What is he looking for? Why is he so angry?

Seven lay the tip of his spear against Rune's neck. Rune blinked and released her, looking at her oddly, as if he hadn't realized he had taken hold of her. He rubbed a hand down his face and walked off into the night.

"Rune, please!" she called after him. "I'm sorry!" And she was. Sorry that she'd let Lark walk out of his bedroom the night after their birthday without trying to stop him, sorry that she'd gone after him, sorry that she'd tricked Seven into coming. She'd just turned twenty, and all she had done so far was build a pile of regrets which she could never undo.

A single tear ran down her cheek, and she swatted away the unwelcome sentiment. Tears would not serve her—at least, that's what Seven would say. He put a hand on her shoulder as Rune disappeared into the night. "You cannot make a man do what he does not have the heart to do."

But the next morning at first light, Bren and Seven spotted Rune at the edge of the forest—waiting.

"Maybe he has a heart, after all," she said.

Seven humphed. "A man's heart does not change so easily. There is something else he wants."

"Money," she offered. But she knew deep down that Seven was right. There was something more that Rune hoped to gain by helping them, and it wasn't money.

CHAPTER 21

BREN

By late-afternoon, Bren, Seven, and Rune arrived at a city protected by a wooden rampart. Rune called the place Simms Branch. It was the last populated town before they passed over into the area of desolation and on to Ruritania. Bren and Seven had ridden their horses, but Lark's horse, Dash, had refused to let anyone ride him, so Rune had to walk. Kia had taken to riding on Bren's shoulder like a monarch. Between Lark's massive horse, Gotz's crafty hawk, Seven's imposing stature, and Rune's crusty demeanor, Bren worried they might draw unwanted attention. Bren and Seven dismounted at the city gates, and armed guards asked Rune what their business was in Simms Branch. Rune mumbled something about supplies, and they were waved in amongst a steady flow of people of all walks of life who were coming in from the countryside—some in horse-drawn wagons, others pulling small carts or leading their tethered goats, pigs, and other animals.

The dirt streets of Simms Branch were alive with commerce—merchants, taverns, and inns, all bustling with people who strode about the town like people who knew they were born of the same earth that they plowed. There was no sense of class or station—no leisurely walkers bidding friends a good day and speaking of fair weather. Kings and queens didn't rule here. Gangling merchants swept out storefronts. Sweaty craftsmen sat replacing worn horseshoes and pounding new blades. Store owners bargained with wayfaring traders for their wares— wagons of hay, wolf pelts, shorn wool, carts of goats' milk, herbs, and leather sheaths. Somewhere in the middle of town, a simple church spire could be seen rising above it all like a beacon for the weary.

Bren squirmed in her belted vest and tunic, feeling slightly out of place, but Seven was relaxed and enamored by it all. Lark's expensive warhorse drew a few stares, as she led Dash along, but, to her relief, most seemed indifferent to their arrival. They were nobodies in a land of nobodies.

Seven approached a woman who was sitting on a stool with a basket of mushrooms at her feet. "How much for a pottle of the Hen-of-the-Woods?"

"A halfpenny," she murmured, keeping a careful eye on the hawk perched on Bren's shoulder.

He pressed a small coin into her hand, and the woman wrapped the rubbery-looking delicacy in cloth and tied the small bundle with string. Seven stuck the package in his saddle pack.

Rune grumbled something foul and waved them along, leading them through the thick crowds until they arrived at the far side of town at a small barn. A fenced area next to it was occupied by a handful of thick-legged, rouncey horses, good for plowing and pulling carts.

"We'll sell the bird and horses here and use the money to buy supplies for the rest of the trip," Rune said.

Kia dug her claws into Bren's shoulder, screeched loudly, and flew away.

"We have money," Bren said, rubbing and rolling her aching shoulder. "We don't need to sell the horses. And *clearly* selling Kia is not an option."

Rune squinted against the sun. "Have either of you been to Ruritania?"

Bren looked to Seven.

"No," Seven answered in his usual flat way.

"We're not selling our horses," Bren said. "Lark would never forgive me for selling Dash. Do you have any idea how expensive a horse like this is?"

Dash whinnied and pulled on his lead as if confirming the notion.

"Then the horses will die at your feet," Rune said coldly.

Bren crossed her arms, tucking the leads of Dash and her horse under her armpit.

"Maybe if you explained," Seven suggested, as if fearing the disagreement was about to escalate.

"The area of desolation is barren, and the water undrinkable," Rune began. "Meaning no water until Ruritania. What will you give your horse to drink?" he asked her.

"We can—"

Rune held up a hand. "A horse can't carry enough water for three days. It's too heavy."

Bren studied Rune's face. "How does Ruritania get supplies if no horses can make the trip?"

"Workhorses can pull carts that can carry enough water, but you can't put these horses in front of a cart. Besides, we need to sell at least two of the horses for supplies."

She grimaced. Rune was right. Lark had his birthday coins on him, and she and Seven needed to save the little money they had between them for when they reached Ruritania. Who knew what price she'd have to pay to find Lark?

Bren rubbed Dash's nose with regret.

"You could board him," Rune suggested. "But if you don't show up and pay the boarding fees within thirty days, they keep the horse."

Dash nudged Bren playfully in the face. "I can't sell him."

Rune's jaw clenched.

"Bren and I will sell our horses," Seven said.

"Are you sure?" Bren asked him.

He gave her a quizzical look. "It will make Six angry. Of course I'm sure."

They shared a knowing smile.

Rune made quick business of the selling the two horses, nodding his satisfaction to the hostler who offered way less than the horses were worth. Bren insisted on boarding Dash, much to Rune's dismay. As soon as an attendant loosed Dash into the fenced area, he bucked and snorted like a child throwing a fit. Kia swooped in and landed on a fence post and watched Dash with rapt attention as if she was enjoying his misery.

"Dash will be fine," Seven said to Bren. But even stoic Seven didn't sound so sure. Though Lark had complained constantly about Dash's bad behavior, she knew deep down that the horse meant the world to him.

Rune asked for Lark's pack. He rummaged inside and pulled out the jeweled-hilt knife. "We can sell this to make up for Dash."

Bren reached out and snatched the knife. "You can't sell that."

"You'll have to come up with twenty shillings, then. Water and food won't buy itself."

Bren sighed and looked down at the bejeweled knife. She'd never seen it before until the night they stayed in the tree hut. She wondered where Lark had gotten it.

"We can sell my knife," she said.

"It won't bring the same coin. It's either Lark's horse or his knife. Your choice."

She reluctantly handed Lark's knife over. If it meant saving Lark, she'd sell everything she owned.

Someone shouted from down the street and people scattered. The three of them turned toward the parting crowd. A young woman with an eye patch appeared with a blade across her back and an ax in her hand. Her braided hair hung loose over her fur shoulder mantle. Though Bren had only seen her in the dim light of the fire, she recognized her right away.

Gilla.

Bren drew her sword. Her heart pounded savagely against her ribs. Seven set his feet and pointed his spear.

Lark must be nearby. She scanned the crowd, though Gilla would likely have him safely stowed away. *If she hasn't already killed him.*

"The two of you stay back," Rune warned.

Seven kept his position. "I can beat her."

The crowd regathered tentatively, curious and thirsty for some entertainment.

Gilla's one eye was as sharp as Kia's. She moved slowly toward them with fists clenched. "You have a lot of nerve showing your face, Rune!" she called above the crowd murmurs. "Draw your sword!"

"Rune," Bren murmured, "what's going on?" Her stomach soured. *Gilla and Rune know each other?* Rune had failed to mention it.

Seven twirled his spear then banged the end of its shaft on the ground—his way of accepting her challenge.

Rune clenched his jaw and threw an arm over his shoulder and drew his sword from its scabbard. "Stand down, Seven."

Gilla laughed. "You're using children now to fight your battles?"

Seven took a step forward. Bren stayed him with her hand.

The braided warrior drew back her arm and threw her short-handled ax with a fury. It landed square at the ground at Seven's feet. He bared his teeth at her.

Bren knelt and swiped the ax off the ground.

Gilla drew the knife at her waist. "Shall we play?" she asked, teasing Seven.

"What did you do to her?" Seven asked Rune.

"I may have killed her pig."

"That's it?" Bren asked, her hand tightening around Gilla's ax. "She wants to kill you for a pig?"

"He was a pet. Name was Oscar."

Bren glanced over at him.

Rune shrugged. "He was worth his bacon."

Seven gave Rune a confused look.

"Are you going to let the *princess* and her friend fight your battle?" Gilla called out, lacing a knife between her fingers.

Bren's heart raced, and a fire lit inside her.

"Bren . . ." Seven warned.

Nobody called her princess. She set her feet and moved her grip higher on the ax. "I'll fight her," Bren said to Rune through clenched teeth. "I'll end her with her own ax."

Rune grimaced. "I don't think that's a good—"

"I'm not asking," she said.

Rune returned his sword to his sheath. "Be smart about this. If you strike and miss, change hands and cut back upwards or your side will be exposed."

Bren nodded and handed Seven her sword.

"Show her what you've got," Seven said, nodding his approval.

She locked eyes with Gilla. *What am I doing?* Suddenly the idea seemed absurd. She was acting like Lark. Impulsive. Spontaneous. Her heart raced with excitement.

Maybe Lark and I aren't so different after all.

"Come on, princess. Fight for your brother. Maybe I'll let him go." Gilla gripped her knife like a stake.

Lark is still alive!

Bren ran toward her with the ax firmly in her grasp. She sifted through every thrust, stroke, and trick that her parents had taught her. The venom of hatred coursed through her, and she knew it was the battle fever her father had spoken of.

Gilla charged, her braids swinging across her back. Once Gilla was within reach, Bren swung the ax in one wide-sweeping stroke meant to split her open. Gilla ducked. On her ax's downswing, Bren changed hands and swept the blade back up. Gilla caught the handle with one hand and kicked, landing a boot in Bren's stomach.

Bren stumbled backward, clutching at her stomach. The crowd cheered and money quickly changed hands.

Gilla switched her knife to her other hand and grinned.

Give the situation time to develop before deciding how to react. Gideon's words instructed her, even now.

They circled each other—ax and knife. Bren twirled the ax and waited for the right moment.

"Go ahead!" someone yelled. "Give it to her!" Laughs rippled through the crowd like stones skipping across a lake.

Bren lunged at Gilla over and over, striking out with the ax, testing her, but Gilla evaded the blows and seemed more interested in entertaining the crowd. Bren backed away, while Gilla pranced in front of the crowds. It was clear to Bren that this was just a game to Gilla—a show—something to amuse herself with while humiliating Bren. She grabbed the ax high on the handle and threw it just as Gilla turned away from the admiring crowd and faced Bren. The blade whistled by Gilla's head and landed in the side of a wagon right behind her. Gilla looked back at the ax, then at Bren. Her face reddened.

Bren smiled. *I can play games, too.*

Making a blade stick was a little trick Bren's Aunt Kidron had taught her. She was glad to see she still possessed the skill. She strutted back toward Rune and Seven, feeling a keen sense of satisfaction in wiping the grin off Gilla's face.

The crowd groaned their disapproval. They wanted more.

Seven's eyes grew large. "Watch out!"

Before Bren could react, Gilla had jumped on her back and locked her legs around Bren's waist. Gilla wrapped her arms in a death grip around Bren's neck. Bren stumbled and tugged at Gilla's arms, her face swelling and growing hot as she struggled to breathe. She turned in circles, trying to throw her off. The crowd cheered, their cries growing louder and louder as Bren spun out of control. She fumbled for the knife at her waist. Gilla squeezed harder.

Her eyesight blurred, and her knees began to buckle. The

cheers faded into the background and became muffled, indistinct noises. On the brink of losing consciousness, Bren fell to her knees. Gilla untangled herself and let Bren fall face forward into the dirt. Bren gasped, her lungs filling with air. Light returned, and sound came back abnormally loud. She coughed into the dirt and poured her gift of healing into her pain.

"You've got guts, I'll give you that." Gilla looked down at her with a touch of admiration and sheathed her knife. "Don't trust him," she said, nodding in Rune's direction.

Seeing that no blood was going to be shed, the crowd began dispersing and grumbling their disappointment.

Seven ran to her side and helped her stand. "Are you hurt?" he asked.

"I'm fine," she said, brushing herself off.

Gilla looked Seven up and down. "When's the wedding?" she asked Bren.

Bren glared at her. Seven stepped in front of Bren with his spear pointed at Gilla.

"If I don't return, Lark is dead," Gilla said pointedly.

Seven lowered his spear.

Gilla cast a look of disgust Rune's way and disappeared into the dispersing crowd. Rune approached with narrowed eyes. There was no softness there, no concern for Bren.

"Never turn your back on an opponent!" he said savagely.

"I wasn't going to play her little game," Bren retorted. "Besides, I don't need or *want* the counsel of some hedge-born squatter!"

"You know what your problem is?" he asked with clenched teeth. "You're spoiled. You think just because you've sparred with your parents you can survive out here? Gilla called you a princess because your demeanor *reeks* of it. Of course she toyed with you—because she knew you were no competition."

The words stung more than she cared to admit, and she immediately regretted her harsh words to Rune. As long as Gilla had Lark, she needed Rune.

"I'm sorry," she said, though there was no real sincerity in the apology.

"What good is being sorry if you're dead?" He stared at her for few beats then turned and walked away.

Tears threatened to come, as Rune walked away. Seven put a comforting hand on her shoulder, and she shrugged it off. Seven hadn't refuted Rune's words. That told her all she needed to know. She truly didn't know much about life outside the comfort of the king and queen's court. She was in over her head. Rune knew it. Seven knew it. And now, so did she. How was she ever going to save Lark?

CHAPTER 22

LARK

Lark lay helplessly on the floor of a dark room with his wrists tied behind his back and his ankles bound. The only light came from a small sliver that seeped under the door frame from the hallway. The guard posted outside the door was snoring and mumbling in his sleep about how the squash was all wrong for the pottage he was making. The slant of the ceiling suggested he was in the eave of an attic—perhaps once a servants' room or storage. There were no furnishings, but there was a hint of brown soap and hot ash in the air that suggested the floors had once been swept and scrubbed with care. Now cobwebs occupied the corners and rodents scampered all around him, exploring the room's murky depths. A threadbare curtain hung crooked over a small dormer window. Seven would have considered the accommodation barbaric.

He drifted in and out of sleep despite the hard floor and tight restraints. Night had brought with it a woeful regret that he couldn't shake. Gilla had caught him by surprise in the meadow. He was supposed to be keeping watch, and he'd fallen asleep instead. If it hadn't been for his mistake, he'd be on his way with Bren and Seven to Ruritania to find the queen's treasure.

It was this fitful state he found himself in when someone

shook him awake. He blinked. The first signs of morning glimmered through the forlorn window. Gilla was crouched beside him with a snide look on her face. "Your sister put up a good fight."

He wiggled his way into a seating position. "You better hope she's still breathing," he growled.

Gilla stood up. "You think me so coarse as that?"

"Worse," he retorted.

She smiled wryly. "Maybe you're right. But I have no need of her. She's no threat to me, and you'll do just fine for my purposes."

"Where is she?" he asked.

Gilla paced in front of him. "She's taken up with a real loser, I can tell you that."

"Seven isn't a loser."

She stopped and stared down at him. "I'm not talking about him." She fiddled with the pommel of the knife at her hip.

"Who, then?" he asked.

"He goes by Rune," she said. "Heard of him?" There was a spark of curiosity in her eye.

A lump rose in Lark's throat. *Had Rune come back to their camp, or had Bren and Seven sought him out again?* It was best to downplay Rune's importance. "We hired him as a guide, nothing more."

"I see," she said, pacing again. "A guide who just happens to be family?" She paused and stared at him.

"What are you talking about?" he asked. "Rune's not family. My father's brothers are both dead."

She laughed a little. "Who said anything about your father's brothers?"

Lark shook his head. "Whatever mind game you're playing—"

"Come on. Think!" she shouted. A fire lit up in her eye—one of bitter satisfaction. "Surely you still have family in Ferran."

Lark was growing tired of her insanity, so he shut down and stared at his boots.

"Of course Wynter's parents are dead," Gilla continued, "but . . ."

"Stop!" he shouted. The mention of his mother sent his blood boiling. The thought of never seeing her again was more painful than he cared to admit.

His anger didn't seem to faze Gilla. She waited a few moments then headed toward the door.

"Who is he, then?" Lark knew she was probably just toying with him, but he wouldn't leave anything to chance.

Gilla spun around. "Rune is Wynter's long-lost cousin, you fool!"

Lark gritted his teeth. "She doesn't have a cousin named Rune."

She smiled. Her eye sparkled with whatever venom she was holding back. She was playing with him like a cat with a dead mouse.

Lark's mind spun. The only cousin of his mother whom he knew about was the cousin whom Wynter had banished for his treachery and betrayals twenty-one years ago. *It couldn't be.* He looked up at Gilla. "Jack," he whispered expectantly.

"I'm clearly not the only one with a score to settle," she said. "Let's hope your sister is cleverer than you are, because I can promise you that Rune won't think twice about stabbing her in the back." With that, she slipped out the door.

Lark's whole world was coming undone. His mother's cousin, Jack, had betrayed her to the Uluns. He had declared her the kidnapped Alrenian queen when, in fact, she had just been a simple transporter. Eventually, she had come to realize that the real queen had given her healing powers right before she'd died in his mother's arms. When she finally accepted her station as queen, she'd banned Jack from Isidor. As far as Lark knew, no one had seen or heard from her cousin since.

Could it really be true? Rune is Jack? The age seemed right.

Rune's sudden interest in being their guide after learning who they were certainly gave Lark pause. If Rune was Jack—his mother's scorned cousin—who knew what his real motives were in offering his services? And Bren and Seven were out there with him, unaware of his true identity.

Lark pulled at his restraints and scooted toward the door on his behind. "Gilla! Gilla!"

Her laughter echoed down the hall.

Lark slammed his heels into the floor in frustration. He had to get free and find Bren and Seven before it was too late.

CHAPTER 23

BREN

Bren's night in Simms Branch hadn't been a pleasant one. She'd spent the night tossing and turning, worrying about Lark and lamenting all the mistakes she'd made in her fight with Gilla. She had wanted to search the town for Lark after the confrontation with Gilla, but Rune insisted that it was too risky to start asking questions in a place like Simms Branch. But secretly she wondered how many other enemies Rune had there besides Gilla that he wanted to avoid. He assured her that Gilla was headed for Ruritania and would eventually make a mistake. Then and only then would they attempt to rescue Lark. It stung to be beholden to Rune, but what other choice did she have? After her performance yesterday, her confidence had been severely bruised.

Now they were headed to the general store to buy supplies before departing for Ruritania. Rune strode ahead of them with purposeful, determined steps, but Bren found herself lagging. Kia had made herself scarce. She didn't blame the clever hawk. If Rune had gotten his way, she would have been sold, tethered, and made to kill barn rats for the rest of her life.

Seven remained quiet and dutifully at her side. And as always when the mind was unsteady, errant thoughts seem to abound. *Why did Gilla look at Seven and ask when the wedding was?* She knew it was ridiculous to give the words any credence, but Lark had insinuated that Seven had unspoken feelings for her. The last thing she needed was for her best friend to have visions of something besides friendship.

"Seven," Bren said. "I need to ask you something."

He furrowed his brow. "Then why don't you just ask instead of announcing your intention to ask?"

She sighed. "This is how people talk, Seven. There is such a thing as social graces."

He gave no response.

"Never mind." She was having second thoughts on broaching the delicate subject anyway.

Seven whistled a happy tune as they walked.

"Don't you want to know what I was going to ask?" she asked, annoyed at how easily he had dismissed the conversation.

"No. You will ask, or you won't."

She grabbed him by the arm, bringing them both to a standstill.

"Ask," he said, looking put out.

"That woman, whom I won't name—"

"Gilla?"

Bren grimaced. "She thought you were my . . . a . . . suitor."

He stared blankly.

"You wouldn't happen to . . . have feelings for me?" She practically choked on the word *feelings*.

He studied her face for a few seconds. "Does this really need to be asked?"

She pressed her lips together. "Yes, Seven. Things like this need to be asked if there is confusion as to what the answer might be."

He scratched his cheek and considered. "Jutta don't discuss these things."

"Technically, you're a Ferrian. You were born in Isidor." She knew the argument was thin. Seven was Jutta through and through.

He rubbed the bit of black stubble on his chin. "Well, my feelings are that you're a bit spoiled, you rush into things only because Lark does, and you lean to the lazy side when it comes to cleanliness."

She fumed.

"What?" he said. "You asked if I had any feelings about you."

"No," she said, waving a finger, "Not about me. *For* me!"

"There's a difference?" he asked.

She laughed and shook her head. "Forget it."

"Forget what?"

"Nothing. Forget I said anything."

"My memory is also better than yours so it will be hard to forget you said anything."

Bren clenched her fists and stomped past him, angry that she'd opened the door for an absurd idea that Gilla and Lark had likely made up to amuse themselves. The whole idea of anything romantic between her and Seven was absurd, of course. She was a year older. He was barely nineteen. She was a princess. He was —well, he was Seven.

He rushed up next to her and slid an arm around her shoulders. "We're family," he said with a big grin on his face. "Is that better?"

She smiled wearily, surprised to find that a small part of her was disappointed. "Yes," she said, pushing his arm off her shoulder. "So much better."

"Good," he said, then started whistling again.

They ate a quick breakfast of porridge and spring berries that a woman on the street was serving up for a penny, then Rune impatiently motioned them into a general store which sold *water*. Bren had never heard of such a thing as buying water. They exchanged the money they'd made from selling the horses and Lark's fancy knife for nine waterskins and enough food for three days. Each of them would have to carry three gallons of water, along with their packs.

Bren grunted and groaned as she tried to adjust the waterskins across her back, trying to find a good balance. Seven insisted on carrying one of her waterskins, and they left Simms Branch on foot. Their three-day journey would take them across the area of desolation to Ruritania. Any thought of the treasure had been extinguished. The only thing Bren cared about now was finding and rescuing Lark. She prayed Rune knew what he was doing. He'd sworn that Gilla was keeping Lark alive for a reason, or else he'd be dead by now. She'd just have to hope he was right.

I'm coming, Lark. Stay alive.

CHAPTER 24

BREN

When Bren stepped out of the woods into the area of desolation, her throat swelled with emotion. She stared in dismay at the barren landscape. The sun was fiery and bright, but the icy breeze that swept across her cheeks brought with it the smell of death and decay. Black, branchless trees stood frozen in time. This was the destruction that came from pride, division, and war.

The landscape enveloped her soul, sending a shudder down her spine. She pulled her cloak tighter around her and looked at the blue skies which were pristine and unaffected by what had once happened there. No birds dotted the skies; nothing moved in the heavens. How would Kia manage the journey if she decided to follow?

Rune stood silently as the three of them took in the indescribable view. There was no smart remark or words to hurry them along. She knew he had also stood here for the first time once. Those who had lived through the Great Destruction had suffered a great loss not only of land, but also of life, and Bren couldn't help but feel like the charred trees stood as a memorial to the thousands upon thousands who had been lost that day. The Great Destruction had never felt real to her until now.

Seven's fingers touched hers, and she took his hand. The three of them walked silently into the strange land, and she had the uncanny feeling that she was walking across a bodiless grave.

"You'll eventually get used to it," Rune finally said.

By the end of the day, the blackened trees had faded away and were replaced with rocky plateaus dotted with short shrubs. Only now and then did a copsewood of healthy trees appear. Just before nightfall, they reached an abandoned village where some woods and ancient trees remained. Rune called it Kapson.

"We'll make camp here for the night," Rune said, shrugging off his waterskins under a large oak tree.

"Why can't we stay in one of the abandoned buildings?" Seven asked.

Rune squinted at Seven. "It's not safe."

Seven scowled.

"You better be more specific," Bren said.

Rune dumped his pack. "A creature lives here."

Bren and Seven exchanged a look.

"Morbid?" they said together.

Bren had heard about the monkey-like creatures, but she'd been told that once the Iron Gate of Isidor had been opened, they had all disappeared.

"No," Rune said. "Something else. Man, beast, or something in-between."

"Then why are we staying in Kapson?" Seven asked.

"Did you see any other accommodations out there to your liking?" When Seven didn't answer, Rune continued. "You'll be safe as long as you stay out of the buildings where he roams. It hates the light. Start gathering kindling. We'll be safe by the fire."

Seven reluctantly unloaded his gear and tromped off into the underbrush with his spear.

Rune bent over and began clearing away debris to prepare a place for the fire.

"There's been no sign of Gilla since we left Simms Branch," Bren said.

"Patience would serve you well," he said, placing a few rocks together to start a fire pit. "I imagine you're used to getting what you want rather quickly."

She didn't know if it was Rune's constant rudeness or the fact that Lark was still missing, but a fire ignited inside her. "Do you care about anyone or anything besides yourself, Rune?" she asked. "Because I've seen what's in you, and it's ugly. You're hardly one to judge."

He straightened and glared at her, his fingers briefly balling into fists. For a moment she was afraid. What else lay there simmering beneath the surface that she hadn't seen when she'd touched his hand?

"If it will make you feel better to insult me, then go ahead. I suspect it's something your servants are used to," Rune said. Then he returned to arranging stones.

Her face flushed with heat. She stomped off to help Seven before she said something she'd regret. Rune seemed to thrive off insulting her, and she was starting to wonder if asking for his help had been a mistake after all.

She wandered for a while between the trees and under-growth, swatting away low-hanging tree limbs. There was no sign of Seven, and the sun was falling well below the tree line. It would be dusk soon. Just as she turned to head back, a sliver of white between the trees caught her eye. Curious, she stepped over a decaying tree and pushed through some bramble to get a better look. A white church with peeling paint stood in a weeded-over clearing. A single octagon-shaped turret covered in narrow windows rose above its tall double doors.

When was the last time I prayed?

Bren considered Rune's warnings about the creature. But had God not led her to this very place? It was doubtful any beast would make its home in a church.

She waded through the knee-high weeds. The church was

encompassed by a rusty, iron fence, so she opened the creaky gate, and proceeded cautiously up a narrow dirt path that was just visible through the overgrowth. The doors of the church were slightly ajar which gave her pause. She drew her sword and sidestepped up the splintered steps, keeping a close watch both ahead and behind her. She slipped between the doors. The pews had all been removed. The decorative wall coverings that hung above the church's windows had shredded with age. At the far end of the room stood an altar with an open Bible on it. Behind the altar was a single, empty candlestand. It was as if someone had arranged the only ceremonial objects left of the church.

Quite unexpectantly, a shaft of light from the multi-windowed turret above her spilled across the leaf-strewn floor. She looked up, and there in its ceiling was a peeling painting of Jesus looking down at her, a crown of thorns on His head.

Feeling something strange shift inside the building, she lowered her eyes. At the end of the room, a cloaked figure had appeared behind the altar, its face hidden inside a hood.

The beast!

A small gasp escaped her lips. She gripped her sword tighter. They stared at each other silently. Who, or whatever, it was turned to leave. "Wait!" she called out.

It stopped and turned her way but made sure that the edge of its hood covered its face. Dark eyes stared back at her. Human eyes.

This isn't a beast. It's a man.

Bren slowly sheathed her sword, then held her hands up to show that she meant no harm. She took a few tentative steps. "I don't want to hurt you," she said.

"Hurt me?" he growled. "Haven't you heard?" he asked in a gravelly voice. "The beast kills anyone who crosses his path."

"Then why am I not afraid?" she asked, continuing to move forward. The truth was, she was terrified, but she sensed something broken about him, and her gift of healing had a strong pull that she couldn't always ignore.

"Perhaps you're foolish," he retorted.

"You wouldn't be the first to say so." She stopped when she was eight feet away. "Will you let me approach?" she asked, her heart beating in her ears.

The man turned his back to her. "How do you know I won't kill you?" He pulled back the sides of his cloak and revealed two swords—one hanging on each hip.

"Would you kill a princess?"

He spun around, still carefully guarding his face. "Who are you?" he grumbled behind the protection of his hood.

She hesitated. Her mother and father had many enemies, but something told her the truth was better than a lie with this man.

She stood a little taller. "My given is Bren. Daughter of the king and queen of Ferran and of Isidor."

His eyes narrowed with suspicion.

"Do you know of them?" she asked. "They united the Alrenians and the Uluns many years ago."

"Your mother? What's her name?" he barked.

Bren found the question strange. But then again, if he'd been living here in this godforsaken place away from people, how would he have received news?

"The queen's given is Wynter."

"Was she from the line of Alrenia?" he asked.

"No, she was not."

He turned away from her.

"Sir, may I see your face?" she asked gently.

"Please leave. You're not safe here with me."

But when he didn't move, she approached him slowly. She reached out with a trembling hand and touched his shoulder. He spun around and pulled back his hood.

She jumped back and gasped at the sight of his deformed face.

"Leave this place and never come back!" he bellowed.

"No," she stammered. "I'm not leaving."

"There's no cure!"

His face was knotted and swollen with large, distorted nodules. She knew of the condition but had never actually seen it up close.

Leprosy.

He stared at her through dark, soulless eyes. A beard and mustache covered much of the deformity.

"I can heal you." Bren didn't know if she could. It wasn't as if she'd had a lot of practice outside of her and Lark's own bumps and bruises. Wynter had forbidden her from healing, but the pull to heal was becoming stronger every day.

To her surprise he laughed. And, for a moment, she saw under the disease a man who had at one time been handsome and strong but whose youth had faded long ago.

"I'm a Healer," she said.

He studied her face, while she clenched and unclenched her hands.

"You said your mother wasn't from the line of Alrenia. How is that possible?"

"The Alrenian queen from long ago was dying and gave her gift of healing to my mother. I was born with the trait."

Though his face was disturbing to look at, she forced herself to maintain eye contact. Tears pooled in his eyes.

She crept closer until she was standing face to face, willing herself not to shake, for he was a man of some stature. The warmth of his breath fell faintly across her face. She reached up to place her hands on his knobbly cheeks. He gently grasped her wrists. "I'm not worth it," he said softly, gazing woefully into her eyes. "Save your healing for someone more worthy."

"The Lord of the house we are standing in says you are worthy."

He resignedly lowered his hands.

She closed her eyes and pressed her hands against his cheeks. Immediately she was struck with a pain like a sledgehammer to her chest. The force of it took her by surprise. Her body stiffened. Never had she felt such dark power. Her instincts screamed for her to pull away. It was as though she had set her hand to a fire, but there was an overriding primal drive to fight what sought to destroy her.

A storm of sickness was raging inside the man—a whirling mass of darkness was in every part of his being. It coursed like an angry storm, anxious at her arrival. Her breathing quickened as she tried to figure out where to start, what to do. The man tensed beneath her fingers. She sensed his strong desire to back away. She dug her fingers into his face and held on, for she found herself hungry for the darkness. The disease attacked her, probing her for a way into her soul. But there was a shield there of strength that protected her, and she used it to push back, pouring her lifeblood into the man. The sickness rolled backward upon itself, screeching at such a high pitch that she found her knees weakening and fear taking hold.

There's too much of it. How can I destroy it all?

But even as she thought the words, other words came.

Do not let your heart be troubled. I am your source.

She took a deep breath, digging deep inside herself, pulling every bit of life and light she could muster. Then she lashed out with it like a whip, and a flash like a bolt of lightning struck the sickness. Pieces of the darkness crumbled, turning to ash. Her confidence grew. She pursued the illness, capturing it now like a sponge, even as it retreated from her. She sought every nook and cranny she could find. The evil seemed endless, yet she pressed on, unable to stop. She destroyed the man's sickness—years and years of twisted disease that had made itself at home. She would fight to the death, for there was no other path for a Healer. Heal or die. The truth of who she was came as a startling revelation.

"Get your hands off of her!"

The voice was muted. Someone else was in the church. She didn't have much time. Desperate, she threw a wide net of everything left in her. She could no longer draw a breath. She was drowning in an airless void. Her world exploded into pinpricks of light like stars. Her knees buckled beneath her. Then she sank into darkness.

CHAPTER 25

LARK

The day had turned gray, night stood at the edge of the western horizon. A cool breeze blew dust across the dry ground. The area of desolation was true to its name. A vast nothingness full of earth, rock, scraggly brush, and occasional trees. Nowhere to run.

Lark's stiff shoulders ached. Having his wrists bound while walking for miles with heavy waterskins slung across his back had taken its toll. Thankfully, Gilla had stopped to make camp for the night, and he'd get a much-needed reprieve.

She was busy rolling out her blanket while one of her men unslung one of the waterskins off Lark's aching shoulders. "I'd appreciate it if you'd also remove these restraints," he said. "It's not like there's anywhere for me to go."

Gilla's man pushed him hard, and he landed face first on the dry ground. The remaining two skins of water on his back rolled to the side. He coughed and sputtered, spitting out a mouthful of dirt.

Gilla laughed. "You think I'm stupid," she said, standing over him. She pressed her boot into his cheek, crushing his face into the ground. Lark grimaced and squeezed his mouth shut to avoid taking in another mouthful of dirt. "Get up," she said, grinding his face into the ground one last time.

Lark rose to his knees then wobbled to standing. He glared at Gilla scornfully. "Why not just kill me? That's what you want, isn't it?"

Gilla smiled. "And miss the chance to parade you in front of my mother?"

Lark clenched his teeth, and fought the urge to charge at her, despite the foolishness of such a move. He was about to tell Gilla what he thought of her when he found himself feeling light-headed. Gilla faded away and a vision came in bits and pieces.

Bren.

An old church.

A creature—deformed and unnatural.

No, Bren! Run!

Pain. Bren's pain.

The vision faded as quickly as it had come. "Bren," he whispered, as Gilla came into focus again.

Gilla laughed, clueless as to what he'd just experienced. "You think your sister will save you. Not as long as she's with Rune."

Lark's anger grew. He'd gotten Bren into this mess and now his hands were tied. He had to do *something*. The vision had to mean Bren was in danger or was going to be soon. "You're right," he said to Gilla. "You should keep me tied up. Because if I were free, I would kill you *and* your two thugs without even breaking a sweat." He looked up at the darkening sky. "How embarrassing it would be for you if I finished what Gideon started when he killed your father in the court of swords by cutting off his *head*!" Lark locked eyes with her and set his lips. "Valen never stood a chance and neither do you." He waited as the words did their work.

Gilla's face burned a bright red. She was practically breathing fire through her crooked front teeth. "Cut him loose!"

Her two men looked at each other uneasily.

Lark laughed. "They fear me more than you!" he shouted to the heavens.

She reached over her shoulder and drew her long sword from her back.

Lark planted his feet. This might be his only chance to get free and find his sister. Was she hurt? Dying? His visions were too cryptic to tell.

Gilla marched up to him, pulled off his remaining water bags and tossed them to the ground, then sliced through the ropes on his wrists behind his back with her sword.

Lark closed his eyes and searched inside for wisdom. His father's words came to him. *Use the enemy's anger, it will cloud their judgment.*

As soon as his hands were free, he spun around.

Gilla was ready with her blade.

CHAPTER 26

BREN

Bren was stuck in a confusing twilight of angry voices, hushed tones, and blurry wakefulness. When her head finally cleared and she opened her eyes, she was lying on the ground by a roaring fire. Night had fallen, stars dotted the sky, and her memories of the church in the woods came back to her like a dream. Seven was hovering over her, looking concerned.

"I'm fine," she said, slowly sitting up. "What happened?" Her whole body was heavy and weak.

Seven pushed a steaming mug of what smelled like mushroom broth into her hand. Rune was sitting across the fire from them, cutting off a piece of apple with a knife.

"You should have seen Rune when you fell on the floor," Seven said.

I fell? She didn't remember falling. *Pain. I remember pain.*

"The creature drew two swords, but Rune charged."

Her heart raced despite her fatigue. "Is he alive?"

"Of course, Rune's alive," Seven said as if the answer was obvious.

"I meant the man at the church," she said weakly.

Seven furrowed his brow. "The beast, you mean?"

"He's not a beast," she snapped.

"Nor a man," Rune retorted.

"He has leprosy!" she shouted at Rune.

Seven placed a hand on her shoulder. "Bren, Rune was trying to protect you."

"Except I didn't need his protection." She pushed Seven's hand away, gave him the mug back, and stood up. Her head swirled.

Rune popped an apple slice in his mouth.

"Is he still alive?" she repeated.

Rune chewed absently and stared at her over the fire. "As far as I know."

She glared at him.

"I assume what you really want to know," Rune said, cutting another slice, "is whether or not you healed him?"

She hadn't told Rune she was a Healer, but he'd likely realized it when she'd touched him with her gift the night she'd begged him to stay and help find Lark.

"That's what you were doing?" Seven asked with a touch of agitation.

She ignored Seven and looked pointedly at Rune. "I'm not sure we'll be needing your services anymore."

"Bren!" Seven said.

Rune wiped his knife on his shirt and sheathed it. "I spotted tracks."

"What?" she asked.

"My best guess is that Gilla has half a day on us."

She stared at him stubbornly. Rune was giving her the opportunity to take back her bitter words. As much as she wanted to be rid of him, Lark was more important than her wounded pride. Perhaps Rune had only been trying to protect her in the church. But she had to wonder why he acted like he loathed her, but would risk his life to save her. He was a man of contradictions.

"When do we leave?" she asked begrudgingly.

"You better sleep," Rune said. "Healing takes away your strength. You'll need the night to recover." His words rang sincere for once, though she wondered what he knew of Healers.

She nodded wearily, then let Seven coax her into taking a few sips of broth before he helped her lie back down and covered her with a blanket.

"It will be okay, princess," Seven whispered in her ear. Then she felt him settle his back against hers.

Sometime during the night, she dreamed of the beast she'd found in the church. Only now he was no longer beast but fully man, and he was finally free from his suffering.

CHAPTER 27

———————

LARK

"You'd fight an unarmed man?" Lark rubbed his rope-burned wrists. He didn't have a chance without a weapon and Gilla knew it.

She glowered at him—her sword gripped firmly in her hand. Her two men looked nervously between Gilla and Lark, their hands on the hilts of their undrawn swords.

"Perhaps it's better this way," Lark said. "When I kill you, the victory will be all the sweeter."

He kept his eyes trained on her and waited. *Come on, Gilla. Pride cometh before the fall.*

"Give him a sword!"

Lark suppressed a smile.

Her men shuffled their feet and exchanged wary looks. Gilla marched up to the blond one and pressed the tip of her sword into his belly. "Give him your sword or I'll cut you open like the churl you are and spill your guts on cursed ground."

The man quickly drew his sword, muttered something unsavory to his friend, and tossed it on the ground by Lark's feet. Lark swiped the hefty blade off the ground, relishing the feel of having a weapon in his hand again.

"Now, you die!" Gilla rushed toward him and swung her sword.

Their blades crashed together and a jolt like lightning ran up his arm. *Sons of Ferran, she's strong.* She lunged, he parried. Blades locked together. She bared her teeth, pushed off his blade, then swung again. He ducked and came up under the cut, landing a quick elbow to her nose with a satisfying crunch. Despite the blow, she managed to pull the knife at her waist and slash it across his arm as he retreated.

They stared at each other, breathing heavily. Gilla's nose dripped blood. She licked it with her tongue, smeared it across her teeth, and smiled.

She's better than you, he realized. He looked down at the gash in his shirt. The wound stung like a thousand bees.

Gilla grinned, spun her knife between her fingers and sheathed it. She flipped her braided hair out of her face and lifted her sword. "Beg for mercy and maybe I'll grant it," she teased.

Lark's temper flared. His father had always said the true nature of man was found on the battlefield. He'd always told Lark to *fight smart not angry. Fight with honor.* But Lark wasn't Gideon, and he couldn't afford to be honorable.

He charged, and their swords clashed once more. He batted away her high strikes, low strikes, and every trick she used in-between. Finally, his blade came within a breath of Gilla's throat as she jerked back her head to avoid his sword. Her eye widened but quickly narrowed with anger as the reality set in of how close she'd come to having her throat slit.

"The only one standing after today will be me," Lark growled.

She raised her sword with both hands, pointing the tip to the sky, and bared her teeth. He had her on the defense how. He charged, only to find himself flat on his back as his feet came out from underneath him. For a moment he lay stunned, staring up at the sky's pink hues. The grip of the sword was still warm in his hand.

"Hardly a fair fight when your man blindsides him," an unfamiliar, deep voice said.

"Move on, stranger," Gilla snarled.

Catching his breath, Lark quickly rolled to his side and gingerly pushed himself to his feet only to find the tip of a sword at his throat from Gilla's dark-haired man. Lark dared a small turn of his head to see who had spoken. The man was shrouded in a hooded cloak and had a short sword in one hand and a long sword in the other. For a brief second he thought it was his father. But the voice was deeper, older than his father's.

"Let him go, and I'll let you live," the man said.

Lark didn't know why the stranger was helping him, but his timing was impeccable. Lark carefully, without moving (for fear of the blade at his throat), steadied his grip on his sword. Gilla's man was distracted by the intruder and had failed to ask Lark to drop it. If Lark played it cool, he might just forget Lark still had it firmly in hand.

Gilla smiled. Traces of blood remained in her teeth. "Who are you?" she asked with a lift of her chin.

"Someone who knows a man should never be bound unless he's done something to deserve it." His eyes flicked over to Lark.

"His father killed my father," Gilla said.

"I don't care."

The blond man who had given Lark his sword pulled a knife. Lark hoped the mysterious stranger was as sinister as he looked or they'd both be dead before nightfall.

"Kill Lark!" Gilla commanded. Then she charged the hooded man.

In one quick move, Lark sprang backward, swept his sword up and blocked her man's blade. He lunged at Lark with careless, powerful swings that, left unchecked, would soon weaken him. Lark blocked left then right, his shoulder aching from the hefty weight of the unfamiliar sword. "Come on, coward!" Lark shouted at Gilla's lackey. "Is that the best you can do?!"

The man tried to thrust, but Lark had nimble feet and quickly escaped his attempts. His opponent returned to hacking while Lark expended as little energy as possible, hoping the man would tire. Fighting defensively wasn't Lark's strategy of choice but he was emboldened, by the arrival of the stranger, to stay the course.

"I'll be spitting on your grave before sunset," the man growled at Lark. He rushed forward and swung his sword like a hammer. Lark gritted and blocked. With blades locked, the man pushed forward with all his weight, hoping to throw Lark off-balance. As the man and his blade pressed closer and closer to Lark's face, battle fever ignited within Lark. He yelled out, and with all his strength, pushed the man and his blade off. Then he went on the offensive, unleashing a relentless barrage of sword mastery. Lark became one with his sword, and the man struggled to block at the speed at which Lark attacked. Finally, the man stumbled, and Lark knocked away the man's last feeble swing, then plunged his blade deep into his gut. He removed the blood-drenched sword and staggered back in a haze of disbelief.

The man dropped his sword and stared down in shock at the blood pouring from his belly. He toppled over and went still. For a moment, Lark thought it was all over, but Gilla's other man bared his teeth and charged at Lark with a knife. Lark was not afraid, for he had tasted blood in the air, and nothing would stop him now.

He grabbed the man's arm mid-air, kneed him in the groin, then sliced his sword's edge across the man's throat. The knife dropped from the man's hand as he grabbed his neck and fell to the ground. Lark spun around, surprised to see Gilla running west into the night.

He was alone with the mysterious, hooded man.

Lark stared at the two men he had killed. Blood dripped from his sword and stained the ground. He should have felt *something*.

But he was surprised to find he was numb, as if someone else had done the deed.

"Killing is never easy. No good soldier will tell you otherwise."

The stranger pulled his hood back from his face. He was an older man, but one who still carried the strength of his youth.

"You were a soldier?" Lark asked.

"A long time ago."

"Ulun or Alrenian?" Lark asked. He was glad to be free, but he wasn't about to trust a man he didn't know. He could just as easily escape one snake only to be bitten by another.

"Would it matter?"

"Some people might say that it does. Why did you help me?" Lark asked.

The man sheathed his weapons and looked down at his hands as if seeing them for the first time. "Someone helped me recently."

Lark ran a hand through his dark hair. Water bags, packs, and weapons were strewn about. Wood had been set for a fire that hadn't been started. He hadn't thought past getting free of Gilla.

"You're a good fighter," the man said. "You must have had someone with skill teach you."

Was the man fishing for information? Lark wasn't about to tell him who he was. He grabbed one of the dead men's packs and rummaged through it. "I worked for someone who took the time to teach me the sword."

"You're very fortunate."

Lark stifled a laugh. *If he only knew.*

"Where are you headed?" the man asked.

"I *was* headed to Ruritania."

"Was?"

"I need to find someone first. Maybe you've seen her? Brunette, stubborn." Lark turned to him expectantly. If Bren was following (and he knew she would follow him to the ends of the earth), it *was* possible they had crossed paths.

The man narrowed his eyes. "I passed a girl traveling with two men."

"Is she well?" he asked.

The man seemed to be considering Lark's motive for asking.

"She's my sister," he added.

The man finally nodded. "The braided girl will return. You killed two of her men."

Lark considered the man's words. If he tracked back to find Bren, that would give Gilla time to return with a small army. And out here in the middle of nowhere, Lark, Bren, and Seven wouldn't stand a chance. Especially with Rune in the mix. The vision he had of Bren was disturbing, and the thought of her with Rune was driving him mad, but the man said she was well, and Lark also knew that there was one thing he could rely on to a fault. Seven would protect his sister at all costs. And from what Lark knew of Rune's past, he was an opportunist. If Bren and Seven told him about the treasure map, perhaps the hope of finding the queen's treasure would waylay Rune's plans for revenge. The best course was to continue to Ruritania.

"What did you say your name was?" Lark asked.

"I didn't." The man sheathed his weapons and headed west.

Lark laughed a little. *Okay, Hood. Have it your way.*

CHAPTER 28

BREN

"I don't trust Rune," Bren said, watching him disappear into the woods. The sun had broken the horizon and was warm on her face.

Seven was sitting on the ground tightening the laces of his boots. "Because Lark didn't trust him."

He said it as fact, not a question.

"No. It's not because Lark didn't trust him."

Seven pushed himself to his feet and brushed himself off. "We can't make it to Ruritania without Rune."

"I know."

"Then what's the purpose of this conversation?"

Bren turned and faced Seven. "Would it kill you to be on my side for once?"

Seven studied her face for so long that she became uncomfortable and looked away.

"I'm always on your side. You should know that by now." There was a hint of exasperation in his voice.

"Well, I don't *know* that," she said with touch of agitation. Seven's rare moment of honesty had caught her by surprise. Was he trying to say he cared for her? Or was she reading too much into it? He was always so cryptic with his words it was hard to tell. The word *beau* was still floating around in her head, and she was angry at Lark for planting a dead seed.

Seven grunted dismissively then picked up his waterskins and slipped his left arm through the straps and over his head so that they rested against his hip.

Rune returned from relieving himself.

"Pack it up. Let's move!" Rune barked.

She snatched her pack off the ground and punched her arms through its straps. "What's the plan?" she asked, testily.

"We continue to Ruritania."

"No. I mean what's the plan to get Lark back?" she asked, tying her long hair back with a leather cord.

Rune ignored her and headed west.

"See what I mean?" she said to Seven.

"You're angry because he doesn't bend to you."

Her heart raced with anger. "Because I'm spoiled. Is that it?"

Seven handed her two water slings and followed Rune.

She fought the urge to cry. Lark was nowhere in sight. Rune hated her. Seven teetered between concern and indifference. Was she really just a spoiled princess? She thought she knew who she was, but the truth was she had no idea. She may have healed a man. Possibly. But even the thrill of that had faded in the light of everything else. Following Lark suddenly seemed like the worst mistake she'd ever made.

CHAPTER 29

WYNTER

"This is Simms Branch?" Six asked Wynter. "I thought it was supposed to be some fancy city."

"It was at one time," Wynter said as the three of them walked down the dirt streets of the last populated area before the area of desolation. "That's why we need to find the queen's treasure, so we can rebuild all of Ferran's great cities."

"Well, it better be one big treasure if you're going to fix this."

"We don't need your commentary, Six," Gideon said. He broke off from them, leading his horse by the reins, and headed toward a supply store.

"Some things never change," Six said.

"What's that supposed to mean?" Wynter asked.

"It means same old grump he's always been."

"He's not a grump."

"Maybe not with you."

Six and Gideon had never really meshed, even after all these years. Six didn't filter her words and Gideon was a man of few words, so inevitably they clashed whenever they were together. Wynter didn't look forward to playing peacemaker the whole trip.

"Tie off the horses," she said, handing Six her reins.

"Why are we going ahead of the army?" Six asked. "We need to bring a show of force *with* us."

Wynter took a deep breath. "Our children are involved here, Six. We can't just march in there with swords drawn until we know what we're dealing with. Do you really want to start a war without knowing where our children are first?"

Six shook her head. "But I still say it's a mistake not riding with the army."

"Noted," Wynter said bitterly.

Leaving Six behind, Wynter crossed the street to look at a street vendor's woven scarves. She smiled at the wrinkle-faced woman and lifted a brown woolen scarf from one of her baskets.

"Dyed with acorns, that one. One of a kind." The old woman smiled. Both of her front teeth were missing. "But if ye be wanting something finer I have ribbon dyed with blackberry and bilberry that me keeps just for special customers." The woman reached into a basket behind her and draped a beautiful piece of lavender-colored ribbon across her gnarled hands. Wynter had never seen any color quite like it.

"I'll take both," she said, digging into the pouch tied to her belt.

"Really?" Six said quietly behind her.

Wynter dropped two coins in the woman's hand. "Thank you. Your handiwork is exquisite," she said, admiring the weave of the scarf and finery of the ribbon.

The woman's face lit up as she examined the coins. She bowed her head. "Thank you, my lady."

Wynter headed back across the street. Several vendors called out to her to come look at their goods.

"You overpaid," Six said.

Wynter stopped in the middle of the street and faced her. "Have you ever heard of being charitable? You might try it with Gideon once in a while."

"Wow," Six said, grinning.

Wynter sighed. "Wow, what?"

"You're still in love with him, aren't you?"

"Why wouldn't I be? He's my husband."

"I don't know. Because he's *him*."

Wynter closed her eyes and took a deep breath.

"Don't get me wrong. He's one good-looking man, but he's got the personality of a turnip."

Wynter's face flushed. "And your personality is as prickly as a porcupine!"

Six pursed her lips and nodded. "Okay. I deserved that."

"Please just try and get along with him. This isn't about us, it's our children that matter right now."

Six held up her hands in surrender. "You're right. I'm sorry."

"Thank you."

"Wynter!" Gideon called, waving her over.

They hurried over to him. He held out a jewel-handled knife for them to see.

"Your brother's knife," Wynter breathed.

"They're definitely on their way to Ruritania. Probably sold the knife to buy supplies."

Wynter touched the cool hilt of the knife, remembering the Lark she once knew and the one that was now her son. She pulled her hand back as if it were hot to the touch.

"Fools," Six grunted.

"The purveyor of the store says the same man who sold him this knife had sold two horses to the hostler down the street and boarded a black destrier stallion."

"Lark," Wynter breathed.

"Apparently, it was an older man who did the selling— perhaps a guide. There was a tall, dark man and a brunette woman with him."

Six seethed. "They've sold two of my best horses to hire some down-on-his-luck guide."

"Sounds that way," Gideon replied.

"I have to admit, I'm surprised they parted with their horses," Wynter said. "Lark is so attached to Dash."

"Supplies are expensive. Especially water," Gideon said. "They probably didn't have a choice. Without a cart you can't carry enough water for the horses."

"Daughters of Alrenia," Six spat. "Lark *had* a choice! He acts just like all the Glasser men act. Irresponsibly!"

Six stormed down the street. Passers-by cleared out of her way in a hurry lest they crossed paths with her.

Gideon frowned and stowed Lark's knife away in his horse satchel. "We don't have time for temper tantrums," he grumbled.

"She'll simmer down," Wynter said. "What about Dash?"

"What about him?"

"We can't leave Lark's horse here. You know what it means to him."

"Fine. I'll see what I can do, but we have to buy a cart and a draft horse to pull it. Don't expect me to spring both of Six's horses."

Wynter could tell by his dark expression that there was no point in arguing. Six didn't have the means to buy her horses back, and Gideon knew it.

All these years, and the two of them are still at it. This is going to be a very long trip indeed.

CHAPTER 30

GILLA

There were only two kinds of people in Ruritania: the nobles who owned the land and controlled the city, and the peasants who served the nobles. The second group included farmers, blacksmiths, woodworkers, cooks, musicians, and a myriad of others who helped turn the wheels of commerce in the city. And above all was the ruling governor—Gilla's mother, Alith.

Declaring Ruritania's independence was the first step in her mother's plan to ultimately rule Ferran. But first, Alith had to find the treasure that the late Queen Zara hid when she'd fled to Ruritania after her husband's ominous last oracle and death. Once Alith found the queen's treasure, she planned to buy for-hire foreign armies to help her reclaim Ferran. Alith would ride in on a white horse as the savior of Ferran, bringing lumber and laborers to rebuild the destroyed cities and return them to their former glory. Alith would be adored by the Ferrians who had waited years for their country to be restored to its former glory. Gilla's mother would be the new queen of Ferran with her sights set on the ultimate prize. *Isidor.*

Gilla had hoped to arrive with something even more valuable than the queen's treasure map—the king's son. Lark. The map would certainly win her mother's favor, but Lark would have won her mother's respect—something Gilla had still yet to do.

She had only herself to blame for arriving without Lark. Had she not cut him loose in a fit of anger, she and her men would have taken care of the hooded stranger, and she'd be marching into Ruritania with her head held high instead of slinking in with wounded pride.

She was still some distance away, but the oasis of trees and the green waters of the large lagoon that were central to Ruritania stood out among the endless vista of red rock that served as the backdrop to the city. Bristlecone pine trees dotted the cliffs, finding refuge in soil-rich shelves. The people of Ruritania existed on a small piece of preserved land on the edges of the great desolation while Gideon and Wynter enjoyed the riches of Isidor. If her father, Valen, had won the court of swords against Gideon all those years ago, she would be a princess now, not some fatherless child doing her mother's bidding. The remnants of Valen's followers had tried to secure Ferran, but ultimately, they were forced to flee to Ruritania after they were defeated by Gideon's combined force of Uluns and Alrenians at the White Mountain gorge.

Her memories of her legendary father were fuzzy at best. She had been just a few years old when he'd died. All she had was a vague memory of his bald head and strong arms as he'd gleefully tossed her on his knee.

She made her way past acre upon acre of flat fields where millet would soon be planted—a cheaper grain easier to grow in harsher conditions. A sheep herder watched her pass by as his flock grazed on grass and weeds amongst the rough terrain. She ignored him as she was a noble and he a peasant. She emptied the last of the water in the one skin she'd managed to swipe off the ground before fleeing from the mysterious attacker. The hooded stranger who had come to Lark's rescue was a skilled fighter, one she'd quickly realized she couldn't beat. Running had been her only option.

She entered the city and meandered through the streets past the sawdust of the woodworkers and the smelting of the blacksmiths. The scent of spiced goat meat roasting over a spit permeated the air along with the putrid smell of horse dung left behind by the horses of noble owners. Two boys followed the trail of droppings with an oversized shovel and a wheelbarrow. The dung would be sold to peasants to mix with straw so they could make plaster for their thatched-roofed homes.

Ahh. The wretched smells of home. The forgotten city of Ruritania would soon be behind her. Alith would reclaim the throne of Ferran, and Gilla would no longer have to travel down these foul streets.

She took a sharp left into noble territory and immediately came under the scrutiny of noble landowners starting their day. She may have been the daughter of Alith, but she still dressed in animal skins like her father once had. Her mother had conformed to the more delicate linens of Ruritania nobles. Gilla fought the urge to bare her teeth and snarl at the stares and whispers of the finely dressed women and men. Her eye patch didn't help. Losing an eye in a fight wasn't exactly a *noble* endeavor.

She hastened to her mother's two-story stone villa. Its tiny, cobblestone courtyard was brimming with sweet violet and primrose—her mother's favorite. Gilla climbed the ashen gravestone-sized steps to the arched entryway. A guard stepped forward to block her path, but upon seeing who she was, moved aside and opened the door.

Gilla passed through the wood-beamed foyer that her mother had sparsely decorated in noble fashion with a white settee, oversized rug, and elegant tapestry. She took the spiral stone staircase up to her mother's quarters. The four-poster bed had long been made, the curtains tied back, and the goose feather pillows fluffed.

A shadow passed by the windows from the balcony. Gilla

removed the map tucked underneath her bear-skinned stole and stepped outside.

Alith was standing at the railing of the large, columned balcony looking across Ruritania at the green lagoon beyond. She was dressed in a shimmering blue gown tied with a gold cord just below her breasts. Her raven hair was braided and pinned into a regal bun on the top of her head. Alith was still a beauty, even though she was well into her forties.

Gilla cleared her throat, and her mother turned.

"Gilla," she said warmly, lowering eager eyes to the parchment in Gilla's hand.

Nice to see you, too, Mother.

"You must be famished," Alith said, motioning to a pewter tray sitting on the table. The flatbread and goats' cheese looked tempting, and the steam of the mint tea, enticing.

"I'm fine," Gilla said. The truth was, she was starving, but she wouldn't give her mother any sign that she'd run into trouble. She had to present a well-fed, well-rested front.

Alith lifted the teapot and held it a foot above a small cup and poured a stream of tea with long-practiced precision. The tea pouring was a noble custom that Gilla never understood the point of.

"Surely you'll have some tea," Alith said, offering her the cup.

Gilla accepted and sat down at the end of the table while Alith repeated the process with a second cup. Her mother sat and crossed her soft shoes, cupping the hot tea with her hands.

Gilla slid the map over to her.

Alith took a quiet sip of tea. "I pray this is the map to the queen's treasure."

"I wouldn't be here if it wasn't."

Alith studied Gilla's face. "You look tired."

"It was a long trip."

"Any problems?"

Gilla's jaw tightened. She fought the urge to confess, but

instead she stretched the truth. "My men are dead. We were ambushed on the plains by drifters."

"All five?" Alith asked, raising an eyebrow. "Yet you managed to escape without a scratch." Her eyes brushed suspiciously over Gilla.

When Gilla didn't respond, Alith placed her cup on the table, unfolded the map, and studied it for a few silent moments. She placed her finger on the initials next to the scarlet X. "D.R.," she said thoughtfully. "How clever of Zara, though I wonder how she managed to hide treasure there." Her mother refolded the map. "Nothing else from the old man you purchased the map from?"

"No. He refused to speak, so I killed him."

Alith didn't need to know it was because Gilla had found him dead in an alley along with three of her best men. Thankfully, a patron of the tavern where she was supposed to have met the old man had identified Lark as the man who had purchased the map.

"He was faithful to Zara to the end, I suppose," Alith said.

Gilla nodded. Many years ago, the old man had served as a young servant for Zara. After her death, the servant had gone missing, and had only recently resurfaced, offering to sell Alith what he claimed was the queen's treasure map.

"What about Zara's niece? Lira?" Gilla asked.

Alith took a sip of tea before speaking. "Our little Lira still claims that neither her mother nor Zara told her anything of the treasure."

"And you believe her?"

"For now," she said. "Lira was just a child when Zara died." Alith tapped the folded map lightly on the table. "I still can't help thinking that we're missing something. Those caverns are miles deep."

"Well, if there was something else," Gilla said, "Zara took it to her grave."

Her mother cringed slightly. "Your father's legacy must be

preserved. With this map we have a chance to regain all we've lost. Ferran will be ours, and I will dance on the graves of those who took my husband from me."

"May the sons of Ulu prosper," Gilla said, using her mother's favorite phrase.

"May the sons of Ulu prosper," her mother repeated.

Retaking Ferran was her mother's one ambition. Alith had worked years at obtaining a position of power just for this moment. Gilla would go along with her mother's plans if only to continue to enjoy the benefits of being a noble. It certainly wasn't because she held hope that Alith would love her. That hope had been extinguished long ago. That's why a small part of her found pleasure in the possibility that Alith would fail. The thought brought a small smile to her face.

"Your mood has improved," Alith said, noting the smile. "Anything you'd like to share?"

"I'm just glad to be home, Mother."

But the sentiment couldn't have been further from the truth.

CHAPTER 31

GIDEON

Gideon stared at the ashes of a recent fire.

"Do you think it was them?" Wynter asked, rubbing Dash's nose. The horse nudged her hand playfully.

He walked around the perimeter, studying the ground patterns. The town was abandoned, but travelers to Ruritania often stopped to make camp for the night in Kapson. The fire could have been anybody's.

"There were three people here as far as I can tell," he said.

"Three?" Six asked. "There should be four if you count the guide."

Gideon glanced over at Wynter. Her face was ashen white. "The supply store owner never mentioned anyone who fit Lark's description," she said, worry creeping into her voice.

"Just because the man didn't see Lark doesn't mean he wasn't in Simms Branch."

Wynter nodded, but there was clear tension in her shoulders.

"I'm going to look around," he said. "You and Six stay put."

Gideon walked through the rutted, dirt streets. Several buildings still stood on what was once a main street, but all of them had weathered to a dull gray. Porches sagged; window frames had long fallen away. Wooden steps that had once welcomed someone home had rotted and turned into deep black loam. He was surprised that this small remnant of humanity remained. Yet there were no signs of life. No sign of Lark, Bren, or Seven.

Wynter's marked anxiety over Lark in particular seemed strange. This wasn't the first time he'd noticed how overprotective she was of him. From the moment Lark and Bren were born, she'd favored Lark. At first, he thought it was because Lark was a fussy baby, but the extra attention continued through his whole childhood. Gideon never gave the disparity much credence because he never once doubted that she dearly loved both of their children. But now, for some reason, her constant angst over Lark had started to gnaw at him, dredging up feelings he'd tried to leave in the past. Had she clung to their son because he reminded her of Gideon's brother, Lark? Their carefree son was more like the old Lark than Gideon cared to admit.

My brother is gone. Wynter chose me.

But had she? She'd hardly been given a choice. It was clear that Wynter and his brother Lark had shared feelings for each other. If Lark hadn't been killed . . .

He angrily dismissed the jealous thoughts. They would not serve him well. Gotz would certainly have told him so.

He backtracked and took a small road that was almost completely grown over with weeds. At the end of the lane was an abandoned white church surrounded by a rusted, iron fence. Surprisingly, the place of worship looked structurally sound, despite its peeling paint.

He passed through the gate and slowly climbed the steps with a hand on the hilt of the sword strapped to his back. He stood in the open-door frame and squinted, surprised to see a dark-haired woman kneeling at the end of the pewless church.

"Bren?" he called out.

The woman rose to her feet and spun around.

"Gideon?"

"Wynter," he said with a growl. "I told you to stay put." He marched toward her, his boots thudding against the wooden floor.

"Should I not pray for our children?" she asked.

"Lark, you mean."

"Lark, Bren, and Seven," she said with a confused expression.

"We should get back to camp," he said, regretting the remark. "By the look of the fire ashes, our children are at least three to four days ahead of us." He turned and strode toward the door.

"Wait!" Wynter cried out.

He stopped without turning around.

"Why don't you just say what's on your mind?"

Gideon's shoulders tensed. This was not a conversation he wanted to have. Not now. Not when so much was at stake. "Another time," he murmured.

"Then I'll be here a bit longer if you don't mind."

He spun around. She had already turned to begin praying again.

"Why did you want to name our son Lark?"

She turned to him with a strange expression on her face. "What?"

"It's a simple question."

She pushed a strand of hair away from her face. "To honor your brother, so his memory could live on. We both agreed on this, Gideon." She took a step toward him.

He put a weary hand on his hip and peered at the dust motes dancing in the light coming from the broken glass of the lancet windows. He could feel the heat of Wynter's discontent but was unable to temper his own obstinacy. He looked to her as one would a stranger. "Did you name our son Lark so that my brother's memory could live on, or was it so *your* memories of him could live on?"

Wynter's lips pressed into a hard line. "I don't like where this is going."

The fire of jealously ran through Gideon's veins as he pressed on. "Would things have been different between us if my brother hadn't died?"

Wynter laughed and rubbed her forehead. "What is it that you're searching for?"

"The truth," he said sharply.

She shook her head and looked away. "Of course things would be different. He'd still be alive."

"That's not what I meant."

"Then what did you mean?" she hissed, clenching her fists.

"Would you be with Lark if he were still alive?"

Her anger quickly extinguished, like a flame in the wind and was replaced with an expression of disbelief. "How can you ask me that?" she asked woefully. "He's dead. What purpose do *what ifs* serve?"

This is where he should have ended it. But jealously is a cruel bedfellow, and he'd slept with it long enough. "Maybe you're unaware," he continued. "but you've favored our son his whole life. And I think we both know why."

Her body trembled.

"Tell me I'm wrong, Wynter," he begged. "Tell me I'm wrong, and we'll go back to Six and pretend we never had this conversation."

She shook her head and turned away, wrapping her arms around herself. "*You're* my husband. Not your brother," she said flatly.

He waited—waited for her to deny what he'd always felt was true, but no words came. He smiled and looked at the ceiling. "I didn't want to believe it. All these years I told myself it wasn't true."

Wynter turned to face him, throwing up her hands. "Believe what?"

He looked at her now, calmly and unflinchingly. "You were in love with my brother. And if he hadn't died, you'd be with him now."

Wynter's expression hardened, her chest heaving with indignation.

"I guess we're done here." He turned to leave.

"We're not done!" she shouted.

He stood still, staring at the floor. She came around to face him. "How dare you insinuate that I settled for you because Lark died."

"Isn't that how it was? Be honest, Wynter. You hated me from the moment you met me."

"Of course I did! You were an unfeeling, stubborn fool!"

"So, I'm right?"

Wynter sighed. "Right about what?"

"You preferred my brother from the beginning, and that's why you've always preferred our son over Bren, because he reminds you of the man you fell in love with."

Wynter's set her lips and slapped him hard across the face.

He placed a hand on his jaw.

"How dare you," she said bitingly. "You insult me, our marriage, *and* your brother." She shook her head unbelievingly, tears forming in her eyes. "I thought I knew you . . . but . . . maybe I never did." She ran from the church.

"Wynter!" he called from the doorway. "Wynter!"

As she disappeared into the woods, he looked up. The forlorn face of Jesus stared down at him from the domed rotunda.

CHAPTER 32

BREN

The heat of the midday sun shimmered across the dusty plains of the area of desolation. Bren and Seven walked in a kind of trance behind Rune, lost in the monotony of the dull journey to Ruritania. Bren dragged her feet forward. Her boots were heavy-laden, and her body ached. Whether it was due to her attempt at healing the man from the day before, or just emotional exhaustion, she did not know. But the price of healing had become real to her for the first time. It had taken something from her. She could feel the empty place and knew it would never be filled again. She understood now why Wynter could no longer heal. The very thing that saved lives also took life.

Bren focused on the two dark rocks she spotted ahead, using them as an anchor to keep her moving. Had she healed the man who had been called a beast? She'd probably never know. Kapson was well behind them now, and she needed to leave what happened there in the past and turn her thoughts to saving Lark.

Rune stopped walking, and she was grateful for the chance to finally rest. But when she and Seven caught up and followed his gaze, she understood with sudden clarity that what looked like rocks ahead were, in fact, bodies. Bodies on the ground. Unmoving. Her stomach dropped. *No!*

She frantically pulled off her waterskins, shrugged off her pack and ran. *Please don't let it be Lark. Please.*

"Bren. Wait!" Seven called after her.

She reached out to the dark silhouettes with her gift, searching for any sign of life, but nothing came back. No feelings. No life. No breath.

"Lark!" she screamed, knowing her words were futile. For death bred a void of darkness and its sting was bitter to the soul.

Seven's boots pounded against the ground behind her.

Kia came out of nowhere and swooped past Bren's head. Bren had been too tired to even notice that the bird had been following them. Kia landed next to one of the bodies with wings spread wide and cried out.

Lark's not dead. He can't be.

Bren's breathing became shallow, her fatigue slowed her steps, stopping her just short of the makeshift camp and its carnage. A blond man was flat on his back. His throat had been cut, and his eyes stared blankly into the sky above. Another dark-haired man, who could have been Lark, was on his stomach with his face turned away. She took a tentative step toward him and stopped—her heart racing.

Seven showed up at her side, breathing heavily. "Wait here," he said, touching her shoulder.

She nodded, but her eyes never left the body.

Seven walked past the remains of a fire and dropped to his knees. Kia flew away. He shoved his hands under the body, then rolled the dead man over.

She closed her eyes. "Is it—?"

"It's not Lark."

Bren rushed over. Blood had drained from the man's stomach wound, leaving a dark stain on the ground.

"It's the two men we encountered outside the gorge," Seven said.

"Gilla's men," Bren breathed. She looked around as if Lark might appear out of the dust. But there was only Rune inspecting the other man's wound.

Seven stood and put an arm around her shoulders, and she folded into him, pressing her face against his large chest. He smelled of earth and sweat and the broth he'd made for breakfast. He held her close and rested his chin on top of her head. "We're going to find Lark. I promise."

Seven had always been a man of his word. He was as solid and sound as the ground beneath her feet, and that was the thing she loved the most about him.

Rune invaded their private moment, bending down to examine the body at their feet. He did it with the callous calmness of someone who'd seen his share of death. "Same blade killed both men," he said, rising to his feet. "It's possible Lark escaped, or at least managed to get through these two before Gilla stopped him."

"If he'd escaped, he would have come back for us," Bren said. Even as she said the words she was reminded of Lark's words.

I left to be alone.

Rune treaded carefully around the camp, squatting to look at the ground here and there. He walked west several feet and came back.

"There's an extra set of footprints leading away from the camp."

"Extra?" Bren asked. "What are you saying?"

Rune squinted. "I'm saying three people left this camp."

Bren stared at the two dead bodies. Gilla, Lark, and an unknown third person had left there alive.

"It's hard to say what happened," Rune said. "There was clearly a scuffle, but Gilla could still have Lark."

Bren bit her bottom lip and forced herself to study the wounds on the bodies. They were vicious and calculated. The attacker had meant to kill and had done it with unfeeling precision. Could Lark have killed these men? He'd never killed anyone before.

Her stomach twisted in a knot of despair. She reached for Seven's hand. He took her hand and gently squeezed it, like he knew exactly what she was thinking. Why did she feel small and afraid? If the time ever came, would she be courageous enough to kill someone? Would she be able to do *this*? She looked over at Seven.

"I promise," he said, reminding her of what he'd said a few minutes ago. She dug inside him with her gift and drew on the strength of his steadfast heart.

CHAPTER 33

WYNTER

Wynter was brushing Dash's coat with fervor when Six walked up and placed a hand on the horse's rump. The horse snorted and whipped its tail. "What crawled up your leg?" Six asked, reclaiming her hand. "Ever since you came back from praying, you've been in a foul mood. Isn't it supposed to have the opposite effect?"

Wynter looked at her pointedly. "I want you to listen because I'm only going to say this once. I don't want to discuss it, so leave it be."

Six chuckled. "You know I can't *leave it,* as you like to say. What happened? Did you tell Gideon the secret you've been keeping?"

Wynter gave her a look that could split logs. "You promised to keep that between us."

"Fine," Six said, holding up her hands in surrender. "But I'll figure out what's going on eventually." She wandered back to the carthorse and tightened its straps.

Wynter went back to brushing Dash. A handful of strokes later, Gideon showed up at her side. She ignored him and kept to her task.

"We need to talk," he said.

"You've done enough talking today for the both of us. There's nothing left to say."

"What do you want from me?" he said tersely. "I'm trying here."

She laughed and stopped the horse's rub down. "Trying to do what? Ruin our marriage? Congratulations, you're succeeding."

Six cast an inquiring eye their way. Wynter turned and focused on brushing the horse. She needed something to hold onto, an anchor to keep her grounded. Thankfully, Dash had taken a liking to her. Gideon stood there speechless and child-like. He'd never been good at expressing his emotions. She knew he carried many burdens from the past, but she was having a hard time mustering up sympathy. He'd wounded her far more than she thought possible.

"How long have you felt this way?" she asked calmly.

"I don't know."

"Do you think so little of me—?"

"You didn't deny it," he said, interrupting her.

She stopped brushing Dash and looked at him, feeling the sting of his accusation all over again. "I shouldn't have to *deny it!*"

Dash whinnied.

"We could resolve this right now if you'd just—"

"Just what?" she asked, throwing her hands up. "Confess that I have pined away for your brother all these years, secretly wishing you'd been the one to die instead of him? Is that it? Is that what you want to hear?"

Gideon stared at her. His expression was hard and unfeeling.

"What happens after that, Gideon? I confess something that's not true and we go back to the way things were? You'll magi-cally be over it?"

"Yes, that's what I'm saying."

"What if I tell you that you're wrong?" she asked stubbornly.

He looked away, his eyes betraying him. She could see that as long as he believed his accusations were true, it didn't matter what she said. He didn't trust her heart. They'd never be able to go back to the way things were.

"You won't get what you desire!" she snapped, fire coursing through her veins. "I won't grovel, bow, or submit to your lunacy. If you want to live in the past, then there's nothing I can do about it, but I won't go back there with you. I *can't* go back. And as long as that's where you want to stay, then there is nothing left for us to say to each other."

Gideon's jaw worked back and forth. He was as stubborn as he'd always been.

"When all this is over," she continued, "I'll find other accommodations in the castle. We at least want to keep up the appearance of a *united* Ferran." She gave him another moment to think, hoping he'd come to his senses and realize how hurtful and foolish his words had been. But his expression remained unmoved.

"You ready to go, Six?" Wynter called out.

"Ready."

She stowed the horse brush in her saddle bag and mounted. She tapped Dash with her heels and headed west. For the first time in a very long time, she felt alone—the same way she'd felt as a lowly transporter who'd just lost her father. And on top of everything, there was the burden of keeping a secret from Gideon. With so much else at stake, she had no choice but to keep it to herself until the time was right. But with the strife between them, would there ever be a right time?

Chapter 34

Lark

Lark's first glimpse of Ruritania came a day later at dusk. The city's large lagoon shimmered like jadeite, and the rocky cliffs of the landscape glowed orange in the sun's fading light. There was some beauty in it, but there was also an unabating coarseness that screamed caution. But he wasn't afraid: he was free. He was walking into Ruritania unburdened from his life. No Bren. No king and queen. No Gilla.

At least for now.

He had enhanced the stable boy clothes with some of the dead men's things—a short-sleeved leather tunic, belted sword, fingerless leather gloves, and a knife hidden at his ankle. The transformation had turned him into someone who would be taken more seriously. He didn't want to arrive in Ruritania as a peasant, but as a man of at least some standing.

A wooden palisade, nearly twenty feet tall, surrounded the city with a single watchtower at the gate. Wispy chimney smoke rose up from all over the vast city and drifted away with a westerly breeze that came from the far shores of the ocean. The log walls were enough to keep out unwanted visitors, but it would never hold up to an actual invasion. Not that Ruritania was under any kind of direct threat. The city existed on the threshold of nowhere and offered little lure. According to Seven, it had been fifty years since Zara, wife of the late King Rodolf, had fled to Ruritania with half of Ferran's treasures. Zara had died long ago. Who knew if the treasure remained? It had crossed his mind that the treasure may not even exist, or if it had existed, had been found and pillaged long ago. But Gilla *had* come all the way to Isidor to purchase the map, so that meant she believed the treasure was still out there. All he had to do was get to it first. That thought was followed by another.

With humility comes revelation.

Gotz and his ridiculous words, always spinning and speaking in riddles. What good had any of his advice done for Lark? It wasn't like Gotz ever gave him a straight answer about anything. Lark still didn't know how to fully use his gift of prophecy. The snippets of visions were as confusing as Gotz. Even the knife and hawk that Gotz had given him had come to nothing. Both had been lost to him and neither had served a purpose.

He approached the city gates with caution. The cover of dusk would help, but he couldn't be sure if Gilla had someone watching for him. He hoped the change of clothes and his missing rescuer, Hood (as Lark had named him), might throw off any potential assailants.

He took up alongside a large, horse-drawn wagon full of fieldworkers coming in from spring planting. The dusty faces of the men and women were flat and expressionless as they bobbed to the rhythm of the cart's rickety wheels. He lowered his head as they all passed through the city gates, keeping his senses sharp and ready. The two guards waved through the driver and its human cargo, barely giving them notice. They were more interested in sharing a waterskin that, by the look of their unsteady legs, was likely filled with something other than water.

As soon as Lark was sure that neither Gilla nor her men were lurking in the shadows, he broke away from the wagon as it turned right, down a dark street.

"Hey, you there!"

Lark squared his shoulders and turned around, placing a hand on the hilt of his sword.

One of the guards motioned him back while the other tipped up the wineskin.

"State your business."

Lark had prepared for this. He'd chosen a name more suited to his taste and a profession he actually knew something about. "My given is Wyot. Blade for hire."

The guard elbowed his buddy and they chuckled. "Did you hear that, Jep? He's a *blade* for hire. Wy-hoot," he said, maligning the name.

"Oooo I'm shakin in my boots, Mule!" Jep replied with a wobble in his knees.

They both burst into a fit of laughter.

Mule narrowed one eye. "I think he might be lying."

"I think you're right, Mule. I'm willing to spit on my mother's grave that he is."

They were drunk, and incompetent. Lark didn't need to be a seer to know that. Their swords hung slack in their sheathes and they reeked of mead and a day spent sweating in the sun.

The men tightened their stances and drew their swords.

Lark inwardly sighed and pulled the sword at this hip. This was not how he wanted to make an entrance. *So much for going unnoticed.*

Mule and Jep sliced through the air a few times.

"I'm not looking for trouble," Lark said.

"That's what a true troublemaker would say," Mule said.

"Fine. Have it your way."

Both guards stumbled toward him like a couple of rickety ships. Jep lashed out, Lark batted his sword away. Mule came with a little more verve, but Lark deflected his strike with a simple flick of his wrist. The men turned in a drunken circle then came at him together. Lark blocked to his left, then right, then left again. He was barely breaking a sweat and considered yawning for added effect. He was feeling quite confident that the two would soon yield when someone stepped out of the shadows. And not just any someone. A tall, dark someone with long, brown hair and a chest as broad as a barrel.

"Move aside!" the new arrival bellowed as he marched toward Lark with a thick blade in his large hand.

Mule and Jep stumbled backward, turned to the voice, then scrambled out of the way.

Wary of the new threat, Lark held up his hands and let the tip of his sword drop and point to the ground. "Your men started the trouble. I came to the city peacefully."

"They're not my men," he growled.

"You must be relieved." Lark's attempt at humor was met with a glare and bared teeth. He lifted his sword and set his feet.

So what if he's large and has arms as thick as my head?

The man took two giant steps and swept his blade out fierce and wide as if to take Lark's head with a single cut. Lark bent backward at the waist, barely avoiding the blade's tip.

"Can't we talk about this?" Lark asked, taking a few steps back.

Another couple of steps and the giant was back swinging. Lark held his sword with both hands and blocked. The man was strong, but his strikes were all dependent on strength. It was time for Lark to school the man in the fine art of swordsmanship.

When the man swung out again. Lark ducked under it then came up and rammed his elbow into the man's chin. Stunned, the man stumbled a few steps backward. Then Lark went on the attack, unleashing a barrage of precision strikes. The man's counterstrikes felt like being hit by sledgehammer, but they were sloppy at best. The man could barely keep up, and his strikes weakened.

All brawn. No brains.

Lark pressed even harder, quicker, forcing the man back further and further until the big lout lost his footing and dropped to one knee. Lark set his jaw and pulled back his sword to deliver the death blow.

"Stop!" a woman shouted from behind him.

Lark stopped his sword mid-air and stared blankly as the giant's expression transformed from battle anger to fearful respect. The man dropped his sword, quickly pushed himself to his feet, and bowed to someone.

Lark turned.

Just inside the city gates, a dark-haired woman, perhaps a bit older than his own mother, stared down at them from atop her horse. Her hair was bound and as tight as her tailored black pants and tall riding boots, giving her a poised regality. She had a dark scabbard belted around a white fur vest, and she wasn't alone. Two armed men on horses flanked her as if she were someone of importance.

Lark lowered his sword.

"My lady," Lark's attacker said, eyes lowered.

"You're dismissed, Arnulf," she said, keeping her hawkish eyes on Lark.

The man shot Lark a look of disdain, swiped his sword off the ground, then lumbered off, pushing Mule and Jep along with him.

Feeling the threat had been neutralized, Lark sheathed his sword. "I want no trouble."

"What's your business here?" she asked.

"Work."

"What kind of work?"

"Blade for hire," he said. "*Legal* hire of course."

She dismounted, triggering her mounted guards to do like-wise. She stayed them with her hand.

"I've never seen Arnulf brought to his knees," she said with a touch of admiration.

"I'll take that as a compliment, My Lad . . . ?"

"Lady Alith," she said. "Governor of Ruritania."

Lark nearly chocked. He only had a rudimentary knowledge

of Ruritania, but he knew enough to know that the title of *governor* meant she was the city's version of royalty and rule. She was definitely *not* the kind of attention he wanted to draw to himself. He quickly made a show of deference by bowing with a sweep of his hand. "My given is Wyot, Lady governor."

She came closer in the fading light and walked around him. A hint of jasmine trailed her. His heart was already racing from battle and her close scrutiny was not helping. It took everything he had to stand still and not run.

She completed her circle and stopped in front of him. "Where are you from?" she asked.

He set his jaw and avoided looking her straight in the eye. "Ferran."

"Not Isidor?" she asked, playfully touching the hilt of her sword.

"No."

"I could use a man like you."

"My lady?" he asked, daring to look her in the eye.

"For security. I have many enemies, as you might imagine."

He knew he shouldn't be staring at her, but it was as though her eyes held a thousand secrets, and it was all he could do to keep from reaching out to touch her to see what visions might lie beneath her façade.

Quite suddenly he had an epiphany. If he could land a job with the governor of Ruritania, the things and places he'd have access to would be well beyond what he could have hoped for. And he was going to need all the resources possible if he was going to find the queen's treasure. There was risk, of course. There was Gilla to keep in mind, and if his identity were to be discovered, Alith could decide to use him to obtain something from his parents. But what was a little risk with the potential for so much reward?

"It would be an honor to serve you, governor," he said with a short, stiff bow.

She gave him a tight smile. "Very good." She took her horse's reins from her guard, mounted her horse, and galloped away into the streets of the city with a guard on her heels.

For a moment, Lark thought she'd changed her mind about him, but the second guard trotted up next to him and bent down, handing him a small piece of parchment. "First Light." He tapped his horse with his heels and sped away.

Lark read the fine piece of paper. *Alith Rising. Governor of Ruritania.*

It was her calling card.

CHAPTER 35

———

LARK

Lark tucked the calling card inside his leather tunic, fighting the urge to whistle as he walked up the cobblestone street into the city. He'd basically just been given a free pass into the city, and what he thought was possibly the worst thing that could have happened had ended up being a stroke of luck. Of course, Gotz would say that things like luck and chance didn't exist, only God's providence and plans. But Lark was a man who made his own way and threshed his own path. He wasn't going to live on prayer alone.

It was nearly night now, and candles flickered from inside windowsills. The city was settling with the sun and the streets were emptying. *Curse the night.* Lark felt like celebrating.

A woman, dressed in a simple linen gown and cap, came scrambling down the opposite side of the street with a handful of blankets.

"My lady," he called out.

She stopped. He walked over to her. "My lord," she said, with a small curtsey and bowed head.

"Where's the nearest tavern?"

She pointed up the street, avoiding eye contact. "On the left, past the Bloated Pig."

Lark glanced up the barren street.

"Will that be all, my lord?"

"Yes," he said.

"Thank you, my lord." And she raced away from him like he had the plague.

He found the Bloated Pig up the street, around the corner. The pig-shaped sign hung out over a darkened display window, though candlelight flickered from within the owner's residence on the second floor above the butchery. Just ahead, two men stumbled out of a door, casting light into the street. They sang loudly as they lumbered up the street. A few windows opened from above them threatening bodily harm, but the men laughed and sang even louder as they stumbled into the night. The sign that hung over the door was a simple silhouette of a black wolf with a white eye. Lark jogged across the street and caught the door, just before it swung shut, and stepped inside.

The place reeked of sweat, stale mead, and smoke. But it was no small hole-in-the-wall like the Prickly Pig in Isidor. The two-story tavern was supported by large ceiling beams where antler chandeliers hung on pulleys. Barmaids bustled around a dozen full tables with fists of mugs, some stopping on the way back to the bar to warm their hands by the huge stone fireplace. Mounted heads of boar, wildcat, deer, and big-horned mountain goat stared blankly across the room from the plastered walls from which they hung.

He quickly made his way to the long bar and sat down at the only stool left on the end. A long-bearded man wearing small spectacles and a dirty apron approached and placed his hairy-knuckled hands on the edge of the bar. "Welcome to the Vomit Repository! What will it be?" he asked with mock enthusiasm.

Lark gave him a blank stare.

The man sighed and in a much more formal tone said, "Welcome to The Wolf's Den. What will it be?"

"Your best mead?"

"No one appreciates a sense of humor anymore," he grumbled to himself with a small shake of his head. He turned and grabbed a stein from a shelf on the wall behind him and filled it from a large cask. He slammed it down in front of Lark. Foam ran over the sides. "Halfpenny."

Lark handed him a gold coin. Fortunately, Lark had been able to retrieve his pouch from Gilla's abandoned pack when she'd fled from Hood. But unfortunately, she must have kept the treasure map on her person.

The man raised an eyebrow when he realized what coinage it was that he was holding. He clearly understood that Lark was after more than just a pint. A few of the patrons seated closest to him eyed him from their perches. Lark lowered his voice. "You can keep the rest of that if you'll point out someone who has their ear to the ground." He wanted to find someone who knew Ruritania. Its past, its present, and its future.

"Over there." He motioned across the room with his chin. "Mose. Smoking a pipe by the fire."

Lark scanned the room. Not far from the fireplace sat an older man with long, silver hair and a cascading mustache and beard that rested against his chest. He was sitting alone, puffing on a long-stemmed pipe. Lark took his mug and weaved between women bearing trays of dirty dishes and mead held high as they spun and bowed out of the way of bungling patrons. As he strode across the room, he couldn't help thinking of the last time he'd approached an old man at a tavern. That man had ended up dead in an alley. He buried the thought. *No time for regrets.*

"Is this seat taken?" he asked, eyeing the two vacant chairs at the man's table.

Mose shifted and propped up his boots on the empty chair closest to him.

Lark was going to need more than a friendly gesture. He set down his mug, put both hands on the table, and leaned in. "I can make it worth your while," he said quietly.

Mose took a puff on his pipe and exhaled it slowly into Lark's face.

Lark held his breath, suppressing a cough, then reached inside his tunic, pulled out the governor's card, and slid it under the man's nose.

Mose glanced at the note, then removed his feet from the chair.

Lark sat down and took a sip of the mead. He immediately spat it across the table. "Sons of Ferran!"

The edges of the man's mustache lifted slightly—a smile lost somewhere within all that hair.

"What the devil *is* this?" Lark asked.

"Likely goat piss."

"Then what are you drinking?" he asked, wiping his mouth on his sleeve.

"Goat piss."

Lark pushed the mug to the center of the table.

"I suggest you return to wherever you came from," Mose said, sizing him up.

"Is that right?"

"What you seek you may not find."

The blood drained from Lark's face. Those were almost Gotz's exact words to him before he left Isidor.

"What business do you have with the governor?" Mose asked.

"She needs someone with my skills."

"Which are?"

Lark put his hand on the hilt of the sword at his hip.

"I'll be needing that chair back now," Mose grumbled.

"What do you know about the queen's treasure?" Lark hoped that question would spark some emotion, but Mose remained calm and collected.

"Probably about as much as you do."

"The barman said you could help me."

"Did he now?"

Someone started playing a happy tune on a lute and the room cheered heartily.

"What makes you think you can find it?" Mose asked.

"Who said I was looking?"

The man leaned forward and rested his elbows on the table. "Because *everyone* is always looking."

Lark tapped his fingers on the table. *This is a waste of time. He knows I'm an outsider. Unless . . .* He lowered his voice and leaned in. "Your king and queen would be most grateful for your assistance."

Mose's mustache twitched, but he didn't seem at all moved by Lark's bold proclamation.

Lark slumped back in his chair.

The old man spotted someone across the room, and his eyes lit up. "Perhaps the young lady headed our way might be of assistance."

Lark sighed. He started to stand when a hand slid onto his shoulder. The distinct shape of a woman in brown pants and a belted leather tunic drew up alongside him. He didn't bother looking up.

He pushed off her hand. "I was just leaving."

She kicked over his chair with her boot, and he went sprawling to the floor. He lifted his head, catching a glimpse of a tall blond as she snatched up his now empty chair and sat down with a satisfied scrape of the chair. He gritted his teeth and slowly pushed himself up on one knee. A patron stumbled into him, barely breaking stride as the man's long cloak swept over Lark, further illustrating his insignficance. Lark stood and jerked back the third chair and planted his wounded pride. He opened his mouth to give this mystery woman a few choice words when he locked eyes with her. His stomach dropped.

"Aunt Kidron?"

"What are you doing here?" she hissed.

"I could ask you the same thing," he answered.

Kidron scooted her chair closer to the table and leaned in. "Gideon sent me. But I'm willing to bet he didn't send *you*."

Gideon sent her? Why?

"When he didn't hear from you, he sent me," Lark said. "And good thing he did, because it looks like you've been spending all your time in taverns in the presence of questionable company." He glanced over at Mose.

Mose chuckled between puffs, his eyes twinkling.

Kidron sat back. It was clear by the exasperated expression on her face that she didn't believe his lie. "Do you know how dangerous it is here?" she asked.

The encounter at the city gates was still fresh in his mind. "As a matter of fact, I do. Do you?"

"Stop with the word games," she said. "You're leaving at first light."

Lark put his elbows on the table and interlocked his fingers. "No. I'm not."

Kidron set her lips and closed her eyes for a few seconds.

Mose took a final draw on his pipe then tapped out the ashes on the side of his chair.

"Who's your friend?" Lark asked, motioning over to Mose with his eyes.

She frowned and folded her arms across her chest.

Stubborn. A Glasser family trait. The truth would likely serve him best. "I'm here to find the queen's treasure."

Kidron's already red face turned even redder. She sat up a little straighter. Mose, however, stayed as stoic as a statue.

Lark suppressed a smile. She'd unknowingly shown him her hand.

She's here for the treasure.

That meant his parents were searching for the queen's treasure. If they'd only trusted Lark and Bren enough to share their plans, he could have delivered the map to them the night of his birthday party. He scoffed at the irony.

"You're in over your head," Kidron said simply.

"Not as over as you might think. At least I can say I've *seen* the map."

"Right," she said with a smug smile.

"Believe me. Don't believe me."

"Fine," she said, crossing her arms. "Let's hear the story."

So he told her how he'd bought the map from an old man at the Prickly Pig, and how he'd been ambushed on the way to Ruritania and no longer had it. He left out the part where Gilla took him captive—*twice*, and how Bren and Seven were likely on their way with Wynter's spiteful cousin, Rune, in tow.

"That's a touching story, but without the map, you've got nothing."

"I know the general area where the treasure is."

"Everyone knows the treasure is near Ruritania, Lark. There's more to it than that. There's . . ."

She trailed off, leaving Lark with the feeling she was holding something back. Could it be that the small piece of paper that was with the map was the key to finding the treasure? He had left it in Seven's care. He prayed Seven and Bren still had it and that they were on their way to Ruritania with it. But until then, his plan was to get as close as he could to the governor and find out everything he could about the treasure. Perhaps Alith had sent Gilla to buy the map.

"You need to go home, Lark. I can't do my job and worry about you, too. The governor is mounting forces to oppose the Crown. If they were to get wind that you were here—" She reached out to put a hand on Lark's arm. "They could use you as bait, as ransom. Can't you see how your being here is jeopardizing everything?"

"She's right," Mose said.

Lark's face flushed with heat. "As future king of Ferran, my duty *is here*," he said between clenched teeth. "So let me remind you of your place, *Auntie*, lest you forget who you are speaking with. I'm the only one sitting at this table with any real authority. And since I won't be leaving, I suggest you stay out of my way."

"Lark," she said, deflating.

He pushed his chair back and stormed out of the tavern in a rage. He took a deep breath of fresh air and tried to calm his racing heart. But instead of replaying the scene with Kidron, something innocuous played at the edges of his mind. When Lark had been rudely knocked to the tavern floor by Kidron, a cloaked man had bumped into him. Had the man sat down at the table next to them? His face had been covered with a hood, but Lark had been too angry to take more than cursory notice. Could it have been his Hood—the man who had saved him from Gilla? He considered going back in, but the further away he was from Kidron, the better. If everything went as planned, by noon tomorrow he'd be working for Alith, and she'd have no idea that the son of the king and queen of Ferran had just infiltrated her ranks. If Alith *was* planning something against his parents, as Kidron had suggested, he'd find out well before his aunt, and in the process, Alith just might lead him right to the queen's treasure.

CHAPTER 36

BREN

It was midday when they approached Ruritania. The city had risen like a ghost out of the ashes of the Great Desolation. Bren's stomach had clenched at the sight of the city gates. Her predicament was becoming more and more real. She and Seven were out of reach of their parents and Lark was missing. She had no idea what awaited them in Ruritania.

"What's the plan to find Lark?" Bren asked Rune, wiping nervous sweat from her forehead.

"I'll take care of it," Rune replied.

"Take care of what?" she asked. "As far as I can tell, you've yet to take care of anything. Lark is still missing, and the city looks huge!"

Seven was strangely quiet. She glanced over at him, but his face betrayed nothing.

Is he feeling the same trepidation I am?

"Listen," Rune said, slowing his pace a bit, as they closed in on the city gates. "Things don't work the same here as they do in your beloved little Isidor."

Again, Bren didn't like the tone he was taking.

"You can't just go poking your head into a hole in the ground until you know what kind of snake lives there," he said.

"That's a true statement," Seven said.

Bren sighed. "He doesn't mean actual snakes, Seven."

"We'll find Lark," Rune mumbled.

Bren was beginning to wonder if they were already too late to save Lark. She couldn't feel his presence. She couldn't feel anything for that matter. Fear had a way of diminishing her gift. Seven put a reassuring arm around her shoulders as they approached the guards at the gate.

"State your business," one of the two lanky guards said to Rune.

"It's him, Mule," the other guard said, elbowing his friend.

"What's him?" Mule asked, sounding annoyed.

"You know," he said, slicing a finger across his throat. "*Him.*"

Mule took a closer look at Rune. His eyes widened. "You're right, Jep. We have a man on the run here, we do."

"Rune, what's going on?" Bren asked nervously.

"I'm not on the run," Rune grumbled over his shoulder.

"Might as well be. Isn't that right, Jep?"

Jep laughed. "I wouldn't be showing my face in here if *I'd* taken Gilla's eye."

"Rune," Bren said, grabbing his arm. "I thought you said you killed her pig!"

Mule and Jep burst into laughter. "Did you hear that? Killed her pig!"

Seven set his feet and pointed his spear at the guards.

Both of them lost their smiles. "Now wait just a minute, young lad. We don't want any trouble. We had enough of that last night," Mule said.

"What about last night?" Rune asked.

Mule and Jep shared a look.

Rune took a step toward them, reaching behind him for the hilt of his sword. "I said, what about last night?"

"We can't say." Jep swallowed, looking at his friend.

Seven took two steps forward.

Mule broke. "Just some no good blade for hire marching in

here like he owned the place. But we handled him. Didn't we, Jep?"

Jep nodded nervously.

"What did he look like?" Bren asked.

"Leather tunic, black gloves, big sword. The same as they all look."

Her heart sank. Even if Lark had escaped Gilla, he had been wearing stable boy clothes.

"Come on," Rune said, stepping around the guards.

As they walked up the street, one of the guards called out. "Good luck!"

"You're going to need it!" the other added. Then they both broke out into laughter again.

The heat of anger rose to Bren's face. If Rune had lied to them about Gilla, what else was he lying about? She stomped up beside Rune. "Is there something you'd like to share?" she asked with as much sarcasm as she could muster.

"No."

"You took Gilla's eye!"

"It's irrelevant."

"To what?"

Rune stopped in the middle of the road and turned to her. "Listen, princess. We don't have time for your temper tantrums. If you want to find your brother, I suggest you let it go. I can handle Gilla."

Bren put a hand on her hip, stuck her tongue in her cheek, and sniggered. "Oh really? Like you *handled* her when you watched her take Lark, like you *handled* her in Simms Branch when you just let her walk away?"

Seven stepped between them. "Enough of this. It does not help us find Lark."

That part was true enough, but Rune was feeling more and more like a millstone around her neck.

"Fine," she said, crossing her arms. "Where do we go from here?"

Rune pointed to a two-story building not ten paces away. A white sign with a silver spoon on it hung above its door. "Get us some rooms at the Silver Spoon and wait for me there. I have some business to take care of first." He turned and headed up the street.

"We should forget about Rune and go our own way," Bren said, trailing him with her eyes.

"Why? Because he called you princess?" Seven asked.

"No. Because we don't need his help anymore. We're in Ruritania now."

"You might have a point. Those guards at the gate seemed to think he was wanted here."

"So, you're finally with me on this?"

"I don't know. Maybe," he said, rubbing the back of his neck.

"Come on," she said, grabbing his arm. "Let's get out of here."

"What about the money we owe him for getting us to Ruritania?"

Bren sighed, tugging on his arm. They walked in the opposite direction until they were out of sight. Bren pulled Seven into a side alley so they could figure out what to do next.

"What if he comes back looking for us?" Seven asked. "He knows the city better than we do."

"Then it will be two against one," she said, peering around the corner. Ditching Rune was the best decision she'd made since their journey began, and a bit of hope crept back into her heart.

"Bren," Seven said.

"What?" she said, still watching the street.

"Bren," he said a little louder.

"What?" she spat, turning around. The words were barely out of her mouth when she spotted the cloaked figure in the alley behind them. Watching.

Chapter 37

Lark

Lark had booked a room from a local innkeeper, filled his stomach with a hot supper, and rested soundly. Upon rising, however, he'd realized that he'd left Alith's calling card behind at the tavern. Standing here now at the stone steps leading to the entrance of Alith's dwelling, Lark prayed he'd made a lasting enough impression that she'd remember him. He took a deep breath, ran a hand through his thick hair, and was about to run up the steps, when a sharp whistle sounded behind him. He glanced back to find a man sitting on a small, two-seat cart that was tethered to a donkey.

"You Wyot?" the man asked.

"Yes," Lark said tentatively.

"Hop on."

"Sorry," he said, motioning back with his thumb, "The governor is expecting me."

"Right you are. I'm supposed to take you to your new post."

Lark looked at the arched door of the governor's home and clenched one gloved fist. *Blazes! I was hoping for a meeting with Alith.*

He backtracked and grabbed the edge of the cart seat, causing it to creak and slant toward him as he climbed aboard.

"Tsk tsk," the whip said, tugging the reins. The donkey took off like an obedient servant.

Lark memorized the route as they traveled farther and farther from the governor. He wasn't giving up on getting close to Alith but, for now, he'd play his assigned part.

In the light of day, Ruritania looked different. Normal. There was no sign of a calculated uprising like Kidron had inferred. No organized armies marching through the streets. In fact, as they rode farther from the more lavish area where the governor lived, the city was decidedly peasant—merchants and laborers. How could Alith raise an army from this? Could Kidron have been wrong about the city preparing to challenge the throne? He needed to focus on finding the treasure, not some imagined coup.

"Here you are," his whip said after a rather long and bumpy ride.

They had stopped in front of a stone building so completely overrun with ivy one would hardly know it was there. There were no windows to be seen, only a large, ominous door.

"There must be some mistake," Lark said.

"No mistake." The man jerked the cart forward a bit—a subtle hint for Lark to disembark. He jumped down from the cart, and the man quickly left as if he were afraid of the place.

Lark took a quick look around. The area was shadowed and deserted like it was purposely hidden on the back side of the city. The street was in disrepair—half stone, half dirt. Pools of stagnant water gathered in large holes. A few weary eyes of the poor watched him from the front of their crumbling homes. This wasn't a place one wanted to linger in for too long.

He made haste to the large door and lifted the heavy knocker, striking twice. People of questionable dress were gathering across the street, intently watching him. He ran a hand over his face and knocked again, harder this time. A small square in the door slid open. "State your business," a woman snarled.

He hesitated. *What is my business?*

"Come on, I haven't all day!"

"The governor sent me."

"Name."

"Wyot."

The little window slammed shut.

He glanced behind him. Two men were heading across the street. Both had one hand hid behind their backs, marching toward him with determined faces. Lark reached for the hilt of his sword. Two thugs with knives would be no match for his sword, but he hardly wanted to start the day like *this*.

The door slowly creaked open. Lark pushed his way in past a short, old woman, shoved the door shut, and slid its large bolt into its locked position.

"Well, I've never seen someone so eager to get in," she said with a cackle.

He placed a hand on the door for a few seconds and tried to calm his racing heart. "What is this place?" he asked, turning around. The women had disappeared down a dark corridor lit by torchlight. With his hand on the hilt of his sword, he followed cautiously, breathing in thick, fusty air. Crying mixed with laughter echoed off the bare, stone walls.

What is this place? And why did the governor send me here?

He was starting to wonder if some kind of trap had been laid for him.

What if Alith knows my true identity?

At the end of the passage was a hall that extended to the left and to the right. Lined up down the left hall were prison cells—barred and bolted. His heart pounded as he spun on his heels and fled back down the corridor to the entrance. *You idiot! Alith knows who you are. You've been duped.* He fumbled with the dead-bolt of the door, his hands shaking.

A woman's scream snaked down the corridor, raising the hairs on the back of his neck. He tugged at the bolt, gritting his teeth. It wouldn't budge.

"You're not going *anywhere,*" a gruff voice said from behind him.

Lark swallowed.

Sons of Ferran, what have I gotten myself into?

CHAPTER 38

BREN

Bren pulled her sword. Seven set his feet and pointed his spear. The cloaked figure in the alley approached them slowly, drawing two blades so fast that it set her heart racing. He swung a short sword in his left and a long sword in his right. He stopped five feet in front of them and stilled his swords, his face hidden deep within his hood.

She stared at him with cold eyes. "What do you want?"

To her surprise, he sheathed his weapons and drew back his hood. He was an older man with dark hair and a full beard. She studied his face. Something about him was familiar. Then it hit her.

"You," she said, sheathing her sword.

"You know this man?" Seven asked, still in combat stance.

"Yes, and so do you. He's the man I healed in Kapson."

"The beast?" Seven asked, sounding uncertain.

"Not a beast. Man," she said, smiling.

"And I have you to thank for that," he said with a slight bow of his head.

"I didn't know if I . . ."

"Healed me?" he asked.

"Yes," she said, feeling her face flush.

Seven stood down and rested the butt of his spear on the ground.

"What are you doing here?" she asked.

"I have some unfinished business in Ruritania. Thanks to you, I can finally see to it."

She nodded. "I'm glad."

"We better go before a certain someone comes looking for us," Seven warned.

The man frowned. "You shouldn't be alone in the city."

"We'll be fine," she said.

"There's something you should know," he said, growing serious. "I believe your brother is here."

Her stomach dropped. "What? How do you know about my—"

"I rescued him from a braided woman on my way here."

Bren grabbed Seven's arm and smiled.

"We parted company, but he mentioned a sister. A stubborn brunette."

"It's definitely Lark, then," Seven said.

Bren gave him a gentle shove.

"So, he's here. In Ruritania? Free of Gilla?" she asked.

The man nodded.

"Where?" she said, filling with hope.

"I saw him last night in the tavern they call The Wolf's Den."

"Why am I not surprised?" Seven said sourly.

"Be careful," the man said, then skirted around them back out into the street.

"Wait," she called after him. "You never told me your name."

He hesitated for a minute, then turned around. "Someone once called me *Hood*."

"Where can I find you?" she asked.

Without a word, he slid his hood back on and joined the bustle of the streets.

CHAPTER 39

LARK

Lark turned around slowly, preparing to fight his way out of the prison if he had to. A man stepped out of the shadows, into the glow of a torch.

"Mose?" Lark asked, recognizing the old man from the tavern last night. Lark had been unable to determine if he was friend or foe, so he kept his hand on the hilt of his sword.

"You should have gone home," Mose said.

"What is this?" Lark asked. "What's going on?"

"This is your new post. Welcome to the governor's secret prison."

"The governor assigned me to a prison to look after a bunch of knaves?"

"That's right. What were you expecting? To be the governor's personal guard?"

Lark hated to admit it, but that was exactly what he'd expected.

"You can leave your pride at the door," Mose said, walking away.

"Wait!"

Mose turned.

"Why aren't you—?" Lark ventured.

"Revealing your true identity?"

"Well . . . yes."

"There's one thing you need to know about old Mose. He always lands on the side of whoever holds the power and the money."

"I see," Lark said. "You play both sides until you see who wins."

"Something like that."

"Well, don't worry. The throne will find the queen's treasure. Your silence won't be forgotten."

"Hmph," Mose said, then ambled down the corridor mumbling about being too old, a fool, and a myriad of other complaints that Lark was unable to follow.

At the end of the passage, the bent old woman who had answered the door arrived with a tray of wooden bowls steaming with some foul-smelling gruel.

"Breakfast time," Mose said. "Push a bowl through the small opening at the bottom of the cell."

Lark examined the stone ceiling and walls while Mose conversed with the woman. There was a tiny crack in the ceiling where water trickled through and snaked down the wall. *Well, that doesn't look good.* A tray was unceremoniously shoved in one of Lark's hands and a key in the other.

"Don't open the cell unless they're dead." Mose took off down the hall in the other direction and the old woman toddled after him.

Lark stood there in a mild state of shock not believing that he was expected to deliver prisoner meals. *So much for being a blade for hire.* He considered leaving, but there was that other voice compelling him to stay. *With humility comes revelation.* He looked down at the porridge. *You better be right, Gotz.*

He made his way down the dimly lit hall, stooping to push a bowl through each cell slot. The thin-faced prisoners snatched the meager food and tipped the bowls to their mouths like ravenous wolves, and Lark could do nothing but watch with abject horror.

Surprisingly, there were only thirteen cells. But Mose *had* said it was the governor's secret prison. What had these men done that they had to be hidden away?

Arriving at the final cell, he slid the bowl through the slot at the base and backed away, but no one stirred inside the terrible abode. He peered inside the shadowy cell. In the back corner was a woman lying on her bed of hay with her knees drawn to her chest. Her blonde hair was matted, her simple shift dirty.

"Hey!" Lark called out.

No movement.

"The porridge will get cold!"

Still nothing.

Lark bit his bottom lip. It wasn't like he hadn't seen a dead body before, but not like this. In a place like this. He propped the empty tray up against the wall behind him and fumbled the key out of his pocket. He unlocked the cell and drew the knife at his ankle in case it was a trick. He moved toward the body with cautious steps, watching for any sign of life. She was a slight thing. The soles of her feet looked like she'd walked through fire ash.

What could she have possibly done to deserve to die in a foul prison?

He knelt and gently pulled back the tangled mess of hair from her face. *So young.*

She bolted straight up, taking Lark by surprise. His knife tumbled out of his hand as he scrambled to stand.

"Blazes!" he said, swiping his knife off the ground. "You scared me."

She stood and stared at him, blinking several times. Her face was smudged with dirt, but her eyes sparkled like an icy, blue lake. "You came," she said.

"Of course I came. Breakfast is served," he said with a dismissive wave of his hand.

"I dreamed of this day," she said, stepping toward him.

Sons of Ferran. She's off her head.

"I think you've confused me with someone else," he said, taking a step back toward the door.

She smiled and shook her head. "No. I know who you are."

He tucked away his knife and held up both hands. "Just stay calm, everything is going to be all right."

She continued to smile and suddenly he found himself entranced by her. There was something familiar about her, though he'd never seen her before in his life. "I'm leaving now," he said, not meaning to speak aloud.

"You're free to leave."

"Do I know you?" he asked, staring into her eyes.

"No. But I know you. You're seeking something."

She moved toward him until her face was within inches of his. He should have left then. *Should* have slammed the cell door shut, locked it, and walked away. But something was compelling him to stay.

"Will you accept what I give you as truth?" she asked.

"What?"

"You must accept what I give you or I cannot give it."

"Are you . . . are you saying you're a . . . seer?"

"I prefer prophetess."

"I can't do this," he said, yet he remained where he stood.

"It won't hurt, I promise."

And for some inexplicable reason that went against all his better judgment, Lark stood still. She lifted her hands and slid her soiled fingers across his cheeks and through his hair until she had cupped his head in her hands.

In a flash, his world went dark.

He floated down a long, dark tunnel and landed on the bank of a river. His lungs immediately filled with thick smoke. The forest around the river was engulfed in flames. Glowing embers floated down from the sky like dark snowflakes.

Where am I?

He scanned the woods for signs of life, but nothing could survive such carnage. His heart pounded; his breath quickened. He was about to call out for help when something caught his eye. Just downriver, a small section of the woods had yet to catch fire. Something or someone was there. There was a glow to the place. He hurried along the river-bank, drawing closer.

Is that a chest?

The closer he got, the more he could see. Cases full of gold, silver, jewels.

The queen's treasure!

The fire hadn't reached it yet. He could save it and all Ferran.

"Lark. No!" A woman's voice echoed around him.

"I can save it!" he shouted to someone who sounded like his mother.

He ran to the treasure and fell to his knees. Much of it had spilled on the ground. He dug his fingers into a pile of coins but when he lifted his hands, the coins turned into sand and fell through his fingers. He tried again, diving deeper, but his hands sifted through the coins like a winnowing fork.

"NO!" he cried, trying again and again.

He tried picking up a silver goblet, but his hand incinerated it. He grabbed a jeweled necklace. This time it stayed in his hand. He laughed and placed the necklace around his neck. It crumbled and fell in bits to the ground.

He clenched his fists and screamed at the sky. He stood and turned in circles, looking for help. But in his lust to save the treasure, he had failed to notice that the flames of the fire had surrounded him. His head swirled.

Is this real?

Lark was losing himself, his thoughts were muddled and confused. The horror of his situation was becoming real. The flames snaked across the ground and claimed the treasure as if it was nothing more than a stack of papers. The fire lapped at his feet.

"Lark!" a woman called in despair.

Mother?

"Mother!" he screamed, searching desperately for her—for a way

out. But it was too late. The fire showed no mercy. It took and destroyed without feeling. He closed his eyes and waited for the end to come.

I'm sorry, Mother.

Suddenly he was snatched from the flames and plunged headfirst through a dark tunnel. The heat of the fire lapped at his heels. Then, quite violently, he was sucked through a small pinprick of light. His feet landed beneath him. He gasped for air as if taking his first breath of life.

He was back in the prison cell, and reason returned to him.

The girl released him and took a step back, looking tentative. He patted his chest and arms and looked at his feet, making sure he wasn't on fire. He cast his eyes to the girl, who had wrapped her arms around her small frame. Her body trembled as if she were cold.

"Who are you?" Lark demanded.

"What you seek."

CHAPTER 40

RUNE

"You've got some nerve showing your face here again," the guard said.

Rune resisted the urge to slit his throat. "Just tell her I'm here."

"I'm going to need your weapons."

Rune unsheathed his sword and removed his belt knife and handed them over.

"*All* of them."

He bent over and removed his ankle knife. What he was about to do was a calculated risk, but one he hoped would pay off.

"After you," the guard said, motioning him forward. "She's in her study."

Rune walked past the staircase that led to her upper rooms, then down a back hall to her study on the right.

The guard skirted around him, grabbed the iron pull ring, and pushed opened the thick-paneled door. "Wait here."

Rune took a deep breath. The guard left the door ajar. Rune listened to a brief muffled exchange of words.

The door swung open. "She'll see you," the guard said with a wry grin.

Rune stepped inside.

She was standing with her hands clasped in front of her, looking out a side window at spring's first blooms. She was wearing a noble blue gown with fine decorative sleeves—her hair neatly pinned up.

"I didn't think I'd ever see you again," she said without turning around.

"I never thought I'd come back." *How long had it been? Five? Six years?*

She turned to face him. "I should kill you where you stand," she said with tight lips.

"There are two sides to every story, Alith."

"It's governor to you."

He ignored her attempt at humbling him. "Gilla provoked the fight."

She grabbed part of her dress and charged toward him.

"How dare you," she said, inches from his face.

"I didn't want to fight her. She persisted," he said tiredly.

"So you took her eye?! For what? To teach her a lesson?"

"It wasn't like that."

She laughed woefully, taking a step back. "You were a fool to come here."

"Love makes one a fool."

She turned her back to him.

"I loved you, Alith. I still do." That last part was a lie, but a necessary one. He wasn't here for love; he was here to make sure Lark and Bren paid the price for Wynter banishing him.

She spun, her face burning with indignation. "Do not speak to me of love!"

"And pretend there was nothing between us?" he asked. "Is that what you really want?"

"You betrayed me. You betrayed me like Valen betrayed me when he foolishly agreed to fight to the death with Gideon. No thought of what his actions would do to me."

"I didn't betray you. I left."

"Valen left me. You *ran*. Ran like you've done your whole life."

He *had* run his whole life. From everyone, from everything that mattered.

Alith paced and pushed back the bits of hair that had escaped her bun. "Why are you here, Rune?"

"I want to make amends."

"Why now?"

"Because I finally have something to offer."

She stopped and stared at him, resting a weary hand on her desk that was full of papers and ledgers. "What could you possibly have that I would want? You've never been anything more than a lowly transporter."

He ignored the biting remark. "How about Gideon and Wynter's daughter, Bren? Would that be something you'd want?" He didn't mention Lark. Not yet. Not without knowing what Gilla had done with him.

Something lit in her eyes. "You have Bren?" she asked with expectation.

"She's close by."

She dismissed the comment with a hand. "If this is some scheme you've made up to try to get back in—"

"Bren's here. I swear it."

Alith closed the distance between them and studied his face with a careful eye. "You're telling the truth."

He nodded.

Her eyes softened as she traced the lines of his face with her eyes. "I hate to admit it, but a small part of me *has* missed you."

He reached out tentatively and brushed his fingers against hers. She pulled her hand away.

"Bring her to me, then maybe we'll talk," she said sharply. She returned to her desk and sat down. "Guard!"

The guard entered the room and gave Rune a push toward the door.

"And Rune," Alith called out, "don't disappoint me."

Rune bowed slightly. When he raised his eyes, she was looking straight into his soul.

Chapter 41

Bren

Bren and Seven were scouting out The Wolf's Den, looking for Lark, when Rune showed up.

"So much for losing Rune," Seven said.

Bren sighed.

Rune headed straight for them. If he was angry that they hadn't waited for him like he'd asked them to, he didn't show it.

"I found Lark," Rune said.

"What?" Bren asked. "Where?"

"He appealed to Ruritania's governor, Alith Rising, for protection. He's safe," Rune said with a rare smile.

"Did you hear that, Seven? He's safe!"

"I heard," he said flatly.

"I'll take you to him," Rune said.

"What about Gilla and the trouble you're supposed to be in?" she asked.

"It's been taken care of."

Seven narrowed his eyes. "Taken care of? How?"

"Come on," Bren said, squeezing Seven's arm. "He said he took care of it. Let's go."

Seven didn't budge.

"Rune, can you give us a minute?" Bren asked.

He scowled at her. "Don't take too long. The governor is expecting us." He left and planted himself by the door.

"I don't like it," Seven grumbled.

"*Now* you don't like Rune? You're the one who wanted to hire him."

"Because we'd never been to Ruritania."

"I know we agreed to do this on our own, but as much as I loathe Rune, he finally came through."

"Why didn't he bring Lark with him, then?"

"Maybe because Gilla is still lurking about. Who cares?"

"It smells of deception. What do you know about this Alith woman?"

"You stay here, and I'll go."

Seven glanced over at Rune. "It's my job to look after you."

"I can look after myself."

He grunted his displeasure.

"We'll meet back up here," she said. "If I don't return, you'll come find me."

"What will be my reason for staying behind?"

"I'll make something up. Don't worry." She shoved her pack into his hands. "Take care of this for me."

She turned to go. He reached out and stopped her. "Meet me at the small church down the street instead, but don't tell Rune."

"I'll be back soon," she said, then joined Rune at the door.

"What's Seven doing?" Rune asked.

"He wants to get his spearhead sharpened. That thing is like his pet. I've told him we'd meet him back here at the tavern later."

She told the lie just like Seven asked her to. If Rune *was* lying about Lark, at least Seven would be safely tucked away at the church along with the cryptic note from the treasure map.

She took one last look at Seven before passing through the door. He raised a hand but there was a forlorn look on his face. *Family*—he had said about their relationship in Simms Branch.

She gave him a reassuring smile and tried to ignore the sick feeling in her gut.

"Let's go," she said to Rune. She couldn't let doubt or fear keep her from Lark.

Chapter 42

Lark

Lark avoided the strange girl's cell for the rest of the morning. The vision had rattled him, and its effects were lingering. Worse, he had no idea what any of it meant. He had hurried from the cell before she could say any more.

What had she meant when she said she was what he sought? She was a prisoner. A nobody.

Yet she knew of the treasure—*knew* Lark sought it. *She's lost her mind.*

Mose limped down the opposite hall toward him. Maybe Lark could ask to be reassigned.

"There's a prison wagon outside that needs an extra guard for a prisoner pick-up," Mose said.

Lark rubbed the back of his neck. Well, it wasn't exactly the reassignment he'd been hoping for, but at least he'd get away from the stifling confines of the prison. Get away from *her*.

"You'll ride in the back."

"With the prisoner?"

"One guard with the driver. One in the back with the prisoner. Governor's orders."

He didn't relish the idea of leaving one prison for another, wagon or not, but if the governor had her eye on this prisoner pick-up, he wanted to do a good job.

Mose held out his hand for the cell key. Lark slapped it in his hand.

"Any issues with the prisoners? Anything I should know about?" Mose asked, squinting one eye with suspicion.

"No. Nothing," Lark said with a straight face.

"I'm surprised number thirteen didn't give you a scare."

"Number thirteen?"

"The girl at the end of the hall. Doc says she's got the prison madness."

"She was sleeping when I delivered her food."

"Aye?" he asked, looking uncertain. "On with you, then. And don't mess this up."

Lark nodded and marched down the corridor.

Prison Madness.

He breathed a sigh of relief, but even as he told himself the vision had meant nothing, he felt the treasure slipping from his hands, the flames lapping at his feet, and heard his mother's voice all over again.

CHAPTER 43

BREN

"This is it," Rune said, waving a hand up the steps of a two-story stone building tucked inside the city's noble section.

Bren's palms were sweating. *Why am I nervous?* She was more uncomfortable being without Seven than she cared to admit. Plus, she was having a hard time shaking the seeds of doubt Seven had planted about Rune's intentions. Despite Rune's prickly demeanor, hadn't he been true to his word? He'd gotten them to Ruritania and found Lark. Just like he said he would.

She rubbed her hands on her pants. She was getting ready to be reunited with Lark and that was all that mattered. She marched up the steps with Rune on her heels. The guard asked for their weapons. She hesitated, but Rune gave his up freely, so she followed suit. Of course, someone of the governor's position had to be careful.

"This way," the guard said, leading them through a stone foyer sparsely decorated with white furnishings and a floor candelabra.

They were led down a back hall and waved into a room. Rune gave her a small nudge.

Bren stepped into what looked to be a study with its large

desk, walls of books, and ornate fireplace. An older woman, perhaps in her fifties, was seated at the desk rifling through some documents, stopping to make notations. Bren scanned the room. There was no sign of Lark.

"Governor," Rune said.

The woman placed her hands on her desk and stood, giving them a welcoming smile.

"I'd like you to meet Bren Glasser, princess of Ferran and Isidor."

Bren cringed slightly at Rune's formal introduction.

The governor raised an eyebrow and glided toward them in her flowing, blue gown. "Please call me Alith," she said, offering Bren a rather limp-looking hand.

Bren stared at the hand, considering if she should try to look at what was inside her heart, but decided against it. She shook the ends of the governor's fingers quickly.

Alith gave her a tight-lipped smile.

"I have to admit. I doubted you," Alith said to Rune.

"Doubted? Doubted what?" Bren asked, glancing back at Rune.

"Oh my. Rune, you're much cleverer than I thought. She has no idea."

A sick feeling was forming in Bren's gut. "Rune," she said uneasily.

Alith tittered.

Rune's silence and stoic expression told Bren everything she needed to know. She shoved him and made a break for the door. He grabbed her from behind and spun her around. Alith lifted the hem of her blue dress and bent to draw a long, slender knife from her ankle.

Bren pressed her lips together and struggled to free herself from Rune's grip. He squeezed her even tighter.

"You're a dead man, Rune!" Bren spat through gritted teeth.

Alith took a step forward and gently grazed Bren's cheek with her knife. "How easy it would be to end it all right here."

She closed her eyes and took a deep breath as if savoring a bite of sweet custard.

"But," she said, opening her eyes, "you're much more valuable to me alive than dead." She spun on her heels and paced in a small circle. "Can you imagine what Gideon and Wynter would be willing to pay to spare your life?" she asked, tapping her finger on the knife's tip. "Ferran itself, perhaps?"

Bren struggled to free herself. *Daughters of Ferran. Does she mean to take Ferran?*

"Mother?" Someone had entered the room behind Bren.

"Gilla!" Alith exclaimed. "Come in, darling. We have guests."

Gilla? Bren's mind raced. Gilla was Alith's daughter? Then that meant . . . *Valen was Alith's late husband*—the Ulun traitor Gideon had killed in the court of swords.

Gilla came around and stood in front of Bren and Rune. Her lips were drawn tight. Her face seethed with anger. "What is *he* doing here?"

"Rune and I have made amends," Alith said.

"Amends?" Gilla asked, turning to her mother.

"Your eye was an unfortunate accident. It's time to put all that behind us."

"I see." Gilla laughed bitterly. "I bring you the queen's treasure map just like you asked, but he brings you the princess and suddenly all is forgotten?"

"Not forgotten. Forgiven."

"He took my eye, not yours! What have you to forgive?"

Alith silently returned her knife to her ankle strap.

Gilla looked between Rune and Alith and shook her head. "You two deserve each other." She spat on the floor then stormed from the room, knocking shoulders with Rune on the way out.

Bren's heart sank as she realized her predicament. Seven's intuition about Rune had been right. Now she was trapped in a hopeless situation, not only for herself, but also for her parents. Alith had the queen's treasure map *and* the daughter of the king and queen. It was the perfect recipe for revenge. If Alith found the treasure, it would give her the means to hire mercenaries and take Ferran. It all made sense. Alith would be able to fulfill her late husband's plan to rule Ferran and she would claim the Crown under the Ulun flag of the wolf. The only consolation was that it didn't appear that Lark was in Alith's hands, or she would have thrown that in Bren's face, too. The thought that he was still out there somewhere gave her a small glimmer of hope.

"Guard!" Alith called out.

The guard stepped into the room. "Yes, governor?"

"A wagon is coming. Prepare the prisoner."

Bren kicked backward, making contact with Rune's knee. He buckled long enough for her to escape his grasp. She sprinted for the door. Almost immediately, she was struck in the back of the head and collapsed to the ground. The last words she heard were Rune's.

"There's someone else who needs taking care of. His name is Seven. You can find him at The Wolf's Den."

CHAPTER 44

LARK

Lark had a very limited view from the back of the enclosed prison wagon. Through the tiny, barred window on the far end he got to see the heads of the guard and driver, and through the other in the door on the back of the wagon, barely a glimpse of the road. The old box smelled like rotting compost. The air was stifling and the bench hard. It was like riding in a large coffin with wheels.

Why am I continuing with this charade? I'm no closer to finding the treasure than I was when I left Isidor.

Working for the governor hadn't exactly gone as planned. So far, all he had to show for his efforts was a confusing vision from an imprisoned, half-mad woman and old Mose (who was hardly a reliable ally).

The wagon jostled him uncomfortably about as it hit holes in the street. He grabbed the edge of the boxy bench he was sitting on and stared at the dark stains on the floor. *After this prisoner pick-up, I'm moving on.*

The wagon came to a slow stop. Unable to fully stand, he crouched to look out the back window, but the voices were out of his sight line. From what little he could see, it looked like they were at the governor's home. The guard who had been riding in the front came and unlocked the wagon door. Lark took a step back, blinking against the sudden light as the door swung open. One of Alith's men came around the side of a wagon with an unconscious woman in his arms. Her limp head was covered with a cloth bag and her clothes were little more than a wool shift and soft felt shoes.

They need an extra guard for this waif?

The man lifted her up to Lark. Luckily, she wasn't very heavy. Lark lay her on the floor because she'd likely end up there anyway on the bumpy ride back.

The guard driver slammed the door shut and clicked the lock into place.

The woman lay still. Unconscious.

Just what I need. Another woman prisoner.

Lark sat and rested his head against the wall and closed his eyes. For a while, he drifted in and out of blissful consciousness until the wagon abruptly stopped and jolted him from his hazy slumber. There was a shift in the wagon as the driver and guard disembarked. Lark rubbed the back of his stiff neck. The ride hadn't seemed very long. Were they back already?

Shouts ensued.

He crouched and peered out the window behind the driver's seat, but he couldn't see anything except the horses shifting nervously in their harnesses. He stepped over the prisoner and peered out the back. Whatever was happening was out of sight.

More shouts came, then the clang of metal weapons. *Sons of Ferran!* Lark pulled at the door, but it was securely locked. The woman moaned, shifted, and grew still again.

Something slammed into the side of the wagon—a body by the sound of it.

Blazes! We're being attacked.

Lark pulled his sword and shimmied it through the crack of the door, trying to break the lock. There was another, stronger thud against the side of the wagon. A spearhead pierced the wagon wall. Lark stared at it in disbelief. It was quickly pulled back through, opening a hole of light. There was a guttural groan, then all grew still. Lark quietly stuck his eye to the splintered hole. The guard and driver were on the ground, blood pooling beneath them. Someone was risking their life to save this woman. This was no ordinary prisoner.

He sheathed his sword, drew the knife at his ankle, and sat in the shadows by the door, pressing himself back as far as possible. He didn't want whoever was on the other side of that door knowing there was another guard in the back. Surprise was his only advantage. He braced himself.

The attacker grunted while he worked the lock.

What if there's more than one of them? Lark's heartbeat pounded in his ears.

The lock snapped.

He took a deep breath and gripped his knife tighter. The door swung open. Wasting no time, Lark pounced. Both he and the masked assailant landed hard on the ground. The fall momentarily stunned the man. He stared up at Lark with large, brown eyes and pulled frantically at the black mask he was wearing.

You picked the wrong wagon, lad. Lark drew back his arm ready to slit the man's throat when the mask came down and the man stared bewilderedly at him.

Seven?

Lark took a quick glance around him. A small crowd of horrified onlookers had gathered in the street and were anxiously watching. He placed the knife's edge against Seven's throat and leaned in. "What are you doing here?" he hissed.

"Bren," he said, breathlessly.

"Bren?"

Seven's eyes flashed past Lark, toward the wagon. Lark glanced over his shoulder at the lifeless body in the back of the wagon. If that was Bren, that meant Alith had somehow found her out, and Seven had let her get taken. Lark drew back a fist and punched Seven in the face as hard as he could. He told himself it was for the crowd, but deep down he was angry at

Seven for not protecting his sister. Seven stopped the next punch with his iron grip and pushed back.

"Get out of here," Lark said fiercely. "I'll take care of Bren."

Seven being quite a bit larger than Lark, rolled them both over, stripping Lark's knife out of his hand in the process. He straddled Lark, grabbed him by the throat, and squeezed with both of his hands. Lark's face swelled and reddened as he dug frantically at Seven's grip.

"Seven," Lark sputtered, unable to draw full breath.

Seven held his grip, baring his white teeth.

Lark's vision blurred.

Seven pulled him closer so that they were forehead to forehead. "That's for the punch." He roughly shoved Lark back to the ground, pulled up his mask, swiped his spear off the ground, and ran off.

Lark pushed himself to his knees, coughing and gasping for air.

Blazes, Seven! You almost killed me.

Women, men, and children stood aghast, mumbling to one another and looking in the direction of Seven's escape then back to the prisoner lying on the floor of the open wagon.

Lark stumbled to his feet and waved off the crowd. "Go home!" He ambled to the wagon door.

I'm sorry, Bren.

He slammed the door then climbed into the wagon seat and drove the horses toward the prison.

CHAPTER 45

SEVEN

Seven ducked inside the small church he had told Bren to meet him at. Large candles flickered and smoked in bronze candle holders on an altar at the end of the sanctuary. A single aisle ran between two rows of benches. The place was empty—quiet. Only the greasy scent of the sheep tallow permeated the air. He leaned up against the back wall, trying to catch his breath. What was Lark doing in the back of a prison wagon? He clearly wasn't a prisoner. He was armed and ready to defend the attack.

He ground his teeth together.

I should have never let Bren follow Rune without me.

After he'd fled from Lark, Seven had followed the prison wagon all the way to what he suspected was a prison, cleverly hidden at the edge of the city. He'd watched from the shadows as an old man opened the door and Lark carried Bren inside. Lark would never hurt Bren, he knew that. But what game was he playing?

Seven strode slowly down the aisle toward the candlelight and plopped down on the first row. *What do I do now, Lord?*

The door opened behind him. He jumped up and readied his spear.

A man stepped in and removed the hood of his cloak.

"Hood." Seven lowered his weapon.

"Most people aren't expecting a fight in a church." He came down the aisle and sat on the bench across the from Seven. "Where's Bren?"

Seven sat. "Prison."

"What happened?"

"Our guide, Rune, betrayed us to the governor."

They were quiet for a few moments.

"What's this prison like?" Hood asked.

"One way in. One way out. No windows." Seven gave Hood a questioning look.

"I owe her," Hood said softly, looking down at his hands.

"Trying to break her out would be a death sentence," Seven said.

"I was dead," he replied. "Now I live again."

"What about your unfinished business?"

"No luck, so far."

"I'm sorry," Seven said.

Hood nodded. "Perhaps I will serve a different purpose."

"You sound like my mother."

"Your mother sounds like a wise woman."

"She is Jutta. She says the Almighty directs the path of our lives, so there is no point in worrying. That is the Jutta way."

"But you're worried?" Hood asked.

"Yes. My faith is weak."

"Said the man whose first thought was to find a church and pray."

Seven gave him a weak smile. "What you say is only half true. I have not yet got to the praying part."

Hood came and sat next to Seven. "Then perhaps you can start by asking God to help us deliver Bren from the enemy."

"Even if that enemy is Bren's brother?" Seven thought perhaps the shocking news of Lark's involvement would sway Hood, but the man didn't flinch.

"Even then," Hood said.

CHAPTER 46

LARK

Lark held the limp body of his sister, her hair spilling over his arm. "Mose, there's got to be somewhere else we can put her." Lark wasn't comfortable with the idea of Bren being in the same cell as the blonde woman.

"Thirteen cells are all we have." Mose looked at him with mock sincerity. "Unless of course you think she would be better off with one of the men?"

The blonde woman was sitting on her pile of hay with her legs crossed, staring at him with her sparkling, blue eyes.

Lark talked quietly out the side of his mouth. "But that one in there is not right in the head."

"None of them are," Mose retorted. He unlocked the cell and pulled the barred door open.

A fresh pile of hay had been tossed on the other side of the cell. As soon as Lark stepped inside, he felt the same strange connection he'd had earlier with the woman.

Blazes! What is this hold she has over me?

He knelt and gently placed Bren on the hay bed. He smoothed her hair back from her face and placed her hands by her side.

"Enough of that," Mose said.

He sat back on his heels. *Can I really leave her like this?* "She's been unconscious for a long time. Maybe we should call a doctor," Lark said.

Mose guffawed.

Lark stood up and looked down at Bren. The lump of regret rose in his throat. *She shouldn't be here. Not like this.*

"Come on. You've got other prisoners to attend. Number five threw up."

"I'm not cleaning up vomit!"

Mose cocked an eyebrow. "There's a hundred men who would kill for your post. So, if you want to surrender it, you know the way out." He tossed Lark the cell key and left.

Lark ran a hand through his hair. The girl crawled over and felt Bren's forehead. He was about to protest, but there was a gentleness to her touch that put him at ease.

"She'll be fine," the woman said. She took Bren's hand into hers as a caring friend would.

He locked the cell and headed back down the hall, wondering how he was going to get himself and Bren out of this mess.

Mose was waiting for him at the end of the prison hall.

"What now?" Lark asked.

There was concern in Mose's face that hadn't been there a few minutes ago. "The governor wants to see you," he said quietly.

Lark cleared his throat roughly. "Why?"

"Why do you think? There's a guard and a driver dead in the streets, and you're the only one who saw the assailant up close."

An inquiry into the incident made sense, but he had to wonder what else Alith might know. Had his identity been compromised now, too?

"The old woman is bringing you a horse out front."

Lark pinched the bridge of his nose. Should he grab Bren and run? Should he meet with Alith and keep up the ruse? He needed time to think.

"Oh, I'm sorry," Mose huffed. "Did you have a prior engagement?"

"Who's going to take care of number five's . . . vomit?" he asked, stalling for more time to think. *What if Bren wakes up while I'm gone?*

Mose didn't seem to know that Bren was royalty, but that didn't mean he wouldn't find out. So far, Mose had kept his mouth shut about Lark, but would he continue the charade if he saw the tide turning in Alith's favor?

"It's just an inquiry," Mose said, seeming to take notice of Lark's trepidation. "You saved the prisoner, didn't you?" Mose gave him a light tap on the arm. "You're a hero." He winked and headed toward prisoner five with a bucket and a broom.

Yes. A hero.

CHAPTER 47

BREN

Bren sat up and winced as she touched the painful knot on the back of her head. *What happened?* She looked around her dark surroundings. The straw beneath her was coarse and the ground hard. A young woman in a threadbare shift was standing next to her, wringing her hands. As soon as Bren spotted the cold iron bars of the cage, her memory came flooding back.

Rune betrayed me. Alith is Valen's widow—Gilla's mother.

Bren slowly pushed herself to her feet. She wobbled unsteadily. The blonde woman reached out and caught her by the arm. "Careful, you've got a nasty bump on your head."

"I'm fine," Bren said, waiting for her head to clear. She reclaimed her arm and took a closer look around the cell. *Daughters of Ferran! This place is a rathole.*

"Lark was concerned about you," the woman said.

Bren turned to her. "What did you say?"

"He's a guard here."

"Oh," Bren said. For a minute she thought the woman had said *Lark.*

"He'll be back to check on you later."

"I'm sure he will," she said, taking a few careful steps up to the prison bars.

The woman reached out as if to help Bren if she stumbled. Bren held up a hand to stay her. But in truth, she was unsteady.

"My given is Lira."

"Bren," she said absently. She peered out of the cell but couldn't make out anything other than the wretched smell of the other prisoners.

Imprisoned. Betrayed.

She began a meticulous search of the cell walls, looking for any structural weaknesses, but the place was built like a fortress.

"There's only one way in and out," Lira said.

Bren gritted her teeth and grabbed the bars of the cell. *What is Seven going to do if I don't show up at the church? Probably something foolish that will get him killed. And where is Lark?*

"We will be free soon," Lira said. "Don't fret."

Bren laughed a little. "Don't fret?" she asked, turning to Lira. "Of course. What was I thinking? Because this place is such a pleasure!"

"There is one more powerful than the bars of this cell."

"Do you think angels will come and open the door for us, Lira?" She knew her words were spiteful, but they came nonetheless. "That we'll waltz out of here like Peter did in the bible and be reunited with our friends?"

Lira stared at her, unblinking.

Bren turned back to the bars. She needed something to hold on to because her world was spiraling out of control. She closed her eyes and took a deep breath. Her words had been cruel. "Listen, Lira," she said, turning around. "I'm sorry."

But Lira had curled up into a ball facing the wall and was humming softly to herself.

Bren deflated. At least Lira was holding on to hope instead of the hopelessness Bren was nursing. She pressed her back up against the cell bars and sank to the dirt floor. There was nothing to do now but wait—wait and hope Seven would find her. She should have been afraid, but she wasn't. Not anymore. A fire had been lit inside her the minute Rune had betrayed her. No one was going to take away her birthright and everything her parents had fought for. She would defend Ferran and Isidor to the death, and nothing and no one would stop her. Not Rune. Not Alith. Not even Lark.

CHAPTER 48

LARK

Trying to maintain a calm demeanor when he was angry was not one of Lark's strong suits. He wanted to march into Alith's home with his sword swinging for what she had done to Bren. But Bren's life hung in the balance, so he buried the burning desire and plastered on the stoic face of a blade for hire. He was certain that Alith didn't know his real identify, because if she did, he'd be in a cell next to Bren already. That was something, at least. His quest for the treasure would have to wait. He needed to play his part until he could figure out how to get his sister to safety. Why did she have to follow him?

His weapons were confiscated, and he was escorted up a stone stairwell, through a richly appointed bedroom, out onto a long balcony that overlooked the city with views all the way to the green lagoon. Alith was standing at the railing in a long, green dress with a matching sheer sleeve. Her long hair was no longer bound but pinned back from her face and hanging smoothly down her back. She wore her nobility today.

"Governor," he said with a slight bow.

"Please, Wyot," she said, motioning to the table of food. "Have something to eat. It's such a lovely evening that I asked for dinner to be served out here. I can't possibly eat all of this."

The food was tempting—flatbread, meat sauce, goat cheese, wild berries, sugar cakes. His stomach growled, but he wouldn't eat from the enemy's table. "Thank you," he replied, "but I should get back to the prison soon."

"Of course," she said, folding her hands in front of her waist. She stepped over to the table, lifted a slender pitcher, and poured wine into a goblet.

"I wanted to thank you personally for preventing what could have been an embarrassing . . ." She paused with the pitcher, searching for the right words. ". . . mishandling of an important prisoner."

This was Lark's opening.

"If you don't mind me asking, governor, who is she? I'd like to know who I risked my life for."

Alith took a tentative sip of her wine. "Mmm," she said, tightening her lips. "The grapes of the Sea People never disappoint. Did you know that they grow their grapes on the slopes of the mountains?"

Lark had heard of the Sea People, of course, but mainly in context of their reputation as seafaring pirates. They lived by the ocean west of Ruritania. He shouldn't have been surprised that Alith would trade with people of such ill repute. "Will that be all, governor?" he asked. He was anxious to return and check on Bren.

"The girl prisoner is someone very important to the future of Ruritania."

Kidron had said that if he was found out, the governor would use him as a pawn against his parents. Only Bren had become the pawn, and it was all his fault.

"I might have another position for you, if you're interested," Alith continued. She took her drink to the railing and looked out over the city.

This was not good news. He wanted to stay at the prison so he could keep an eye on Bren.

"Surely I'm more use to you at the prison," he said. "After

what happened this morning . . ."

She spun around and smiled. "All the more reason to use you for an important mission."

"Mission?" he asked.

"The details aren't your concern. I need a man like you in my guard. One who thinks on his feet."

He shuffled through a myriad of reasons he could use to turn her down but couldn't come up with anything that wouldn't rouse suspicion.

Someone stepped out onto the balcony behind him and cleared their throat. He was grateful for the interruption. It would give him more time to create a believable reason to return to his duties at the prison.

Alith scowled. "What is it, Gilla?"

Lark stiffened. He'd been so tied up with his own predicament, he'd completely forgotten about her. All he could do now was hope that she stayed behind him and didn't look too closely. He edged his fingers toward a small knife on the table.

"Is Rune still here?" Gilla asked.

Rune?

Lark seethed as he put the pieces together. *That scoundrel must have turned Bren in. After all these years, his mother's dear cousin Jack was finally getting his revenge for being banished.*

"Rune left," Alith said, "and as you can see, I'm in the middle of something."

"Who's this?" Gilla asked.

Lark stealthily slid the knife off the table's edge and up his sleeve.

"No one who concerns you."

Gilla stepped around to face Lark. She turned and smiled at Alith.

Alith raised an eyebrow. "Do you two know each other?"

Gilla smirked at Lark. "You always were one for a pretty face, Mother."

Lark's face colored. *Mother?* The truth came rushing at him like a tidal wave. If Alith was Gilla's mother . . . that meant that Alith was the beheaded Valen's widow. It was all just as Kidron had said. Alith had a motive for mounting forces against the Crown. She had picked up Valen's mantle to reclaim the throne of Ferran, and Lark had just handed her more fuel—Gideon and Wynter's son. He cursed himself for not learning more about Ruritania and its governor before stepping foot into the wretched city.

Gilla smiled and drew her sword slowly as Lark squirmed. He felt a fool. Without realizing it, he'd walked straight into the wolf's den—Valen's den. And he'd brought Bren with him.

"Gilla," Alith warned.

"Mother," Gilla said mockingly, placing the tip of her sword at Lark's throat.

He swallowed gingerly and held up his hands.

"This is Lark," Gilla said. "The *son* of Gideon and Wynter."

Alith's eyes lit up as she took a sip of wine. A faint smile spread across her face as she studied him over the rim of her goblet. "I know who he is," she said coldly.

Lark clenched his jaw. How long had she been playing him?

Gilla lost the smile and shifted uncomfortably. "What do you mean, *you know*?" she asked, keeping her eye locked on Lark.

Alith sat her goblet down. "I know you had Lark in hand and lost him. I would have hoped to hear that information from you, but alas…it came from other lips. Now you've ruined my little ruse with Lark which, I must admit, turned out to be more fun than I'd even hoped." Her eyes glimmered with satisfaction.

Lark raged inside, heat rising to his neck and face.

"Poor, foolish Lark. Can you imagine what a delight it was to watch you discover that your sister was your prisoner?" she asked him. "And you *still* sacrificed her safety for your own ambition. I don't know whether to be impressed or disgusted." Her face hardened as she swiped her goblet off the table. "Guards!"

Everything in him screamed to fight, but a table knife wasn't going to get him out of this. He had no choice but to stand down while two men entered the patio and bound his hands. They searched him and quickly found the knife he'd slipped up his sleeve.

Gilla lowered her sword and turned to her mother. "You had me followed all the way to Isidor?"

Alith folded her hands. "Only out of concern for your safety. You are my only child after all."

Gilla shook her head in disbelief, as if she wasn't buying the motherly sentiment.

Alith picked up her goblet and returned her gaze to the view. "Be a dear and see that he's locked him up in the basement until morning. I'll send word to the prison to expect you at first light. I'm sure you'll want to personally see to his . . . *safe* arrival."

Gilla's grip on her sword tightened. "Of course, governor," she said bitterly.

Lark struggled against the men who held him, though he knew it was futile.

"Oh," Alith said, with a slight turn and flit of her hand. "While you're at the prison, Gilla, bring back our little, fair-haired prisoner. Lira may prove useful yet."

Lira? Lark's face paled and his knees weakened. Alith narrowed her eyes and gave him a curious look as if trying to determine why he had reacted to Lira's name.

When Lark asked the woman who she was, she had said *what you seek*. Her words finally made sense. She was the woman from Gotz's vision.

Lira.

CHAPTER 49

SEVEN

The hour was late. The city was shuttered up tight for the night. Seven wasn't sure this plan of Hood's was going to work, but he wouldn't leave Bren in prison. Seven was going to get her out, even if he had to fight Lark. This time there would be no running away.

"Are you ready?" Hood asked, loosely tying Seven's hands behind his back.

"This question does not need to be asked."

Hood placed a hand on Seven's shoulder. "And you're sure there's only Lark and the old man inside?"

"One can never be sure of anything."

Hood reached around Seven with an exasperated sigh and pounded the iron knocker on the prison door four times. "Remember, wait until we have confirmation on Bren."

Seven closed his eyes for a brief moment. *Please let this work, Lord God.* Because if it didn't, he would be taken prisoner, too, and there would be no way out for any of them.

The small window in the door slid open. A scowling, old woman peered out at them from the light of her lantern. Seven breathed a silent sigh of relief that it wasn't Lark.

"State your business!"

"New prisoner," Hood said, pushing Seven a little closer to the door.

"There's been no word of a new prisoner," the woman said, eyeing Seven up and down.

"This is the man wanted for the prison transport ambush this morning. I want to claim the reward the governor is offering in exchange for the prisoner."

"Wait here," she growled. The small window slammed shut.

Seven grunted. He wasn't relishing the idea of giving himself up voluntarily even if it was a ruse to get inside. Plus, there was no guarantee that if they got in, they'd be able to get back out.

After several long minutes the window slid open again. This time a gray-bearded man appeared. "So, you have the assailant, do you?"

"I want the promised reward money," Hood said.

The older man held up his lantern and studied Seven with small, crinkly eyes almost hidden between his bushy eyebrows and beard. "The door gets opened to no one without the governor's approval." The window slid halfway shut. "Come back tomorrow."

Seven shifted uncomfortably. The plan had failed.

"Wait!" Hood barked.

The door slid back open.

Hood slipped a piece of fine parchment between the slender bars. "I'm guessing the governor's calling card will be sufficient?"

Sons of Ferran! Where did he get that?

The man took one look at the paper and then held the lantern a little higher as he peered out between the bars.

Hood displayed Seven's spear for the man to see, then roughly pushed Seven's head against the barred window. The window slid shut again. Hood removed his hand from Seven's head.

"Was that really necessary?" Seven asked, working his jaw.

The bolt of the door clicked.

"This question does not need to be asked," Hood said with a sarcastic whisper.

Seven bristled.

The door swung open, Hood escorted Seven inside like a common criminal, and the old man quickly bolted the door.

"Who's in charge here?" Hood asked.

Seven glared at the wiry, old prison keeper.

"My given is Mose," the man said, taking a few wary steps back from Seven.

Good. He fears me. He should. I could break his neck with one hand.

"I'll just take my reward and be on my way," Hood said evenly.

"We don't have the money here," Mose said. "But we can send for it in the morning."

"Then I'll be staying the night," Hood said.

The man shook his head. "I'm afraid that's impossible. Prisoners only."

"No money. No prisoner," Hood said gruffly.

It took everything Seven had not to headbutt the old man and race down the darkened corridor. But Hood was right. They needed to be sure Bren was still there and Lark hadn't grown a conscience and set her free. He buried his impatience.

"Suit yourself," Mose finally said. "But you'll have to be locked up with the prisoner."

Hood gave him a quick nod.

"This way," Mose said, leading with his feeble light.

As Seven and Hood followed Mose through a dark, stone passage, Hood untied Seven's hands and slipped him his spear.

Seven's heart pounded with the anticipation of battle. Now that he'd had a taste of real battle outside the gorge against Gilla's two men and with the guards in his attempt to rescue Bren, his desire to fight for justice and honor was like unsatiated hunger.

"I heard the prisoner from the wagon transport made it here

safely, despite this rogue's failed attempt to free her," Hood said casually.

"That she did."

Seven glanced back at Hood and nodded once.

As soon as they reached the end of the corridor and Seven saw the row of cells and heard the snores of the prisoners, he slammed the long shaft of his spear into Mose's back, sending him to his hands and knees.

"You dung-eating guttersnipe!" Mose shouted.

Hood grabbed Mose by the collar, pulled him up to his knees, and spoke gruffly in his ear. "Big words from a fool-born leech."

Seven picked up the felled lantern and placed it on the small table. He nervously glanced down the darkened halls. To the left was a row of cells; to the right, a long hall where two figures glided toward them from the unhallowed shadows. The ring of two blades being pulled from their metal scabbards pierced the darkness.

"Hood," Seven said, his heart pounding.

But Hood had already drawn his weapons—a blade in each hand. "Watch the old man."

"If it's Lark—" Seven leveled his spear at Mose.

"I'll do my best." Hood planted his feet and stood like an impenetrable fortress.

A rush of feet followed. Two men with swords sprang out of the darkness. Neither was Lark. The men attacked simultaneously. Hood parried a slash to his right, then to his left. He ducked under the swing of one man and lunged at the other with his short sword, burying it between the man's ribs. Before the man had even registered that he'd been wounded, Hood withdrew his blade with a grunt, blocked the other man's blow with both blades crossed, then turned and dragged his short blade across the neck of the wounded man. After seeing his partner fall, the remaining man hacked desperately, but was quickly overcome by Hood's frenzied two sword blows. At last, Hood's long sword speared the man in the gut like a fish. The guard dropped to his knees and toppled over with a look of shock on his face.

Hood withdrew his bloodied sword and turned to Seven. His eyes suddenly widened. "Behind you!"

Seven turned just in time to catch a glint of lantern light on the edge of a sword. He ducked, lifted his spear and lunged, feeling the tip sever tendons and crash through bone.

The shadow groaned and collapsed.

Please. Not Lark.

In a panic, Seven grabbed the lantern from the table and held it over the dead man's face.

"It's not him," Hood said, placing a hand on Seven's back.

Seven closed his eyes and sighed with relief. How would he have explained to Bren that he'd killed her brother?

Hood wiped his swords clean with some rags on the table, while Seven tied Mose's hands behind his back.

"You won't get far," Mose grumbled.

"Far enough," Hood said. He dragged Mose to his feet and searched his pockets. He proffered a key and tossed it to Seven. Seven unlocked the first cell, and Hood pushed Mose inside.

The old woman who had answered the door earlier came from the opposite hall with a raised lantern and cried out at the sight of the dead men.

"Go back to your room!" Hood growled. "And stay there!"

She was startled, then hobbled back down the hall.

"Hail, friend," the prisoner inside the first cell said, stepping forward.

Seven held up the lantern. The man was rugged and fit despite his filthy prison rags.

"We're not your friend, mate," Hood said, attempting to close the cell door.

The man stayed the door with his hand. "That may be. Unless you fight for the Crown. Then we might be friends indeed."

Seven and Hood exchanged surprised looks.

"You are?" Seven asked.

"My given is Wyck. As you are now seeing for yourselves, Ruritania's governor imprisons the voices of dissent."

"What dissent?" Seven asked, glancing at Hood.

Wyck let out a short laugh. "For Ferran's sake, lad! Have ye had your head buried in the sand? Alith is looking for the queen's treasure so she can take back Ferran and the crown."

Seven had no idea what burying his head in sand had to do with anything, but if what the man said was true, there was more at stake here than he or Bren had realized.

Seven needed to know more. He motioned with his head for the man to come out of the cell.

"Are you sure?" Hood asked Seven.

"Yes."

Wyck turned and spat at Mose's feet before he left the cell.

Seven slipped the key into the door and locked it.

"You'll all hang for this," Mose said grimly.

"Shut your hole, you back-stabbing goat!" Wyck shouted.

Cheers and jeers erupted from the darkened hall as the prisoners woke to the sound of Wyck's voice.

"They're good men," Wyck said, looking down the hall. "We'd owe you our lives if you'd be inclined to let us all go free. All of us are loyal to the Crown of Ferran."

Seven's mind spun through the possibilities. He'd found a den of men loyal to the Crown just as he learned of a planned coup. It had to be providence. God had brought him *and* Bren to this place just for this moment. He handed Wyck the lantern and unlocked the cells one by one. Each ragged man came out in a state of disbelief and embraced their fellow prisoners in subdued elation.

Seven's heart sank as they neared the end of the hall and there was still no sign of Bren.

Hood spoke to Wyck. "We're looking for a brown-haired girl."

Wyck pointed. "Cell thirteen. But you may be getting one more than you expected."

Seven quickly unlocked cell twelve and rushed to the last remaining cell.

"Seven!" Bren cried out, as she clung to the bars of her cell.

"Bren," he said with a heart-pounding whisper. There was another woman in the cell with her—a blond woman who appeared to be of similar age.

As soon as he unlocked the cell, Bren rushed into his arms. Seven held her tight. Never had he felt such overwhelming relief. "I'm sorry," he said across the top of her hair. "I should have never let you go alone with Rune."

She backed away a bit and shook her head. "No. This was my fault. I should have listened to you. Rune's going to pay for what he did."

Bren embraced him once again, and they stood there in the gloom and filth, clinging to each other as if they'd found home. Then, quite suddenly, he realized that he didn't want to let go of her. He wanted to hold her for as long as she'd let him, and he wondered what it could mean. He rested his head on top of hers and closed his eyes. Was this not the little girl he hid in the bushes from or scared with large spiders he'd fished out of the barn—the girl whose hair he held back so that she could bob for the biggest apple at the local fair?

"Come on," Hood said, interrupting the moment. "We need to get out of here. I'm not sure we can trust the old woman to keep quiet for long."

"Hood?" Bren asked curiously. She turned, finally taking notice of Hood and the contingent of prisoners who had gathered in front of her.

Seven scanned the group of ragged men—dark, light, young, old. There was a rare opportunity here that Bren had yet to conceive. And with rumors of treason floating about, he knew what he had to do.

"Gentlemen," Seven said, taking a step back from Bren. "Meet your future queen. Princess Bren Glasser of Isidor."

Bren looked over at Seven with a look of shock, and whispered, "What are you doing? Lark will be king."

The men shared shifting glances and mumbled to one another privately. Seven took the opportunity to quietly explain to Bren. "These men say that the governor of Ruritania is planning to find the treasure so she can reclaim Ferran and its Crown. Right now, the future king is not here, but a future queen is, and she has a small army at her disposal."

"There's more, Seven," Bren said, miserably. "The governor is Valen's widow. Gilla is their daughter."

Seven raised an eyebrow. "Then Alith wants more than Ferran. She wants revenge."

Bren nodded and stared out over the troubled eyes of the men.

Wyck cast a look back at his men and stepped forward. "Listen, we're grateful for your help, but you can't expect us to believe that she's *the* princess." He glowered at Bren uncertainly with his clever, blue eyes. Head nods and cries of *Aye* rippled through the men.

Bren shifted uncomfortably.

"It's true, gentlemen." Hood pulled the hood back from his face. "I had leprosy, and she healed me. I serve as a witness to the truth. She is the princess."

"Join our quest to stop Alith and your loyalty will be rewarded," Seven added.

Wyck shook his head. "I can't risk the life of my men on your word. I'm sorry." His men grumbled their agreement.

Seven rubbed his brow. He understood their trepidation. There was no proof, no reason to believe that Bren was who they said she was. She was standing there in a sack, miles from home.

To Seven's surprise, Bren boldly stepped forward and around Wyck.

"Who here is ill?" she said sharply.

Seven reached for her arm. "Bren. *No.*" She shrugged him off.

"Come on!" she said, her demeanor coursing with determination. "Show yourself! By the look of the lot, you've been in this rathole for months."

The men lowered their skeptical eyes. An awkward silence ensued.

"Anyone?" she barked, spinning toward Wyck.

Wyck smirked and held up both hands in mock surrender.

Bren's face colored.

A dark-skinned man from the back pushed his way to the front. His face was moist with sweat, and his eyes were red and watery. "I've got the sweating sickness," he said, avoiding eye contact. "I can barely stand."

"Very well," she said, taking a satisfied breath.

"Bren," Seven said with a pained expression. "You don't have to do this."

"Yes, I do," she said to him softly. "But there is a condition," she said louder, turning to the face the men. "If I heal this man, you will pledge your allegiance to me this day and to the Crown of Ferran."

Wyck, still appearing wary, conferred briefly with the men, then nodded once.

Bren stepped up to the listless man and took a deep breath. "What is your given?"

"Elijah, my lady."

She placed her hands on his face. Her body immediately jerked and went rigid with such violence that Seven lunged to grab her. Hood stopped him by pressing a hand into his chest and pushing him against the prison wall, shoving one of his large arms under Seven's chin to hold him there. "It must be done," Hood said fiercely.

Seven's heart raced as Bren's eyelids fluttered violently. The ill man closed his eyes. His body twitched almost imperceptibly.

Bren's breathing became labored and her legs shook, but she

hung onto the man as if her life depended on it. Her head dropped back, and she gasped for air.

Tears welled in Seven's eyes. "No!" he cried, pushing with all he had against Hood. Other men joined in restraining Seven. "Bren!" he shouted as he struggled against the filth and stench of the men who held him.

Bren suddenly stilled, then collapsed to the ground.

A bewildered shock registered on each of the men's faces. The men holding Seven released him, and he rushed to Bren's side in horror, dropping to his knees. He drew her to him, cradling her in his arms.

"The fever has left me," the sick man said almost in a whisper.

"Are you sure?" Wyck asked skeptically.

"Aye. It's as if I was never ill," he said, examining his arms and torso as if checking to be sure he was all there.

Everyone crowded in around Seven and Bren now.

"Bren," Seven said desperately, stroking her face. "Come back to me." He bent his head to her ear and whispered. "Stop being such a princess, you stubborn maggot-pie."

He held her there, his eyes closed, his lips next to her ear silently praying. No breath came. Her lungs were still. The silence in the somber confines of the prison was deafening as the lot of them seemed to be holding their breaths. After a long, heart-pounding moment, Bren gasped, opened her eyes, and sat up suddenly as if awakened from a bad dream.

The men, cheered by her recovery, rubbed their healed friend's head and slapped him on the back, grinning and joyful.

Seven rose to his feet. "Can you stand?" he asked, extending a hand.

She pushed her long hair out of her face and nodded. She gave him her hand, and he gently pulled her to her feet. The blonde woman rushed to her side to assist.

A moment of quiet reverence fell upon the group as the awe of the miracle reached the heart of every man standing there.

Bren stood weak but triumphant, and together Seven and Bren watched the joy of revelation light up in the eyes of the men. They were standing before royalty. One by one, as the spark of who she was took hold, the men, starting with Wyck, dropped to one knee, bowing their heads in a show of allegiance.

Wyck raised his eyes. "You have our allegiance, Princess Glasser."

"Good," she said, sounding tired but satisfied. Seven had never seen Bren like this—determined—queen-like. His head swam with conflicting feelings. She was the better choice to inherit the Crown. Unlike Lark, she was stable, dependable, smart. But if she were to become queen, what would become of their friendship? For the first time ever, he feared losing her.

"What should we call you?" Wyck asked.

"Anything *but* princess."

Wyck dared a charming smirk. "Yes, my lady."

Bren blushed and for some reason it made Seven angry. He rolled his shoulders, trying to shake his discomfort.

"Let's go!" Hood said, turning and urging the men to their feet.

And just like that they had a small army. Bren turned to Seven, her face turning serious as she embraced her role.

"Do you have our packs? The note from the map?" she asked urgently.

"Yes. They're stowed safely away at the church."

Bren touched Hood's arm. "I need a moment with the men."

"Make it quick."

She pushed her shoulders back and took a moment to compose herself. "Gentlemen, we were once Alrenians and Uluns, but no more. We are Ferrians now. It's clear that Alith wishes to conquer Ferran and reinstate an Ulun Crown. She has the queen's treasure map. And if she finds the treasure, she'll be able to hire the mercenaries she would need to take over Ferran. What I'm going to ask you to do now could change the course of Ferran forever. I've asked for your loyalty and you have given it, but if you choose not to continue on this dangerous quest, I release you and peace be with you. But if you dare to grasp for something nobler, then I bid you to join forces with me to find the queen's treasure so *we*, as a united people, can rebuild Ferran together and secure the Crown for all of time so that we may never again have a divided Ferran."

Her words hung in the air for a brief, austere moment as the men examined their hearts. No one moved. No one scarcely breathed. Though they had already pledged their loyalty, she was giving them a final opportunity to turn back. And Seven understood she needed to be sure of the men who would follow her.

Then a few small voices said, "We are with you, my lady," and the rest followed.

"For Ferran."

"Long live the queen and king!"

"Aye."

"Long live Ferran!" they shouted as one.

Though the men were bedraggled and filthy, their smiles and energy lifted the room and Bren beamed. Though she wore the garments of a peasant, Seven had never seen her look so beautiful, so confident. He didn't need to be a seer to see the future. He was looking at the face of the future queen of Ferran.

CHAPTER 50

LARK

Early the next morning, with hands still bound behind his back, Lark was unceremoniously plucked from a stone cell in Alith's basement by two of her thugs, dragged outside, and pushed up onto a black stallion. Gilla attended the whole scene with clear agitation. By yesterday's accounts, she and Alith didn't appear to have a loving mother-daughter relationship. And by the tone of Gilla's question as to Rune's whereabouts, she didn't seem to have much affection for him either. Perhaps that was her way with everyone, but Lark got the feeling there was something more to the story with her mother and Rune.

Gilla led the way to the prison on a strong, brown mare. One of the guards rode alongside Lark, leading Lark's horse by its reins, while the other guard brought up the rear. Lark pressed his thighs against his horse, fighting to maintain his balance, but beyond that, he was barely aware of the city streets, the stares, the whispers. He was numb to the wind in his face, the girth of the saddle. He licked his parched lips, lamenting his mistakes. He'd thought he had everything under control—instead he'd been a fool. Gotz's words rang true for the first time since he'd left Isidor.

What you seek you may not find.

And what was worse was that his Aunt Kidron had been right about everything—he had jeopardized his whole family with his scheme for glory—for treasure. He had come to Ruritania unprepared and with little to no information. Now he was now paying the price.

When they arrived at the prison, Lark's stomach twisted into a knot. What was he going to tell Bren? He'd failed her, his parents, and Ferran.

Gilla jerked Lark out of the saddle, letting him fall to the ground with a thud. The guards chuckled. She went to grab the door knocker and stopped mid-air. The door was ajar.

Lark scrambled to his feet. Something was wrong. He tried to summon a picture of Bren, a vision, anything. Nothing came.

Gilla drew the sword strapped across her back and pushed the door open with one hand. A waft of stale air escaped. She stepped inside, motioning to the men to follow. They pulled their blades and pushed Lark along, causing him to stumble through the threshold. The hallway torches were out. Every muscle on Lark's body tensed.

Gilla closed the door and bolted it shut, then proceeded with caution down the stone corridor toward the meagerest of lights.

Lark listened for the voices of the prisoners, the old lady's hobble, Mose's grumbling. There was nothing but silence.

"Mose!" Lark called out, his heart racing.

"Keep him quiet," Gilla hissed.

Lark grimaced as the tip of a sword was pressed uncomfortably into his back.

If something had happened to Bren, he would never forgive himself.

I should have never brought her here.

"Mose!" he yelled louder.

Gilla's man grabbed him roughly by the collar.

"Here!" the old man's voice cried out.

A flicker of lantern light broke through the cave-like darkness as they reached the hall of cells. Gilla picked up the lantern that had been left on the table and held it up.

Lark smelled the blood before he saw the bodies. A man lay dead to his left—a single gaping wound in the abdomen. *Spear?* There were two dead to his right—one with a cut throat and a puncture to the lungs, the other a blow to the stomach. *Sword.*

This is the work of two men. His heart pounded fiercely.

"I'm here," Mose cried out from the first cell.

"What happened?" Gilla asked, pulling at the locked cell door.

"They're gone," he said wearily, rubbing the top of his head.

"Who's gone?" Lark asked anxiously, glancing down the hall.

"The prisoners. The cook."

Lark didn't wait for further explanation; he bumped roughly into Gilla to avoid the dead guard with the spear wound and ran down the hall toward cell thirteen, only vaguely registering that all the cell doors were open.

Please, no!

He stopped and stared at the empty straw pallet where he had left her. "Bren," he whispered. *Where are the prisoners? Where is Bren?*

One of Gilla's men gruffly grabbed him and shoved him back toward Mose's cell.

"Tell me what happened," Gilla said to Mose. "And don't leave out any details."

"A hooded man with a beard showed up with Alith's calling card and a man who fit the description of the prison wagon assailant. He wouldn't leave the prisoner without receiving the reward. I let them in. You can figure out the rest," he said, throwing a furtive glance at the dead guards.

Lark balled his hands into fists. "Was this prison wagon *assailant* a tall man with a large spear?"

Mose nodded.

Lark should have guessed Seven would try something like this. But who was the hooded man? Was it possible that it was

Lark's *Hood*? A man with a beard and a hood could describe half of the city. And why had Seven let *all* the prisoners go? His head spun with questions.

"Who were they after?" Gilla asked.

"Who else? The *princess*." Mose cast a scornful look at Lark. It was clear that Mose had not known who Bren was when she'd first come to the prison but had since learned her identity.

Gilla's teeth clenched. "Why did they let the other prisoners go?"

Mose's brow furrowed. "You don't know who your mother imprisons here?" When he was met with silence he added, "The prisoners were all men loyal to the Crown of Ferran."

Blazes! How had Lark missed that? He grimaced to think he'd barely given the men a glance.

"Get me out of here," Mose grumbled.

"I should let you rot in here," Gilla said. "Key?"

Mose pointed. "On the table."

Gilla nodded to one of her men who quickly snatched up the key and unlocked the cell. Mose ambled out, grimacing as he arched his back. He avoided eye contact with Lark.

He's chosen his side, Lark thought with disdain.

"Do you have any idea where the prisoners went?" Gilla asked.

Mose shrugged.

"*Lark,*" a small voice came from the hall on the right.

Gilla spun round, brandishing her sword.

Lark squinted in the dim light. "Lira?"

Lira ignored the sword and rushed to Lark, embracing him, even though his hands were tied. He found himself relieved to see her.

"Thank God you're well," she said softly.

"Bren?" he asked next to her ear, hoping her seer abilities were working better than his.

"She's safe."

He breathed a sigh of relief.

Lira backed away as if just noticing they weren't alone.

Facing her again, he now understood that he was looking into the eyes of the woman from Gotz's vision—a much thinner, dirtier version. Why hadn't she left with the rest of the prisoners? *Because she knew I was coming back*, he realized. She was somehow part of his future. But with the circumstances being what they were, what kind of future could he hope to have?

"Let's go," Gilla said, motioning to Lira with her knife. "Alith wishes to see you."

There was no hesitation on Lira's part, no surprise, she slipped her hand under Lark's elbow as if aligning herself with him. His heart ached as he looked into her crystal blue eyes. Now Lira was caught up in his mistakes, too. He swallowed the knot that had risen in his throat.

"Don't worry," Lira whispered. "What they intend for evil, God will use for good."

He marveled at her faith even while he thought, *We're dead. Both of us.*

Chapter 51

Bren

Before they'd left the prison, Wyck had named a meeting place, then sent two of the men to fetch Bren's and Seven's packs from the church. To keep from drawing too much attention from Alith's night patrols, he had the rest leave the prison in pairs except for herself, Seven, and Hood. They were now following Wyck stealthily down dark, cobbled streets and piss-filled alleys. Their journey through the city ended in an alley beside a two-story inn called The Goose Feather. Wyck lifted a hatch in the ground, and Bren descended with the others down rickety wooden steps below the street into a large cellar whose crumbling stonework had seen better days. The underground bunker was already buzzing with activity. The newly freed men had set right to work, tossing their prison garb and washing away the grime by dumping buckets of water on each other with a joviality that marked a close brotherhood. Others were sharpening weapons and ushering in food and supplies being sent to them from the streets above. Bren surmised that The Goose Feather must be a hideout for the resistance in Ruritania. Even though Alith had control of the city, there was a small, organized faction who had stayed loyal to the Crown—to her parents. With these men's help, she thought they could have a real chance at thwarting Alith's devious plans.

Wyck tossed her a green linen dress and a pair of tall, suede boots with ties that wrapped around the calves. A dress wasn't ideal, but she'd have to make do. She quickly pulled the dress over her prison shift. Hood handed her a knife and a sword belt then ran off to help with a large crate that had just arrived.

"Bren," Seven said. "Lark is—"

"Now is not the best time," she said, setting the knife down while she tied the scabbarded sword around her waist. She was still trying to wrap her head around her newfound situation. Hood had assured her that Lark was walking freely in Ruritania, but Lark had chosen to go on without Bren, so perhaps it was time she went on without him. She drew the sword, spun it once in her hand and shoved it back in place.

Seven massaged his forehead. "I tried to rescue you from the prison wagon when they picked you up at Alith's residence."

"I know," she said, shoving her feet into her boots. "You told me on the way here."

"I didn't tell you everything. I wanted to wait until we were alone."

"Well, we're alone." She wiggled her toes. The boots were a surprisingly good fit.

"When I opened the back of the prison wagon, Lark jumped out and attacked me. He was ready to slit my throat until I pulled down the cloth I was wearing on my face. I told him you were in the wagon, then he punched me in the face. He told me to leave. Lark was working at the prison—for Alith."

Her face flushed. "You're mistaken," she said, refusing to believe Lark would do such a foolish thing. But deep down she knew Seven never embellished anything. She sat down and laced her boots.

"He *drove* you to the prison, Bren. I followed him."

She shook her head. "Why would he do that?"

"I don't know."

She stood defiantly. "He must not have had a choice."

Seven's face darkened. "I do not accept that. He was the only guard left after I took care of the other two."

"Took care of? How?"

Seven ignored her inquiry. "Lark could have saved you," he said. "He could have let *me* save you."

"He had his reasons," she said, knowing the argument was thin.

"You're blind when it comes to your brother," Seven said, then stormed away.

Bren bit her lip. She couldn't believe that Lark would take her to prison, much less leave her there, without good cause. Nevertheless, the revelation stung. What was Lark doing in the back of that prison wagon? And why had he fought Seven? She wanted to be angry, but if she hadn't been taken to that prison, and if Seven and Hood hadn't rescued her, she wouldn't be standing in a room with a band of men loyal to the Crown ready to follow her. Then where would they be?

She shook her head. Everything with Seven was black and white. He'd never understood the gray areas, and Lark was about as gray as they came. No, she would withhold judgment until she heard Lark's side of the story. *If* she ever got to hear his side. Her brother grew more distant with every waking day. As much as she hated to put thoughts of Lark aside, she had to. The men who had sworn their allegiance to her were expecting her to lead, and for the first time in her short life she felt like she was doing what she was meant to do. Only she never expected it would be without Lark.

"My lady," Wyck called from across the room. "We're going to need you to draw what you can remember of that treasure map."

CHAPTER 52

LARK

Lark kept his eyes straight ahead as Alith called for Mose to be taken back to the prison and thrown into a cell. She was livid about the loss of her prisoners and apathetic to Mose's begging. Mose gave Lark a hard look as if everything that had transpired had all been Lark's fault. Lark was helpless to do anything about Mose's plight. Nor did he want to.

That's what you get for playing both sides, old man.

Alith barked orders to have Lark and Lira scrubbed down and given clothes more appropriate to their station. Lark was taken in one direction and Lira in another. He was shoved into a room in Alith's basement, stripped down as if he were a child, and manhandled into a wooden tub. He sat naked and shivering as his dark locks were hacked off with a pair of sheep shears. Buckets of cold water were dumped over his head while a plump woman with strong arms and a scowl scrubbed him down like she was doing laundry on a human washboard. She had gotten some pleasure over leaving his skin red and raw, for she smiled and left the room with an air of satisfaction.

Just as soon as he stepped out of the tub, the guard threw wool trousers, a beige linen shirt and scuffed boots at him. Lark wasn't immune to Alith's mind games. She'd meant to demean him, and she'd succeeded. His chopped hair would give him the look of a peasant desperate to rid himself of lice, and his attire would mark him as nothing more than a common street urchin.

He'd barely finished tucking in his shirt when the guard took him by the arm and ushered him out of the room. He was gruffly told that if he tried to escape, Lira would be killed. For a common criminal this wouldn't have been a deterrent, but Alith was clearly counting on Lark's nobility.

His guard escorted him down the basement hall to where two guards were chatting outside the door of another room. One of the guards shoved a thick paper package into Lark's hands, while the other guard opened the door and nudged him inside. They chuckled as the door shut. A key scraped in the lock.

A thin, young woman stood shivering, clutching a dark robe around her neck. Her blond hair had been chopped pitifully short, but her skin was like porcelain and her eyes a lapis blue.

Sons of Ferran! Lira?

"Is that for me?" she asked, eyeing the package.

He stepped forward awkwardly and handed her the brown package.

"Thank you," she said, ducking behind a privacy screen.

He surveyed the room. Other than the privacy screen and the large basin of dirty water where Lira had bathed, there was nothing else in the windowless space except for a small table that currently held a steaming pot of tea and two cups. He leaned against the table with one hand and pinched the bridge of his nose. Surely *this* was not supposed to happen—being captured—imprisoned. He was supposed to be a seer, yet he'd seen none of this coming.

Gotz's vision. Lira. What did it all mean?

He poured some tea into a cup and stared into it, looking for words. "Listen," he said. "I'm sorry—"

"What do you think?" Lira asked, stepping out from behind

the screen. She held out the folds of her salmon-colored dress like a fan.

Lark dropped his cup. The tea spilled across the floor. She was wearing nothing more than a peasant's linen dress, but Lira could have worn a potato sack and he wouldn't have noticed anything but her angelic face.

"You look . . . you know," he said, rubbing the back of his head. "Fine?"

"It's been so long since I've worn a dress," she said, twirling around once.

He marveled at her gratitude for something as simple as a dress. It deepened the lump of regret growing in his throat. His choices had led Lira to her current predicament. She should have fled instead of waiting for him at the prison. And though Alith had provided them with a bath and clean clothes, he didn't expect her show of charity to last.

"Listen, Lira. I'm sorry."

Her brow knit in confusion.

Lark ran a hand through his short, cropped hair. "Why didn't you leave the prison when you had the chance?" he asked miserably.

"Where else would I go?"

"Not here!" he said, with a wave of his hand.

"Will I not fulfill God's purpose?"

"What purpose?" he asked with a sigh.

Lira glided over to him and placed a tender hand on his face. She studied it, seemingly marveling at his features—his mess of a haircut, his dark eyes, his nose, his mouth. "Our lives are bound." She searched his eyes as though she knew every part of him. Something strange awakened inside him. He reached up and gently grasped her hand. It was warm and surprisingly soft to the touch. "Who are you?" he whispered.

Her cheeks colored, and she backed away. "When do we leave?" she asked, straightening the folds of her dress as if to distract herself from what had just transpired between them.

"Leave?" he asked, still feeling the warmth of her hand on his fingers.

She looked away. "To find the queen's treasure. That is what Alith seeks, isn't it? What *you* seek?"

Alith hadn't shared her plans yet, but Lira seemed to already know them. The hair prickled on the back of his neck. What did he really know about Lira other than that she was a seer? He hadn't imagined the vision she had given him at the prison. What if Alith had planted Lira at the prison to gain his trust? Alith had known who Lark was from the beginning. She would have had plenty of time to plant Lira and create the illusion of her being a prisoner.

His jaw tightened. *Alith thought me a fool for a pretty face.*

Lira strolled over to the table and poured a cup of tea.

How old was Lira, anyway? Eighteen? Nineteen? He needed to find out who she really was and what she knew about the treasure. The situation wasn't ideal, but perhaps he was right where he needed to be. He'd let Alith think he'd fallen for Lira's act, but he'd be the one acting. In fact, Lira might be exactly what he needed to gain an edge.

A key turned in the door. One of Alith's men entered. "We leave within the hour," he said.

"Where?" Lark asked.

"Devil's Rock."

The guard backed out and closed the door.

Lira peered at him over the top of her tea.

She's watching to see how I react. The marked location on the treasure map had the initials D.R. next to it. Now he knew what they stood for. But did Alith have the small piece of paper that had been hidden within the map? Lark had put it in Seven's quill and ink box back in Ferran. But did Seven still have it? Or had he given it to Bren? Bren had been taken prisoner by Alith, so there was a *chance* Alith had it now. The words on that paper could possibly be the key to finding the treasure. Lark regretted that he had not memorized its strange words when he'd had the chance.

"You know of the caverns beneath Devil's Rock?" Lira asked.

"No," he said truthfully.

She set her cup down on the table, looking slightly paler. "Beneath Devil's Rock is a maze of underground tunnels rumored to be overrun by the only remaining Morbids in Ferran. There are many stories of men and women who have entered but never returned."

Lark swallowed. Hard. Even though he'd never seen one, he was undeniably, unequivocally, and hopelessly afraid of Morbids.

CHAPTER 53

BREN

After Bren finished drawing a rough sketch of the treasure map, Wyck frowned and the faces of the men watching went pale. Hood and Seven stood on either side of her, like bookends made of stone.

"What's wrong?" Bren asked.

"Devil's Rock," Wyck said with a sigh. The other men grumbled to one another then fell silent.

"The initials on the map?" Hood asked.

Wyck nodded.

"What's Devil's Rock?" Bren asked.

Wyck's expression darkened. "Cursed ground." He stabbed his finger on the X she had drawn. "If the treasure be in Devil's Rock, it won't be had by anyone."

"I don't understand," she said, looking around at the dejected faces of the men who only moments earlier had been in high spirits.

Wyck frowned. "The caverns within the Devil are impossible to navigate and full of Morbids."

"Morbids?" she asked in disbelief.

"Even if you get in and find the treasure," Wyck said, "you'll never get out. It's a fool's errand."

Ayes rippled through the men.

Morbids. How was it possible?

After a few moments of uncomfortable silence, Seven leaned forward and put his large hands on the table. "There's a way."

Wyck scoffed. "Sorry, lad, but you're mistaken."

"Your pack, Seven," Bren said, understanding Seven's meaning.

Wyck snapped his fingers at the man she had healed, Elijah, and he ran off to the other side of the room, retrieved Seven's pack, and brought it over to him. Seven dug out his ink and quill box, removed the note, and pressed it open on the table for all to see. The men crowded in, and the room fell silent as Wyck read it aloud.

For this is left of that fair Oracle

Bottomless seas, caverns deep

The soul shall find itself alone amid the Morbids creep

O Great Destruction, eternal flame

Yet there is still one whom the treasure will claim

Look, great wanderer, for only you will see, the crown of jewels at the bottom of the sea

Alas, the hour has finally come. Extinguish the flame of the evil one.

Wyck looked back at Bren. "A riddle? *That's* your way in and out?"

Bren fought to maintain her composure. Wyck had a way of making her feel like a child, and her first instinct was to fight back. Instead, she pushed her shoulders back and hardened her demeanor. "It was with the map. It must mean something," she said stiffly.

"Yeah, it means the death of the lot of us if ye fool enough to believe such trite." He turned and pushed his way through his men as if the issue had been decided.

She burned with indignation. How dare he dismiss her so quickly after pledging his allegiance. "Wait!" she shouted.

The men gingerly drew back so that Wyck was on full display to everyone in the room. He turned around and faced her. Bren didn't know which was worse—the self-righteous look on his face or the dispassionate way he held himself. It mattered not. She'd been surrounded by stubborn men her whole life, and with men like Wyck, one had to be like a hawk. Though the raptor glided gently through the air, its real power came when it dove for the kill.

She snatched the paper off the table and clutched it in her fist. "This is the key to finding the treasure!" she exclaimed, waving it around for all to see. "Alith doesn't have it! We do."

No one spoke. Some of the men hung their heads or looked away to avoid eye contact. Others stared at her blankly. Her heart pounded fiercely, and her fingers ached. Seven nodded ever so slightly as if to remind her who she was.

"Where is your faith?" she asked, laying a charge against the men.

The room stilled. The men stood like mute puppets. She did not need sorrowful, defeated men, she needed kingdom warriors.

"Was it not the providence of God that brought us to this place?" She looked from man to man as she talked, calling each to task. "Do you believe it was by *your* hand that you were set free from prison? Yet here you are running like rabbits when put to the test. If we stand back and do nothing and let Alith succeed, what then will we say to our families and friends when she takes Ferran and divides us once more into Alrenians and Uluns? Will we fight against our brothers and sisters?" Bren's body shook with indignation and fear.

Wyck ambled back to the table and placed a weary hand on the table. His expression had softened, and his shoulders no longer held the contempt they had just moments ago. He looked at Bren with tired eyes. "I'm afraid we lost our faith a long time ago, my lady."

Bren realized then that, even though these men had once spoken out against Alith, prison had taken its toll. She needed to inspire, but more than that, she needed to help these men find hope again. She reached out and placed her hand over Wyck's. "A king is not saved by the size of his army, but by the size of his God," she said.

"And a companion of fools shall be destroyed," he said with woeful eyes.

"I don't see any fools here," she said, withdrawing her hand.

The room held its breath, waiting to hear what Wyck would say. He stared at the map—biting his lip—rubbing a hand through his hair.

Bren held her breath but maintained a strong, confident posture.

"We're going to need horses," he finally said.

Relief coursed through Bren's veins as she breathed a sigh of relief. "Then let's get horses."

Wyck nodded. "Aye."

The room exploded with sudden activity as everyone scrambled away from the table to prepare for the journey ahead. Bren placed a hand on her stomach and took a deep breath.

"My lady," Hood said. She hadn't realized he was still standing next to her.

"Hood," she said, smiling. But the seriousness of his face told her that what he was about to tell her was not something she wanted to hear.

"This is where we part," he said.

She shouldn't have been shocked, but she was. Somehow it felt right to have him by her side. But his debt had been repaid. She had freed him from his disease, and he'd freed her from her prison cell.

"I shall miss you," she said, reaching for his once-withered hand.

He lowered his eyes and gently, almost reverently, held her hand. "You shall always have my sword if you ever need it."

"I know." And she did know. "Thank you," she said, willing herself not to cry.

"You're in good hands," he said without much conviction.

She nodded. The healing had connected them in some way she couldn't explain.

"Perhaps . . ." he said, as if he might change his mind.

But she would not have him beholden to her for his healing. "Goodbye, Hood," she said, releasing his hand. "You deserve a second chance at life. May God make your path straight."

He took a step back and bowed slightly. Then he was up the stairs and gone from her sight. She took a moment to shed a few tears, then quickly wiped them away and joined her band of brothers in the preparations.

CHAPTER 54

GIDEON

"Daughters of Ferran," Six muttered as she and Gideon crested the top of a hill with the wagon. Wynter rode up next to them on Dash. After miles of traveling rocky, infertile land, Ruritania rose from the earth in a valley of flat farmland. Surrounding the city were wide vistas of red rock and sun-kissed cliffs where bristlecone pine trees grew like a legion of demons.

"What's the plan?" Six asked.

Gideon's jaw tensed. He was not accustomed to having to discuss plans with Six.

"Yes, my lord. What *is* the plan?" Wynter asked with icy formality.

The truth was, he hadn't thought past saving his children. Yes, he was prepared for the worst. The Crown's army was behind them, but they would not come within battle range unless word was sent. He needed time—time to find Kidron and assess the rumors of a coup, time to find the children. Though he'd known for some time that Valen's widow, Alith, governed the city, she'd hardly been a major concern. She was miles away in a forgotten city, with little means to become a real threat. But now, with word that Alith may have the queen's treasure map, the past was suddenly becoming quite real again as echoes of Uluns vs. Alrenians resurfaced. He couldn't let the country divide again, not after all he and Wynter had fought to mend.

"We stick together and try to find Kidron." He looked over at Wynter. She was staring forlornly at the city as if her heart ached. He knew it was probably concern for the children, but accusing her of loving his dead brother had probably added to her pain. If only she had denied it. But she'd refused. He assumed the formal tone she was taking with him now meant she'd go about the kingdom's business and put her feelings aside until the children were safe and back home.

"You really think it's a good idea for the king and queen of Ferran to go marching into enemy territory without an army?" Six asked.

"She has a point," Wynter said.

Gideon frowned. As king and queen of Ferran, they were expected to put country above everything else, including their children. Six was right this time. If he and Wynter were found out, there would be nothing they could do for Ferran or their children. There was too much to lose.

"I'll go in and find Kidron," Six said. "No one will give me a second look."

Wynter's forehead creased with worry.

Gideon nodded. Six was right. It would have to be her.

"If you don't hear from me by tomorrow at sunrise, you know what to do."

"Gideon," Wynter pleaded. "Surely we can't let her—"

"Godspeed," he said to Six, cementing the moment.

Six jumped down from the wagon and ran toward Ruritania. Gideon and Wynter stared silently until Six was just a speck on the horizon.

A loud screech broke the silence. Gideon shielded his eyes against the setting sun. A lone hawk circled above them, gliding on top of the warm, rising air.

"Daughters of Ferran!" Wynter said. "You don't think it's Gotz's hawk, Kia, do you?"

"It doesn't matter," he answered, lowering his eyes to hers. "Our ancestors believed that a circling hawk was a warning. Beyond this point lies death."

Chapter 55

Lark

Lark relaxed into his horse's saddle, letting the slow rhythm of Alith's caravan lull him into a kind of trance. If he didn't think, he didn't feel. He was a mote among the long line of fur-clad men and women who snaked along the shores of a large lake that sat at the edge of a forest, miles from Ruritania.

"What is wrong?" Lira asked. "You have been silent ever since we left Ruritania."

Lira's voice pulled him back to reality. There *was* something wrong. He had an unnatural fear of Morbids. As a child he'd had nightmares where they'd crawl out from under his bed and surround him, snapping their sharp teeth and clawing at his face. Now he was going to a place called Devil's Rock that was filled with the vile creatures. What if Alith meant to use him as bait? He knew the old stories. Morbids killed without feeling. Knowing they had once spared his mother and father did nothing to alleviate his panic. That was a long time ago, different time, different place.

"I'm fine," he said.

"You are not. But I won't pry."

"Thank you."

Bren wouldn't have afforded him the same kindness. She would have worried him to death until she'd torn the truth from him. *But she would have known the truth,* he realized. Bren had been the one to climb into his bed when they were kids and hold his hand when he was afraid. She'd soothe away his tears with stories of how she'd protect him from the monsters beneath his bed with her invisible magic sword. She was so sure of herself that he had believed her.

Bren.

Thinking of her made his heart ache. Remnants of guilt lingered over taking her to Alith's prison when he could have let her escape with Seven. Lark had chosen to do Alith's bidding by convincing himself that it was all for a greater cause. Now there was little chance of making a claim to the queen's treasure so he could be the one to save Ferran.

He turned slightly in his saddle and stared at Lira. Her cheeks were pink, her eyes clear and serene as if they'd only ventured out together to enjoy a day at the lake. *It's because she knows she's safe. A spy doing Alith's bidding.* He ground his teeth. *How did I not see through Lira's façade earlier?*

He was supposed to be a seer, but his gift was no gift at all, just rare, unformed glimpses into the future that meant nothing to him. Perhaps that's all it would ever be.

"Who are you, Lira?" Lark asked suddenly. The question was bold and laced with accusation. He regretted the question immediately. He had wanted her to believe he bought her act. If Lira suspected he was on to her . . .

"There will be time for that later," she said.

CHAPTER 56

WYNTER

Wynter woke up curled in a ball next to Gideon. She had not wanted to share his pallet, but Gideon was always ten degrees warmer than the air, and she needed his warmth for the cool, night temperatures. He rolled over and draped an arm across her. His warm breath fell against her face. She could tell by the fall and rise of his chest that he was still sleeping. She longed to erase the words he'd spoken to her in Kapson. Had she'd shown preference to their son, Lark?

Perhaps.

But it was not for the reasons Gideon had accused her of. She should have told him about the vision she'd had of Lark a long time ago, but they were strangers then. She had been Gideon's captive, and she'd loathed him. Why she hadn't told him about the vision the caged Morbid had given her since that time, she did not know. People sometimes held things within their hearts without realizing it. Perhaps that's what she'd done—forgotten, but not truly.

She could still remember the vision vividly. Fire and smoke surrounded her while a baby cried somewhere in the distance. Her heart had ached for the child. What was this baby to her that she should care? Then Gideon's dead brother, Lark, appeared with the baby boy in his arms, and she was afraid. Deep down she knew it was her son—a son on the edge of a world falling apart around her.

That was the real reason she had always doted on their son, Lark. She was afraid for what the vision might mean for his future. Gideon couldn't be more wrong about her still holding onto feelings for his brother. The only candle she was holding onto was for her son. She only hoped it would not be a candle for his funeral. She knew she should explain it all to Gideon—clear the air between them, but she was too hurt by his accusations.

She slid out of his embrace, just as the sun peeked above the horizon. A reddish glow ushered in first light. She rubbed her arms for warmth and looked toward Ruritania. If Six didn't show up soon . . . what then?

Gideon came up quietly behind her and placed a blanket over her shoulders. "Any sign of Six?"

"No."

He left her and walked back to the wagon. Gideon cursed loudly.

Wynter looked over her shoulder. He was standing next to the wagon, scanning the horizon all around them.

"What is it?" she asked.

"Dash is gone."

"What?" she asked. She'd only had one thing on her mind that morning, and it wasn't the horses. She frantically checked around the wagon. She lifted the frayed end of Dash's reins that had been tied to the wagon. Her stomach sank.

"There's nothing to be done for it now," Gideon said, resignedly. "I'll make us some breakfast. Dried fish, or dried whatever else we have?"

On a normal day that would have made her smile, but not today. Today she was that naive young girl back in the trees. Her children were missing, she didn't know who her husband was anymore, and now her son's beloved horse, Dash, was gone. The world she had held so close to her heart was falling apart. The things that she'd feared the most in life were happening right before her very eyes. In a rush of frustration, she untied the small piece of Dash's rein that remained attached to the wagon and threw it as far as she could.

"Two riders coming this way." Gideon quickly grabbed their swords and handed Wynter hers. "Just in case," he said, slinging his scabbard across his shoulder. She quickly buckled hers around her waist.

As the pair of riders got closer, Wynter could tell by the way they rode that it was Six and Kidron. *Where are Lark and Bren?*

"Don't draw any conclusions," Gideon said, as if reading her mind. "We've taught the children well."

She found her heart beating faster as the horses drew closer. *Please let the children be all right? Please, Lord God.*

Six and Kidron rode up and dismounted.

"Brother," Kidron said, sounding relieved to see him.

"I'm glad you're safe," Gideon said.

"The children?" Wynter pleaded. Gideon placed a reassuring hand on her arm.

"She doesn't know where they are," Six growled.

"What does that mean?" Wynter asked, pushing Gideon's hand away.

Kidron sighed. "Lark showed up in Ruritania at the tavern, *alone,* with Alith's calling card. He boasted about having seen the queen's treasure map. I haven't seen him since."

"Daughters of Ferran," Wynter cried. "Why didn't you stop him?!"

Kidron scowled. "I tried, but he said you sent him."

Wynter blustered and took a step toward Kidron. "Why on earth would we send—?"

"Bren and Seven?" Gideon asked, interrupting the exchange.

"I didn't know Bren and Seven were in Ruritania until Six told me they might be," Kidron explained. "There *are* stories circulating at the local tavern that two men broke a woman and several men out of one of Alith's secret prisons."

There was mild concern on Gideon's face, but nothing more.

"There's something else," Kidron said.

"What else?" Wynter snapped. "We sent you here to find the map, and all you've managed to do is to let our children slip through your fingers! And no map, I presume?"

"Wynter," Gideon said, "we are talking Lark and Bren here. They are not innocents in all of this."

He had a point, but she was in no mood to be logical. She folded her arms, knowing she should apologize to Kidron, but she simply didn't have the heart for it.

Kidron cleared her throat. "Alith was seen leaving Ruritania with a large contingent of soldiers. The word is that she has the queen's treasure map, but they're only rumors."

"Lark instigated all of this," Six said scornfully. "Surprise. Surprise."

"We have to send word to the army," Gideon said. "They're following behind us."

Kidron nodded. "I'll go." She turned to mount her horse.

"Wait," Wynter said, reaching out to stop her. "Any idea what direction Alith was headed?"

"No. But money in the right hands might bear fruit at The Wolf's Den tavern."

Wynter held her hands over her rolling stomach. War may yet come to Ferran again, only this time her children were right in the middle of it. Memories of the old vision that haunted her resurfaced.

The treetops burned like giant torches and flakes of leaves fell in golden wisps all around her.

A baby's cry pierced the crackling of the trees.

CHAPTER 57

RUNE

They'd traveled through forests and rock-laden pastures and were now making the gentle descent into the valley at the base of the lofty peaks of the White Mountains. A strange orange line marked the horizon as the sun dropped below the trio of rocky pinnacles called Devil's Rock. Small farmsteads could be seen far from its shadow, huddled fearfully together.

The blustery wind numbed Rune's cheeks and whipped away the white plume of his breath. He shuddered, but not from the cold. The jagged monoliths evoked thoughts of ancient legends and fairy tales, but none as fearful as the Morbid inhabitants who lurked inside the Rock's gloomy dens.

Alith rode next to him, unflustered, with a confidence he did not have. Her white stallion was huge and beastly. Torment was his name—a name befitting to how Alith governed. Her dark hair hung smoothly outside of the hood of her white, fur cape. She looked very much the queen she longed to be—a vision of primness and grandeur, with eyes of fury that matched the harshness of the terrain around them. He rode by her side like he used to in the days of old—a dutiful sycophant. When Wynter had banished him from his own people, he had been the one who had brought Alith a message from Gideon's traitorous cousin, Finn, to send the Ulun army to the White Mountain gorge to fight Gideon. She'd readily accepted his immediate pledge of loyalty, and before long, they became more than friends. But all of that had been destroyed when Gilla confronted him in a drunken rage over a pig he'd slaughtered for one of Alith's noble galas. It was during that fight that Gilla had lost her eye. Even though Gilla had started the confrontation, he often wondered if he'd maimed her on purpose so that he'd have a reason to break his bond to Alith. Though he'd loved Alith, she was like a flame—beautiful to look at, but to touch her was to burn. He'd only come back now to see that Lark and Bren paid for what Wynter had done to him. Maybe a small part of him also wondered if he might be able to make amends with Alith, even if it meant pretending to have feelings for her. He had missed the lifestyle with her—one he'd become accustomed to. But now that he was about to get what he wanted, he found himself losing his heart for revenge—and Alith. The repurecussions of what he had been doing was beginning to leave a sick feeling in his gut that he couldn't explain. A man's sins had a way of festering, he supposed, and he wondered if it was possible for him to ever be free of them.

He twisted in his saddle and quickly surveyed the three hundred men and women in Alith's army. The motley crew followed by foot, horse, and cart. By the look of the carts, Alith had brought enough supplies and food to last a month, even though Devil's Rock was not far. *What dark secret are you keeping from me, Alith?*

"You didn't have to come," Alith said, breaking the comfortable silence.

Rune loosened his grip on his horse's right rein and moved closer to Alith. "My place is by your side, governor."

"So, you say," she said flatly.

"Haven't I proven myself?"

She gave him a thin smile. "I suppose you have. Bren would have been the icing on the cake if it hadn't been for that fool Mose. But Lark is a far better prize."

"What are your plans for the boy?"

"I haven't decided," she said with an air of satisfaction. "Perhaps I'll fight him in the court of swords, cut off his head, and serve it to Gideon and Wynter on a pole. It's fitting, don't you think?"

"You're assuming you can beat him."

She looked Rune up and down with a discerning eye. "I suppose you think you could show the boy his place?"

"I'd never suppose anything. You can be sure that, as the future king, he has been well trained."

"Perhaps. But he won't be fueled by twenty-one years of pent-up vengeance."

Rune didn't dare tell her of the emptiness of revenge—the dark hole that it left in the soul.

An approaching horse abruptly ended their conversation. Rune turned in his saddle. A dark woman with a long braid and a bow and quiver of arrows bouncing against her back rode up in a hurry next to them.

Rune and Alith drew rein. "What is it, Orilla?" Alith asked.

"Our scouts have spotted a small band of people following us."

"How many?"

"Five."

Alith scoffed. "Keep an eye on them."

Orilla gave a small nod of her head and retreated to the rear.

Rune shifted uneasily on his saddle as his horse danced sideways. "There'll be a lot of people just as eager as you to find the treasure. Secrets don't stay secrets long in Ruritania."

Alith's teeth gleamed. "I'm counting on it." She heeled her horse, brazenly quickening her pace now that they were in the valley and the land had leveled out. Rune raced after her, an uncomfortable feeling forming in his gut. The wind gusted, lifting Alith's hood back. Her hair unfurled and drifted upon the wind. There was something in the bitterness of the cold and the wind that he felt deep in the marrow of his bones.

Death.

CHAPTER 58

BREN

Bren and her entourage were traveling on horses across open pasture, when a group of Wyck's men, who had been sent ahead to scout out Alith's location, returned.

"Alith has a large army," one of them said, relaying the news.

Bren bristled slightly and tightened her grip on her reins. "God will provide," she said uncertainly.

"Aye, a noose," Wyck said. The men laughed despite the dreary presentiment.

She glanced over at Seven who had a scowl on his face. He had no patience for misplaced humor. His horse even whinnied as if it understood his scorn.

"May we speak in private?" she said quietly to Wyck.

They lightly heeled their horses and walked them through tall grasses and spring's first crocuses. The red glow of the setting sun bathed them in soft light. When they were away from prying ears, they drew rein and dismounted. Wyck stood next to her, and they stared at the shifting shadows on the horizon.

"I can't do this without you," she said.

"Aye."

"What is it you want?" she asked, looking over at him.

His brow knit in confusion. "Want?"

"Money? Land? Power? What's your price?"

Wyck scoffed. "You think this is about money?"

"Well, isn't it? You may have pledged your allegiance, but you clearly have your heart set on something else. You've undermined me at every turn."

Wyck's face hardened. He stepped close to her—his face inches from hers. He stared defiantly into her eyes—his breathing rough. She stealthily slipped out the knife at her waist and pressed its tip into his soft underbelly. He didn't even flinch. "Are you prepared to use that, princess?"

Her heart pounded fiercely, and her cheeks reddened. Wyck may have lacked certain charms, but his bold confidence was magnetic. His fingers wrapped around her grip on the knife, and he leaned farther into the blade's tip. "Aye?" he asked, dangerously close to her lips.

"I'll gut you where you stand," she whispered harshly, "and your men will thank me afterwards."

They were caught in a battle of wills and the heat of each other's breath. Just when she thought he might kiss her, he smiled, released his hand, and stepped backward. "Good," he said, sounding satisfied. "You'll need that fire if we have any chance at all." He pressed a boot into his horse's stirrup and lifted a leg over his saddle. "We'd best make camp for the night." With that, he pulled reins to the right and raced back toward the men.

She closed her eyes, placed a hand over her racing heart, and poured calm into it. *Daughters of Ferran. I have to stay focused. I can't let Wyck distract me with . . . with . . .* She opened her eyes, Seven was looming above her on his large stallion like a dark cloud.

"Are you all right?" he asked, as if he were ready to fight for her honor.

She nodded, and they returned swiftly to the others.

The men were already busy setting up camp under Wyck's watchful eye. Seven gave her a hand down from the horse, though she didn't need it.

Always the gentleman—Seven. Wyck could learn a thing or two from him.

Wyck looked her way, and her face involuntarily flushed despite her great efforts not to react to him.

"What's wrong?" Seven asked.

"Nothing," she said. "Wyck is stubborn, that's all."

Seven coughed a little into his hand—almost a laugh.

She knew it was a dig at her own stubbornness.

"These men are going to want a plan," Seven said. "It would be unwise to think we can march right past Alith and into Devil's Rock."

Bren was immediately struck with a thought. She beamed at Seven. "That's exactly what we're going to do."

CHAPTER 59

____

LARK

Alith and her army had hastily made camp in the valley with Devil's Rock towering above them like a phantom. Lark knelt and rubbed his hands together over the small fire that had been made for him and Lira. Armed men and women were stationed around them for the night, abiding by their own fires. He was given a final reminder that if he tried to flee, Lira would be killed. The warning was hardly necessary. Without a weapon, Lark didn't stand a chance of escaping.

Lira sat on a tattered blanket across the fire, staring up at the first stars as if she'd never seen them before. She was certainly playing the part of a prisoner who hadn't seen the light of day in a long time. How long would she keep up the ruse of the mistreated prisoner? He was angry with himself for falling for her act, but even as he had the thought, he found himself wanting to be wrong—wanting her to be something other than Alith's pawn. He was inexplicably drawn to her but, at the same time, he found her presence unsettling.

Blazes, Gotz! Why couldn't you have been a little clearer about this girl.

He sat down on his threadbare wool blanket. "You said you'd tell me who you were when the time was right."

She continued staring at the stars, almost as if she hadn't heard him.

He tried again. "You said before that our lives are bound. How?"

When she looked at him from across the fire, it was as though he were looking into the face of an angel. Her golden hair shimmered, even though it was cut short, and her pale face was like a full moon.

"Yes. We are bound," she said. She stood up and came and sat beside him, lacing her arm in his. Having her next to him felt as natural as his own skin. He cursed himself again for feeling anything at all.

"I dreamed of you," she said, "a long time ago. That dream is what kept me alive in prison. I knew you would eventually come." Fire danced in her eyes.

His stomach twisted into a knot. He looked into the fire.

"Our fates are intertwined," she added.

"How?"

"I don't know. Only that they are."

A war was raging inside him. He wanted to believe her, care about her, even. But even moths were drawn to the flames of a fire. It was time to confront her with her lie.

"Listen," he said, turning to her. But as soon as he turned, she placed a gentle hand on his cheek and kissed him softly. And then he was gone, enveloped by a vision.

Darkness. Deep blackness. A void.

Screeches. Mountain lions? No. Something else. Something darker.

Water.

Lark! No!

Lira?

Flames. Fire.

Gold.

The queen's treasure!

His eyes flew open, and he frantically stumbled to his feet, trying to get his bearings.

Lira was standing now, clutching her stomach—her breath clouding in the night air and disappearing like mist.

They had just shared another vision, and Lira seemed just as surprised by it as he was.

"Who are you?" he asked.

For the briefest moment she touched her lips as if they held some curious, unknown power.

"The truth, Lira!" His jaw tensed.

She took a deep breath and nodded. "You know of King Rodolf?"

"He was king of Ferran. His final oracle led my parents to Isidor."

"King Rodolf's wife, Queen Zara, fled to Ruritania when he died, for she knew from his last oracle that her children would wage war against each other."

"Zara brought treasure with her to Ruritania and hid it. I know!"

She bristled slightly under his harsh words.

His breathing came rapidly now. A fire burned inside him— one for Lira. He was desperate for the truth. "Please," he said miserably. "Tell me if you're working with Alith."

"What?" she asked, sounding surprised. "No, Lark. I'm Zara's niece. My mother was Zara's sister. The last oracle was written by my uncle. King Rodolf."

Stunned, Lark could only stand there and stare. He knew of Queen Zara, but of Zara's sister and family he knew nothing. *Lira is Queen Zara's niece.* It took a minute for the revelation to sink in.

A few tears ran down Lira's face. "Alith put me in prison after my mother died. She believed that because my mother was Zara's sister, Mother had told me where the queen's treasure was." She swatted away the tears as if angry they were there. "Alith thought she could break me."

"She didn't," he said, softly, taking a step toward her.

"No," Lira said, shaking her head. "Because I knew you would come for me."

"So, you're not working with Alith?" He shouldn't have asked again, but he had to be sure.

"No," she said, looking hurt.

The sorrow in her face sealed the truth for him. He suddenly found himself angry at Alith's cruelty. "How long?"

Lira's brow knit in confusion.

"How long had you been in that prison?" he asked fiercely.

She shook her head, refusing to answer.

He approached her slowly, taking her tenderly by the arms. He drew her close, so that their foreheads touched. Their breath mingled in the cool night air.

He closed his eyes. "How long?"

"Ten years," she said, barely above a whisper. "I was only nine years old."

Chapter 60

RUNE

It was late, but Rune needed to see Alith. She was keeping him at arm's length, and he wanted to know why. He had taken a big risk by returning to Ruritania, but he hadn't come empty-handed. He'd brought Alith a prize like a hunting dog looking for praise. And not just any prize—*family*. He had betrayed Wynter, once again, and for what? Love? He laughed at the thought. Who could love a woman like Alith? No. Every choice he'd made had been for his own benefit. Power and position had always driven him. But now that he was back with Alith, he was bereft to realize that he was tired—tired of trying to please her.

Candlelight flickered inside Alith's tent. Soft voices could be heard. There were two guards posted at the entrance, so he made a wide arc and approached her tent from behind. He crept up close and listened.

"What do you want, Mother?" Gilla asked.

"To make peace between us," Alith answered. "There is much ahead for us."

Gilla scoffed. "You chose Rune over me. There will be no peace between us!"

"Gilla, Gilla," she tsked. "Perception can be deceiving."

"Stop playing games, Mother. It's tiresome."

"I've only tolerated Rune because he's been useful to me." She laughed softly. "He's done his worst by betraying Wynter's children. I have no more need of him. He's yours to avenge, my dear."

"I thought you loved him," Gilla said bitterly. "Why the change of heart?"

There was a short pause before Alith spoke. "Wait until the heat of battle so his demise appears to be a casualty."

Rune had heard enough. His whole body shook with fury as he stormed away. He'd been a fool. What was worse, was that Alith had done nothing more than he'd done his whole life—used people to serve his own purposes. Wasn't that what he had done with Wynter, Alith, and now Wynter's children? He was finally reaping what he'd sown at the expense of Lark and Bren. He might have deserved what Alith would do to him, but they certainly didn't. The look on Bren's face when he'd betrayed her to Alith played over in his mind—her questioning stare that didn't want to believe he would do what he had done. She had trusted him to help her find Lark.

His steps slowed. He stumbled, holding a hand to his aching heart. He dropped to his knees in the damp grass and lowered his head. He had come to the end of himself. There was no one left to turn to.

God forgive me. Is it too late?

Perhaps Gilla would destroy him in the end, but before that happened, it was time he destroyed the demons of his past and found the one thing that had always eluded him.

Redemption.

CHAPTER 61

BREN

Bren's sleep had been fitful, even though she'd slept with her back against Seven's. Normally, the childhood habit brought her comfort, but not even Seven's presence was able to bring her peaceful rest. There was much at stake, and she was feeling the weight of the responsibility for the men who were following her. It wasn't just her and Seven's lives she was playing with now. She couldn't afford to make mistakes. According to Wyck's scouts, they were half a day behind Alith.

After a drinking a sweet cup of tea that Seven had made from the roots of wild fern, she forced down a piece of dry bread he'd pushed under her nose. While the men were packing and finishing their meager meal, Bren took Seven and Wyck aside to share her plan.

"The Sea People live to the west by the ocean," Bren began. "If we approach Alith and pretend—"

Seven caught on immediately to what she was suggesting and frowned. "I will not pretend to be a pagan pirate," he said matter-of-factly.

"Sea merchants," Bren corrected, though Seven was right. They offered "protection" on the high seas, but at a price. If that price wasn't paid, then the ship was for the taking.

Wyck plastered on a skeptical scowl, the one that made her feel like a child. "You want us to pretend we're Sea People?"

"Why not?" she asked, trying to sound confident. "It's as good a plan as any. They live close by. That's reason enough for them to be in the area. The men might have to braid a few beards and apply a bit of face paint, but it will work."

"I will not wear face paint," Seven grumbled.

Wyck shook his head doubtfully. "What makes you think Alith would welcome the Sea People?"

Bren was shooting in the dark here, but with the close proximity of the Sea People to Ruritania, Alith must have had some dealings with them. "Where does Alith get supplies for the city?"

The scowl on Wyck's face was replaced with resignation. "Wine," he said. "They supply Ruritania with wine."

Seven grunted.

"It's a good idea," she said. "It will work."

Wyck's jaw worked back and forth. Obstinance simmered in his eyes.

"I do not agree to this plan," Seven interjected. "Plus, there is one small problem. Alith has seen your face."

Bren's heart raced. How could she have forgotten such an important detail?

Wyck sighed. "Not if she cuts her hair and adds the face paint the women of the Sea People wear."

The suggestion to cut her hair took her aback. She'd been growing it since she was a child. It would take years to grow back.

"But if it's beneath the Lady to do so . . ." Wyck said.

"I'll cut my hair," she said defiantly.

"Bren," Seven said, looking concerned. "You don't have to—"

"I do!" she said, trying to calm her racing heart. "I must do what's best for Ferran regardless of the sacrifice."

"What happens after they let us pass through the valley?

Then what?" Wyck asked. "Are we to just waltz into Devil's Rock and escape with the treasure?"

"My parents are on the way with an army." It was out of Bren's mouth before she realized what she had said.

Wyck raised an eyebrow. Seven narrowed his eyes as if she had been withholding information from him.

"I'm sure of it," she added, though she was not sure at all, and the plan she had just suggested was born out of desperation. "I know my parents better than anyone. They'll come, and they'll bring an army with them. In the meantime, we can pretend to be passing through, then stay hidden and keep an eye on Alith."

The more she thought about it, the more she was sure her parents would have figured out what happened—all of it—the map, the treasure, Ruritania. There was a trail to follow. She just prayed they'd found it and were on their way.

"Are we all in agreement, then?" she asked hopefully.

Wyck gave a sweep of his hand back toward Ruritania. "Aye, pretending to be pirates and hoping this invisible army shows up. How could I refuse such ingenuity?"

It was said with sarcasm, but the hope of the Ferran army had been enough to sway him.

"Seven?" she asked.

He was gripping his spear so hard his fingertips were turning white. She pleaded with him with her eyes and his grip finally relaxed. He huffed. That was as close as she was going to get to actual consent.

A feeling of triumph shot through her. She was doing what she was born to do. She only wished Lark was there by her side.

"I'll fill in the men," Wyck said. He pointed to her dress. "You're going to have to do something about that, too," he added as he strode away. "Women of the Sea People don't wear dresses."

She turned to Seven with a smile on her face but was met with a frown. "You're upset with me," she said.

"That is not it."

"What, then?" She unsheathed her knife and checked the sharpness of the blade with her thumb. The hack job she was about to do on her hair wouldn't be pretty. When Seven didn't answer her question she became annoyed. "I can't read your mind!"

"What we're about to do is dangerous."

"We both know it must be done." She pulled her long ponytail through her hands, feeling it one last time.

"Things have been left unsaid," Seven said.

Bren knit her brow in confusion. "What things?"

They stared at each other for a few seconds. His posture was stiffer than usual. He seemed like he wanted to say something but was holding back.

"Come on, princess!" Wyck called out.

"We'll talk about this later," she said to Seven.

To her surprise, his shoulders relaxed as if relieved to have the conversation waylaid. She was reminded that he hadn't even wanted to come on the trip. She had blackmailed him into it. *I'll find a way to make it up to him when we get home.*

"We'll do this together. Family, just like you said," she said cheerfully.

CHAPTER 62

LARK

Lark was prodded awake by the sharp tip of a sword. His eyes sprang open. *Blazes!* He'd meant to stay awake to keep watch over Lira. To his relief, Lira was on her pallet a few feet away from him, rubbing the sleep out of her eyes. She smiled at him.

Only a woman like Lira could smile in the face of Devil's Rock.

Gilla abruptly grabbed Lark by the collar and forced him to his feet. "Alith wishes to see you both."

An ominous dread crept over him.

What's Alith's plan? Why are Lira and I here?

Whatever his and Lira's fate, it had already been sealed. He walked with heavy steps, like a man facing divine judgment. If only he had worked on developing his gift of prophecy. Gotz had tried to help Lark—over and over. But Lark had resisted. Maybe if he hadn't, he could have seen what lay ahead. He couldn't look at Lira. He was powerless to protect her from Alith.

"Have faith, Lark," Lira said suddenly.

Gilla laughed.

Lira, Lark thought. *How innocent you are—believing, even now, that God will save us from this impenetrable mountain.* He envied her. She had surrendered her will to something greater. Lark had always relied on himself—his sword skill, his stubbornness, and his station as prince. Now he'd been stripped of everything that he'd believed made him a man.

Maybe if you lived by the spirit, you'd be able to see.

Gotz's words were a bitter reminder of Lark's failures. Thinking of how disappointed Gotz would be in him pained Lark more than he'd thought it could.

If I live, Gotz . . . I'll make things right between us. I'll be the seer you always believed I could be.

He was so lost in the trappings of his mind that he hadn't noticed they'd arrived in front of a large tent with two armed guards. Gilla parted the tent flaps and spoke to someone inside.

"Whatever happens . . ." Lark said without looking at Lira.

"Will be a victory," she finished.

He studied her. Her shoulders were square. There wasn't a single quiver of fear in her demeanor. Her inner strength was even more beautiful than she was.

Alith emerged from the tent in a belted white tunic and black pants. A white fur cape was draped across her shoulders. Her hair was braided and secured at the back of her neck in a bun. Lark immediately recognized the gold ring on her left finger.

The seal of the Wolf. The old Ulun crest.

Her intentions were right there on her hand for all to see. She meant to return the throne of Ferran to Ulu's heirs and once again divide the kingdom between wolf and eagle—Ulun and Alrenian. His blood simmered, and his palms ached to draw a sword. Misty pieces of a vision danced around his head, but nothing materialized.

Rune showed up with his sword strapped across his back and a pack slung over one shoulder. He stood beside Alith. That was the first Lark had seen him since he had talked Bren into sending him away. It took every ounce of self-control he could muster not to rush at him and go for the knife belted at his waist. It was ultimately Rune's betrayal of Bren that had put him and

Lira here. His only consolation was that Bren and Seven had escaped his treachery. He gave Rune a self-satisfied look. *You didn't get Bren or Seven, you goat's turd.*

Rune held Lark's eyes stubbornly without any hint of regret, but Lark sensed in the shifting of his feet and the clenching of his jaw that he'd received Lark's silent message.

He betrayed my mother, now he betrays her son. Surely God will avenge my faithful mother.

Alith was oblivious to the silent exchange between Rune and Lark. Her focus was on Lira.

"I hope you two slept well. Though I'm not sure how much sleep you got expending all that energy on romantic notions that will never come to fruition."

Lark's face reddened. *Sons of Ferran. She knows about the kiss?*

Alith gave Rune a flirtatious grin, but Rune's face remained unmoved.

"What do you want, governor?" Lark asked.

"Want?" She gave a little laugh and then began walking in a circle around Lark and Lira. "Oh, I want many things," she said, tracing a finger across Lark's back, "and I shall have them soon enough. But I'm in no hurry. Watching you squirm is rather . . . enjoyable."

A few of those in her security entourage chuckled.

Lark grinned as she came around to face them once again. "Yes," he said, "I imagine my father also found cutting off your husband's head rather *enjoyable*."

"You know nothing of honor," she said bitterly.

"Nor do you!" Lira said with more bite than Lark expected from her.

"Fight me if you have an inch of honor!" Lark challenged.

Alith laughed. "If this is some vague attempt to goad me into repeating Gilla's mistake, then you have underestimated me." She sidled up to Lark like a slithering snake. "I'm giving you what you came for," she whispered next to his ear. "The queen's treasure."

Lark balled his hands into fists. Her breath was hot in his ear, and it sickened him. "If you two bring me proof of the treasure, I'll let Lira live. Return with nothing and she dies slowly by my hand while you *watch*." She paused. He could smell the perfume in her hair, the gruel she'd had for breakfast. Bile rose in his throat. "That is . . ." she hissed, ". . . *if* you return at all."

Alith pulled back with a self-satisfied look and studied Lark's face. "Do we understand each other?"

Lark's heart pounded. *She's going to send us into Devil's Rock?* Now he understood what he and Lira were doing there. When Lark did not answer her, Rune punched him in the gut.

"Perfectly," Lark said, between gritted teeth.

Alith smiled, took one final look at Lira to make her point, then withdrew into the camp with armed escorts at her side.

Gilla took Lira by her arm. Rune took a hold of Lark.

"You don't have to do this, Jack," Lark said desperately, using Rune's real name. "You can make things right with Wynter. It's not too late."

Gilla eyed Rune, looking for his reaction.

"Be quiet," Rune growled in his ear.

An uncomfortable knot formed in Lark's throat. What Alith was asking him to do was impossible. If the rumors were true, and the tunnels in Devil's Rock were full of Morbids, he and Lira didn't stand a chance of finding the queen's treasure.

If only I hadn't exchanged my birthday coins for the map. God forgive me.

They were marched out of camp and up to the entrance of Devil's Rock—a mammoth opening that went at least a third of the way up the side of the center rocky pinnacle.

Rune gave Lark a little push forward and dropped the pack he'd been carrying on his shoulder at Lark's feet. "There are torches and water in there for two days."

Lark stared at it like it was a rattlesnake. If he picked it up, he was as good as dead. "I need a weapon," he said.

"You think we're stupid," Gilla said. "No weapons."

"Rune, please!" Lark pleaded. "You can't expect us to face Morbids without weapons."

Rune's jaw worked back and forth, but he remained stoic.

Lark burned with rage. Rune was as ruthless as his mother had made him out to be. "Once a traitor, always a traitor," he said bitterly. He spat on the ground.

Gilla laughed as though she agreed with the insult. Rune turned and walked back toward camp.

Lira picked up the pack and took Lark by the arm. "Come on, Lark. Let's go."

Gilla drew her sword. "There will be guards posted at the entrance in case you get any ideas of running."

"We won't run," Lira said. "We'll find the treasure."

Lark considered rushing Gilla, but it would be foolish without a weapon. She would gut him before he even got close. He was no good to Lira dead.

Lira tugged on his arm again and they walked into the mouth of darkness—Devil's Rock.

Chapter 63

Bren

As they rode toward the White Mountains, Bren touched the ragged edges of her hair at the base of her neck. Her long, brown locks were gone. It would be months before she'd need a leather hair tie. The black, delicate swirls of paint on her face had hardened and cracked from the cool wind. The sword around her waist drummed lightly against her thigh, keeping time with the cadence of her horse. She was no longer Bren, princess of Ferran. She was a warrior in disguise—eagle like her mother, wolf like her father. Seven rode next to her, his face marked with thick, black smudges under his eyes—symbols of the power and strength of the Sea People. Wyck and his men followed with their axes, spears, and swords—each one looking battleworn and fierce. Some men had shorn their heads, others had braided and trimmed their beards. All had black marks below their eyes. She prayed quietly that Alith would believe them to be Sea People.

If only Lark could see her now. She was no longer the scared girl chasing after her brother and his dream of finding treasure. She was becoming something else. A Healer, yes, but more than that. The flames of her love for Ferran had ignited, and the desire to save everything her parents had fought to build drove her.

They had united the Uluns and the Alrenians under one ring—one Ferran. She would do whatever she had to do to preserve their legacy. Courage welled up inside her, threatening to burst forth like the brilliance of the stars and the fierceness of a roaring river. The feeling was like madness. She couldn't control it, and she didn't want to. She knew in her heart that she would risk everything with no compunction, all for the sake of Ferran, even if it meant her death.

"Guards ahead!" Wyck cried out in warning.

A band of three men and two women sat atop their horses just ahead of them, overlooking the shallow valley of Devil's Rock.

Bren exchanged glances with Seven. There was drive and determination in his face that mirrored the determination Bren felt in her heart. He gave her a slight nod. They'd do this together—just like they always had.

There are things left unsaid, he'd told her.

"Halt!" one of the women cried out.

Bren slowed her horse to a walk, and the others followed suit. Wyck took up along her other side, tightening the reins of his horse. Bren raised a hand of peace. What looked to be Alith's crew drew their weapons. A dark woman wearing a scaled, leather vest and wrist cuffs strung an arrow on her bow and aimed it at Bren. She surveyed their troupe with suspicion. "You're early and coming from the wrong direction."

Daughters of Ferran! The woman spoke as if they were expected. Bren's heart raced. If that was the case, their cover wouldn't remain a cover for long. She opened her mouth to speak, but nothing came out.

"We had to make sure you weren't bringing the armies of Ferran with you," Wyck said gruffly. "If you think we're going to trust you just because you buy our wine, you're sadly mistaken."

Bren inwardly sighed, grateful for Wyck's quick thinking.

Alith's soldiers talked quietly among themselves.

"Let us through, you rat's ass," Wyck added. "We're tired

and hungry. We had to kill a band of thieves ten miles back who were trailing you. You might want to tighten your perimeter."

They scowled at Wyck's gruff words.

Bren dared a small smile. *Of course.* Alith's people would have seen the scouts Wyck had sent ahead. She silently thanked God for Wyck's quick wit and wisdom.

"Killing makes him grouchy," Bren added.

The men behind her all laughed, lightening the mood. A few beat their swords on their shields.

The arrow set on Bren was lowered, though begrudgingly. The rest sheathed their swords, and the women waved them through, though they all continued to watch Wyck like he was a wild boar.

The real test was yet to come. Would their cover hold? Would Alith recognize her? If so, she would have just handed Alith back her pawn.

CHAPTER 64

GIDEON

Gideon and Wynter were careful to keep their faces hidden beneath the hoods of their cloaks as they approached the city. It was unlikely anyone in Ruritania knew what their king and queen looked like, but Gideon would take every precaution to ensure their safety.

He slipped the guards at the city gates a few coins along with a story that they had come from Simms Branch to buy sheep pelts. The guards did a customary look through the cart's meager contents and waved them through. They immediately headed to The Wolf's Den, and Wynter paid a boy at the tavern to tend to their horse and cart while they went inside.

The establishment stank of strong mead, smoke, and the sweat of the city laborers. A tavern was usually the heart of the city—the place where tongues were active—where farmers talked of seasons, builders of wattle, and women from the local wash houses complained of smelling of soapwort. This was the place to discover secrets if there were any to be found.

Six broke away from Gideon and Wynter and headed straight for the barman. She had refused to continue concealing her face with her hood.

"She doesn't waste any time," Gideon said quietly to Wynter.

"Seven is all she has," Wynter replied.

Before they could even make it to the bar, Six was walking toward them, pointing to a man across the room wearing a hooded cloak. He was sitting alone at a table in the middle of the room. "They said he's been coming around," Six said, "but no one seems to know who he is."

"Wait here," Gideon said, sliding his hand beneath his cloak to rest on the hilt of his sword.

Six, being Six, pushed past him and headed straight for the man's table.

"I'll wait here and keep watch," Wynter said.

Gideon stomped after Six, cursing under his breath. Her strong headiness was going to draw unwanted attention. To his complete dismay, she plopped down at the man's table without invitation or introduction. Gideon arrived at the table and pulled back his hood.

The hooded, mystery man was twisting his mug of mead in a circle with his fingers and staring darkly at Six's scowl.

"Where are they?" she blurted out.

Gideon bowed slightly to the man. "I apologize, my lord. She speaks out of turn."

The man gestured to an empty chair, and Gideon sat down.

Six opened her mouth to speak. Gideon quickly covered her hand with his own to keep her from speaking. "We're looking for someone," Gideon said.

"Isn't everybody?" the man asked.

"We can pay."

"Not interested."

A man who couldn't be bought was either a man of honor or a man being paid handsomely for his silence. Gideon would have to figure out which this man was. He shifted in his seat and leaned forward. "We've been told you may have information about some young people who recently came to Ruritania. Perhaps you even guided them here."

"Tall, dark one with a spirited brunette and her hot-headed twin brother," Six growled.

Gideon shot Six a look of disapproval.

"Not here," the man muttered. He immediately rose and darted for the door. Gideon caught Wynter's eye, and she trailed the hooded man outside.

"If you don't mind," Gideon said to Six as they dodged barmaids and patrons on the way out, "Let me do the talking."

Six huffed. "I'll speak as I please."

When they reached the door, Gideon stayed her with a hand. "Please."

Six considered for a few seconds, then nodded. Perhaps a little humility was needed with Six. He held the door open and waved her through.

Gideon's heart skipped a beat when there was no sign of Wynter or the hooded man on the street. "Sons of Ferran!"

"This way," Six cried, and they ran up the street looking into alleys and through doorways. A few alleys up, Gideon and Six stopped cold and drew their weapons.

The hooded man had a sword in each hand, his firm grip a warning and a clear sign that he was not interested in talking. Wynter had not been deterred. She was facing the man, crouched for battle, holding her sword with both hands in front of her.

"Wynter," Gideon said very calmly.

"I've got this," Wynter said firmly.

"We can take him," Six whispered to Gideon. "There are three of us."

Gideon raised his arms and let his sword tip fall and point to the ground. "We just want to talk," he said to the man. Gideon flicked his chin at Six, and she reluctantly sheathed her sword.

"Who are you?" the man asked, keeping his eyes on Wynter and her sword.

Gideon struggled with what to say. If he lied, the man might see through it. If he told the truth and the man worked for Alith, they'd be found out within minutes. He'd seen soldiers on the street who could easily be summoned with a shout.

"You have drawn sword on the Queen of Ferran . . . my wife."

The man shifted his feet uneasily. He studied Wynter's face and seemed to be weighing up Gideon's words.

"We're risking everything by telling you the truth," Gideon added.

To his surprise, the man sheathed his swords. "I apologize, Your Majesties." He made a low bow. "I see the resemblance now."

Wynter cautiously sheathed her sword, and Gideon and Six joined her.

"Hood at your service," he said, pulling back his hood. His was an older man with dark hair and eyes and arms that were thick and muscular. He was clearly a man of strength and skill, for no man drew two swords unless they were an expert swordsman.

"How do we know you're not working for Alith?" Wynter asked.

"Your daughter, Bren, healed me."

Gideon and Wynter shared a look of shock. When Bren was a child, they had discovered her gift after she'd healed a bird with a broken wing. Wynter had forbidden her to heal again, as too many healings could take a Healer's life. The thought of Bren finally being called to use her gift was sobering, for it seemed only a moment ago that Bren was a child and Gideon had carried her on his shoulders so she could touch the leaves on the trees.

"I've had leprosy for many years," Hood continued. "People who passed through Kapson spoke of me as a monster. But your daughter was not afraid of me." He smiled a little. "She has the heart of a true Healer. I owe her my life."

"She is well?" Wynter asked, as a concerned mother would.

Hood nodded.

Wynter smiled and touched Gideon's arm.

Hood looked at Six. "Your son, my lady, I assume is Seven?"

Six managed a nod, but Gideon could see the fear in her eyes and stiff posture.

"He is a brave and loyal friend. A man of great faith. You would be very proud if you knew all he has done here."

Six turned her head away. She'd always said that crying was not the way of the Jutta. But perhaps even Jutta needed a moment to temper their emotions.

"What of our son? Lark?" Wynter asked desperately.

Hood's brow furrowed. "I helped him escape from Alith's daughter, Gilla, when I encountered him while traveling from Kapson to Ruritania. At first, I did not know who he was. He is very skilled in the sword. You have taught him well."

"Daughters of Ferran!" Wynter cried.

"Where is he now?" Gideon asked.

Hood seemed reticent to continue. "I'm afraid the rumors in the city are that Alith has the king's son. I do not know how it came to be. Seven said Lark was working for her. Perhaps she discovered his identity."

Wynter grabbed Gideon's arm. "You know what she'll do to him. You cut off the head of her husband!"

Gideon clenched his teeth. Based on what Kidron had said, that Lark had Alith's calling card, Gideon did not doubt that the rumors of his capture were true. "How can we find our children?" he asked.

"We can pay you handsomely," Wynter said, taking Hood's hand.

"No payment is necessary," he said, staring strangely at her hand. "I'm sorry. I'm not accustomed to being touched."

Wynter withdrew her hand quickly. "I didn't mean to offend—"

"On the contrary," Hood said. "It is my honor. I'm used to people fearing me. I'm afraid it's going to take me some time to become accustomed to my new . . . life."

"One I hope you'll be spending with us in Isidor," Gideon said. "You'll always be welcome there. What can you tell us of Alith's plans?"

"Bren and Seven have a band of twelve men with them that are loyal to the Crown. They've left Ruritania to follow Alith in hopes of finding the queen's treasure. They do not know of Lark. I only heard the rumors of his capture after we had parted ways."

"How can this be?" Wynter asked, looking at Gideon.

"Bren has become quite the leader," Hood said.

Wynter sighed but Gideon's chest lifted with pride.

"Where is Alith headed?" Six finally asked.

"The queen's treasure is inside the caverns of Devil's Rock."

Gideon's muscles stiffened. Wynter's face paled. They both knew what was in Devil's Rock—the one thing they hoped never to encounter again. Their children were not just headed into Alith's *wolf den*, they were headed straight into a Morbid den—a den no one had ever come back out of alive.

CHAPTER 65

LARK

J

ust inside the mouth of the cave, before they ventured into the darkness, Lark knelt and rummaged through the supplies Rune had given them.

If only I had memorized the words on the paper within the map. Perhaps they would have proved useful.

He was relieved to find ten dry torches and a tinderbox inside the pack. At least they'd *see* the Morbids coming. He moved aside the waterskins but there was nothing else. Every decision Rune had made since the day they had knocked on his cabin door had been calculated to hurt Wynter's children. Lark handed Lira a torch.

"I thought perhaps Rune would give you a weapon," Lira said.

"He's a traitor, and he always will be."

"People can change," Lira offered.

"Not him," Lark said, slinging the pack over one shoulder. He took the flint and steel out of the tinder and lit her torch.

"You ready?" he asked.

She nodded.

He put on an air of confidence, but in truth he was terrified. Terrified of the Morbids, yes, but more than that—terrified of losing Lira. The kiss had meant more to him than he'd cared to admit. He swallowed and tried to muster courage, but there was none there. *Lord, I know I don't deserve to live, but Lira does.*

Lira plowed ahead—torch lifted high. Their footsteps echoed on the stone floor. The air was cold and musty and had a sullen smell, redolent of a damp vegetable cellar. The towering cavern was filled with moist, glistening stalactite and stalagmite formations that resembled melted candles. Some had joined together between ceiling and floor to create large, deformed pillars. The silence was ethereal, broken only by the constant drip of water.

"This is incredible," Lira said, holding up her torch to examine the height of the ceiling.

Lark didn't share her sentiment. The place was cold and informal, leaving a dull feeling in the pit of his stomach. He counted five tunnel accesses. "How do we decide which way to go?"

"We follow the river of five colors," Lira said, lowering the torch. She walked slowly, examining the cave floor.

"Wait," Lark said, trailing after her. "River of five colors?"

Lira kept moving, sweeping her torch over the floor.

He reached out and stopped her, his brow furrowing. "I thought you said you didn't know anything about where the treasure was."

"I never said that."

"So your mother *did* tell you where the treasure is?"

"As much as she knew about it."

Lark rubbed a hand over his face. Perhaps Lira was not the innocent damsel in distress she seemed to be. "You stayed in jail ten years and pretended to be . . . what? Weak and helpless so Alith didn't suspect anything?"

"You would have done the same thing," she said icily. "If I had showed any strength of character, she would have known I was hiding something. She wants Ferran, Lark. All of it. I couldn't let that happen."

Her face was stern and determined. Where had the young,

naive girl gone who he'd found curled up in a ball in a prison cell?

"So all this, *I knew you'd come for me. Our lives are bound*? Was that an act, too?" he asked testily.

She drew her lips into a hard line. "Put your pride away. There's no room for it here."

Heat rose from his neck to his ears. Her words had stung because they were true. Finding out she wasn't someone who needed rescuing *had* hurt his pride. Why wouldn't she be strong and independent? Look at all she'd endured for the sake of Ferran.

"I'm sorry," he muttered.

"Save your apologies," she said. "We've wasted enough time on trivialities. Set your heart on why we are here."

"Why are we here?" he asked, throwing up his hands. "To do Alith's bidding? To die?"

Lira's brow wrinkled. "You saw the same vision I did by the fire last night."

"Yes, and it wasn't pleasant!" The words were out of his mouth before he realized what he'd implied. "Lira . . . I didn't mean the kiss was unpleasant . . . I meant the vision was—"

"Don't concern yourself over it," she said impatiently. "It was foolish of me to kiss you." She went back to searching the floor with the torch, leaving him in the dark.

"Lira . . ." He wanted to say more—tell her that the kiss *had* meant something to him, that *she* meant something to him, but he was surprised to find that this new Lira intimidated him.

"Look for water," she said. "We follow the water."

CHAPTER 66

BREN

The woman with the quiver full of arrows on her back escorted Bren and the men into the valley. The sun shone above the soaring spires of Devil's Rock and bathed the sunken valley in light. Her resolve was wavering. Why were the Sea People meeting Alith at Devil's Rock? Had they agreed to help her find the treasure in exchange for a portion?

Wherever there is a carcass, there the vultures will gather.

There was no way to know for sure, but one thing Bren did know was that her father would have disapproved of riding into Alith's camp with no plan. Bren and Lark had rushed into the alley back in Isidor to save a man who was being attacked. It was only after they'd rushed in that they realized they were outnumbered. She'd thought then that her parents had overreacted, but now she understood their concern.

Lark and I could have died that day because we didn't think. We just rushed in without considering the consequences.

Oh, how she wished Lark was next to her, riding by her side. But Lark needed to find his own way, and she needed to find hers. Now that the Almighty had given her men to lead, she was surprised to find that leading felt as natural as healing did. Her parents had earned their stations, but Bren had so far only lived the rewards of their sacrifices. Now it was her turn to prove herself worthy. But as each step brought her closer to Alith's camp, her confidence waned. She was leading men into the enemy's camp with a plan that would likely no longer work. They were facing insurmountable odds with little hope of victory.

Only God can save us now.

Wyck must have sensed her mood, for he rode close by her side, offering a kind of silent reassurance. Wyck was proving to be more than just some zealot who had fought in a resistance. She looked over her shoulder. Seven rode on her flank, towering above her like a dark knight.

There are things left unsaid, he had said. *What things, Seven? What things?*

As soon as they reached the valley floor, she realized that Seven and Wyck would fight to the death to save her, and the thought was sobering.

Very rarely will anyone die for a righteous man, though for a good man someone might possibly dare to die.

Thankfully, the camp showed no signs of Sea People. Bren briefly closed her eyes and poured calm into her racing heart. She needed to be controlled and confident. Alith was as shrewd as a snake and would sense any small sign of deception.

Alith was easily spotted. She stood out like a white wraith among her band of demons who, unlike her, were dressed in animal pelts and leather breast armor. Their weapons at their waists and backs varied between bow, ax, sword, and spear. Alith was gesticulating wildly and shouting orders. Tents were coming down and fires were being dosed with water.

What are you preparing for, Alith?

There was no sign of any impending danger. In fact, there was nothing in the face of Devil's Rock except for serene pasture and distant homesteads with small herds of sheep and cattle.

Alith took notice of their arrival and was now watching them approach with curious interest.

Bren and her crew dismounted their horses, and each gave a small bow of their head in greeting.

Alith looked to the woman who had escorted them to the valley and raised an eyebrow. "Orilla?"

"They came from the East. Said they wanted to make sure you weren't bringing an army with you."

"Is that right?" Alith asked, studying them with a careful eye. "And did you find one?" she asked, addressing Bren.

"No."

"And who sent you to look for this . . . army?"

She's testing us.

Bren sent more calm healing through her blood. She couldn't let her face betray her fear. To her relief, Wyck spoke. "Who do you think?"

"So, he doesn't trust me? Is that it?" Alith asked.

"Why would he? You're planning to invade a country that doesn't belong to you."

A knot formed in Bren's throat. Wyck's hatred of Alith was spilling over, and she worried that he was taking things too far.

"But it will belong to me," she said. "Will it not?"

Wyck shrugged. "We shall see."

Bren had to give Wyck credit. He acted as though he knew exactly what Alith was talking about, though she was sure he had no idea what the involvement of the Sea People entailed. Bren was becoming more uncomfortable by the minute. What if Alith could see past the face paint and was toying with them to amuse herself?

"We shall see? What a marvelous idea!" Alith said with a clap of her hands. "How about we see right now?"

Wyck's brow narrowed in confusion. The horses whinnied and pawed nervously behind her as her men grew anxious.

"Orilla, fetch our guest. He just arrived last night. I'm sure he'll be relieved to see that all of you have arrived safely."

Bren's heart sank as Orilla walked back toward a group of men and women packing a tent into a cart. If the guest was Sea People . . .

This is it. It's over.

Alith had a smug, self-satisfied look on her face.

Orilla came walking back toward them with a tall, muscular, dark man whose long beard was braided with feathers and small rodent skulls. One eye was encircled in black paint, a sign that he was the leader of the Sea People. His clothes were cut loosely from wool, and he carried a spear that had a small animal skull and black fox tail secured to the top of its shaft. If this man held the authority he appeared to, they would be found out immediately.

Bren's hand slowly moved toward the sword belted at her waist. Out of the corner of her eye, she saw Wyck do the same. The horses whinnied behind them. They would fight to the death.

I will die with honor.

She set her eyes on Alith who was watching the man approach. Bren knew Alith carried a knife at her ankle, but she would not be able to draw it before Bren pierced her through.

The man of the Sea People was almost upon them. Bren tightened her fingers around the hilt of her sword and drew it ever so slightly.

It's now or never.

She wet her lips, ready to draw when Seven suddenly reached out and stayed her with a hand. She stared angrily at his hand, but he held on, urging her with his eyes. The man was ten feet away. Wyck looked over anxiously at Bren, waiting for her command. Bren quickly reached inside Seven with her gift, searching his heart, for she did not understand why he would have them surrender. She was immediately seized with his panic, fear, and uncertainty. But why? She dug deeper but kept hitting walls.

Release yourself to me Seven, or nothing will stop me from fighting Alith.

Almost immediately, a wall came down inside him, and a flood of his emotions poured over her. *Loyalty. Steadfastness. Order. Family, Family, Family* came almost like a scream. And finally, *Love.*

Love?

Her heart slammed uncomfortably against her ribs.

Seven pulled his hand away, but she snatched it back and held his eyes. *Love?*

Wyck cleared his throat, breaking the spell Bren had fallen under.

The imposing figure of the man of the Sea People was standing there staring at them with big, brown eyes and crossed arms. She let go of Seven's hand. Now she understood what Seven had meant before. *There are things left unsaid.*

It no longer mattered now because, by the look on Alith's smug face, they would all soon be dead.

CHAPTER 67

SEVEN

Seven bared his teeth as Alith's men whisked away his spear. Then they searched the rest of the group and confiscated every weapon. Bren's eyes and flaming cheeks conveyed her internal disquiet. He should have told her sooner that his feelings for her had changed. In the moment where they should have been one in purpose, he found he could not draw upon himself to watch her die in a fight they could not win. Perhaps that had been a mistake, and something much worse would befall them all, but as long as he had breath in his lungs, he would do whatever he could to preserve her life, even if it meant only an hour more.

Alith made a dramatic sweep of her hand for the Sea People leader. "Damson, your people have come from the east!"

The fearsome man made a show of looking their crew over, barely skimming their faces. "These are not my people. They're imposters. Isidor spies," he growled.

Alith smiled.

"Bring the tall one for questioning," Damson said, referring to Seven. "Keep the others under guard." He made a show of checking the sharpness of his spear tip, then turned and walked away.

Seven was pushed from behind with the long shaft of his own spear by one of Alith's goons. He grimaced as the hard wood was pushed into his back. Damson led them away from the inner workings of the camp.

"Wait over there," Damson said, motioning to the guard.

The guard hesitated, but Damson was a large man and very imposing. He twirled his spear so that its tip faced up.

Alith's guard did as he was told.

"What are you going to do with us?" Seven asked.

Damson got right up in his face. "I'll be the one asking the questions."

Seven clenched his hands into fists. Damson took notice and backed up a few steps.

"Anger will not serve you," Damson said stiffly.

"How would you know?" Seven retorted. "What do you know of Jutta?"

Damson raised an eyebrow. "Jutta?"

Seven grunted. "What do you want? Kill me, don't kill me. What does it matter?"

"And your father's name?"

The question surprised Seven. Why would a man of his position care? "I have no father," he answered, his throat swelling with emotion.

"And your mother?"

"Her given is Six."

There was a long, awkward silence. Damson studied Seven, but for what reason, he did not know, nor did he care.

"Despite what you might think, I'm a man of honor," Damson finally said.

"A man of honor would not be in business with Alith."

Damson smiled, his teeth white as morning snow. "You are wise for your age, Son of no father."

"Then let us go free," Seven said miserably. "Do this and I'll believe you are a man of honor and not a wretched pirate out to fill his pockets."

Damson's demeanor darkened. "Guard!" he called out. When the guard returned, Damson looked directly at Seven. "Keep him with the others until I decide what to do with them."

CHAPTER 68

LARK

"Did you know that Ferran was once an ocean?" Lira asked.

"Fascinating." Lark couldn't understand why Lira was so calm. The tunnel they were navigating seemed endless, and he was having a hard time imagining that it led to anything other than their impending death.

"Is it me or is it getting colder?" he asked. A foul, sour scent was in the air. Something felt . . . wrong. A sudden gust of cold air extinguished their torch, and a piercing screech followed.

Morbids.

Lark cursed under his breath, his heart thrumming savagely against his chest. He dug inside their pack for the tinderbox, searching with his fingers.

"Hurry," Lira whispered.

He fumbled open the box and quickly struck the flint against the steel. A spark ignited long enough for him to see a wide-eyed Lira holding the torch out to him. The sparks fizzled out.

"Sons of Ferran!" he shouted.

Something that sounded like claws scraping against rock was moving toward them with the quickness of a spider.

"Lark!" Lira said urgently.

He struck the flint over and over at the torch, his hands shaking.

No flame.

Lira's rapid, warm breaths puffed across his face.

Strike.

Spark.

Lira's face.

Strike.

Spark.

Lira's face.

"Another torch!" Lira cried. The old torch hit the cavern wall and clattered to the ground. Lira's hands grappled for the pack at his hip. Their hands collided as she removed a torch, and Lark dropped the steel. He fell to his knees, groping, and splashing about in the shallow water.

"I have the torch. Hurry!" Lira cried.

His fingers finally hit cold steel, and he quickly dried it off on his shirt.

"Lark?" Lira's voice was strangely calm now. "Lark. Something sticky just fell on my face."

Strike.

Spark.

Lira's terrified face.

Strike.

Spark.

The torch burst into flames.

They stood there waiting for their eyes to adjust. Lira wiped her face, then studied her hand.

That's when they heard the breathing—rough, raspy, gurgling breathing. It was coming from above them. Lira's eyes widened, her body shaking as the realization struck.

He pried the torch from her fingers, then slowly raised the flame. He instinctively held his breath, trying to draw his sword

—a sword he didn't have. The torchlight landed on a furless, monkey-like creature baring razor-sharp teeth. A thin line of goo dripped from its mouth and fell into the water.

"Sons of Ferran," he whispered as it hissed at him.

The Morbid let out a long screech and leaped, landing on Lark's chest. Lark fell backward against the tunnel wall and dropped the torch.

Lira screamed.

He stumbled forward, grappling to get a good hold on the Morbid. The creature's sharp claws dug into his chest and face as it scampered to avoid Lark's frantic fingers. It leaped onto the tunnel wall and back onto Lark's back, wrapping its spindly legs around Lark's neck, and digging its sharp claws into his cheeks. It tightened its slimy legs, cutting off Lark's breath.

"Lark! Hold still!" Lira cried out.

Lark pulled madly at the creature's arms and legs. Blood was spilling down his cheeks. He felt the heat of the torch on his back as Lira tried to scare off the Morbid with its flame. The creature screamed but held on. Lira prodded the Morbid over and over with the torch as Lark pulled helplessly at its tiny limbs. Twisting and turning, Lark lost all sense of direction. Heat raked his side and the air filled with the scent of seared wool and burning flesh.

Lira gasped. "Fire!"

Lark immediately fell to the ground and rolled to his side in the water while he fought to get the creature off his back. The Morbid's legs constricted even tighter around his neck. The thing was getting stronger while Lark was getting weaker. He was close to losing consciousness, only vaguely aware of Lira yelling. Everything sounded muffled, as though he had gone underwater. Then in a haze of slow motion—a flash of metal—a small splash of water next to him.

Lark gasped violently—oxygen filling his lungs. His eyes slowly refocused. The Morbid was next to him with vacant, wide eyes—blood oozing into the water. Whether it was his own blood or the Morbid's, he did not know, but the air was putrid. He stared into the creature's open mouth of sharp teeth. It was as if it had died mid-shriek.

Lark coughed, grasping his throat with his hand. "Lira?" he croaked.

She dropped to her knees in the water in front of him, examining his face with her torch. He shut his eyes against the sudden light. "You killed a Morbid," he croaked. His voice sounded like gravel.

"No," she said.

Lark opened his eyes, confused.

"He did," she said, holding up the torch behind her.

Lark rolled to his back. Standing above him with a bloody sword in his hand was the one man he'd hoped to never see again.

Rune.

Without thinking, Lark sprang to his feet and charged at Rune, but the Morbid attack had weakened him more than he'd realized, and he quickly lost footing and fell at Rune's feet with a splash.

Rune reached down with one hand and grabbed him by the arm, helping him to stand. Lark took two wobbly steps back and licked his bloodied lips. "I should kill you."

Rune knelt and rinsed the blood off his sword, then stood and sheathed it. "I'd like to see you try."

Lark laughed. "If I had a weapon—"

Before he could even finish his sentence, Rune began removing his knife belt. He tossed it at Lark's feet. "You're going to need this. There could be more Morbids ahead."

"How do you know the knife won't end up in your back?"

"Because you need me. You both do." Rune glanced at Lira, and Lark immediately understood his meaning. If he didn't come back with proof of the treasure, Alith would kill Lira. As much as it pained Lark to admit it, Rune was right. They did need him, and two blades were always better than one. He'd have to put aside his contempt for Rune despite what he'd done to Lark's family.

"How do you sleep at night?" Lark asked him.

Rune skirted by, plucked Lira's torch from her hand, and plowed into the dark. "I don't."

CHAPTER 69

GIDEON

Gideon sat on the cool ground with his arms on his knees—away from Wynter and Six who were resting. The sun was high in the sky, but thick waves of clouds were rolling in, blanketing the sky in shades of gray and white. The picturesque White Mountains stood regal in the distance, while the three jagged peaks of Devil's Rock towered dark and rigid. They had ridden the horses hard, hoping to catch up with Bren, but there had been no sign of her and the men she rode with. He feared they may have been captured, too. They had no choice now but to wait for Ferran's army out of eyesight of Alith's camp below. Much plagued his mind. How long before Ferran's army arrived? Were his children still alive? How long would Wynter continue her icy demeanor? She had always been his voice of reason—his anchor when his mind threatened to drive him mad. The brief moment of relief they'd shared together in Ruritania after they'd discovered that their children were still alive had done nothing in the way of mending what he had broken between them. He plowed his hands through his hair and pressed his palms against his eyes.

"You messed up, didn't you?" a voice behind him asked.

Gideon grabbed his sword and spun toward the voice. When

293

he saw it was Six, he stabbed the tip of his sword into the ground and stared out at the horizon. Six plopped down next to him—*right next to him*. Never had she dared to come so close. He gave her a curious look. She had a wild kind of beauty—like a bracken-covered moor that overlooked an angry sea.

Six wrinkled her nose at his brazen stare.

"What do you want, Six?"

"Whatever is going on between you and Wynter needs to be resolved before we go into battle." She looked him squarely in the face and waited.

"I've tried," he said, looking away.

"Try harder."

He worked his jaw back and forth. "It's complicated."

"That's a huge pile of horse manure! Whatever you did or said—take it back."

"I can't," he said stubbornly.

"Don't be a fool. No one, and I mean no one, would put up with your pompous, self-righteous ego. Wynter is a saint!"

Gideon wanted to get angry, but he didn't have the energy, so instead he turned the tables. "How about we talk about who Seven's father is so I can show him what happens to a man who abandons a woman and child?" Regardless of how Gideon felt about Six he would avenge her honor if he ever had the chance. She deserved better, and so did Seven.

Six's mouth closed quickly into a hard line.

"That's what I thought," he said.

They both heard the rumble of horses coming at the same time and rushed back over to their camp. Wynter had roused from her sleep and was throwing off her blanket. All three of them waited with weapons drawn. A rider tore across the meadow toward them.

"It's Elias," Six said.

Behind him came a glorious sight and sound—the thunder of Ferran's army.

At last!

But Gideon's moment of elation quickly evaporated when the horses suddenly stopped coming.

His lieutenant, Elias, rode up and slid off his saddle. The mournful look on his face told Gideon all he needed to know.

"Where are the rest of them?" Gideon asked. "Six hundred left Isidor."

"Only 300 made it out of Kapson. The others drank the water. They will recover, but they weren't fit to ride. Kidron has taken command in hopes they'll quickly recover and join us."

It was all Gideon could do to maintain his composure. Wynter's face had paled. Six stood there with a kind of shocked stupor on her face. Their children's lives were at stake. Gideon thought about how many loved ones he'd already lost in his lifetime. As the spirits of the dead began to surround him, he wondered if his children were fated to join them.

"I'm sorry, my lord, Elias continued. "I take full responsibility. I told them not to drink the water, but our water supply was not what it should have been."

Gideon's rising anger at the incompetence of his men in not following direct orders only deepened his sense of despair, but he hid it all behind a mask of confidence. Kings were called to lead, to stand firm in the face of obstacles. Elias had been Gideon's lieutenant ever since Brendle had disappeared in the battle in the White Mountain gorge, twenty-one years ago. He couldn't blame him for this, for the fault lay with Gideon. If he had ridden with the army instead of going ahead to look for his children, things might have turned out much differently. He had put his family above Ferran, and now he was suffering the consequences of that decision. His gross misjudgment could ultimately cost him his children and the throne.

"I'll need a minute to consider our next course." He headed for the woods where the horses were tied off. Ever since he'd left Isidor he'd made one misstep after the other. First, by riding in front of the army, and second, with Wynter, when he accused her of favoring their son because she still held a torch for his name-sake—Gideon's deceased brother.

He entered the woods and began hacking at limbs and underbrush with his sword while he cursed the day he was born. The thought of losing his family and everything he'd fought for—everything his father before him had fought for—was too much to bear. What if 300 men weren't enough to defeat Alith?

"You're going to hurt yourself."

Gideon spun around with an angry sweep of his sword that came within inches of Wynter's face. He planted his feet, teeth clenched, breathing heavily as he held the sword steady.

"What you're doing right now isn't going to help," she said.

He lowered the sword. "Let me be," he said miserably.

"Why?" she asked. "So you can convince yourself that all is lost?"

"It is!" he shouted, tossing his sword to the ground. He bent over and put his hands on his knees. Sweat pooled on his fore-head. *I'm not the man you thought I could be. God help me, I tried.*

"I loved your brother," Wynter said.

Gideon straightened and stared at Wynter in disbelief.

"Isn't that what you wanted to hear?" she asked coldly.

Gideon wiped his forehead on his sleeve. "Why are you telling me this now?" he asked.

"Because it's time we cleared the air."

He laughed. "So, you're telling me what I want to hear, is that it?"

"Stop this!" she spat. "Those men and women back there are counting on us to lead them." She stormed up to him, grabbed his hand, and held it roughly over her heart. "The only person my heart belongs to is you."

Her heart pounded angrily beneath his hand. The heat of her breath caressed his face. He dared not move lest she flee from him again.

She looked lovingly into his eyes. "As much as I cared about your brother, the truth is, he couldn't hold a candle to you. You had my heart long before I even knew it was yours."

A single tear fell down her cheek, and he longed to wipe away the pain he had caused her.

"I love you more than I ever thought I could love anyone," she continued. "But you hurt me, Gideon. You didn't trust what we've had all these years, and it made me wonder if all this time you've just been going through the motions with a heart that has been stuck in the past."

"Wynter," he whispered. "I'm sorry. I . . ."

She dropped his hand and took two steps back. "If your brother came back today, it would not matter."

"I beg you to forgive me," he said, stepping toward her.

She shook her head and took a step back. "Not yet," she said, keeping him at bay. She wiped at her tears and hugged herself. "It is true that I have favored our son."

"But why?"

"I had a vision of him before you and I were together."

Her tears were coming faster now, and it took all the restraint he had not to go to her.

"It was when your men had captured and caged the Morbid in the northern forest. I went to give the creature some water, and it grabbed my wrist and gave me a vision."

"Sons of Ferran," he said. "And I came and killed it. I thought it was hurting you."

Wynter shook her head and continued her story. "The woods were burning all around me. A baby was crying, but I couldn't find it. Then your brother came from out of nowhere with a baby boy and handed him to me. The baby was so beautiful." She smiled through her tears. "Your brother said Lark was a good, strong name." She laughed a little and pushed a stray hair out of her face.

"Why didn't you ever tell me this?" he asked.

"I don't know. I'd told myself that the vision didn't mean anything. But after Lark and Bren were born, I remembered the vision—our baby boy—the danger around him—the fire. I didn't tell you because it seemed foolish to believe that something from so long ago could matter." She covered her face with her hands.

Gideon's heart ached. He rushed to Wynter and wrapped his arms around her. "Forgive me," he said into her hair.

She held onto him fiercely and with abandon. "I love you, you fool," she mumbled.

"I'll never hurt you again," he said softly.

She took a step back and placed her hands tenderly on his cheeks. "You're stuck with me, my lord. If you still want me."

Her formal address was a tease at what they had once been— she a lowly transporter and he a future king.

"I've never wanted anyone else," he said. He kissed her then, and she clung to him as she once had, as if they were the only two people in the world. Memories of Wynter raced through his mind. The scared young child who'd fallen from the trees into his arms, the strong confident woman he'd married under the golden leaves of a cherry tree, the mother of his children smiling up at him from sweat soaked sheets as he held their twins for the first time. No longer would his love-haunted heart doubt her. He stopped and rested his forehead against hers and savored the sweet reunion.

"There'll be time for this later," she said softly.

He kissed her forehead. Feeling renewed strength and determination, he gathered his sword. "Let's go save Ferran and get our children back."

Chapter 70

Bren

Bren, Wyck, and their men were taken to the mouth of Devil's Rock. It was genius really. No one was going to run into the dark caverns of Devil's Rock only to be ripped apart by Morbids. Death by sword was cleaner—more honorable. Only there was still no sign of Seven.

Bren purposefully stood apart from Wyck and his crew. She was the reason they were here. She was the reason they would die.

The sun had begun its afternoon descent. The band of guards appointed by Alith to keep watch over them had grown bored and had wandered within a safe distance to play a game of dice. The constant click-clack of the dice and the roars of the guards had lulled her into a reflective trance.

How could Seven have kept something so important from me? Love. Love. Love. He lied to me when he said I was like family. Why?

She bit her lip in frustration.

Wyck approached warily. "How fare ye?"

"Not well." She sighed.

"I'm sure Seven will be fine," Wyck said with a kind smile.

He had misunderstood her brooding as concern for her friend, and she didn't correct him. Because more than feeling hurt by Seven's omission, she was pained that she would be the reason that Wyck and his men would die. "I should have never asked you to come," she said regretfully.

"Aye," he said with a nod. "Maybe. But will you give up so easily when you become queen?"

She laughed so loud that she drew the attention of the guards. They paused briefly to look her way, then quickly returned to their jovial game-playing.

"I can't be queen if I'm dead," she said. "Besides, I don't deserve to be queen. I failed."

A bird of prey cried out somewhere above them.

"See," she said. "The vultures are already circling."

Hood shaded his eyes with a hand. "It's a hawk, my lady. Not a vulture."

For a moment, she wondered if it could be Gotz's hawk, Kia. She didn't dare look up, because even if it was Kia, Gideon had taught Bren that a circling hawk was an omen of death.

"There's something I need to say." She wouldn't hold back anything from Wyck. Not now. He needed to know how sorry she was.

Wyck smiled at her and held up a hand. "I already know."

She narrowed her eyes. "You do?"

"Yes," he said, putting his hands on his hips. He looked at the ground and shook his head then peered up at her with a darkened brow. "You're madly, deeply in love with me and want to declare your love before we die."

She couldn't help but smile. He returned a crooked grin that was more charming than she cared to admit. But she wouldn't be swayed by his attempt to distract her.

"This is serious, Wyck."

The smile faded from Wyck's face. "Aye?"

"I'm sorry I got you and your men into this mess. We both know what will happen next."

Wyck rubbed his chin. "Perhaps Seven will convince the Sea People man to spare us."

It was a long shot, and Wyck knew it, but she admired him all the more for keeping up the ruse of hope. She lowered herself to the ground and sat back against the sheer rock wall. Wyck sat next to her and put an arm around her. "It's not over yet, princess."

Instead of being angry that he had called her princess, she folded herself into his arms and let him hold her. He rested his head on top of hers and stroked her arm for a few minutes. "Hey," he said, lifting her chin so he could look in her eyes. "Don't worry. I'd follow you to the moon if you asked me to."

"You would?" she asked, feeling her heart flutter at the warmness of his breath.

"Aye."

And just when she thought he might kiss her . . .

"Bren?"

Startled to be caught in such an intimate moment, she sprang to her feet.

Seven was standing there between two guards with a scowl on his face.

To Bren's relief, Wyck stood up, brushed himself off, then returned to the other men who had moved just inside the lip of the cave.

"I hope you two will be very happy together," Seven said flatly.

Bren marched up to Seven and slapped him across the face with every ounce of strength she could muster. It was like hitting a statue, and a sharp sting coursed through her hand. Seven, being Seven, remained stoic, registering the slap with nothing more than a wince. His guards chuckled then turned and retreated.

"You lied to me," she said tersely.

Seven's eyes glimmered with the threat of tears. "And you betrayed my heart."

His honesty took her by surprise and rendered her speechless. He had called her family back in Simms Branch. He had laughed at the idea of any real feelings for her. Then, just moments ago, when she had searched inside him.

Love. Love. Love.

"Seven," she said with a sigh. "How can I betray a heart I didn't know I had?"

"It doesn't matter now," he said, looking back toward Alith's camp.

"What did Damson say?"

"Very little."

Her anger over Seven not telling her about his feelings seemed a trivial thing now that she could see how defeated he looked. She walked into his arms and embraced him. "I'm so sorry, Seven. About everything."

At first, Seven remained stiff in her arms, unfeeling. Without thinking, she poured a small amount of love into him—that he might forgive her for being angry—for leaning on Wyck.

Release yourself to me, Seven. Please.

Then ever so slowly his body relaxed. His arms enveloped her, and he bore her tightly to him until he had fully surrendered to the embrace. She was surprised to find that being in Seven's arms felt very different than being in Wyck's. Wyck was like a pleasant dream, but Seven felt like home.

A horn sounded a long, mournful note that echoed off the mountains.

They stepped back from their embrace and looked toward the valley.

"That's a Sea People shell horn," Seven said.

"What does it mean?"

"War."

"War with who?"

That's when they saw the white flag waving on the precipice above the valley, and it wasn't a flag of surrender. There were flickers of red and yellow—the colors of Ferran—the colors of the eagle and the wolf.

"Daughters of Ferran, Seven! The Ferran army is here."

CHAPTER 71

LARK

"If I kill Rune now, it will save me the trouble later," Lark whispered to Lira. The Morbid attack had left him feeling bruised, burned, and brutish.

"I can hear you," Rune said, plowing through the dark ahead of them with the torch.

Lira reached over and gave Lark's arm a squeeze. "Try to think of finding the treasure and not revenge."

She was right, of course. Now wasn't the time to make Rune pay for his treachery. But the danger lurking ahead had put him on edge, and thoughts of killing Rune were a good distraction. Or maybe it was because Lira had become noticeably quieter since Rune had come to their rescue. He hoped she wasn't reverting to the old Lira he'd first encountered in the prison. He was starting to like the new Lira. More than like, if he were truthful with himself. She'd stood up to him. No woman had ever dared to stand up to the king's son. They were too busy trying to win his hand in marriage.

They came to a crossroads in the caves. Three possible paths.

Rune glanced over his shoulder. "Which way?"

Lira left Lark's side and took a hold of Rune's fist that held the torch. She guided his hand closer to the ground. "Left," she said. A thin ripple of green water beneath their feet was flowing from that direction.

Rune took off, taking strides as big as a giant's. As the torchlight drifted farther away, the darkness abounded. Lark's hands began to tremble as he felt his way along the cold, damp walls. Memories of his childhood nightmares surfaced—the ones where Morbids sat on his chest and ripped him open while he still breathed. At least in the darkness Lira wouldn't be able to see how frightened he was. One knife against a brood of Morbids was little comfort. If only he had listened to Gotz and worked harder on becoming a seer, perhaps he would be able to see what lay ahead. Surely there was something he could do to ignite a vision. He took several deep breaths and tried to clear his mind.

"You're wasting your time," Lira said.

He could not see her face, but he heard the exasperation in her voice, even in the dark.

"Now you read minds?" he asked mockingly.

"No," she snipped. "But taking deep breaths isn't going to bring on a vision."

"How do I make it work, then?"

She humphed. "You don't. Power comes from God alone."

Lira was starting to sound like Gotz. "Then how do I get it from Him?" he said testily.

"You don't *get* it, He gives it."

I'm doomed, he thought. "I give up, then."

"Good. Now maybe God can do something with you."

Lark bristled. Something in what she said had a ring of truth to it. He had knowingly pushed his gift away—pushed God Himself away because he was prideful and didn't want to acknowledge his weaknesses. Something inside him shifted as if the wall he had built around himself had finally cracked. *Is this what humility feels like?*

The torch stopped moving. Rune had stopped just outside a large opening. A strange, green glow was coming from inside.

This is it. There was nowhere else to go except back from where they had come. Lark's stomach lurched. He readied the knife Rune had given him.

Rune drew his sword. "Let me go first and see what's inside."

"No," Lira insisted. "Whatever fate awaits, awaits us all."

Lark clenched his jaw. Rune didn't deserve to be lumped in with whatever Lark's fate was. Rune was a back-stabbing traitor who had done nothing good with his life. What purpose could he possibly serve now? Rune's future was already written on Lark's heart, and he would see it done before they left these tunnels.

To his surprise, Rune acquiesced to Lira's plan, and they all crept forward, staying close together.

Lira whispered a prayer that Lark couldn't discern.

Lark swallowed. *Lord, if you decide to return my gift to me, I will honor your name with it for all of my days.* He knew it was a prayer of desperation, but he meant it. And though Lark was nothing like his father, they shared this. They were men of their word.

The glow became brighter as they entered the vast cavern. They stopped just inside the entrance. Once their eyes adjusted to the strange aura, Lark was able to take in the massive, circular cavern. In the center was a lake with greenish-blue water that glowed as if illuminated from below. Rune lifted the torch toward the ceiling. Its recesses went beyond what they could see, but on a ledge about twenty feet above them was a flame. A flame of fire.

Oh, eternal flame!

That line he did remember from the small paper that had been with the treasure map.

This is where the treasure is! It has to be. Only what else lurked about? His heart raced. "Rune," Lark said quietly. "I'd really prefer the sword." He tried to steady his trembling hand. He searched the dark recesses nervously, looking for creature eyes.

Where there's one Morbid, there must be more.

Rune ignored him and led them farther inside.

"Sons of Ferran!" Lark exclaimed, taking in the strange surroundings. Then just like in the tunnel earlier, there was a sudden gush of air, and the torch flickered out. They were left standing in the bright, hazy glow of the water and the light of the mysterious flame above them.

Lark listened intently for gnashing teeth or scratching claws. To his relief, the only sound was a trickle of water that fell from somewhere unseen. It was so quiet that he could hear the rush of his heart in his ears.

"I don't see any treasure," Rune said. "Are you sure we went the right way?"

Lira brushed past Rune without answering and trailed the edge of the water as if she were looking for something. Lark followed, keeping a close eye on their surroundings. "Perhaps someone has already found the treasure," Lark said.

"I don't understand," she said, becoming more reflective. "My mother was so clear. Follow the river of five colors."

"Except . . ." he said, looking at the water, "there only seem to be two colors. Green and blue."

She bit her lip and looked across the water.

Lark had an idea. After all, his parents had opened the Iron Gate of Isidor with a kiss. "Perhaps . . ."

"Perhaps what?" she asked, still intently staring at the water.

"Perhaps we should try the kiss again?" His face flushed with heat as his words hung in the air. Even in the eerie, green glow he could make out a scowl forming on her face.

"Are you really choosing *now* to make romantic overtures?" She glanced annoyingly toward Rune.

Lark scratched the back of his head. "I was only thinking of the vision we shared before . . . back there . . . before." He gritted his teeth to stop his stammering.

"Oh," she said, looking slightly embarrassed. "Well, it's not the worst idea you've had. I haven't had a vision since then."

Lark's spirits lifted.

"Don't flatter yourself," she said. "This isn't about you."

"I never said it was." His voice came out an octave higher. He cleared his throat. "I never said it was," he said, deeper than usual.

A smile spread across her face, and he realized he'd give every coin he had to see her smile at him that way again. He tucked the knife in his belt, and they inched toward each other, feigning to kiss one way then the other. They were in a kind of awkward dance of who was going to take the lead.

Lira sighed and took a step back.

"Could you just . . . let me handle this one thing?" he asked with a sigh.

She smoothed down her hair (though she had little hair to smooth), squared her shoulders, and held her chin high. "Proceed," she said flatly.

Lark shook his head a little. This was not the way he saw this going. Lira was acting as if this was some formal ceremony, and he was feeling anything *but* formal. He looked nervously back at Rune, but he was occupied with probing the water with the tip of his sword.

He stepped up to Lira. She closed her eyes. Her posture stiffened as he took her by the arms and pressed his lips against hers. Her lips were hard and cold—like kissing a wall. Nothing happened. No vision. He stepped back and coughed into his hand.

Her eyes flew open. She pursed her lips with dissatisfaction.

"It helps if both people actually participate," he said quietly.

"Fine," she said. Wasting no time, she took his scruffy cheeks into her hands, and kissed him—really kissed him—with abandon to ceremony or purpose. His arms seemed to have a mind of their own as they wrapped around her waist. He became lost in the moment and visions became the last thing on his mind. His only thought was of her. *Lira.*

A flash of light severed his connection.

He was standing on the edge of the cavern lake, Lira by his side, staring confusedly at the water. He was unsure if this was real or a vision. He looked for Rune, but he was not there.

Sons of Ferran! This is a vision!

"Lira?" he asked, wondering if she were in this with him, or whether this was just him experiencing it.

She stared at him wide-eyed.

"So, you're here? In the vision with me?"

She nodded.

"And we're back in real time . . . kissing?"

She nodded again.

"Sons of Ferran," he grinned. Beat this one, Gotz, you old goat.

The surface of the water gurgled and burped.

"Lark, look!" Lira pointed at the water.

There was something just beneath the surface shining bright—like a star. They both dropped to their knees and peered into the water.

"I think I can reach whatever it is," he said, stretching out his hand.

Lira grabbed his arm. "We don't know what it is," she said, sounding concerned.

"It's the treasure, it has to be!" he exclaimed.

Lira reflected for a moment, then said, "Look, great wanderer, for only you will see, the crown of jewels at the bottom of the sea."

"Wait," he said, sitting back on his heels. "That's from the paper that was with the treasure map?"

"What paper?" she asked, looking over at him.

"You failed to mention you've had the key to the treasure this whole time!"

"You never asked," she said stubbornly.

He clenched his jaw.

Lira scoffed. "Are you really going to pick a fight inside a vision!"

He took a deep breath. It was hard to stay mad when just on the other side of the vision, they were in the middle of kissing. He was mildly aware of the pleasant sensation, though it was very faint.

"We'll discuss this later," he said, searching for his knife. Realizing he didn't have it, he rolled up the sleeves of his shirt, and leaned over, reaching into the water.

"Be careful," she said.

The water was freezing but became warmer as his hand drew nearer to the light. He searched with his fingers and found something hard. He wrapped his fingers around it—the nondescript edges of something. The queen's crown! But the crown resisted as he pulled, and it slipped out of his fingers. He stretched himself out flat on the ground and reached into the water up to his right armpit, taking hold of the crown. He used his left hand to brace himself on the rock, took a deep breath, and pulled with all the strength he could muster. The crown sprang out of the water, but something came with it. He slung the entire mass behind him and scrambled to his feet.

Lark and Lira stared in shock as a Morbid shook itself off and bared its teeth like a rabid wet dog. It dropped the crown in its hand and sprang.

"Sons of Ferran!" Lark cried out. He reached for the knife that wasn't at his waist and swore under his breath. The Morbid launched itself into Lark's chest and climbed up to his shoulders.

Lira screamed as the creature wrapped its legs around his neck from behind and dug the claws of its spindly hands into Lark's eyes. He blindly pulled at the Morbid. Blood streamed down his face as his eyeballs slowly tore from their sockets. His scream was followed by a burst of light.

The next sensation was of Lira's lips pressed against his. He released her, his heart pounding against his ribs. He frantically grabbed at his face with his fingers, searching for blood, for his eyes. *I can see.* He stumbled backward, backing away from the water.

It wasn't real. It wasn't real.

Yet, the vision had *felt* real. The pain of having his eyes ripped from his head was more real than any nightmare he'd ever had. He wiped a hand across his mouth and looked at Lira.

The terror in her face and her rapid breathing matched his own.

"Perhaps we should save the kissing for another time," he said.

Lira rushed into his arms and held him tight. "Oh, Lark."

Rune came and pulled them apart. "Knock it off! We have a treasure to find."

Lark drew the knife that was now tucked safely in his belt. Rune, misunderstanding, drew his sword and pointed it at Lark. "There are Morbids in the water," Lark said, motioning with his head.

Rune glanced at the water while keeping his sword aimed at Lark. "I don't see anything," Rune said.

"We give you our word," Lira said.

Rune gave her a sour look.

"We shared a vision," Lark explained. "The treasure is in the water, but it's being guarded by Morbids."

Rune lowered his sword. "Then I suggest you figure out how to get to the treasure without getting yourself killed."

CHAPTER 72

WYNTER

From Wynter's bird's-eye view of the valley that snaked around Devil's Rock and spread between the White Mountains, she quickly realized that their predicament was worse than she and Gideon had thought. She gripped her horse's reins tightly, wondering what turn of events had occurred that the Sea People would stand with Alith. More than likely, she had filled their heads with the promise of treasure.

Gideon guided his horse a little closer to Wynter. "We're outmanned," Gideon said quietly. "And if the Sea People fight in their traditional pike squares, we won't be able to outmaneuver them."

His words sounded ominous. Wynter had a rudimentary understanding of pike squares. They were closed square formations of up to a hundred men wielding eighteen-foot, sharp poles on all four sides, making it virtually impossible to penetrate. Charging a pike square was akin to poking a porcupine—only much deadlier.

Anger boiled up inside her. She and Gideon had spent years reuniting Ferran and working tirelessly to find a way to bring it back to its former glory. The injustice of their predicament ground against her bones. She wanted nothing more than to heel her horse and charge into the valley, wielding her sword with the unbridled rage that was coursing through her veins.

Gideon must have sensed her mood and added, "No king is saved by the size of his army."

His uncharacteristic optimism surprised her. "Gotz?"

"No," he said, looking back down into the valley. "Psalm 33."

A small smile crossed her lips despite her foul mood. If Gideon was quoting scripture, then anything was possible.

"Elias!" Gideon called out. "Flag!"

Elias wasted no time unfurling the white Ferran flag. The yellow eagle and red wolf whipped in the wind as an announcement of their arrival and their wish to negotiate. Wynter held no hope in it, but for the sake of the men and women who rode with them, they had to try.

"I should be the one to go," Wynter said.

Gideon nodded. It was unusual for him to agree so readily, but they both knew he'd be tempting fate to show his face after he'd beheaded Alith's husband, Valen, in the court of swords. After further discussion, it was decided that Elias and Six would accompany her. Gideon would stay behind with the army. The anger she'd felt just moments ago quickly morphed into fear. She had no idea if Alith would honor customary negotiations. But she thought of Lark down there with Alith, possibly even Bren and Seven, and she found that a mother's courage was a very strong weapon indeed. She said a silent prayer as they began the descent.

"If she has done anything to Seven, I will gut her," Six said, from atop her horse next to Wynter. "I will cut her open while she watches and place her guts into her hands."

"Six, this kind of talk doesn't help."

"It helps me," she retorted.

Elias let out a little snort.

The closer they came to the valley floor, the more anxious Wynter became. She was desperate to catch a glimpse of her children, but there was nothing but a blur of faces, some with the tell-tale black eye marks and face paint of the Sea People, and others clad in leather armor, beating their swords against their shields in a slow, rhythmic beat. The lot of them glared at Wynter's party with furrowed brows and gritted teeth.

Intimidation tactics, she thought anxiously.

The noise made by Alith's army was making Wynter's horse uneasy, and she had to tighten the reins to steady her gait. They reined in their horses a good distance from Alith's army. After what seemed an eternity, the beating on the shields stopped, and the army parted to make way for a woman with a long, dark braid, riding forth on a beast of a horse at full gallop, along with two others. The woman was wearing brown armor plate over a white tunic with black fitted pants. A sword bounced on her hip. Though Wynter had never met her in person, she knew who it was.

Alith.

Six grunted.

Wynter also recognized the large, dark man with a black circle around one eye—Damson, the leader of the Sea People. They'd met with him years ago when he tried to sell them his sea protection for incoming cargo. The other woman who rode with Alith wore an eye patch and had long, dark blonde braids. A mantle of fur was draped over her leather shoulder braces, and a sword was strapped across her back.

Wynter briefly closed her eyes and took a deep breath. Old feelings of being nothing but a transporter surfaced, and she shook them off. *I'm the queen.* And then that lingering voice. *A queen who can no longer heal.*

She straightened her shoulders as Alith and her riders slowed, coming within a stone's throw.

A slow grin spread across Alith's face as she eyed Wynter up and down.

Six's horse started and whinnied.

"Finally, we meet," Alith said.

"We came to offer terms," Wynter said. Her face flushed.

Alith chuckled. "You are in no position to offer terms." Her eyes trailed to the precipice above where Ferran's army waited.

"There's no need for war," Wynter said.

Alith laughed and looked over at the man of the Sea People. "We couldn't agree more. There is no need for war."

Wynter could *feel* Six seething next to her.

"But you must first meet our terms," Alith added.

"Which are?" Elias asked.

"Surrender Ferran, and we'll let your prince live."

Wynter's whole body lit like a flame. "If you have harmed him—!"

Alith raised a hand and cut her off. "He's alive as far as I know. But who can say for how long," she said with a mocking smile.

"What have you done?" Wynter asked hotly.

"Someone had to find the queen's treasure. Who better than the prince of Ferran?"

It was Wynter's horse that bristled now, for she had unknowingly dug her heels into its side with her fury.

"You're nothing," Six hissed at Alith. "You're a desperate widow of a traitor, who has somehow convinced the Sea People to fight her battles!" Six spat on the ground and bared her teeth, though it seemed like the spitting was directed more toward the Sea People's leader.

Alith responded with a small smile of amusement, but the young woman next to her shifted uncomfortably in her saddle.

That must be Gilla. Wynter knew *of* her, of course—the only child of Alith's union with Valen. Hood had said he'd freed Lark from her grasp. The mother-daughter duo made the perfect revenge-seeking pair. But it was Wynter's duty to at least try and make an offer of peace.

"If you stand down now," she said, "we'll allow you to leave Ruritania peacefully and find sanctuary in another country." She then spoke to Damson. "Whatever treasure you seek here belongs to Ferran for the rebuilding of our country. Leave now and perhaps we'll look past this small transgression."

Damson's face remained stoic.

"Oh, Ferran will be rebuilt," Alith retorted gleefully. "Just not by you and your murdering husband."

Wynter placed her hand on the hilt of her sword. The desire to draw blood was stronger than she'd ever felt it. Lark was inside Devil's Rock, Bren and Seven were still missing, and the woman responsible was right in front of her. She could end Alith now.

"We're done here," Elias said, clearly sensing that the meeting was about to go awry. He nudged his horse toward Wynter's, and her horse responded by turning back willingly. Even her horse seemed to understand that Wynter was in no position to launch an attack.

The three of them galloped back up the hill, out of the valley. The future of Ferran was at stake. Her son's life was at stake. They would fight despite being outnumbered. The fate of Ferran would be determined today and written about in books for millenniums. There was a part of her that wanted to surrender to save her son, but she could not. Lark was a man now. He was no longer hers to lose. She prayed fervently, as the wind whipped across her face, that God would protect him and preserve his life.

Take my life if you must, Lord, but keep Lark safe.

When Gideon saw her face, no words were needed. Six rode past them in a fury, not even stopping to discuss the battle plan.

"Elias," Gideon said with authority. "Get the men ready."

"Yes, Your Majesty," he said, then rode back along the ranks barking commands.

"Alith sent Lark into Devil's Rock to look for the treasure," Wynter said, now that they were alone. "But there was no mention of Bren or Seven."

The news didn't seem to surprise him. "Then there's hope," he said. "Lark and Bren are smart. Perhaps Bren is even close by."

His confidence touched her: whether it was genuine or not she did not care. She cared only that he had tried to give her hope.

"I love you," she said softly.

He only nodded, for he could not lead their army without first hardening his heart. That warrior of long ago would fight once again—for Ferran and for their children.

Gideon steadied his horse and drew his sword, facing the men and women behind him. "We fight for Ferran!" he called out to them.

Weapons were raised overhead, one by one as his words made it down the line. Chants and battle cries sounded. The battle fever had begun.

CHAPTER 73

LARK

Lark's hand hurt from gripping his knife so tightly. He considered burying it in Rune's back as Rune walked away. Lira reached out and touched his arm. "We'll figure this out," she said calmly. "*Together.*"

He relaxed his grip and nodded. He'd have to pretend Rune wasn't there. He took a deep breath, but cleansing his thoughts of Rune only reignited the memory of having his eyes ripped out of their sockets by a Morbid. *The vision wasn't real,* he reminded himself. Yet his eyes burned as if a shadow of the memory remained.

"The answer to finding the treasure must be in the key," Lira said quietly.

As far as Lark knew, Rune knew nothing of the key. It was best to keep it that way. "And the key is?" he asked.

"Bottomless seas, caverns deep," she began.

Lark closed his eyes and put her words to memory, but, to his surprise, the next words came to him in a whisper. "The bones of the Great Destruction lie asleep," he murmured.

"O Great Destruction, eternal flame," Lira continued.

Lark opened his eyes. "Yet there is still one whom the treasure will claim!"

"Look, great wanderer," Lira said, smiling, "for only you will see, the crown of jewels at the bottom of the sea."

"Alas, the hour has finally come," he said excitedly.

"Extinguish the flame of the evil one!" Lira was grinning at him. His heart skipped a beat.

"Stop dallying!" Rune suddenly cried out from the entrance to the cavern.

Lark looked up at the flame that burned high above them. "The evil flame?"

"Could it really be that simple?" Lira asked uncertainly.

"There's only one way to find out." Lark handed Lira his knife, took off his shoes and socks, and dug a waterskin out of their bag and slung it across his body to put out the flame. It would be a long climb—a dangerous climb. He rolled up his sleeves while surveying the wall of rock for handholds. Every potential path he followed with his eyes came just short of the ledge where the fire burned. He'd have to hope that there were crevices up at the top that he couldn't see.

"Be careful," Lira said.

Rune stormed over with his weapon still drawn. "What are you doing?"

Lark ignored him and planted a foot in a small recess. He reached up and gripped a small indentation above him, barely big enough to take hold of. Lark wasn't particularly afraid of heights, but it had been a long time since he'd done any serious climbing. There wasn't a tree, cliff, or mountain in Isidor that he and Bren hadn't explored when they were younger. Even Seven hadn't been able to resist the temptation to try and best Lark by climbing faster and higher. But now that the fate of Ferran *and* Lira rested on his shoulders, the adventurous spirit of childhood had left him. A fall from the rock face he was climbing was enough to kill a man.

He grunted, stretching as he searched blindly with his fingers for cracks and crevices, while trying to keep his body balanced over his feet. Each pull of his fingers and push of his feet increased the ache in his muscles. He had to be careful. If he climbed too fast, the burn would intensify, and he would become paralyzed with pain and unable to continue.

"Slow and steady," Lira said calmly from below him.

"If this is some kind of trick—" Rune said.

"It's not!" Lira snapped.

There's the real Lira, he thought with a grin. Her outburst must have shocked Rune into silence for he kept quiet after that, and Lark pressed on with renewed strength.

Left hand, pull, left foot, push. Right hand pull, right foot, push. Lark focused his thoughts. Each cool touch of the wall on his hands and feet spoke a thousand words of the rock's distant birth—one of water and ice and death. The unmoving surface held within itself time before time when there was vast nothingness—before God spoke it all into being. His head swooned.

The ledge was close now. A soft glow was cast upon the rock face just above him. *The eternal flame!* But he reminded himself, lest he'd forget, who this flame belonged to.

The evil one.

Lark swallowed nervously, as he shifted his weight and moved his feet sideways across a narrow ledge, feeling above him for his next handhold. He let one foot come off the wall, and placed it in a hole above his waist, but after he pushed himself up, he could find nothing to grab onto above him. He was a few feet short of the flame's ledge. He clenched his teeth. *Sons of Ferran!* He hadn't come this far only to fail.

"Throw up your waterskin and hook it around that small rock jutting out from the ledge!" Rune yelled up.

As much as he hated to admit it, Rune's idea wasn't a bad one. He shrugged off the water pouch and let it slide down his arm. He tossed it up, attempting to ring it around a small piece of uneven rock that jutted out from the rim of the ledge. It took him several tries, but on the fourth attempt the strap looped around the rock and a quick tug let Lark know that it was secure.

"Be careful," Lira cried anxiously.

Lark took a deep breath and, with both hands on the water-skin strap, pulled up, hand over hand, climbing with his feet against the wall like a spider. His feet were warm from the fire that had penetrated down into the rock. His blood pumped with excitement. *I'm going to make it.* But just as he reached for the ledge, the waterskin strap snapped.

CHAPTER 74

BREN

Bren and Seven stood in amazement at the sudden arrival of Ferran's army. "We can't just sit back and do nothing," Bren said, biting her lip. She kept her eyes on the three Ferran riders on horses who were coming down into the valley to meet with Alith, but the figures were too far away for Bren to be sure of who they were. There would be a battle. *That* she was sure of. Alith wouldn't concede to anything, and Gideon and Wynter surely knew by now what Alith was planning or they wouldn't have come. They would never allow Alith to gain the upper hand by obtaining the queen's treasure.

"The guards have weapons, we don't," Seven replied. "There's nothing we can do."

She cut her eyes to Seven. "Could you just this once try to think beyond the obvious."

He humphed like he always did when he found her disagreeable. But then he looked at her, lingering in a way he never had before. Bren shifted her shoulders a little, feeling something the opposite of disagreeable.

"I make you nervous," he said matter-of-factly.

She scoffed. "No." That was a lie. She knew how he felt about her now. She'd seen his heart. She could see it now in his eyes.

But what did knowing the truth mean for their friendship? He was her best friend. Anything beyond that was . . . unsure. Yes, she'd toyed with the idea of there being more between them, back in Simms Branch, but he'd called her family then, and she'd buried the idea. But now . . .

". . . Is not the time for this," she said, accidentally sharing her silent thought. She felt her face flush. Thankfully, the face art would hide her embarrassment.

Seven appeared mildly confused by her strange remark but continued. "How can we get free from the guards?" he asked.

"A distraction? I don't know."

Seven scowled at something behind her.

Bren whirled around.

"That's not a bad idea," Wyck said, approaching.

Seven's whole body tensed as tight as a coiled snake. Wyck smirked with amusement. She found herself suddenly feeling awkward. Just a few minutes ago, she was about to let Wyck kiss her, and Seven had seen the whole thing. Seven's intense glaring at Wyck could have bored a hole in a wall.

Wyck planted his feet and crossed his arms. "Five of the guards have already been drawn away." Wyck was talking to Bren, but he was maintaining eye contact with Seven like they were in a staring contest. "If we're ever going to try and escape, now would be the time."

"Um . . ." she said, looking back and forth between their blatant posturing. She'd never had two men vying for her, and she was completely clueless about how to handle it.

"A distraction *is* a good idea," Wyck said, eyes still locked on Seven.

"Yes," Bren said nervously. Her heart played a nervous rhythm against her chest. "If we can draw in the guards, we may have a chance to overtake them."

Seven grunted.

Bren touched Seven's arm. "What do you think?" she asked

gently, trying to draw his attention back to her. But he ignored her, and the two men inched closer to each other.

"How about a fight?" Seven said gruffly, when he was only a foot away from Wyck.

"A . . . fight . . . nooo," she stammered.

"Great idea," Wyck said with a bit too much enthusiasm.

Bren swallowed. She immediately understood where this was going, and she didn't like it.

She shook her head. "No," she said, finding her words again. "Someone will get hurt."

Seven finally looked at her. "That's the *point*, isn't it?"

"Aye," Wyck replied heartily.

Bren took a deep, frustrating breath. If the two of them wanted to make fools out of themselves, then so be it. "Fine," she said with a huff.

"I'll let the men know of the plan." Wyck wandered back to the cave.

Bren grabbed Seven's arm. "What are you doing?" she snapped.

He gently removed her hand, his eyes still on Wyck's back. "What needs to be done."

"I rather think there's more to it than that," she retorted. "Do you care to explain?"

"No," he said simply.

Bren closed her eyes and took a deep breath. Seven was as stubborn as a crow. There would be more to this fight than just creating a distraction. But if it helped draw the guards to them . . . . "Don't hurt him," she said. Seven didn't say anything but his jaw clenched several times.

Wyck returned. "The men will wait until the fight ensues, then come out of the cave and make a show of it."

Seven nodded readily, but Bren was feeling less enthusiastic by the minute. "Listen, you two," she said. But before she could get another word out of her mouth, Wyck shoved Seven in the chest and shouted, "Big man carrying a big spear! What are you without that spear, aye? Nothing!" Wyck took two steps back and spat at Seven's feet.

Bren covered her mouth with her hands and backed away. *Daughters of Ferran!* Nobody had ever dared talk to Seven like that before. His eyes widened. And before she knew it, he was charging at Wyck, and the two of them fell to the ground with a sickening thud.

She screamed. It was not an act. She was mortified that the two of them were using the distraction to fight over her. Just as Wyck had said, the men came running from the cave. Seven and Wyck grappled on the ground, each trying to gain the upper hand. Seven quickly pinned Wyck, only to have a knee driven into his groin. He rolled off and Wyck sprang on top of him. The men surrounded the fight, nudging Bren closer to the action. She watched in horror as Wyck landed a punch to Seven's face. The men cheered.

"Give it back to him, why don't ya!?"

"Aye, come on, lad. Cry for your mommy, maybe she'll come!"

The men laughed heartily and jostled each other for a better view.

Seven grabbed Wyck and threw him off like he was tossing a child, and Wyck went flying back into his men, toppling two or three of them, who found the whole thing amusing. They scrambled to their feet and jerked Wyck up by the collar, giving him a jovial shove back toward Seven who was hunched in the shoulders like a wild bear.

"Stop this!" Bren yelled, but her voice was lost in the melee of jostling bodies and shouts for blood.

Wyck lowered his head and bolted into Seven, landing a shoulder right below Seven's ribs. Seven flinched, but that didn't stop him from folding over Wyck and picking him up by the waist, so that Wyck was hanging upside down. Wyck managed a kick to Seven's head and Seven dropped Wyck and staggered back.

Bren's breathing came faster now, her head spun, and her feet felt like they were lifting off the ground. She thought she might faint when two of Alith's guards pushed through the men with weapons drawn. Seven's eyes were wide and angry, and Wyck's face was as red as a fiery sunset. They were both breathless and sweaty, staring at each other as if gauging their next move.

"Stand down!" the two guards shouted, as they placed themselves between the two opponents.

Wyck laughed and wiped a bit of blood off his lip. "Did you hear that, Seven? They want us to stand down."

"I heard," Seven said, cracking his neck.

One of the three guards maintaining the perimeter pushed through next to Bren. His sword was drawn, but there was a knife at his waist for the taking. She clenched and unclenched her fists, anticipating the right moment to make her move.

"Return to the cave!" one of the guards shouted.

Wyck's men turned and moved slowly toward the guards behind them. The guards backed away nervously, holding their swords at the ready.

"What do you say, Seven?" Wyck stepped up to the guard in front of him and spread his arms out wide, letting the tip of the guard's blade rest against his breastbone. "Should we return to the cave?"

Seven glanced quickly at Bren. She lowered her eyes to the knife of the guard standing next to her. He seemed to understand her meaning.

Seven held up his hands in mock surrender. "I rather like it where I am."

The guard lunged at Seven with his sword and everything that happened after that was a blur of bodies. Bren picked the knife from the guard's waist next to her, but he was not to be fooled. He turned on her in a split second and his blade swept out in a long arc that she only barely managed to duck. She scrambled out of his reach, but he was on her again in seconds, and she struggled to dodge his strikes. She ran toward the cave, drawing him away from the others. *Divide and conquer*, she told herself. But she was never going to get near him with her knife as long as he had a sword. She stopped just short of the cave and turned around, letting the knife rest softly in her hand. The guard grinned and stopped running. "Go ahead. Run into the cave. You can join the prince. *If* he's still alive." He laughed heartily and spun his sword in his hand.

Bren's stomach dropped and a sick feeling formed in her gut. *Prince?* She glanced behind her at the ominous mouth of Devil's Rock.

The brute moved toward her. Angry and trapped, she pulled back her knife and threw it like her Aunt Kidron had taught her. To her amazement, the knife landed squarely between the man's eyes. He stopped in his tracks, dropped his sword, and collapsed.

She stared breathlessly at his lifeless body, unable to look away. She was dizzy and disconnected from reality. *I've killed a man.* She was too numb to move.

She looked back at the cave again. Was it possible that Lark was in the caverns? When she turned back, Seven was there standing over the man, pilfering his sword.

"You did well," he said.

She nodded. Her heart was beating strong and savagely. For the first time in her life, she felt the battle fever. It was primal and base, and it frightened her. What else was she capable of doing when pressed?

Wyck and the other men joined them. "The distraction worked," Wyck said, sounding winded. He glanced at the dead man and smiled at Bren. "Well, princess, I wouldn't want to meet you in a dark alley."

She smiled and searched the jubilant faces of the men. This was what she was meant to do. The revelation of what she'd eventually become coursed through her blood. One day she'd be queen. It wasn't a desire or something she hoped for. She was certain of it.

To her surprise, several of the men jostled Seven about and congratulated him on his performance. But *had* it been a performance?

"What now, princess?" Wyck asked, looking ruggedly handsome.

"We help fight to save Ferran. Aye?" she asked. She'd tried to sound confident and composed, but her hands were shaking.

The men responded in unison with a resounding "Aye!"

She smiled weakly. At the back of her mind, the words the man had spoken right before she'd killed him lingered. *Run into the cave. You can join the prince. If he's still alive . . .*

"We can crawl through the underbrush, staying out of sight until we're needed," Wyck suggested. "Alith won't be looking for an attack from behind."

"Seven?" Bren asked.

"I agree with this."

As anxious as Bren was to help her mother and father, there was something holding her back. "I can't go," she said, surprised to hear herself say it.

"What?" Wyck asked. "Don't worry, princess, we'll protect you," he said, placing a gentle hand on her arm.

Seven gave her a confused look.

"There's a chance Lark is inside Devil's Rock," she said.

"How can you know this?" Seven asked.

"The man I killed said the prince was inside those caverns. I must go, Seven. Even if there's a small chance Lark's in there. He's my brother."

"The brute could have just made that up, my lady," Wyck said.

Bren nodded. "The thought did occur to me." She glanced down at her Sea People attire. "Except the man didn't know who I was, did he?"

Wyck's expression softened. "Aye, he did not." He looked away as if her going into those caverns pained him.

"I will go with you," Seven said.

She turned her eyes to Seven and nodded. Of course he would go.

"My lady—" Wyck said, looking uncomfortable.

She held up a hand. "You will go help Ferran's army any way you can."

He shuffled his feet. "Are you sure?" he asked, uncertainly.

"Aye," she said with a smile, looking around at all the men. They all gave her a nod of respect. It was more than she deserved.

"Then may the good Lord make straight paths for you, my lady," Wyck said with an air of sadness.

She stepped up to him and hugged him with all her strength. He held her tightly, undeterred by the presence of his men. She whispered in his ear, "Thank you, Wyck. For everything. Perhaps one day you'll find someone to follow to the moon." She quickly kissed his cheek, then turned away and ran into Devil's Rock with Seven at her side. Wyck rallied the men as she ran, and she prayed she'd made the right decision—about going after Lark *and* leaving Wyck behind.

"Come on, let's get on with it, then! Quit standing around like a bunch of derelicts!" Wyck cried out.

CHAPTER 75

GIDEON

Pike squares, shields, and weapons that were meant to kill formed under dark storm clouds on the valley floor. Gideon's enemies stood before him with Devil's Rock at their backs. Just as he had feared, the Sea People had formed two large pike squares, 10 by 10 ranks deep, with longbowmen secured between the pikes. Alith and the rest of the army waited in reserve at the rear, ready to protect the flank and ward off any cavalry charges. The mountain passes behind them provided a perfect escape if the need arose. Alith had every advantage.

Gideon played out all the military tactics in his head—attack and withdraw, feint and redirect, swift focused blows, speed and mobility. Training and discipline had always been his allies, but how well would that serve him against eighteen-foot pikes and the long range of the Sea People's arrows? Alith had known that he would rely on cavalry and had planned accordingly. Charging horses into a pike square was a death sentence, and she knew it.

But there was more to leadership than carrying a big stick. Alith had brought her big stick—the Sea People. But would they stay the course long enough to win the battle? Alith had one weakness. She lacked the humility that came from battle experience. She would fight from a place of anger and greed and expect all the people under her command to do the same. Gideon would fight like a man after God's heart who stood to lose everything—his family, his country, and the honor of all those who had sacrificed their lives before him to unite Ferran. That is how he would win this battle—not as a dictator, but as a servant of his people.

Wynter, thankfully, had agreed to stay behind the battle lines with the wagons and assist with treating the wounded. Though she was no longer allowed to heal, lest she lose her own life, she was still able to determine if a man could be saved—if the darkness was too great to overcome. They were united in purpose, once again, as they had been when they had fought to save Ferran and unlock the Iron Gate to Isidor.

Six had not showed her face since returning from the meeting with Alith. He got the feeling there was something going on with her beyond concern for Seven. But what did he know of women? He'd almost ruined everything with Wynter over his petty jealousy. Six would fight when the time came. She may be moody and disagreeable, but she had always been loyal to Ferran's cause without fault.

He took a deep breath and lifted his eyes to the sky. The heavy storm clouds grew darker, and rumblings sounded in the distance. The same rain that nourished the ground and fed the rivers and streams rendered bows useless and bogged down men and horses in muddied battlefields. How could something as simple as rain be a blessing and a curse? Such things were the enigmas of man.

Lord God, grant me wisdom.

He emptied himself of feeling and turned in his saddle to his lieutenant to give his first order. "Elias. Charge the pikes."

Elias didn't question the order despite knowing, as Gideon did, that it was impossible to break through a pike square on horseback. Even if his soldiers made it past the arrows of the longbows, their horses would be skewered before the men could get within a sword's blade reach of a pikeman. No, this was a test—a test of the strength and discipline of the Sea People. Would they hold in the face of a battle charge?

"Mounts!" Elias shouted, as he rode in front of Ferran's battle line. Those on horses came out of the line. Gideon observed like a statue as Elias relayed the order. His men charged without hesitation as one large unit, toward the right pike, with swords and shields at the ready. The archers between the pike squares sent up a volley of arrows. Gideon's men changed direction, some veering left while others broke to the right. Enemy arrows hit his men's shields; others hit ground where only seconds before Ferran horses had left their marks.

His men continued the charge, and he watched as the Sea People's arrows dropped two of his horses and struck four of his men. Stretcher-bearers armed with shields ran into the battlefield to retrieve the wounded. The front pike rows stood firm, and his men quickly turned and retreated to the battle line.

With time, and more horses, he could keep up the attacks, perhaps weaken the enemy's resolve, but Gideon had seen all he needed to. The Sea People were seasoned fighters. They did not fear a cavalry charge. He'd have to find another way. If he tried to go around the pikes, Alith would overpower his forces with numbers. But if he broke the pikes, he'd break the Sea People's resolve, and sometimes breaking the mind of the enemy was the only thing needed to turn a battle.

"Your Majesty," Elias said, interrupting his thoughts.

"Not now," he said stiffly.

Elias steadied his horse and motioned with his head. Wynter had approached. He quickly dismounted and Elias followed suit.

"There's a group here from Simms Branch who wishes to speak to you," she said.

He frowned. "Now is hardly the time."

"I think you should hear what they have to say. They're skilled slingers."

Gideon knit his brow. "Slingers? As in David and Goliath?"

Wynter nodded. "They fled from Ruritania when Alith started rounding up those who didn't pledge their loyalty to her. They want to fight."

"Slingers," Gideon repeated.

Elias shrugged.

Gideon was going to need more than a child's toy to win this battle, but a good leader considered all options—even bad ones. He nodded once, and Elias motioned to the men behind them.

"Any word of Six?" he asked Wynter.

She shook her head and gave him a final gentle touch on the arm and returned to the wagons. He had learned over the years that her subtle touch was a way of reminding him to stay calm and hear the new arrivals out.

A large group of men and women, perhaps fifty or more, were ushered through the battle line. They were dressed in wild animal skins and had the rough-and-ready faces of those who had lived hard. All of them had a thin, braided sling tied around their foreheads and another one around their waists. A woman with a shaved head and a scarred lip stepped forward. "Your Majesty," she said with a slight bow. "My given is Ursula. We heard of your journey and have come from Simms Branch to join in the fight."

"Unless you can break a pike square, you will not be needed." He didn't mean to sound gruff, but the interruption was unwelcome.

She untied the sling at her waist, placed a small dark object in its pouch, and twirled it at her side so fast he could barely see it moving. "If we bombard the pikes with lead shot, we can break the pikes," she said with an edge of arrogance.

"Is that so?" he asked doubtfully.

She stopped spinning her sling and spat to the side. "We can beat the range of your archers even on a bad day. The Sea People's longbowmen, too."

Gideon raised an eyebrow.

"A good slinger can hit a target up to 1,300 feet, Your Majesty."

She had pluck, he'd give her that, but he didn't have time to entertain thrill seekers, much less make them part of his battle plan. She took his temporary silence as an invitation to share more.

"A pikeman makes a good fleshy target," she continued. "They need two hands to hold a pike. They have no shield to protect themselves."

"That's why they wear armor." He knew the argument was weak. The Sea People armor was a simple breast plate, but he was anxious to end the conversation. He turned to mount his horse.

Ursula grabbed him roughly by the arm, staying him. Elias drew his sword as well as the other men around him. But the Simms Branch woman held on, gritting her teeth. "A rudimentary breast plate won't save them from having their jaws shattered or their knees blown out." Then she let him go, and she and her men were quickly escorted away under threat of sword.

To his surprise, her words gave him pause. Using slingers was a risk, yes, but if these men and women were as skilled as Ursula claimed they were . . . He was torn between his pride and his humility. "Elias, do we have enough halberds and longswords to make a frontal attack?"

"Yes, but—"

"Bring them back," Gideon said, motioning with his hand.

Elias' brow knit in confusion. "Lord?"

"The slingers! Bring them back!" he said brusquely.

"Yes, Your Majesty," Elias said, looking slightly flustered. He shouted orders, and after a short delay and a few shouts, the group of slingers were ushered back through the battle line, shrugging off the hands of the soldiers who pushed them forward. Their expressions were no longer hopeful, but defiant and sour. Ursula held herself rigidly, and rightly so. He had dismissed her offer of help without giving it serious consideration.

"Ursula, can you use your slings in a coordinated attack without hitting my men?" he asked.

Her scowl softened a bit. "Aye, Lord," she said, standing a little taller. "Any one of us could hit a fly off your ass at 100 yards." Her fellow slingers laughed and jostled her from behind. She grinned. One of her front teeth was missing. Between that and the scar on her lip, he wondered if she had once been a recipient of a sling projectile. When she saw that he wasn't laughing, she lost the smile and cleared her throat. "Lord." She bent her head in submission.

Gideon held out his hand. "Let me see this lead shot of yours."

She gingerly reached into a small cloth bag tied at her waist then placed an eye-shaped projectile in Gideon's hand. It was surprisingly heavy considering its small size but, thrown at a high speed, it would no doubt do significant damage to its target. There was an engraving on it he couldn't make out. "What does it say?" he asked, handing it back to her. Her fingernails were caked with dirt.

Ursula sniffed and suppressed a smile. "*Catch.*" The other slingers chuckled, though it was more subdued this time.

"What's in this for you?" he said.

She furrowed her brow. "Alith has imprisoned my brother, Lord. As well as the brothers of others here. We come as volunteers. We don't expect anything from ye, if that's what you're getting at. We only wish to see our fellow slingers freed."

"Aye!" the other slingers chorused and nodded.

Hood had said that Bren had been broken out of prison along with a dozen men that she was now leading. Was it possible that these men were the families Ursula spoke of?

"I trust you know how to follow orders?" he asked. It wasn't a question. It was a test. To his surprise, she took a knee and bowed her head. The other slingers followed suit. They may have been a rough bunch, but it was clear they had the respect and humility that came with good character.

Ursula peered up at him. The lines around her dark eyes softened. "You have our slings and our allegiance, Your Majesty."

Gideon's heart pounded. Some might consider what he was about to do foolhardy, but he had an unexplained feeling that these men and women from Simms Branch might have come from the very hand of God. With the help of the slingers, it might just be possible to break the Sea People's lines.

"Rise," he ordered. The slingers rose in unison. "Slingers of Simms Branch! You will make a frontal assault on the longbowmen and the front line of the pikes. If the pike starts to break—"

"When it breaks," Ursula said, her face eager and hungry.

"When," he said, "the pike starts to break, you will retreat to the army's wings and support the ground assault."

"You have our word," Ursula said. The others began preparing their slings.

"Elias, bring me a longsword!"

"What's your brother's name?" he asked Ursula as an afterthought.

"His given is Wyck."

He placed a hand on her shoulder. "I want you to pretend that every lead shot you let loose has Wyck's name on it."

"Aye, Lord." For a split second he saw the eyes of a sister who loved her brother very much. Then, as if realizing she'd let her guard down, she began shouting and rousing her fellow slingers into battle fever. They quickly formed a tight circle and sang a song that Gideon had never heard before.

Bred in lust
Born of dust
A Ferrian forever be.
Battle cry

Time to die
Slingers to infinity!

Gideon looked to the skies. A lone hawk circled silently above, its wings tipping slightly in reverence to the sovereign wind. Death seemed to be following him. But he didn't need a portent in the sky to tell him so. The sky rumbled angrily, and the battle-field was bathed in darkness.

CHAPTER 76

LARK

Lark dangled precariously, hanging onto the broken waterskin strap with one hand while his back scraped against the rock wall. Every time he tried to spin around to find a handhold, the strap slipped further. The muscles in his arm were seizing, there was little else he could do. This was where it was going to end for him, and the only thing he could think about was the pain his death would bring his mother.

"Hold on!" Rune yelled out. "I'm coming up."

"I don't need your help!" Lark shouted stubbornly.

But despite Lark's plea, Rune removed his shoes and sword, and began climbing.

"Hold on, Lark!" Lira cried.

He closed his eyes and tried to relax, but the pain in his arm was becoming unbearable. He didn't know how much longer he could hold on. "Rune," he bellowed. He loathed Rune, but he had to think of Lira's well-being. "If I die, make sure Lira gets out of here alive. Promise me, you vile traitor!"

"You're not going to die," Rune growled from somewhere below him.

Lark's fingers holding the strap went numb. "Promise me!" he yelled desperately. His heart ached for Lira; he clung to the memory of her face—of her lips on his. The connection they shared was undeniable. He was stronger—better—when he was with her. "I'm almost there," Rune said breathlessly. But his voice sounded miles away. Lark kept his eyes closed and focused on the image of Lira in his mind. He wanted his best and last thought to be of her.

"Give me your hand!"

Lark opened his eyes. Rune was slightly above him with one hand on the ledge. Rune had found a handhold Lark hadn't seen. It pained him to be beholden to Rune, but he swallowed his pride and reached over and grasped Rune by the wrist. The strap snapped completely, and all his weight shifted to Rune's grip. Swaying precariously, Lark quickly found a place to plant his toes. His freed arm felt like he had stuck it inside a nest of fire ants, and he wondered if he'd even be able to grip the wall.

Rune glared down at him with a painful grimace. "Find a handgrip and let go."

"Gladly!" He mercifully found a crevice he could slide his whole numb hand into. Rune let go of his other hand, and Lark quickly took hold of a knob of rock. Rune climbed and pulled himself up onto the ledge. Lark took deep breaths and waited for the blood to return to his aching arm.

On hands and knees, Rune peered down at him with a breathless grin.

Lark hated the smug look on his face. He knew Rune hadn't helped out of any kind of affection. Rune only looked out for Rune, just like he'd done his whole life. Lark would not mistake his help for anything other than what it was—Rune ensuring they found the treasure for Alith.

Lark was about to begin climbing again when the fire behind Rune suddenly grew brighter. Rune sat back on his knees and looked back just as a ball of fire shot out over the top of his head. But what Lark first thought was an explosion of fire wasn't fire at all. A large bird *made* of fire with eyes as blue as sapphires spread its wings and shrieked. Its body and wings blazed in a swirl of purple, orange, and yellow. Its talons were as red as roses. The mythical phoenix was mythical no more.

Blazes! It wasn't a river of five colors they were looking for. It was a bird of five colors. The Devil's flame!

Lark risked a quick look down. Lira already had Rune's sword and was turning in circles, keeping the bird in her sights as it flew around the cavern, screeching its discontent. The bird swooped and dove toward Lira, but she drove it away with the sword. Without missing a beat, the phoenix flew straight up, setting its glimmering, blue eyes on its next fleshy target.

Sons of Ferran! Fate seemed determined to have Lark die on the wretched rock he was clinging to. He looked up at his only hope. *Rune.*

Rune had pulled a knife at his ankle and was trying to distract the fiery bird by waving his arms.

What's he doing? A knife would be no defense against such a creature. But the distraction worked, and the bird's flames warmed Lark's back as it passed him by and headed for Rune. Lark scaled back down the wall as fast as he could while Rune cursed at the bird and threatened to cut out its heart. Lark dared a few glimpses up while he descended. Rune was keeping the bird preoccupied with wild gyrations and loud cries, but for how long? As soon as Lark's feet hit the cavern floor, Lira was at his side, pushing Rune's sword into his hand. He backed away from the wall and looked up.

Rune was fighting a losing battle. Despite the knife Rune was sweeping out in front of him, the bird was pressing closer and closer, forcing Rune back deeper into the Phoenix's lair.

"Run!" Rune yelled out, as he stumbled a step backward.

It would have been so easy to just run and let Rune finally get what he deserved, but Rune had saved Lark's life *twice* since they'd entered the wretched caverns. Though that would not erase Rune's sins, it was enough to make Lark wonder if perhaps there was some part of Rune that cared what happened to him.

"Hey, down here!" Lark yelled up at the bird, waving his sword back and forth in a large arc. Lira waved her arms.

"Come on, you chicken!" Lark figured that would be an insult to any bird with intelligence. Whether the bird understood or not, he did not know, but the yelling did the trick. The bird turned from Rune with a piercing cry and set its sights on Lark and Lira.

"Maybe that wasn't the best idea," Lark lamented as he readied the sword.

As soon as the flaming bird began its nosedive, Rune took a flying leap and landed on its back. The creature halted mid-flight, rearing and screeching as Rune plunged his knife over and over into the bird's back. Lark watched in disbelief as the bird went into a tailspin, trying to rid himself of his intruder. How Rune was not bursting into flames Lark did not know. After a sudden bolt straight up toward the ceiling, the bird's wings suddenly folded, and it turned and began free-falling to the ground.

"Rune!" Lark cried out. Rune and the bird plummeted, and there was nothing Lark could do. The twisted pair landed with a hard thunk just a few feet away. Rune rolled off the smoldering bird—its flame nearly extinguished. The bird was dull and ordinary, now that its glory had been taken from it. Lark and Lira ran to Rune and dropped to their knees. Most of his clothes had been burned away. Every exposed part of his body was red and raw. His eyes were open, his chest moving with shallow breaths. He was staring up into the endless darkness of the ceiling.

"Rune . . ." Lark said, shaking his head in disbelief. He dared not touch him, for there was no place to touch that wouldn't bring him pain. "Why?" Lark asked, mortified at Rune's wounds.

Why did you help us?

Rune's eyes trailed over to Lark. His lips were moving. He was trying to speak. Lark lowered his ear to Rune's lips and listened to words that came barely above a whisper. "Tell Wynter . . . I'm sorry."

Lark wanted to say something in return, but no words came. Rune was watching him—waiting. The man whom Lark had hated only moments ago had died to save him and Lira. Lark nodded and gave Rune his dying wish. A peace passed over Rune's face as if he'd been relieved of a heavy burden. Then he closed his eyes, and his chest grew still.

Lark clenched and unclenched his jaw. His throat swelled with a weird sense of loss. In a different lifetime, maybe Rune could have been someone he looked up to. He shook his head in disbelief. "I don't understand, Lira. I thought I knew who he was, then he does this."

"Yet there is still one whom the treasure will claim," Lira murmured.

Words that were once a mystery were a mystery no longer. The treasure had indeed claimed its promised victim.

"Perhaps his sacrifice will cover his many sins," Lira added. "His death was not in vain."

Rune's death felt *in vain*. Larked stared at the bird, still lying in a heap. Its flames were all but exhausted, but each exhale brought with it small plumes of purple fire that ignited then flickered out.

The words of the key came flooding back. *Extinguish the flame of the evil one.*

Lark stood abruptly and swiped Rune's sword off the floor. Lira grabbed at his arm, but he shrugged her off and stormed toward the bird. He stood over it, watching it struggle to breathe. One of its sapphire eyes rolled up and looked at him. Lark gripped the sword's hilt in both hands and raised it with the tip pointing down. He set his jaw and brought down the blade, piercing the heart of the creature. The bird burst into a ball of fire, its final, high-pitched cry bouncing endlessly off the walls of the cavern. Lark stumbled backward, leaving the weapon behind. The flames devoured bird and sword until finally only a puff of inky smoke rose from the barren ground. The bird and the sword were gone—as if they had never existed.

"Sons of Ferran!" he said in horror. Lira ran to his side and latched hold of his arm. He had extinguished the eternal flame, and the treasure had claimed its life. Would the treasure now reveal itself?

They both watched the lake. Nothing happened. The treasure was still buried and unclaimed. There was no magical unveiling. No sign of Morbids in the water. This was the end of it.

"Perhaps the treasure has still not claimed its life," Lira said, looking back at Rune.

Lark returned to Rune's body and looked down at his charred remains. "We need to put him into the lake," he said, following Lira's chain of thought.

Lira slid a hand across Lark's back. "It seems wrong, after what he did for us."

"At least now his life will finally be used for something good." It was the best he could do for Rune. Perhaps in the end God *had* forgiven him.

Together, the two of them took a hold of Rune's hands and feet and lugged him to the edge of the water. Lira muttered a final prayer, and they knelt and rolled Rune's body into the water. There was a small suck of air as the body sank and was overtaken by the water. The surface stilled. They stood and waited expectantly. For a moment there was nothing but a peaceful calm. Then the ground beneath their feet began rumbling.

CHAPTER 77

GIDEON

A westerly wind brought with it a salty brine smell. Rain was coming. Alith rode her white horse behind the pike squares, calling to her foot army with her sword raised. Damson sat atop his horse staring toward Gideon's army. She had more men than she needed, and Gideon had too few.

"Slingers!" Gideon shouted. "Forward!"

Elias shifted nervously in his saddle next to him.

The slingers ran into the field shouting war cries at the top of their lungs. Their slings swirled in a blur by their sides. It was like trying to watch a whirlwind. His battle line waited, shouting obscenities at the enemy, and banging their swords against their shields. Lightning flashed across the sky and thunder rumbled in the distance. A spattering of fat raindrops began falling.

The slingers loosed projectiles one after another with a speed and distance Gideon never imagined possible. His hand tightened around his horse's rein as a barrage of lead shot hit the front lines of the Sea People and body after body crumpled. Even at a distance, he heard the sickening crack of shattered bone. The Sea People's longbowmen loosed their arrows, but the slingers were just out of range, and the arrows pierced the ground in a barrage of empty thuds.

"Sons of Ferran," Elias whispered next to him. "I've never seen such a thing."

"Ferran archers!" Gideon shouted, not missing a beat.

The mounted crossbow archers spurred their horses, crashing through the valley undergrowth to charge the pikes. Two groups swept out in wide arcs to attack the sides of the pikes. The horsemen drew the fire of the Sea People archers, allowing the slingers to come in close enough to render the longbows useless against them. The heavy longbow was meant for long-range volleys, not close contact.

The Sea People steadily lost their front row to the slingers' projectiles. They frantically pushed and pulled bodies out of the way and replaced the downed pikemen with others from the second row. But even as the replacement pikemen stepped up, the slinger's projectile barrage continued, and the Sea People continued to fall.

Another volley of arrows came from the Sea People, again targeting Gideon's archers on horses, but most were able to avoid the volley by changing direction. His archers released their arrows into the sides of the pike squares and retreated. Men fell on both sides in the exchange.

Gideon could still make out Alith's white horse at their flank. She was riding furiously back and forth, continuing to stay her army, as the battle unfolded.

She didn't expect me to attack the pikes.

But Gideon knew something she didn't. Break the will of the Sea People and the pikes would break. They had only to believe he had the upper hand.

Gideon dismounted and one of his men handed him a long shield. They would go forward now without horses and archers, for as soon as the rain started, the bows would be rendered useless, and the horses would become mired in the mud.

"With me!" Gideon shouted as he marched in front of the battle line with sword raised. The men beat their shields with their swords and growled and cursed. He joined the center where the worst of the fighting would take place. He would not hide behind his crown. The men would fight harder if their king fought with them. And he would need them to fight harder today than they'd ever fought before.

"Shields!" he cried out. The line locked shields in a thunderous chorus that vibrated in his ears.

The sky finally let loose its fury and a deluge bathed the battlefield. "Forward!" he shouted above the roar of the pummeling rain.

They charged as one—a wall of shields, blades, and men— their single purpose—to destroy and kill. They ran close together, their minds lost to their weapons. The Sea People released what was likely their last volley of arrows. Gideon's army dropped in one accord to one knee, forming a shield wall above and around them that encased them like a cocoon. As soon as the arrows finished pounding against their shields, the men were up and running again.

So Gideon ran. Ran with his men through a thick veil of rain toward an uncertain destiny. Suddenly he felt old. The thrum of his heartbeat in his ears sounded distant as if he were miles away from the battlefield. The faces of all the men he had killed flashed before his eyes—the men whose blood he'd shed and bones he'd crushed. Grave upon grave of fathers, husbands, and brothers. But he knew, even now, once he sensed the enemy's fear, the battle fever would swell, and once he smelled the blood, he would want more. The battle line split and half went left with Elias to attack the left pike, and half went right with Gideon to attack the right pike. The slingers took their attack to the long-bowman whose bows had now been rendered useless by the rain.

Gideon's men charged into the pike squares with long shields, two-handed giant swords, and hooked halberds. His men in light armor, armed with daggers, quickly dropped to the ground and crawled like hidden vipers underneath the forest of tangled pikes, swords, and halberds. They stealthily slashed the ankles and knees of unsuspecting Sea People, then jumped on top of them as soon as they fell and cut their throats. The water beneath Gideon's feet turned red and there was no distinguishing between the rain and the blood.

Gideon numbed himself to the screams, the blood spray, the anguished cries of men calling for their wives and mothers. Finally, they managed to carve out a gap in the pike square—a path of dead bodies and broken pikes that led right into the center of the square. Gideon continued to shield pike thrusts for his men welding giant swords as they cut to his left, then to his right. Gideon called his men forward and they scrambled over dead bodies and broken pikes to hack away at the formation's center. Some pikemen dropped their pikes and fought back with knives, but others began pushing their way out of the squares to escape when they realized the pike square was slowly collapsing.

"Rear!" someone shouted.

Gideon ran back to survey the battlefield. Alith and Damson had finally left the safety of the flank and had circled around the pike squares to attack Gideon's rear. If he and his men got caught between the pike squares and Alith's army, there would be a slaughter. The pikemen would take courage and reignite their efforts. He couldn't let that happen.

"Flanks!" Gideon yelled above the torrential rain. "Flanks!" And the call was passed along the fighting men.

CHAPTER 78

LARK

The ground quaked, and the teal lake churned like an angry ocean, spilling water over the edges and under their feet. They backed cautiously away.

"Any chance your mother gave you more clues?" Lark asked Lira.

"I'm afraid not," she said, her voice filled with apprehension.

"I don't like the look of this." He handed Lira the extra knife Rune had killed the Phoenix with. "Go for the eyes," he said. If the vision they'd shared earlier was accurate, there was a good chance Morbids were getting ready to come out of the lake.

The ground shook more violently now. They fought to keep their footing and weapons steady. The water bubbled as if boiling. A large shadow rose from the depths of the lake. Water fell away as the mysterious silhouette surfaced.

"Sons of Ferran!" Lark cried.

A slab of rock almost as big as the lake itself broke the surface of the watery depths. But it was what was on that rock that sent Lark's heart racing—chest upon chest stacked upon one another in a kind of haphazard pyramid.

"The treasure!" Lira called out over the rumblings.

Lark smiled, even though the whole cave sounded like it was

about to come down on their heads. They'd found the queen's treasure!

The rising rock platform ground to a halt, and they both stood there, paralyzed with shock as water cascaded off the stack of chests. He took a step toward the treasure, but Lira stayed him with her hand. He frowned. "What's wrong?"

"Something isn't right," she said cautiously. "There were Morbids in our vision."

"We found the treasure, Lira! Things couldn't be more right! Besides, how can a creature like a Morbid live beneath the water? They're land creatures." He tucked his knife inside his belt and inched toward what now looked like an island surrounded by a few feet of water.

"Wait," Lira said. She ran to gather their bag and quickly lit a new torch. "Be careful," she said, handing him the torch.

He nodded and jumped over. He was practically bursting with joy. He wouldn't just be a footnote in the pages of history, he'd be much more—he'd be the one to rebuild Ferran.

He tried to hold the torch steady as he flipped the latches of one of the chests. The lid creaked as he lifted it. His eyes alighted as he beheld the dazzling display. The chest was full of a gold coin, diamond-encrusted jewels, gemstones, silver chalices, candlesticks.

Perhaps I will be king after all.

"Lark!" Lira cried.

"This is it, Lira! We found the queen's treasure!"

"Lark!"

He dug his hand into the chest, letting his fingers sift through the cold fortune. "It's marvelous, Lira!"

His joy was met with silence. He turned, expecting to see Lira's smile. Instead, Gilla stood a few feet from Lira, with her sword drawn. Lira was standing her ground with her knife firmly in her hand, but a knife against Gilla's skilled swordsmanship would be like fighting a bear with a stick. Gilla scanned the cavern nervously, keeping a close eye on Lira.

Lark glanced at the treasure and back to Lira. He cursed under his breath. What a fool he was. The only treasure he truly cared about was on the other side of the water, and the thought of losing her was like a knife to his heart.

"Where's Rune?!" Gilla barked, calmly taking in the treasure. "I know he followed you here."

Lark had assumed that Alith had sent Rune, but Gilla's agitation suggested otherwise. Had Rune come on his own volition? Against orders? The idea was sobering.

"He's dead, Gilla," Lark said resignedly. "The treasure is yours. Put your sword away."

"You're lying," she said, baring her teeth. Her eye darted around the cavern as if she expected Rune to pop out of the shadows.

"He's not lying!" Lira said angrily. "We pushed his body into the water!"

"It's true," Lark said.

"You killed him?" Gilla asked skeptically, looking from Lira to Lark.

"No," he said. "He was killed by a bird of fire hiding in the ledge above you."

She took a quick look up the face of the rock. "Then he got what he deserved," she said flatly. "Throw your knife over," she said to Lark.

He tossed his knife across the water. It landed near Gilla's feet with a clang. She picked it up and tucked it inside her belt. She came to the edge of the water and motioned him over with her sword.

He leaped back across the water, keeping an eye on Lira. She still had her knife, but Gilla must have decided she was not a threat and was focused fully on Lark. He held up his hands in surrender. "Let us go, Gilla. You and Alith got what you wanted."

Gilla laughed, her eye patch crinkling. "You think I got what I wanted?"

"The treasure is yours. You won!" he exclaimed.

Gilla pressed the tip of her sword against his gut. Lark flinched. She bared her teeth at him. "You think I care about any of this?" she hissed. "I have no father and a mother who only cares about avenging his death. But you? You've gotten everything you've ever wanted. Haven't you?"

Lark swallowed as Gilla pierced him just enough to draw a trickle of blood. Sweat poured down his back.

She grinned. There were years of contempt etched on her face. She would kill him. "I always finish what I start," Gilla said. "Now neither of us gets what we want." She licked her teeth and was ready to plunge her sword into Lark, but suddenly she stiffened and gasped. Her one eye widened, and she turned slowly. Lira was standing behind her with a bloody knife in her hand—her eyes angry.

"Daughters of Ferran, Lira!" he cried out.

Lira's face was wild and ferocious. "You thought I wasn't a threat," she said to Gilla, who was now swaying and fighting to remain standing. "You thought wrong."

Gilla collapsed to the ground, and her body grew still.

Lark stood with his mouth agape. Yet another layer of Lira had been unveiled. He quickly reclaimed his knife from Gilla's belt and grabbed her sword.

Gilla was dead.

For the briefest moment, he felt sorry for her, and he understood, maybe for the first time, that his parents weren't his enemy. He had exchanged the truth for a lie. There was no glory in self-serving ambition—only destruction. He finally understood Gotz's words. *With humility comes revelation.* With that thought came something else—a knowing. Gotz was dead. Lark felt it as sure as the sun rose every morning. Perhaps he even knew before he'd left Isidor that he would not see Gotz again. Hadn't there been a burning in his heart to stop at Gotz's cottage one last time?

"Lark," Lira said nervously, looking toward the treasure.

He turned.

Dozens of slimy Morbids were crawling out of the water, up, around, and over the top of the treasure, moving toward Lark and Lira.

"Will this torment never end!?" Lark cried out.

The Morbids were multiplying faster than he could think. Would he and Lira be able to fight off a brood of Morbids with just a sword and two knives? He wouldn't give up. Not now—not when he'd finally figured out who he was and what was important. He wouldn't let it end like this.

He readied his sword and handed Lira his knife so that she would have a knife in each hand. Suddenly, fear fled, and anger swelled. A dozen Morbids charged them like wild boars. He slashed every Morbid that came—both high and low. Lira yelled as a warrior in battle would as she kicked and stabbed the spindly beasts. Their accursed bodies screeched and fell to Lark and Lira's blades. But still more came. Lark became lost in a frenzy of blade and blood. He was only mildly aware that he was bleeding. He did not feel his wounds. He felt nothing but bloodlust and a desire to destroy, and he lunged and plowed his sword into another slimy, screaming mass, even as he crushed more with his feet. The creatures became faceless to him. He lost his fear of dying, or having his eyes torn from his face. A Morbid wrapped itself around his neck, and Lark reached back and sliced his sword across its back. The creature fell to the ground. Every hand that sought to kill him he slayed. He was fighting his past, his present, and his future, and he didn't care whether he lived or died, only that Lira lived.

"They're too many!" Lira screamed. But Lark was numb to her voice. He kicked and stabbed, and punched and blood covered him like a wave he might drown in. He was succumbing to madness. Perhaps this was what happened in the end—the loss of all reason and understanding, when man became nothing but primal—instinctive. A dead man walking. His sword arm became heavier and heavier. His legs weaker—as a torrent of

Morbid claws tore and ripped through his pants and dug into muscle, trying to bring him down for the kill. He stumbled and was about to fall, when the Morbids attacking him screeched and ran away. He swayed and sought to steady himself. A wide-eyed Lira glanced his way. She never looked so afraid and so beautiful at the same time.

"Take that, you foul-breathed monkey!" a voice from the abyss screamed out.

He turned listlessly toward the voice, blood streaming down his face and neck.

A woman with short hair and face paint had joined the fight. A dark man spun his spear and sent it through two Morbids at once. They fought like . . .

Bren? Seven?

Of course, it couldn't be them.

I'm dreaming.

It was a wonderful dream of his sister and Seven coming to his rescue. His sword fell from his hand and the clang echoed endlessly in his head. He labored to breathe. His heartbeat slowed. He turned his head to Lira. She was fighting—stabbing a Morbid in the eye that had jumped on her. He smiled at her resolve and opened his mouth to speak, but words would not come.

I love you, Lira.

Then his breath left him, and his world went dark. His spirit departed and flew away into untold light and peace.

CHAPTER 79

GIDEON

The pike formations had been severely weakened and even now were continuing to break apart as Gideon's men on the inside of the pike squares continued fighting. Alith's army had circled around his army and was charging on foot toward Gideon, brandishing their shields, swords, pole axes, and spears.

"Shield wall!" Gideon shouted as rain washed down his face and into his mouth. His men fighting at the ends of the pikes stopped and joined the formation. He ran to the center, knowing Alith's bloodlust would drive her straight to him.

"Shield wall!" He cried out again above the rolling thunder as men continued to join the line from the left and the right pikes.

The long, mournful horn of the Sea People sounded. They were retreating. *Why?*

His men locked shields and waited for the harrowing crash of shields and swords as a river of muck washed over their feet. Despite the retreat of the Sea People, they were still outnumbered. They would live or die in the mud, rain, and blood. He wiped a hand down his face and prepared for the worst. That's when he saw them, above the hills through the thick rain—like ghosts hidden in the veil. He was either mad or salvation had come. The mirage was charging down the hill toward Alith's flank, and she was none the wiser, for the pounding rain had drowned out all sound.

The sky released a thunderous roar and the ground shook with its fury. He gritted his teeth, as Alith's shield wall plowed into Ferran's army. Men on both sides hacked over and under shields with their swords and spears. Blood flowed and the water washed it away as if it were nothing. All Gideon's men had to do was hold the line. Alith's shield wall quickly turned into disarray as half of her army was forced to turn and fight the surprise attack from the rest of Ferran's army. The bloodlust ran through him like a disease. He threw down his shield and parried the desperate attacks of a man, then plunged his blade deep into the man's gut. He ducked under an ax, catching a far glimpse of Six and Kidron, savagely slashing their way toward him. Alith's men and women began surrendering as they discovered they were trapped. Weapons and shields fell to the ground, and one by one Alith's soldiers knelt on the muddy ground and put their hands behind their heads in surrender. Within seconds, the rain stopped as the storm moved past.

The fight was ending, but not without a price. The valley was littered with bodies. Gideon's clothes had been stained with the price of war. By the time he'd made his way toward Six and Kidron, Alith was already on her knees next to the Sea People's leader, surrounded tightly by a band of Gideon's men, who were cursing and spitting at the defeated traitors. Six was threatening Gideon's men with her own sword and screamed for them to move back. Gideon grasped her shoulder, and she spun around. Never had he seen her eyes so filled with hatred.

"We've won," he said simply.

"Damson is mine," she growled quietly.

He studied her face looking for a reason, any reason why she had singled the man out, but he found none. Reluctantly, he nodded to the men, and they moved aside.

Six approached Damson and lifted her sword. He did not cower or flinch. He looked Six straight in the eye, unwavering and stoic. "Seven has turned out to be a fine man."

Gideon flinched. *Seven? How did this man know Seven?* Gideon's men exchanged confused glances.

"How would you know what kind of man he is?" Six hissed, keeping her sword raised.

"Because he's here. I have talked to him."

Six gritted her teeth and tightened her grip on her sword.

Damson motioned with his chin toward the mountains. "He's there, just outside of Devil's Rock."

"Go check," Gideon said, turning to one of his men. He approached Six and gently pushed her sword arm down. She scoffed and turned away.

"How do you know Seven?" Gideon asked the man. Alith remained quiet but her eyes held Gideon in contempt. At first the man only stared into the distance.

"How do you—?"

"He's my son."

Gideon's throat tightened. He looked over his shoulder at Six. Her back was to him, her arms crossed. *She's kept this from me all these years. Did Wynter know?* Gideon's mind raced, trying to piece together the timing. It would have been twenty years ago . . . when . . . Damson had come to Isidor to offer his "protection" services on the high seas. Gideon's heart leaped and anger boiled through his veins. This man had taken advantage of Six under Gideon's own roof! No wonder she'd never mentioned Seven's father. Seven had been conceived in violence and shame. Now he would avenge Six's honor. "You sick—" Gideon raised his sword.

"No!" Six cried out, grabbing Gideon by the arm.

"He deserves to die," Gideon said stubbornly.

"I loved him," she whispered so no one else could hear.

"What?" he asked quietly. He was surprised to see tears in

Six's eyes—tears of a lost love—a future that never came to be. "He didn't hurt—?"

She shook her head. Gideon handed his sword to one of his men and led Six gently out of ear's reach. He needed to understand. They stood there, the two of them—both too stubborn to speak first.

"I fell in love with him," Six finally said, swiping away her tears. "He begged me to go back with him and become his wife, but I said no." She covered her face with her hands and sobbed.

"Sons of Ferran, Six." He pulled her into a gentle embrace and held her as she wept against his bloodied, cold armor plate. "God help me, Gideon. I should have told you," she said miserably. Despite the animosity that had always existed between the two of them, Gideon cared about Six and her well-being. Six and Seven were family in every sense except by birth.

After a few moments, Gideon said, "Crying is not the way of the Jutta, you know."

She nodded and backed away, wiping her face. "Finally, you say something I can agree with."

Gideon spotted Wynter racing across the battlefield, searching frantically among the dead bodies. He waved his arm, and relief flooded her eyes as she ran toward him. She rushed into his arms, but only for a moment. She turned to Six, and the relief on her face turned to a scowl. "What's happened?" she asked Gideon.

"It wasn't me this time," he said.

Wynter touched Six gently on the arm. "What is it? What's wrong?" she asked, searching Six for wounds. "Are you hurt?"

Six shook her head. "No."

"Then what?" she asked, looking to Gideon.

But it was Six who spoke. "The leader of the Sea People is Seven's father," she said quietly.

Wynter looked from Six to Gideon and back to Six. "Daughters of Ferran! You're serious. Did he—?"

"No!" Gideon and Six said at the same time.

"Lord!" one of Gideon's men cried out. "Seven is here."

"That means Bren—?" Wynter ventured.

"Let's hope so," he said.

The three of them returned to where Alith and Damson were being held. "Well?" Gideon asked the man he sent to search for Seven. "Is Seven here?"

"Yes, Lord." The man's face was troubled. He was holding something back.

"Out with it!"

"Seven and the lady Bren were last seen running into Devil's Rock." The man's knees were trembling.

"Bren," Wynter breathed.

"Why would they do such a foolish thing?" Six asked.

Alith smiled. Blood stained her teeth where her lip had been split open. "You've forgotten! I sent Lark into Devil's Rock to find the queen's treasure."

"You worthless creature!" Wynter sprang at Alith, but Gideon caught her by the arm.

Alith tsked. "Too bad Bren and Seven will be too late to save him. If only you had surrendered earlier, perhaps you could have saved them all. You've killed your own children."

Gideon felt the fight drain from Wynter. He released her, and she stumbled backward in a kind of shocked disbelief.

Alith set her jaw and stared at him with soulless, vengeful eyes. "Now you both will know what it is to lose someone you love."

Gideon calmly held out his hand to one of his men. "Give me a sword."

There was an awkward hesitation as the men all around him exchanged uncertain looks.

"Now!"

A sword was placed in his hand. He tossed it on the ground in front of Alith. "Pick it up."

Her eyes widened.

Gideon held out his hand again, and his own sword was

placed in his hand. "Valen died with honor," he said to Alith. "You will die in shame."

"You expect me to fight you?" she asked, horror spreading across her face.

"No, Alith. I expect you to take your own life so I don't have to sully my blade with your accursed blood."

Alith looked over at Damson, but Damson offered no support. He was staring straight ahead, emotionless. She stared at the sword for a moment then reached out a trembling hand. As soon as her fingers touched the bloodied hilt of the sword, she jerked her hand back.

"Suit yourself," Gideon said. He took two steps, Damson instinctively fell to his side, and with a single sweep of his sword, Gideon took Alith's head.

The last thing he remembered of that moment was Wynter's piercing wail of grief for her children.

CHAPTER 80

BREN

When Lark fell, something inside Bren broke, and she knew—she knew he was gone because there was an indescribable pain of despair in her heart.

"Go help Lark!" Lira shouted as she stabbed a Morbid climbing her dress.

Bren mindlessly gutted a Morbid and another jumped on her back. Seven ripped it off and threw it to the ground. She finished it with her sword. "I've got Lira!" he cried. "Go!" So, she hacked her way to her brother, barely registering the sea of Morbids who were clamoring over each other to reach her. Her only thought was of Lark.

Please don't let it be too late, Lord.

She'd never forgive Lark if he died for something so vain as treasure. His journey to find it had been foolhardy from the beginning. Why hadn't she tried harder to stop him?

She skewered a Morbid, then pulled its flailing body off her sword and tossed it into the lake. She dropped to her knees by Lark's side. The Morbids scurried away from her, as if wanting nothing to do with their own kill. His body was bloody, and his face was covered in bleeding claw marks. One leg had been torn open to the bone. Yet he seemed only to be sleeping.

She placed her hands on his body. Emptiness. She closed her eyes and dug deeper. Never had she experienced such utter darkness. Cold seeped venomously into her bones, welcoming her. She spoke into the nothingness. *Lark, come back to me.* Perhaps some part of him, however small, could still hear her. She did not know how to heal death, so she poured her breath into him, willing it into his lungs, his heart, his soul. She gasped for more air, emptying it into dark places. The air vanished inside Lark as soon as she gave it. A fire only needed a spark, she told herself. She would be that spark.

Her life drained slowly, from every part of her. She felt it flee, even from the strands of her short hair. How was it possible to feel such a thing as a single strand of hair? She did not care that she was slipping away. She would not let Lark go without her this time. If this was to be her final act, then it would be an act of sacrifice.

I love you, brother.

And when there was nothing left in her to give, she screamed until her world went black.

CHAPTER 81

———

WYNTER

Three Days Later

Wynter lifted the hem of her black mourning dress and sat on the side of Bren's bed.

"The pyre for the funeral is ready," Gideon said, entering the room.

Wynter rubbed the back of Bren's hand with her thumb. "I should have done better with our children."

Gideon's warm hand slid over her shoulder. "You are a wonderful mother."

"No," Wynter said, shaking her head. She was weary from all they had endured in the past days, and melancholy and regret had set in. "I should have taught her how to use her gift properly. How *not* to use it. I thought I had more time."

"We both did," he said. "What's done is done."

"Look at her hair, Gideon," she said miserably. "Her beautiful hair all chopped off and now it's turned white. Think of what she's endured."

"Think of what she's accomplished," he said. "Her new white hair will make her look wise when she becomes queen."

Wynter stood up and faced Gideon. She'd been keeping her secret long enough. It was time he knew. "There's something I have to tell you."

Gideon's brow wrinkled with concern.

"I've been keeping something from you because I didn't want you to worry."

Gideon took her gently by the arms. "Are you sick? Have you tried to heal Bren? Is that it?"

She shook her head. "No, that's not it. I promised you I would let her heal in her own time, without my help."

"Then what is it?"

She strolled over to the windows and looked out over Ruritania. The city was awake, and its people milled about the streets, smiling and embracing one another. Wynter wrapped her arms around herself and rubbed her arms. She envied the joy they must have been feeling in their hearts now that they were free from Alith's rule.

"I'm with child, Gideon," she said simply. When he didn't say anything, she turned toward him. He was staring at her with a rare look of disbelief.

"Well?" she asked. "Aren't you going to say anything?"

"How?" he managed.

"For Ferran's sake, I think you know how!"

He shook his head. "I mean, how is it possible? I thought the doctor said you couldn't . . . you wouldn't . . ."

She had no answer for him, for she did not know herself. It had been twenty years since the twins had been born. She had long given up hope of having more children.

"How long have you known?" he asked.

"I knew before we left Isidor. I did not tell you because I knew you would not let me come."

She felt herself coming unraveled. Between Lark, Bren, and the pregnancy—how would she keep herself together? And today . . . the funeral. She turned back to the window, and the tears flowed. Suddenly Gideon was at her side, turning her around and wiping her tears away with his thumbs. "I'm such a fool," he said. "I went on about my brother like some jealous adolescent, and all this time you were carrying our child." He put his forehead against hers. "Forgive me."

Wynter sniffed and nodded.

"I love you," he said, pulling her into his arms.

She closed her eyes and took comfort in Gideon's embrace.

"I will love this baby," he said.

"You will?"

"Of course, I will," he said, pulling back. He smiled. "We both will. Is it too soon to hope for a girl?"

She smiled through her tears. He kissed her tear-stained lips.

"Please stop," Bren said, "or I might go blind."

They both were startled and turned. Bren was sitting up in the bed rubbing her eyes.

"Bren!" Wynter cried out, hurrying to her bedside. "Darling, we were so worried." She looked back at Gideon.

"You gave us a real scare," he added.

Bren scanned the room. "Where are we?" she asked, looking confused.

"Ruritania," Gideon said. "We were waiting for you to recover before returning home."

"Ruritania? Alith—"

"Is dead," Wynter finished. "The battle has been won. The treasure—"

"I don't care about the treasure," Bren said gruffly.

Wynter took her hand. "It will take you a while to regain your strength."

Bren's face darkened when she realized they were wearing mourning clothes. "When's the funeral?" she asked.

Bren looked to Gideon.

"Soon," he said.

"I want to go."

"I don't think that's a good idea," Wynter said.

"I'm going!"

Wynter would have preferred Bren to remain in bed, but she hated to refuse her. Gideon left the room, and had soup brought up, but Bren only managed a few spoonfuls then insisted she was fine. Wynter helped her into a green linen dress she had picked up for her at a local shop. It would have to do. She didn't dare tell her about how her hair had turned white or that Seven had left after finding out that Damson was his father. Some things were best left for later, when she was stronger.

Gideon returned and gathered them, and they walked slowly together down the street to a small town square. There was already a large gathering there. Between the army (wounded and otherwise) and the curious citizens of Ruritania, it was a showing that would befit any royal.

A pyre had been built, the body wrapped in linen and clothed with herbs and flowers. Only now that they had arrived would the fire be lit.

Wynter wrapped an arm around Bren's waist. She could feel the weakness in her and wondered how she was even standing. Bren began shaking. "Mother," she said urgently. "I can't do this." Her eyes were watery and wild. "I can't . . ."

Wynter exchanged confused looks with Gideon.

"What's wrong, dear?" Wynter asked.

Bren looked back and forth between Wynter to Gideon. "What's wrong?" she asked, incredulously. "How can you ask me that?"

The pyre was lit, and the flames quickly engulfed the body.

"No!!!!" Bren cried. Her knees gave way and she collapsed to the ground. Gideon lifted her into his arms, and she buried her face into his chest and sobbed. "I couldn't save him, Father. I tried. I really tried."

Then, the realization of who Bren thought had died struck Wynter. She had thought she had no tears left, but more came. That her daughter would suffer with such guilt and sorrow was more than she could bear. She laid a hand on Bren's head. "Look," Wynter said gently. Bren shook her head. "Look, my darling, and let your heart sorrow no more." Bren lifted her head off Gideon's chest.

Lark was standing there, leaning on a cane. He didn't much look himself, for his face was scabbed over from claw marks and his once thick hair had been chopped off. He would have to walk with a cane for the remainder of his days.

Bren's face paled. "Lark?" she asked with a flood of tears in her eyes. Gideon gently set her down but held onto her to keep her steady. "Lark?" she asked again, blinking. She took an uncertain step toward him.

"Sister," he breathed.

Wynter put a hand to her mouth as Bren fell into Lark's arms. He held her gingerly with one arm and they sobbed in each other's arms.

"Oh, Gideon," Wynter said, lacing her arm under his. "She thought Lark was—"

He nodded. There were traces of tears in his eyes. Rarely did Gideon show such vulnerability. But they both knew that it was a miracle that the only loss they were mourning on this day was his lieutenant, Elias, and not Lark. Their children were alive. And though it pained her that Lark and Bren would both carry the scars of their mistakes for the rest of their lives, she understood that they were survivors—they all were.

She placed her hand on her stomach, and Gideon kissed the top of her head. Lark and Bren joined them, and they stood in a line and held hands, together, as a family, as the sparks of Elias' pyre lifted into the sky.

CHAPTER 82

____

BREN

Six Months Later

"Did you hear?" Lark asked. "Father asked Wyck to start training an official Ferran regiment of slingers in Ruritania."

Bren plucked a wildflower petal from its stem and threw it into the river. She watched it float downstream until it disappeared. Everything seemed to be disappearing from her life lately. She lifted her eyes to the trees. The leaves in Isidor were already beginning to change, and soon another winter would be upon them. She was certain it would be a winter of the worst sort—cold, hard, and bitter—snowdrifts as white as her hair.

"Hello?" Lark said.

He was spread out next to her on a blanket, propped up on one elbow, fiddling with his cane. He'd dragged her out of the castle with some lie about wanting to spend time with his sister.

"I heard you," she said. "Wyck will make a fine teacher."

"And what about Six?" he asked. "Did you ever think you'd see the day when Gideon would appoint her as his lieutenant?"

Bren shrugged. "I guess they've finally put aside their differences."

Gotz's hawk, Kia, landed next to her and dropped the small mouse in her beak by Bren's side. Kia belonged to Bren now and the bird was ever trying to please her. Kia began preening her black-speckled feathers.

"And of course," Lark continued, "the biggest surprise of all is that we are going to have a new brother or sister very soon. I suppose you're hoping it's a girl?"

"I don't know."

Lark sighed. "When are you going to stop brooding over Seven? You can't live the rest of your life like this."

Heat rose to her face. "Can't I?" she asked bitterly. She stood up, grabbed the folds of her dress, and stomped up the pathway through the woods that led back to the castle. Kia took flight and called out.

Coming here with Lark was a mistake.

She didn't want to be cheered up, and she didn't want his sympathy.

"Bren!"

She ignored him. It was easy for Lark to go on with life, wasn't it? He and Lira were soon to be married, and after that they'd be moving to Ferran to oversee its rebuilding. She would be left in Isidor, alone, with a head of white hair, and a lonely future as queen.

Lark hobbled up beside her, out of breath. "Stop," he said, taking her gently by the arm. "I'm sorry. I know you miss him."

She pulled her arm away. "It's quite a bit more than that, isn't it? You were the one who saw what was between us even before I did."

Lark rubbed his bearded chin. "There are plenty of men who would have your hand. Wyck, for example." His eyes lit up.

She shook her head in disbelief. "And there are plenty of women who would have your hand, yet Lira seems to be the only one who has captured your heart. Should you settle for someone else?"

He pinched the bridge of his nose. "You're right. I'm sorry. What can I do?"

"Nothing," she said. A small stab of guilt tickled the edges of her conscience. She didn't want Lark to worry about her or feel responsible for her happiness. He deserved a life unfettered from her. "Listen," she began. "I wish you and Lira nothing but happiness. You both deserve to be happy, Lark. I'll be fine." She smiled weakly. "Our parents will have me busy learning warfare, negotiation, and kingdom management. This is my destiny, and you must go on to fulfill yours."

"Seven could still come back," he said, trying to sound hopeful.

She touched his arm. "It's been six months. Perhaps he'll never forgive Six for keeping the identity of his father from him. But it matters not. I'm to be queen one day, and I have much to do to prepare." She put on a happy face for Lark's benefit, but inside she felt nothing but hollow emptiness.

Lark took her hand. "You and me forever. Aye?"

Bren knew he was saying what he thought she wanted to hear, and she loved him for that. She smiled and embraced her brother warmly. "Aye," she said. "Always."

Lark took a step back and stared into the woods with a faraway expression. After a moment, he looked back and said, "Don't be too hard on him."

"What?" she asked.

He smiled and winked at her, then limped up the trail with his cane.

She stood there perplexed, trying to make sense of his words. She scanned the woods where he'd been staring, but nothing caught her eye. *Don't be hard on whom?*

Bren pushed ahead. The first dropping of acorns crunched under her feet. Lark was out of sight now. She was puzzling over his little riddle when she stepped out into the meadow behind the castle and came face-to-face with the last person she expected to see.

"Seven," she whispered, scarcely believing her own eyes. She took a stunned step backward, her heart racing fiercely with the sudden proximity.

He seemed taller, more handsome (if that was possible). He'd let his hair grow longer, and a slight beard was visible on his chin. He towered over her like a dark shadow in leather and fur. His figure was imposing and statuesque, like the warrior he was. She felt her face burning with a fierce flame.

"Bren," he said.

They stood staring at each other. In that quiet moment, the past came flooding back, and the lifetime of memories they had shared together stood between them as if they'd come to a crossroads where they both would have to decide if they would carry on together or go their separate ways.

"You came back," she finally said.

"I forgot something."

"Oh," she said. "Your spear, I suppose. It's . . . up at the castle. They were able to recover it," she said, gesturing vaguely to the stately castle on the hill.

"I'm glad to hear it, but I think we both know that's not why I came back."

"Do we?" she asked, wiping away a stray tear.

"I'm sorry," he said, looking away. "I needed time . . . Six . . . she—"

"I know," she replied. Seven was a man of strong principles, and Bren had no doubt that his mother's omission had hurt him and caused him great embarrassment. "She should have told you a long time ago," she added.

He nodded and rubbed a hand across the top of his head. "I don't know how to do this," he said.

"I've never missed anyone so completely," she blurted out awkwardly.

Seven's eyebrows raised slightly. "Nor have I."

She held out her shaking hand, and he stepped forward and took it gently—almost reverently—as if she might break.

"How does a man go about asking a future queen for her hand in marriage?" he asked.

"Does this man plan to stay in Isidor? And does he find that he is particularly fond of white hair?"

He looked humbly at her hand. "He does plan to stay. And yes," he said, lifting his dark eyes to hers. "He finds himself completely and utterly enraptured by your white hair."

The way he was looking at her sent a chill down her spine, but she was determined to maintain her composure until he spoke the words she'd longed to hear. She squared her shoulders. "Then if that's the case, he need only ask."

Seven knelt slowly, with her hand still in his and gazed up at her. "Bren Glasser," he began. Her heart beat wildly, and her breathing became shallow as she listened to his words. "I think I have loved you my whole life. And if you would have me as your husband, I promise I will never leave you nor forsake you all the days of my life. Will you be my wife and my future queen?"

"Yes, Seven," she said with a smile. "I will be your wife and queen." A single tear fell down her cheek and she quickly wiped it away.

"Are you sure?" he asked, giving her one last chance to take the other path.

"I'm the surest I've ever been about anything."

He smiled his wide, beautiful smile, and she thought she'd never seen anything so perfectly wonderful. He stood, pulled her gently to him and kissed her for the first time. She closed her eyes and breathed him in, and he gripped her all the fiercer as the love between them ignited. Everything that had felt broken in her for all the past months vanished, and her heart filled with new requited love.

"Come," he said, taking her hand again. "I don't want to

waste another minute. We will tell everyone today we are to be wed."

"Wait," she said, suddenly realizing the impact of their decision. "How mad do you think our getting married will make Six?"

"She owes me now," he said simply.

Bren nodded and smiled. Then gasped as he suddenly swept her off her feet and into his arms. "I've never seen this side of you," she said, breathlessly.

"When I passed Lark, he said that I better sweep you off your feet."

"He probably meant it figuratively," she said with a grin.

"Yes, well. I can think of no better place for my fair-haired lady than in my arms."

She smiled and he kissed her again. She lay her head on his chest as he carried her toward the castle. She was in the arms of the man she loved, and she knew he would stay faithfully by her side all her days.

"Wait!" she said, thinking of something more. "Stop."

"What is it now?" he said, coming to a halt.

"You have to promise me one thing."

He gave her a playful scowl. "Only one?"

"If we have a child, you will not want to name him or her Eight."

Seven grinned sheepishly. "We shall see, princess. We shall see."

And he spun her around until she was dizzy, and they laughed all the way to the castle.

This was *not* the way of the Jutta.

Acknowledgments

This novel could not have made it this far without the exceptional team at Blue Ink. They have not only endured my quirks as business manager but have also meticulously edited and supported my work. I am deeply grateful to Stephanie for the countless hours she dedicated to transforming *The Queen's Treasure*.

Writing this novel has been one of the greatest joys of my life. The characters are as real to me as my closest friends and family. I only wish my older sister, Suzette, had lived to read it; she was an excellent proofreader, and was always willing and ready to be that last set of eyes.

Lastly, my heartfelt thanks go to my daughter Cassie. She has read every first draft I've ever written and not once has hesitated to scribble a strong "NO" in the margins. Her incredible artistic talent has also given me the cover designs of my dreams. Thank you, Cassie, for your unwavering support and creativity.

About the Author

A self-described nerdy introvert, Sherry has been writing books for over a decade. Her genres include middle-grade, young adult mystery & Sci-fi, and adult fantasy. Her work has garnered national recognition, earning accolades from IBPA Benjamin Franklin, Foreword Indies, Feathered Quill, Next Generation Indie Book, and the Apparitionist National Ghost Story Competition. Beyond the world of writing and publishing, you'll find her working in her greenhouse, thrift shopping, watching football, or reading through her endless TBR pile of fantasy and classic books.

sherrytorgent.com

blueinkpress.com